A SNAKE LIES WAITING

ALSO BY JIN YONG

A HERO BORN

A BOND UNDONE

JIN YONG

Legends of the
Condor Heroes III

A SNAKE LIES WAITING

Translated from the Chinese by
Anna Holmwood and Gigi Chang

ST. MARTIN'S GRIFFIN
NEW YORK

First published in the United States by St. Martin's Griffin, an imprint of St. Martin's Publishing Group

www.stmartins.com

The Library of Congress Cataloging-in-Publication Data is available upon request.

ISBN 978-1-250-25012-4 (trade paperback)
ISBN 978-1-250-22066-0 (hardcover)
ISBN 978-1-250-22067-7 (ebook)

Our books may be purchased in bulk for promotional, educational, or business use. Please contact your local bookseller or the Macmillan Corporate and Premium Sales Department at 1-800-221-7945, extension 5442, or by email at MacmillanSpecialMarkets@macmillan.com.

First published in the Chinese language as *Shediao Yingxiong Zhuan* (3) in 1959; revised in 1976, 2003

First published in the English language in Great Britain by MacLehose Press, an imprint of Quercus Publishing Ltd., an Hachette UK Company

First U.S. Edition: 2020

10   9   8   7   6   5   4   3   2   1

CONTENTS

CHARACTERS

As they appear in this, the third volume of
Legends of the Condor Heroes: A Snake Lies Waiting

MAIN CHARACTERS

Guo Jing, son of Skyfury Guo and Lily Li. He grows up with his mother in Mongolia, where they are looked after by Genghis Khan. He is now on his first journey to the Central Plains, the native land of his parents.

Lotus Huang, daughter of Apothecary Huang, she is witty and mischievous, a skilled martial artist and extremely fast learner. She befriends Guo Jing early on in his travels, and they now journey together and share many adventures.

THE JIN EMPIRE

Wanyan Honglie, Sixth Prince, also known as Prince of Zhao, has made conquering the Song his personal mission, in order to secure his reputation and legacy among his own people. He is an astute tactician, using rivalries and jealousies within the Song court and the *wulin* to his own advantage.

Wanyan Kang was raised as the son of the Sixth Prince of the Jin

Empire, but only discovers the identity of his biological father at the age of eighteen. Rather than a Jurchen prince, he is in fact **Yang Kang**, son of Ironheart Yang, one of Song China's greatest patriots.

Consort to the Sixth Prince is **Charity Bao**, who is in fact wife of Chinese patriot Ironheart Yang and mother to Yang Kang.

FOLLOWERS OF THE SIXTH PRINCE OF THE JIN EMPIRE

Gallant Ouyang, Master of White Camel Mount in the Kunlun Range, known as the nephew to one of the Five Greats, Viper Ouyang, Venom of the West.

The Dragon King **Hector Sha** controls the Yellow River with his four apprentices, whose lack of skill infuriates their Master, despite the fact that it is most likely his foul temper that has prevented them from learning anything more than their rather basic moves.

Browbeater Hou, the Three-Horned Dragon, so named for the three cysts on his forehead.

Graybeard Liang, also known as Old Liang, the Ginseng Immortal and, more disparagingly, the Ginseng Codger. He comes from the Mount of Eternal Snow (Changbai Mountains) up in the northeast, close to the current border with Korea, where he has practiced kung fu for many years as a hermit, as well as mixing special medicinal concoctions with the aim of prolonging life and gaining strength.

Lama Supreme Wisdom Lobsang Choden Rinpoche, from Kokonor, now known as Qinghai. He is famed for his Five Finger Blade kung fu.

Tiger Peng the Outlaw, Butcher of a Thousand Hands, has command of much of the mountainous region surrounding the Jin capital Zhongdu, which would later become Peking.

SUBJECTS OF THE SONG EMPIRE

Ironheart Yang, descendent of Triumph Yang, one-time rebel turned patriot who served under General Yue Fei. He practices the Yang Family Spear, a technique passed from father to son.

Married to **Charity Bao**, daughter of a country scholar from Red Plum Village.

Yang Kang, son of Ironheart Yang and Charity Bao, sworn as brother to Guo Jing while both are still in their mothers' bellies.

Mercy Mu, goddaughter of Ironheart Yang, takes part in martial contests her godfather stages to find her a suitable husband and is defeated by Wanyan Kang.

THE MONGOLIANS

Tolui, fourth son of Genghis Khan Temujin, and Guo Jing's sworn brother.

Khojin, one of Genghis Khan's many daughters whose names are mostly lost to history, betrothed by her father to Guo Jing.

Jebe, whose name means "arrow" and "Divine Archer" in Mongolian, is a general under Genghis Khan and known for his great skill with the bow and arrow. He has taught Guo Jing archery and wrestling.

Boroqul, one of Genghis Khan's Four Great Generals.

THE SIX FREAKS OF THE SOUTH

Also known as the Six Heroes of the South when being addressed respectfully by other characters. They refer to themselves as a martial family, despite being of no blood relation. They used to be known as the Seven Freaks before the death of Zhang Asheng, also known as the Laughing Buddha.

Ke Zhen'e, Suppressor of Evil, also known as Flying Bat. The oldest of the Freaks, he is often referred to as Big Brother. Blinded in a fight, his preferred weapon is his flying devilnuts, iron projectiles made in the shape of a kind of water chestnut native to China.

Quick Hands Zhu Cong the Intelligent is known for his quick thinking and even quicker sleight of hand. His dirty scholar's dress and broken oilpaper fan, really made from iron, belie his real martial skill. He is particularly knowledgeable in acupressure points, using them to disable his opponents in a fight.

Ryder Han, Protector of the Steeds, only three foot in height but a formidable fighter and an expert horseman. His weapon of choice is a whip.

Woodcutter Nan the Merciful, known for his kind, if not shy, nature, fights with an iron-tipped shoulder pole.

Gilden Quan the Prosperous, Cloaked Master of the Market, is a master of the rules of the marketplace and always looking for a good deal. He fights with a set of scales.

Jade Han, Maiden of the Yue Sword, is the youngest of the group and the only female. She is trained in the Yue Sword, a technique particular to the region surrounding Jiaxing and developed when the Kingdom of Yue was at war with the Kingdom of Wu in the fifth century B.C.

THE FIVE GREATS

Considered the five greatest martial artists after a contest was held on Mount Hua. Only four are mentioned in this third book in the series:

The Eastern Heretic **Apothecary Huang**, a loner and radical who practices his unorthodox martial arts on Peach Blossom Island along with his wife and six students. He holds traditions and their accompanying morals in contempt and believes only in true love and honor. His eccentricity and heretical views make others suspicious of him, an image he himself cultivates.

Double Sun **Wang Chongyang**, also known as Central Divinity, is the founder of the Quanzhen Sect in the Zhongnan Mountains, with the aim of training Taoists in the martial arts so that they might defend the Song against the Jurchen invasion. A real historical figure, he lived from A.D. 1113 to 1170.

The Northern Beggar **Count Seven Hong**, sometimes referred to as the Divine Vagrant Nine Fingers, is the Chief of the Beggar Clan and commands all the beggars in the Song and Jin Empires. He is respected for his sense of righteousness, but few know his whereabouts as he likes to roam the *jianghu* alone. He is also known for his great love for exceptional cooking.

The Western Venom **Viper Ouyang**, known as uncle to Gallant Ouyang, is a master in taming venomous snakes and using poison. He draws inspiration from the deadly creatures he keeps in his martial practice and rarely sets foot in the Central Plains.

PEACH BLOSSOM ISLAND

Twice Foul Dark Wind were apprentices of Apothecary Huang. They fled Peach Blossom Island and eloped after stealing the Nine Yin Manual. Husband **Hurricane Chen**, known as Copper Corpse, and wife, Iron Corpse **Cyclone Mei**, are masters of the Nine Yin Skeleton Claw. They killed Ke Zhen'e's brother, Ke Bixie the Talisman.

They have four martial siblings: an elder martial brother, **Tempest Qu**, and three younger martial brothers, **Zephyr Lu**, **Galeforce Wu**, and **Doldrum Feng**.

THE QUANZHEN TAOIST SECT

A real branch of Taoism, whose name means "Way of Complete Perfection."

The Seven Immortals, students of Wang Chongyang, are in fact real historical figures:

Scarlet Sun **Ma Yu**, the oldest of the Immortals, teaches internal kung fu, based on breathing techniques.

Eternal Truth **Tan Chuduan** had been a blacksmith in their native Shandong before becoming a Taoist monk.

Eternal Life **Liu Chuxuan** is the third student of Wang Chongyang.

Eternal Spring **Qiu Chuji** befriends Ironheart Yang and Skyfury Guo at the beginning of the series and vows to protect their unborn offspring. To this end, he devises a martial contest with the Seven Freaks of the South. He becomes teacher to Yang Kang.

Jade Sun **Wang Chuyi**, the Iron Foot Immortal, befriends Guo Jing after hearing of Qiu Chuji's contest with the Seven Freaks of the South.

Infinite Peace **Hao Datong** had been the son of a wealthy family in Shandong before joining the Quanzhen Sect.

Sage of Tranquility **Sun Bu'er** is the only female of the Sect, and was married to Ma Yu before both found their spiritual calling.

Not one of the Seven Immortals, **Zhou Botong** the Hoary Urchin, sworn brother and student of Wang Chongyang, is in fact their martial uncle and a lay member of the Quanzhen Sect.

Harmony Yin is one of Qiu Chuji's students. He first met Guo Jing on the steppe of Mongolia when he was sent by his Master to test Guo Jing's developing martial skills.

Emerald Cheng, daughter of a wealthy family in Baoying, is Sun Bu'er's martial disciple. She was attacked by Gallant Ouyang, but was rescued by Guo Jing and Lotus Huang, and has since felt undying gratitude to her saviors.

THE BEGGAR CLAN

The Beggar Clan is a fictional group that has nevertheless appeared in countless works of martial-arts literature. Despite having members all over China, its strength lies mostly in the north—territories already annexed by the Jin Empire at the beginning of this novel.

Beneath Chief **Count Seven Hong**, one of the Five Martial Greats, are the Four Elders, each in charge of Clan affairs in a different part of China: **Surefoot Lu**, Elder of the West; **Jian**, Elder of the East; **Liang**; and **Peng**.

IRON PALM GANG

Led by Iron Palm Water Glider **Qiu Qianren**, the Iron Palm Gang are known for their greed and willingness to collaborate with the enemy for strategic gain. Despite his terrible moral reputation, Qiu is regarded as a great fighter. And yet, others suspect these skills to be nothing more than a result of sleight of hand and treachery.

ROAMING CLOUD MANOR

On the shore of Lake Tai is Roaming Cloud Manor, a grand estate with an unusual layout. Its master is **Squire Lu**, a cultured man who has lost the use of his legs, and his son **Laurel Lu** is in charge of the everyday running of the household.

CHAPTER ONE

THE FAKE MANUAL

I

COUNT SEVEN, ZHOU BOTONG, AND GUO JING RUSHED OUT of the cabin and were shocked to find the water already up to their shins. They ran for the mast and shimmied up it. Count Seven snatched a couple of deaf and mute sailors along the way, pushing them up in front of him. From up high, they looked down and watched as the water churned, rushing over the deck and filling the boat. It was all happening so fast, they did not know what to do.

"Old Beggar," Zhou Botong called to Count Seven, "Heretic Huang is quite remarkable. How did he build this boat?"

"I don't know!" Count Seven replied. "Guo Jing, hold tight to the mast. Don't let go."

Guo Jing was about to answer when a loud crack echoed around them. The boat was breaking in two! The sailors lost their grip and fell into the raging water.

Zhou Botong went after them, turning somersaults in the air as he fell.

"Old Urchin!" Count Seven Hong called. "Do you even know how to swim?"

At that moment, Zhou Botong's head popped up from beneath the water. "I'll have to give it a try . . ." he said, and laughed.

The wind was roaring so loudly, they could barely hear each other. The mast was leaning at such an angle that it would surely soon be touching the water.

"Boy!" Count Seven called out to Guo Jing. "The mast is joined to the hull. We need to snap it. Come on!" Together, they struck at the center of the long wooden pole. It may have been honed from one solid trunk, but how could it withstand the combined forces of Count Seven Hong and Guo Jing? After a few sound blows, it let out a loud crack and relented. They held tight as what remained of the mast fell into the sea below.

They were leagues away from Peach Blossom Island. In every direction, waves rose as high as mountains and there was no land in sight. Count Seven was secretly worried. Without food or fresh water, and with no prospect of being rescued by a passing ship, they would be dead within days. Their martial skills were worthless, out at sea. He gazed into the distance. No sign of Viper Ouyang's boat. Just then, laughter interrupted his thoughts. Zhou Botong.

"Lad," Count Seven said, "let's go fetch him." With one hand clutching the mast, they each used their other to paddle in the direction of the sound. The waves towered above them and, for every few feet they moved forward, they were quickly pulled back nearly the same distance.

"We're coming!" Using his internal strength, Count Seven projected his voice over the sound of the roaring water between them and the Urchin.

Zhou Botong's reply came back to them: "I'm now a sea urchin, pickled in brine!"

Guo Jing could not help but laugh. The old man was still able to make jokes in a situation like this? He certainly deserved his nickname. They were still separated by a hundred feet of billowing sea, but Guo Jing and the Old Beggar raged against the waves and slowly managed to edge closer to their friend.

Once close, they saw their friend had tied planks of wood to his feet with some rope from the rigging and was treading the water using his lightness kung fu. The water was getting the better of him, however. He may have looked as if he was bobbing leisurely on the surface, but in fact it was an incredibly tiring way to traverse it. And yet the Urchin looked as if he was enjoying himself, seemingly unaware of the severity of their plight.

Guo Jing looked around. The boat had vanished, its crew buried at sea.

"*Aiyo!*" Zhou Botong suddenly called out. "The Old Sea Urchin might be about to meet a terrible end." The fear in his voice was unmistakable.

"What is it?" Count Seven and Guo Jing cried in unison.

"Sharks! A school of sharks!" Zhou waved his hand toward the distance.

Guo Jing had been raised in the Mongolian desert; he knew nothing of sharks or how fierce they were, but the change in Count Seven's countenance was enough to make him wonder what manner of monster they must be that they should frighten two such mighty men of the *wulin*.

Count Seven gathered his *qi* to his hand and snapped the end of the mast clean off. He then divided this end piece in half, to make two large cudgels. Just then, a sound pierced the air and a shark's head appeared amid the spray, its rows of razor-sharp teeth glistening in the sunlight, before disappearing back under just as quickly.

Count Seven threw one of his makeshift weapons toward Guo Jing. "Aim for the head!"

Guo Jing reached into the front of his robes and felt for his blade. "I have a dagger!" he cried, hurling the wooden cudgel as hard as he could toward Zhou Botong, who reached out and caught it.

By now, there were four, maybe five sharks circling around the Urchin. They appeared to be waiting for the right moment to strike. Zhou bent at the waist, howled in defiance and struck one of the sharks on the head. The others smelt blood, and pounced.

Guo Jing watched as the water seethed and bubbled. It looked like there were thousands of them. Then, with a flash of long, sharp teeth, a lump of flesh was ripped from the dead shark. At that moment, Guo Jing thought he felt something brush against his foot. He pulled back and the water beneath him roiled. A shark. Clutching the mast, Guo Jing ducked to his right and thrust down with the dagger. The blade sliced a deep gash in the top of the animal's head. Blood bubbled in the water and a set of teeth came snapping.

The three men were all masters of the martial arts, and so did what they knew best: they fought. Each strike caused death or injury, but the men remained unhurt. The smell of blood drew more sharks out and, within moments, all that was left of their dead brethren was bones. The sight of it made the three martial heroes tremble, despite their combined bravery and skill. There were so many sharks, it felt as if they would never be done with them, but there was no time to let thoughts wander when the fight required their every ounce of strength. They thrust and jabbed, and within two hours they had killed over two hundred of the majestic animals. Mist clung to the water as the sun started to slip toward the horizon.

"Old Beggar, Brother Guo," Zhou Botong called out, "once the sun has set, we'll be fed to the sharks, chunk by chunk. Let's have a bet as to who'll be the first course."

"And would that count as losing or winning?" Count Seven asked.

"Winning, of course," Zhou replied.

"In that case, I'd rather lose," Count Seven said. He launched a Dragon Whips Tail and struck the back of his hand against a shark, sending all two hundred *jin* of rippling muscle into the air, where it spun twice before crashing back into the sea to lie floating, its white belly up to the dusky sky.

"Wonderful palm technique!" Zhou Botong cried. "I will call you Master if you teach me this Shark-Subduing Palm. And yet, we don't have time. Old Beggar, why don't we exchange a few blows?"

"My apologies, I'm busy."

4

The Hoary Urchin guffawed and turned to Guo Jing. "What about you, boy? Are you scared?"

Guo Jing's heart was nearly beating out of his chest, but, as he looked upon the calm expressions of the two older men, a smile came to his lips. He took comfort from it. "I was, but I'm feeling a bit better now."

Just then, he saw a huge fin and the tip of a tail come slicing through the water toward him. He leaned to the side and lifted his left hand high. It was bait, and the shark took it. It leaped out of the water and snapped its jaws. The dagger in Guo Jing's right hand thrust upward and sunk into the shark's throat. Blood gushed forth, as if from a spring, and the animal was promptly gutted.

Meanwhile, Zhou Botong and Count Seven Hong had each killed another shark. Yet, Zhou was still suffering from the injury he had sustained earlier, following Apothecary Huang's punch, and he was now feeling a severe pain in his chest. "Old Beggar! Brother Guo!" he cried, then laughed. "I'm afraid I will not be able to continue much longer. It is I who will go first into the shark's belly. Fie! What a shame you two would not bet. I would have won!"

Guo Jing could hear the disappointment in his voice, despite the laughter. "Fine—I'll bet with you!"

"Marvelous! At least now death will be interesting!" Zhou Botong turned in order to avoid being pincered between two sharks, and that was when he saw it: a white sail on the horizon. A large boat emerged from the gloaming, cleaving the waves. Count Seven saw it too. The Venom of the West had come to rescue them!

Before long, the boat had drawn close and let down two sampans to collect the three men. Zhou Botong coughed a mouthful of blood and then began to laugh so hard he could barely stand. He pointed at the sharks and cursed.

Viper Ouyang and his nephew, Gallant, were standing on the prow and welcomed them as they came aboard. They had been watching the scene below, the water seething with fins, and, in their hearts, had been most unsettled.

But Zhou Botong was not one to admit defeat. "Old Venom, you came to save us; I didn't call for help. I owe you nothing."

"Indeed not. I saw you were on a merry shark hunt and curiosity got the better of me."

Zhou laughed. "You interrupted our merry hunt, yes, and denied us the pleasure of exploring a shark's belly! So, I think we're even. Neither of us owes the other a thing."

Gallant Ouyang and one of his snake shepherds, meanwhile, were threading chunks of beef onto hooks, and before long they had hauled up half a dozen sharks.

"Ha!" It was Count Seven's turn to laugh. "You couldn't eat us, so now we'll eat you!"

"To avenge Uncle Hong's injuries," Gallant Ouyang said. He ordered some men to prise open the sharks' jaws with spears, wedging open their mouths with wooden stakes. Then they threw the live sharks back into the water.

"They won't be able to eat again!" Zhou Botong said, and laughed. "But it will take them at least ten days to die."

What an evil trick, Guo Jing said to himself. Only Gallant Ouyang could come up with something like that. The poor sharks will starve to death. How cruel.

Zhou Botong saw the disgust on Guo Jing's face and only laughed harder. "You don't look kindly on such venomous malice, I fear, boy? Like uncle, like nephew!"

Viper Ouyang was not disturbed to hear himself called venomous. On the contrary—it pleased him. He smiled at Zhou Botong's words. "Hoary Urchin, this little trick is small fry compared to those I keep up my sleeve! The three of you are quite out of breath after fighting off those little sharks. They may have been many in number, but I wouldn't call it a feat worth talking about." He gestured in the direction of the sea. "Were there ten times as many, I would destroy them without the slightest effort!"

"Aha!" Zhou Botong cried. "The Venom of the West certainly knows how to flatter himself! If you can demonstrate comparable prowess and kill as many sharks as we did, this Old Urchin will kowtow and call you Master three hundred times over."

"I daren't accept such an honor," Viper Ouyang said. "But, if you don't believe me, we can make a wager."

"Marvelous! I bet the very head on my shoulders!"

Count Seven Hong, however, was suspicious. Such a feat would be impossible by conventional means, he thought. The Viper must be planning something.

"I have no need for your head," Viper Ouyang said, with a smile. "If I win, there is something I would like you to do for me—indeed, you would have no choice. If I lose, you may decide something for me to do. How does that sound?"

"Fine—whatever you say!"

Viper Ouyang turned to Count Seven. "Brother Seven, may I ask you to stand as witness?"

Count Seven nodded. "Very well," he said. "But what if the winner chooses something for the loser to do, and he is unable or unwilling to accept?"

"Then he must jump into the water and become shark food," Zhou cut in.

Viper Ouyang gave a thin smile, but said nothing. He signaled to one of his servants, who brought him a small cup. He then released the two snakes from his staff and pinched one by the neck, forcing its jaw open. Venom trickled from the tips of its teeth. Viper Ouyang held the cup beneath it and, before long, it was half filled with a thick, dark liquid reminiscent of ink. Then he took the second snake and repeated the procedure until the cup was full. Thus emptied, the two snakes wrapped themselves limply around the head of the staff, exhausted.

Viper Ouyang then ordered his servants to lure another shark out of the water and place it on the deck. With his left hand, he yanked its upper jaw open and stood with his right foot just behind its central fin. Despite its great size—it was nearly twenty feet long—the shark was unable to resist. Its rows of dagger-like teeth were on full display. Viper poured the venom straight into the shark's mouth, where the hook had ripped its flesh, then made his hand into a fist and punched the shark in the belly, sending all two hundred *jin* of its bulk up over the gunwale and down into the sea with a splash.

"I see!" Zhou Botong cried, and then laughed. "This is how the old monk kills bed bugs!"

"What do you mean, Brother?" Guo Jing said.

"There was once an old monk who made a living selling a special preparation to get rid of bed bugs in the old capital at Kaifeng," Zhou began. "He claimed it was most effective, and that, if the bugs did not die instantly upon ingesting the substance, he would happily give the customer their money back tenfold. He did a roaring trade, of course. One of his customers went home and spread the mixture on his bed. Ha, ha! Well, that night, ten thousand of the little creatures came and bit him half to death. Needless to say, he rushed to the market the next morning to claim his compensation. But what did the old monk say? 'My preparation is most effective. I dare say you did not use it right.' 'How am I supposed to use it, then?' the customer asked." At this point, Zhou paused, smiling and shaking his head.

"How was he supposed to use it?" Guo Jing asked.

With a perfectly straight face, Zhou Botong said, "The old monk told him, 'Catch the bug, prise open its mouth and feed it just a little bit. If it doesn't die after that, you can come back to find me.' The customer was furious. 'If I manage to catch a bug and force open its mouth, I can just as well pinch it to death with my fingers. What do I need your preparation for?' 'I never said you couldn't choose to pinch it to death, did I?' was the old monk's reply."

Guo Jing, Count Seven Hong, and both uncle and nephew Ouyang all burst into peals of laughter.

"My preparation is a little different to the old monk's," Viper Ouyang said, with a smile, when they had all caught their breath.

"I don't see much of a difference," Zhou Botong said.

Viper Ouyang pointed out to sea. "Take a closer look."

The shark who had been fed the venom was now bobbing on the surface, its belly exposed to the sky. Half a dozen of its kin had been feasting on its remains, and, before long, all that was left was a skeleton, which slowly sank to the seabed. The strange thing was, a few minutes later, the sharks that had eaten it were also dead. These were then consumed by yet more sharks, who in turn also died. And so, one shark killed ten more, ten became a hundred, a hundred a thousand, until, before even an hour had passed, the sea was a carpet of floating carcasses. The few living that remained were still feasting on the dead, but soon they too succumbed and all was quiet.

The blood had long since drained from the cheeks of the on-lookers.

Count Seven sighed. "Old Venom, Old Venom. That was an evil trick indeed. Who would have thought that small amount of venom could turn out to be so deadly?"

Viper Ouyang looked at Zhou Botong with a most satisfied expression. Zhou, in turn, tugged on his beard anxiously.

They looked out across the water. As far as the eye could see, sharks were floating on the surface. "I feel sick. And all killed by the Venom's venom," Zhou Botong said. "Be careful. Or the Sea Dragon King will send his army of prawns and their crab generals to fight you."

Viper Ouyang smiled, but said nothing.

"Brother Viper, there is one thing I don't understand. Pray, will you explain?" Count Seven Hong asked.

"You flatter me," Viper Ouyang replied.

"How could such a small cup of venom, no matter how deadly, kill so many sharks?"

Viper Ouyang threw his head back and laughed. "This is a very special type of venom indeed," he began. "As soon as it enters the veins, it poisons the blood. Once this poisoned blood is consumed by another shark, its blood becomes toxic too. This is repeated and continues until none are left alive."

9

"A never-ending chain of destruction," Count Seven Hong said.

"Precisely. I am known as the Venom of the West. I shouldn't dare to claim such a title if my knowledge of toxins was in any way lacking."

The sea around them was eerily calm. The smaller fish had all either similarly perished or else had fled.

"Quick, let's get under way. The air is thick with poison," Count Seven Hong cried.

Viper Ouyang gave his signal and the ship's three sails were set. The wind was moving in a northwesterly direction.

"Old Venom's preparation for killing bed bugs has proved most effective," Zhou Botong said. "What am I to do for you?"

"First, I would like to welcome the three of you into my cabin," Viper Ouyang said. "You must change out of those wet clothes, eat and rest. As for our wager, we can discuss that later."

But Zhou Botong was impatient by nature. "No, no, just tell me! There is no advantage to be gained by keeping it under your tongue!"

"In that case"—Viper Ouyang smiled—"come with me, brother."

2

COUNT SEVEN AND GUO JING WATCHED AS VIPER OUYANG and his nephew led Zhou Botong to a cabin at the stern of the boat, before they were taken to a different cabin to change their clothes. Four young women dressed in white attended to them.

"Poor Old Urchin—he won't be getting this kind of treatment," Count Seven said, laughing. He stripped naked and one of the women toweled him dry.

Guo Jing, meanwhile, could feel the blood rushing to his neck and cheeks. He did not dare disrobe.

"What are you so afraid of? They won't eat you alive."

Two maidens approached him, intending to remove his boots

and loosen his belt. Guo Jing shrugged off his outer layer and dashed over to the bed, where he slipped under a blanket to change his undergarments. Count Seven found his modesty hilarious, and the four young women in white giggled too.

Presently, two more women entered the cabin, carrying trays laden with various dishes and rice, and wine to accompany them. "Please, gentlemen, just a little something to eat."

"You may go," Count Seven said, gesturing with his hand. "The sight of so many lovely ladies will ruin my appetite."

The women smiled and obliged him, closing the door as they left. Count Seven took a glass of wine and sniffed, then did the same with the food. "Don't touch any of it," he whispered. "Old Venom is sly, indeed. Eat only the rice." He reached for the gourd on his back, pulled out the cork and took two long drafts of wine. The two men then guzzled three big bowls of rice each. The poisoned food they hid away under the floorboards.

"I wonder what they want Brother Zhou to do," Guo Jing said in a low voice.

"It can't be good. The Old Urchin has got himself into a tight spot, this time."

At that moment, the cabin door was pushed open and a young woman hovered in the doorway. "Master Zhou has asked for Master Guo to come to the rear cabin to speak with him."

Guo Jing glanced at his *shifu* and then followed the woman. They walked along the port side of the boat, round to the stern. The maiden knocked gently on the cabin door and, after waiting a moment, pushed it open. "Master Guo is here."

Guo Jing entered and the door was closed behind him. But the cabin was empty. How strange! Just then, a small door to his left swung open and Viper Ouyang and his nephew strode through it.

"Where's Brother Zhou?" Guo Jing asked.

Viper Ouyang closed the door with the back of his hand, took two steps forward and seized Guo Jing by the wrist. His movements were quick and Guo Jing was taken by surprise. A sharp pain spread up through his arm and it was instantly paralyzed. Gallant Ouyang pulled his folding fan from his sleeve pocket and tapped its metal blades against one of the acupressure points on Guo Jing's back.

What were they doing? Guo Jing was struck dumb, unable to move.

"The Old Urchin lost our wager, but when I asked him to do something for me, he refused," Viper Ouyang started, his voice icy cold.

"Huh?" was all Guo Jing could say.

"I wanted him to write down the entire Nine Yin Manual from memory. But he refused to honor the terms of our agreement."

Why would he give you the Manual? Guo Jing thought. "Where is Brother Zhou now?" he managed to say.

"He said himself that he would jump into the sea and be food for the sharks if he didn't keep his word. At least, on this, he has been honorable. Ha!"

"He . . . ? He . . . ?" Guo Jing could barely speak. He tried to pull back his hand and run for the door, but Viper Ouyang's grip was too firm. Gallant Ouyang, meanwhile, pressed harder on Guo Jing's Yang Extremity point, making his whole body go numb.

Viper Ouyang pointed to some paper, ink and brushes on a table. "Now, you are the only person in the whole world who knows the full text. Write it for me."

Guo Jing shook his head. Gallant Ouyang sneered. "The food and drink you and the Old Beggar consumed just now was poisoned. Without my uncle's unique antidote, you will both be dead within twelve hours. Just like the sharks. Though, of course, if you comply, we can spare your lives."

Had my *shifu* not been so alert, they would have killed us, Guo Jing realized, a chill running down his numbed spine. A martial master you may be, Guo Jing thought, as he looked at Viper Ouyang, but you are truly without honor.

"You have memorized the Manual, anyway; it is no loss to you to write it down. Why are you hesitating?"

"You have killed my sworn brother," Guo Jing said, his voice hard. "My hatred for you runs as deep as the ocean. Kill me, if you so desire. But you can never force me to write down the Manual!"

"You are a brave young man, to be sure," Viper Ouyang said. "You aren't scared of death, apparently. But does your *shifu*'s life mean nothing to you?"

Just as Guo Jing was about to reply, a loud bang interrupted him, and the cabin door shattered into fragments. Viper Ouyang spun around, only to see Count Seven Hong in the doorway, carrying two wooden buckets. With a flick of his wrists, he emptied them, sending two columns of seawater straight at Viper Ouyang and his nephew. Viper leaped to the side, still clutching Guo Jing and pressing on his pressure point.

The water crashed into the back wall of the cabin and splashed in all directions. Gallant Ouyang cried out; Count Seven had grabbed the back of his robes and he was held suspended, his feet dangling inches from the floor.

"Old Venom, I'm afraid the heavens have refused to accommodate your plans. You won't get the better of me!"

"Brother Hong, are you testing me again? We can settle this once we reach the shore."

"You seem very fond of my disciple," Count Seven said, with a laugh. "You won't let go of his hand!"

"I won my bet with the Old Urchin, didn't I? You were witness to it. The Old Urchin refused to keep his word, did he not?"

Count Seven nodded. "That is correct. Where is he?"

"Brother Zhou is . . . He was forced to jump overboard!" Guo Jing cried.

Startled, Count Seven rushed out on deck, still holding Gallant Ouyang, but it was dark and all he could see were the black waves rising and falling. There was no sign of the Hoary Urchin.

Viper Ouyang followed them out, still holding Guo Jing. "Young man, your skills leave a lot to be desired," he said, letting him go. "I was able to take your wrist without so much as the slightest sign of resistance. Study another ten years under your Master and maybe then you will be fit to wander the *jianghu*."

But Guo Jing was more concerned about the safety of his sworn brother Zhou Botong than these petty gibes, so he climbed the mast and gazed out across the sea.

Count Seven carried Gallant over to his uncle. "Old Venom, you pushed the Urchin to his death. The Quanzhen Sect will come for you. You may be a renowned practitioner of the martial arts, but not even you can overcome all seven of their masters."

At that moment, Gallant slapped away Count Seven's hand and landed gracefully back down on the ground. Stinking beggar! he said to himself. By this time tomorrow, the poison will have taken hold and you will be kneeling in front of me, begging for me to save you.

Viper leered at Count Seven. "But then I'm afraid you won't get away with merely observing our fight."

"Indeed, I'll be there with my Dog-Beating Cane to help finish you off!" Count Seven Hong said.

Viper Ouyang cupped his hands in a perfunctory gesture of leave-taking, turned and strode back into the cabin.

Guo Jing continued to gaze out into the black night. Breaks of white foam were the only thing to disturb the darkness; there was no sign of Zhou Botong. Eventually, Guo Jing climbed down from the mast and told his *shifu* how the Venom of the West had tried to get him to write down the Manual for him. Count Seven nodded but did not reply. Old Venom doesn't let go of an idea easily, he said to himself. He will keep tormenting my disciple until he gets his hands on the Manual.

Guo Jing began to cry at the thought that his sworn brother might be dead. Count Seven was also distressed. The boat was sailing quickly in a westerly direction and they would reach land in a day's time. He did not trust the Venom not to poison their food again, so he made for the kitchen and stole some things for them to eat. The two men ate until they were full, and, before long, they were fast asleep.

Viper and his nephew, Gallant, waited until the following after-noon, nearly eighteen hours after their last conversation with Guo Jing and his *shifu*. They had heard nothing from their two guests. Perhaps Viper Ouyang had used too much poison and killed them? He was not so concerned about Count Seven, but if Guo Jing was lost, so was the Manual. Forever. He approached the door to their cabin and peered through the crack. Inside, *shifu* and student were sitting and chatting. Count Seven's voice was loud and clear. Viper Ouyang was incensed. They were fine! If he was going to dispense with Count Seven but not harm Guo Jing, he would have to think of another way.

Count Seven was telling Guo Jing all about the Beggar Clan, and how, despite their need to beg in order to survive, they were staunch believers in righteousness and justice, serving the weak and those in distress. He then went on to describe the process by which the clan elected their chief. "What a pity you don't live the beggar life, son; otherwise, you have just the right character to be leader. There is no one in the clan who can compare to you. I would happily pass the Dog-Beating Cane into your hands."

Just then, a hacking sound interrupted their conversation, much like an axe being swung repeatedly at the wall.

"Oh! This is not good," Count Seven said, and jumped to his feet. "That slithering snake is going to sink the boat!" He ran to the door and then called back to Guo Jing: "Get to the sampan at the back of the ship!"

At that moment, a loud crash announced a jagged hole in the wall, down near the floorboards. This was followed by the sound of hissing.

Not of rushing water, this time.

"He's attacking us with snakes!"

Count Seven quickly released a rain of needles, pinning dozens of vipers against the wooden boards. They writhed in agony and went still.

"Lotus is accomplished at this Skyful of Petals technique, but she has a long way to go to match her Master."

More snakes were approaching. Count Seven Hong threw yet more needles and killed them. But a flute was playing outside, driving even more snakes forward.

"How kind of the Venom to keep providing me with target practice!"

Yet, as he reached inside his pouch for more needles, he realized to his surprise that he had only a few left. And the snakes were still coming. What should he do? Just then, the wall behind him was smashed into splinters and a palm came hurtling at his back.

Standing beside his Master, Guo Jing felt the gust of air as the palm approached. Too late to turn, he brought his hands together and blocked. He had to use all his strength to withhold the force of the blow. Viper Ouyang yelped in surprise, but countered the move with a horizontal chop. Guo Jing knew this would be harder to stop, feinted with his right hand and aimed at Viper Ouyang's left shoulder. Viper ducked and hacked at Guo Jing's wrist. The situation was critical. If Viper was free to open the cabin door, more snakes would come, putting Master and disciple in great danger. Guo Jing defended with one hand and attacked with the other. His hands moved independently, just as the Hoary Urchin had taught him. This was the first time Viper Ouyang had seen anything like it. It confused him for a moment, giving Guo Jing the chance to land a few hits. Viper Ouyang's skills still made him twice the fighter Guo Jing was, but the novelty of the young man's technique enabled him to gain the upper hand, if only briefly. Before long, however, the Venom of the West had worked out how to counter it. He had not held the title of master for decades for nothing, after all.

Huh! He thrust two palms. Unable to block the move with his left only, Guo Jing stumbled back.

"Marvelous! Wonderful!" Count Seven cried out. "Old Venom—call yourself a master? You can't even overcome my young disciple!"

Launching into a Dragon Soars in the Sky, he flew straight past the two men and kicked Gallant Ouyang, who had appeared behind his uncle, into a sprawling somersault, before elbowing Viper Ouyang in the back. Viper leaned sideways, dispelling the force of Guo Jing's attack.

Shifu is as accomplished in the martial arts as the Venom, Guo Jing was thinking, and I am more than a match for his nephew. Also, he is hurt. Two against two, we will most definitely win.

The thought raised Guo Jing's spirits, and his hands and feet rained on Viper like a violent storm.

Still attacking ferociously, Count Seven glanced around to see writhing snakes closing in behind Guo Jing. Just one bite would be enough to kill him.

"Lad! Get out of here!" Count Seven increased the intensity of his onslaught, returning the full force of Viper Ouyang's blows.

Viper was being attacked on two fronts and was feeling the strain. He ducked sideways, allowing Guo Jing to escape the cabin while he continued to fight Count Seven.

In the meantime, hundreds of snakes had slithered up onto the deck and now had them surrounded.

"Need animals as your backup? Shameless." Count Seven's tone was mocking, yet the sight of the snakes made his heart quiver. Holding his Dog-Beating Cane in his right hand, he killed a dozen snakes before grabbing hold of Guo Jing and making a dash for the main mast.

Viper Ouyang watched in alarm. If they climbed the mast, they would be out of his reach. He rushed forward to block them.

Count Seven met him with a gust of air and two chopping palms. Viper swept his fist sideways to meet them.

Guo Jing made as if to help his Master, but Count Seven waved him back. "Up the mast, quick!"

"I'll kill his nephew to avenge Brother Zhou!"

"The snakes!" Count Seven called desperately.

Guo Jing looked down at the writhing snakes and dared not linger any longer. With a backhand swipe, he caught Gallant's Swallow Shuttles, leaped up and grabbed hold of the mast. Just then, he heard the whistle of another weapon flying at him from behind, so he threw his own to block it. *Clang!* The two projectiles crashed mid-air and fell into the sea. Guo Jing then grabbed the mast with both hands and climbed up, halfway to the summit.

Viper intensified his attack on Count Seven. The Chief of the Beggar Clan was able to keep Viper at bay, but could not inch any closer to the mast. Guo Jing saw the snakes gathered around his Master's feet, cried out and, with his legs gripping the mast, let his torso swing down. He had imbibed such quantities of Graybeard Liang's snake blood that his whole body gave off an odor of herbs. It was enough to make the snakes edge away, giving Count Seven a chance to tap his foot against the deck and fly up, aiming a kick at Viper Ouyang's face. Guo Jing grabbed the bamboo stick from his Master and wrenched his arm upward. Count Seven continued his ascent and seized hold of the mast above Guo Jing.

Now, they were both at a safe height, looking down on their enemies. Viper realized there was no point climbing up to fight them, so instead he called, "Fine—you win, this time. Turn the rudder east!"

Count Seven positioned himself on the crossbeam and began to sing an old ditty beloved of beggars everywhere: "Falling Lotus Flowers." But his relaxed demeanor was but a mask to hide the genuine anxiety he felt. How long would they be able to stay clinging to the mast? Viper Ouyang could cut it down, and they could not descend as long as the snakes were still there. The others could drink wine and sleep in their beds, while all they could do was eat wind and urinate. At this thought, he hauled himself to his feet, pulled down his trousers and watered the snakes below.

"Boy, let them have something to drink!" he cried.

"Yum, yum!" Guo Jing cried, just as amused as his Master, and joined in.

Viper Ouyang leaped back, managing to avoid the spray. Gallant, on the other hand, was treated to a light shower across his cheeks. This only made him even more furious.

Count Seven then pulled out a tinderbox, ripped off a piece of sail, lit it and threw the ball of fire downward.

"Clear the snakes!" Viper Ouyang barked. The wooden flutes began to play and the snakes withdrew, but a dozen or so at the base of the mast had already been burned. The sight of the flames frightened them and they began to writhe and curl in all directions, making them impossible to control.

Count Seven and his disciple laughed as they watched the chaos unfold. Brother Zhou would have enjoyed such a sight, Guo Jing thought. He sighed to think that such a master of the *wulin* should have to die at sea.

3

SOME FOUR HOURS LATER, AS DUSK APPROACHED, VIPER Ouyang ordered the crew to festoon the decks with meat and wine. It was a devious move on his part. How, he asked himself, could a gourmand like Count Seven withstand the delicious aroma of all that food?

That night, Count Seven and Guo Jing took turns keeping watch. The deck below was lit by lanterns and a swarm of snakes guarded the foot of the mast. There was no way to break through such a defense. Count Seven cursed a full eighteen generations of Viper Ouyang's ancestors, adding his own deliciously concocted details. But nothing would draw the Venom out of his cabin. Count Seven could do nothing but continue cursing until his lips were dry and he fell asleep with exhaustion.

Early the next morning, Viper Ouyang sent one of his servants to call to the men up the mast: "Chief Hong! Master Guo! Sir Ouyang has prepared a most sumptuous meal for you. Please, come down to enjoy it!"

"Tell Viper Ouyang to come out here and enjoy our piss instead!"

Before long, a table was set below and steaming dishes of freshly prepared food were carried out. Two chairs were placed at the table for Master and disciple. Count Seven considered sliding down and pilfering some food, but it was sure to be poisoned. "Damn you and your mother," he muttered.

BY THE third day, the two men were so parched and hungry, they were beginning to feel dizzy.

"If only the girl was here. She's whip smart, that one. Surely, she'd come up with a plan," Count Seven Hong said. "All we seem to be doing is sitting here with dry eyes, drooling."

Guo Jing sighed.

As the sun reached its highest point in the sky, Guo Jing spotted two white dots in the distance. At first, he took them for clouds and paid them little attention. But as the dots grew larger and larger, a familiar screech reached his ears. Two white condors!

Delighted, Guo Jing summoned his inner strength and called back to them. The birds circled above the boat before swooping down. It was the very same pair that he had raised on the steppe of Mongolia.

"*Shifu*," Guo Jing began, breathless with excitement. "Perhaps Lotus is sailing this way?"

"Now, wouldn't that be wonderful. What a shame the birds are too small to carry us on their backs. We're thoroughly stuck. Let her know to come here quick and think of something."

Guo Jing took out his golden dagger and cut two five-inch-square pieces from the sails. Then, using the tip of his blade, he scratched *Help* into the cloth, and beneath that the shape of a gourd. He repeated this and tied the pieces of material around the condors' legs. "Come back quickly, and bring the maiden Lotus with you."

The two birds let out a loud cry, flapped their wings and took flight. They circled the boat once before flying west, where they were quickly swallowed by the clouds.

A couple of hours or so after the condors had departed, Viper Ouyang made another attempt to lure Count Seven and Guo Jing down with yet more food.

"Old Venom, this is a dirty trick. You know how much I love to eat. I have only ever practiced external forms of kung fu. I'm not trained to withstand the tug of a good meal. Guo Jing, what do you say we jump down and beat them senseless, then come back up?"

"Have patience; we've sent the birds to find Lotus. Rescue is coming."

Count Seven laughed, then fell silent. "What's the most disgusting taste in the world?" he said suddenly.

"I don't know. What?" Guo Jing replied.

"I once went north. Far north, into the snow. I was hungry for eight whole days and nights. There wasn't a rodent in sight, not even a measly piece of tree bark. So I started digging in the mush and mud, where I came across five little wriggly things. They saved my life and gave me enough strength to live another day. The next day, I caught a weasel and gorged myself full."

"What were the five little wriggly things?"

"Earthworms. Nice and fat. I swallowed them whole. I didn't dare chew."

Guo Jing pictured their squirming bodies and could not help but feel disgusted.

Count Seven guffawed. It was his best hope of forgetting the fragrance of the delicious food wafting toward them from below.

"Lad, I would eat those earthworms right now, if there were any to be had. But there is one very dirty, very smelly thing that I would never eat. Indeed, I would rather eat my own toe! Can you guess what it is?"

"I know!" Guo Jing said, and laughed.

But Count Seven shook his head. "Dirtier than that."

Guo Jing kept guessing, but to no avail.

"Let me tell you," Count Seven boomed. "The dirtiest thing in the world is Venom of the West, Viper Ouyang himself!"

"That's right!" Guo Jing laughed.

BY EVENING, however, Guo Jing could take it no longer. He slid down the mast and slashed the heads of two snakes with his golden dagger. The other snakes could smell the herbal medicine in his blood and slipped away. Guo Jing gave chase and killed two more, then gathered the four dead snakes and climbed back up the mast. Up on the crossbeam, he skinned them and the two men devoured their raw flesh.

Gallant Ouyang emerged and stood among his swarm of snakes. "Uncle Hong, Brother Guo, my uncle merely wants you to write out the Manual for him, nothing more."

"Fie! There's always more," Count Seven Hong hissed quietly.

Just then, an idea came to him. Keeping a straight face, he shouted: "Scoundrel! Your uncle wins. I surrender. Bring us meat and wine and we will talk tomorrow."

Gallant Ouyang was most pleased. Count Seven Hong's word was as steady as a mountain; he would never go back on a promise. He ordered the snakes to retreat, and allowed Count Seven and Guo Jing to slide down the mast and enter the cabin. Gallant's servants brought them a veritable feast.

Count Seven Hong closed the door and grabbed a pot of wine and gulped it down. Then he ripped a chicken in half and began to chew.

"Are you sure the food isn't poisoned?" Guo Jing whispered.

"Silly boy," Count Seven replied. "The Old Venom needs you to copy down the Manual. He couldn't risk hurting you. Now, eat up. I've got a plan."

Guo Jing said no more and guzzled down four bowls of rice, scarcely drawing breath.

Once his belly was full, Count Seven Hong wiped the grease from his mouth with his sleeve. Then he moved closer to Guo Jing and whispered in his ear: "Old Venom wants you to write down the Nine Yin Manual. All you have to do is give him a fake Nine Yin Manual."

"A fake Manual?"

"Indeed," Count Seven Hong said, and smiled. "Write whatever you like. Apothecary Huang has the only other copy, and, come what may, he will never give it to the Venom of the West. His nephew memorized the first few passages, so don't get them wrong. As long as he recognizes the start, he will never suspect a thing. Then, for the rest, you can mix it up. That way, he could train for a hundred years and it would all be a waste!"

What a good trick, Guo Jing thought. We'll get that Old Venom! After a pause, Guo Jing said, "But the Venom is a master of the martial arts. Not to mention very sly. If I write nonsense, won't he be able to tell? And then what?"

"Well, of course, you must write something plausible, but wrong," Count Seven Hong said. "Three correct sentences, and then put in one that's wrong. Or change the numbers, so that nine becomes one, two becomes eight, three becomes seven, four becomes six, five becomes ten, and reverse them too. He'll never be able to catch something like that. I would be happy to go seven days and seven nights with neither food nor wine to watch him try to train from a fake Nine Yin Manual!" A wide grin had spread across Count Seven Hong's face.

"He won't just be wasting his time, he could even cause himself a serious injury," Guo Jing said, with a laugh.

"You start thinking about how you're going to change it. If he gets suspicious, our plan will be ruined." He paused, before continuing. "Remember that scoundrel Gallant Ouyang also read the second volume on Peach Blossom Island, so don't alter too much there. Just put in some wrong words. I'm sure he won't be able to tell the difference."

Guo Jing recited the Manual to himself, trying to think where he could make the changes. Wait could become thrust, up could become down—all that would be easy to alter, without requiring him to write whole new sentences. His Master was right, the changes should be subtle but thorough. Up is down and down is up. Front is back and back is front. Chest is abdomen and hand is foot. Heavens are earth. If he stuck to these simple substitutions, he would be able to replicate the altered version. *Palms toward the sky* would become *Soles of the feet toward the sky*. *Feet planted on the ground* would become *Hands planted on the ground*. In the sections that dealt with the cultivation of internal energy, he could change *Gather the* qi *in the elixir field* to *Gather the* qi *in the chest*.

Guo Jing sighed. It was a ruse that would delight both Lotus and Brother Zhou. What a shame that one is dead and the other nowhere to be seen. I will see Lotus again one day, but I will never be able to tell Brother Zhou this story.

Early the next morning, Count Seven Hong called for Gallant Ouyang. "I, old beggar that I am, have enough unique skills in the martial arts. I don't need the Nine Yin Manual. I have no interest in it; I wouldn't look even if you were to wave it in front of my face. Only a man with the martial skills of a turkey would try to steal its secrets. Wang Chongyang had it in his possession before his death, as does Apothecary Huang now, but neither cared to study it. Is this not the difference between a man and a hero? Tell that dog brain of an uncle of yours that the Manual will be written out just for him. He must shut himself away and train. Then, once he's done, he is to come and find me, Chief of the Beggars, and fight. This Manual is a fine thing, to be sure, but still I will not even glance at it. I want to know if the Manual really can help the Old Venom finally beat the Old Beggar! Or perhaps, after all that work, he will still only be my equal. He could end up taking off his breeches just to fart!"

Viper Ouyang could hear everything from where he was standing behind the door. But, rather than make him furious, Count Seven's speech delighted him. Just as well the Old Beggar is so proud, he doesn't mind me having the Manual, he thought. Much easier than trying to fight him, threaten him with snakes or starve him to death.

"What nonsense! My uncle's martial skills are perfection itself. You could not hope to win one pass against him. Why would he need the Nine Yin Manual? Indeed, he told me once that the Manual's powers must be exaggerated. Otherwise, why didn't Wang Chongyang show the *wulin* what he learned from it? My uncle is motivated above all by the prospect of pointing out its errors and proving once and for all that it is nothing but a hoax. That way, we heroes of the *jianghu* needn't fight over it. Now, that is a true service to the *wulin*, is it not?"

At this, Count Seven Hong could not help but laugh. "What self-satisfied bombast! Boy, write the Manual for them. If Old Venom can find the errors, I will kowtow before him."

Gallant Ouyang led Guo Jing into the larger cabin and produced paper and a stick of ink, which he ground in preparation for him to begin.

Guo Jing had little formal education and his hand was shaky. He had to think hard to remember how to write certain characters, and his progress was slow. More than once, he had to ask Gallant Ouyang for help with characters he had forgotten. By noon, he had barely finished half of the first volume. Viper Ouyang was not present, but, after each page was finished, Gallant Ouyang carried it away to give to his uncle. As for the incantation at the end of the Manual, no one could fathom its meaning, but Count Seven Hong feared it to be a transcription of a western tongue. Viper Ouyang was himself from the west, so Count Seven Hong had told Guo Jing not to change a word of this part, lest the Viper should realize their secret.

Viper read the pages carefully. The ideas contained within them were like riddles, but the words themselves were simple and he could tell that their meaning was profound. Once back in the west, he was sure to be able to use his considerable intellect to unpick their meaning. It may take him decades, but he would master the Manual's esoteric techniques eventually. He was elated. Such a foolish boy as Guo Jing, his writing so clumsy and crooked, would not have the wit to make it all up. Not only that, but his nephew had to teach Guo Jing how to form many of the characters, which he knew to pronounce but not to write. This had to be the real Nine Yin Manual. How could such a stupid boy conspire with his *shifu* to trick him?

Guo Jing wrote without interruption until sunset, under the constant supervision of Gallant Ouyang. As each page was finished, it was whisked away and passed to his uncle. Viper Ouyang did not dare let Guo Jing return to his cabin, lest Count Seven change his mind. He would not be satisfied with an incomplete text, so he ordered a feast to be taken to the boy so that he might continue writing.

Count Seven Hong waited nervously until the end of the eleventh watch. Guo Jing had still not emerged. Had their plan been uncovered? If the stupid boy had let it slip, the snakes would already be crawling all over the deck by now. He crept out of his cabin and was greeted by two snake herders keeping guard outside his door.

Ha! Count Seven chopped with his left. The rush of air from his hand set the rigging aflutter. The two men glanced across at where the sound was coming from, giving Count Seven just enough time to sneak past them, and he was out, stealing along the starboard side, before human or ghost could sense him.

A faint glow came through the window of the main cabin. Count Seven approached and peered in. Guo Jing was still bent over the desk, writing. Two women in white were serving him tea and grinding his ink. Gallant Ouyang stood on the other side, watching.

Count Seven felt relieved at first, until the smell of alcohol assailed his nostrils. There, on the table in front of Guo Jing, was a cup of fragrant, amber liquid. The color was so deep that it resembled that of a block of women's rouge. So, Old Venom serves my disciple his finest liquor, all because he is able to write out the Manual for him. But me, the epicurean, whose knowledge of wine is unrivaled in these lands, I only get the cheap, watery stuff. I must taste it. Old Venom must keep it stored belowdecks. I'll have a drink, then, when I'm finished, I'll pee in the barrel. Let him taste a bit of the Old Beggar's fine wine! What's a little urine compared to our ordeal with the sharks? It won't kill him.

The thought made him smile. If there was one thing at which he excelled, it was stealing food and drink. During one three-month period, he had lived in the rafters of the imperial kitchens in Lin'an. During this time, every dish made for the Emperor first passed his lips. The palace was tightly guarded and yet he had come and gone as he pleased. So, sneaking down under the decks of this ship? A mere trifle. He tiptoed toward the quarterdeck, looked around and then gently lifted the hatch. He slipped inside and eased the cover back into place. A couple of sniffs confirmed his suspicions: this was where the food supplies were kept.

The darkness below was absolute, but he soon managed to find what he was looking for by the power of his nose alone. Once at the food store, he lit a torch. In the corner were stacked half a dozen wooden barrels. He picked up a nearby bowl, chipped at the rim, blew out the torch and tucked the bowl into his robes. Then he approached the nearest barrel. He tried to nudge it, but it was heavy, filled to the brim. He grabbed the wooden stop, but, just as he was about to pull it out, he heard a noise. Footsteps. Two people were outside the store.

Their steps were light; it had to be Viper and his nephew. No one else on board had comparable lightness kung fu. Why were they here at so late an hour? They must be up to no good. Poisoning the food? He shrunk into the corner and curled up behind the barrels. At that moment, the door opened slowly, a light flickered and two figures slipped inside.

They walked toward the barrels and stopped. Are they about to put poison in the wine? Count Seven Hong thought.

Just then, the Venom of the West spoke: "He's finished the Manual. A success. The cabins all have the oil, firewood, and sulfur?"

"It's all ready. As soon as we light the fire, the boat will disappear in a ball of flames and the Old Beggar will be reduced to ashes within seconds."

Count Seven was in shock. They are going to burn the boat?

"Let's wait a little longer, until the Guo boy is fast asleep. You go to the small boat. Be careful; the Old Beggar mustn't find out. I'll start the fire here."

"What about the concubines and the snake herders?"

"It is unavoidable that some people will have to be sacrificed if we are going to catch a master of the *wulin*. It's all in the nature of the difference in their standing."

Count Seven Hong yanked the stopper out of the barrel as they talked, and a pungent smell of oil reached his nostrils. A mixture of tung and vegetable oils. The two men removed a lump of sulfur from a wooden box and covered it with firewood and a large bag of sawdust and wood shavings. Before long, with oil pooling unnoticed beneath their feet, the two men made for the door.

"Uncle," Gallant Ouyang said as they left. "Soon, that Guo boy will have made his grave at the bottom of the sea and the only person in the whole world with knowledge of the Nine Yin Manual will be you!"

"No, there will be one more person. I shall share my knowledge with you. And, of course, Apothecary Huang also has the book. We'll have to think of a way to get rid of him, too."

Gallant Ouyang grinned. "Let's go and wrap the Manual in oil paper and cloth. We can also melt wax over it so that the water can't ruin it."

With that, the men left and closed the door behind them.

Count Seven Hong was both shocked and furious. Had he not by some strange coincidence come down here to steal some wine, he would never have uncovered the Ouyangs' venomous scheme. Once the flames started raging, out on these open seas, how could they escape? He listened as their footsteps receded before sneaking back up to his cabin, where he found Guo Jing sound asleep. Just as he was about to wake the boy and tell him of what was happening, the quietest of sounds from outside the door alerted him: Viper Ouyang was checking to see that they were both asleep.

"Excellent wine! Bring me another ten flasks!"

Viper Ouyang froze. The Old Beggar was drinking.

"Venom!" Count Seven Hong's voice came from inside. "I challenge you to another round. Let's see who's really the better fighter! *Hic!* Good boy. That's it!"

Viper stood listening for a while. What nonsense . . . He must be talking in his sleep! The Old Beggar is about to face a grisly end, and yet still he dreams of drinking and fighting!

Count Seven Hong was himself listening intently, despite his babbling. Viper was a master of lightness kung fu, and yet still the Chief of the Beggar Clan could clearly make out that he had moved to the port side of the boat. He put his lips to Guo Jing's ear. "Guo Jing," he hissed, gently shaking the young boy's shoulder.

"Mm."

"Do as I say, and don't ask why. We're going out on deck. Make sure no one sees you."

Guo Jing rolled out of bed. Count Seven gently opened the cabin door. Then he tugged at Guo Jing's sleeve and stepped out on the starboard side. Rather than walk to the end of the boat, he felt his way over the taffrail and pulled Guo Jing with him. Guo Jing dutifully followed without saying a word. Moments later, they were hanging precariously above the roaring waves. Count Seven began to lower himself slowly, his eyes fixed on Guo Jing. His greatest fear was that the side of the boat would be wet and the boy would slip, the splash as he fell into the water thus alerting Viper Ouyang to their escape.

It was a dangerous climb. The paint finish was glossy and the boards were indeed wet, but not only that, the curve of the hull and the sway of the boat in the water all meant that such a descent required amazing skill. Luckily, Guo Jing's training with Ma Yu at the cliff in Mongolia, as well as his more recent improvements, allowed him to make steady progress by clinging to iron rivets and small cracks that had been filled with putty. The two men climbed slowly downward until Count Seven Hong was half submerged in the water. He then moved carefully toward the stern and Guo Jing followed suit.

There, tied by a long, thick rope, was a small boat.

"Get in," Count Seven called to Guo Jing.

The moment he let go, Count Seven was swept out into the sea. The ship was moving fast and he just managed to grab hold of the small boat in time. He flipped himself over the gunwale without making a sound, and there he waited patiently for Guo Jing to join him. "Cut the rope!"

Using his golden dagger, Guo Jing sliced the boat free from the ship, and instantly they were at the mercy of the waves. Count Seven steadied their boat with an oar and together they watched as the large ship disappeared into the darkness. Not a moment later, a flash of light appeared at the stern. It was Viper Ouyang, carrying a torch. He was shouting. The small boat was gone. He was enraged, but also afraid. Count Seven Hong released a hearty laugh from deep within his abdomen.

At that moment, out of nowhere, another skiff appeared, cresting a nearby wave. It was moving toward the Venom's ship with surprising speed.

"What's that—?" Count Seven cried.

Before he could finish his sentence, the two white condors swooped and circled the Venom's mainsail. A flash of white appeared on the skiff, and suddenly it jumped onto the larger ship. A golden hair band glimmered in the faint starlight.

"Lotus!" Guo Jing gasped.

4

LOTUS IT WAS INDEED. JUST AS SHE WAS ABOUT TO LEAVE Peach Blossom Island, she had caught sight of Ulaan galloping out of the forest. A horse is of no use at sea, she had thought, but the condors can help me find Guo Jing. She whistled and the birds appeared. There, tied to one of the bird's feet, she found Guo Jing's message: *Help.*

Condors have sharp eyes and fast wings, and before long they had again spotted Guo Jing's ship on the vast open waters. She followed the condors, urging her crew to sail her skiff as fast as they could, until, at last, she caught up with them.

As the birds circled above, the two craft pulled up close to each other. Clutching an Emei Needle, she jumped on board, only to find Viper Ouyang jumping up and down like an ant in a hot wok.

"Where's Guo Jing? What have you done with him?"

After lighting the fire belowdeck, he had discovered the small boat he was planning to escape on was gone. At that moment, Count Seven's laugh rang out. He cursed himself. He was the one now suffering the consequences of his own actions. Indeed, the situation made him feel anxious in the extreme. But now Lotus was here.

"Quick, onto her boat!" he shouted.

But the crew of Lotus's skiff were both deaf and mute. They had followed her orders out of fear, but, now that she had jumped aboard the bigger ship, they started to turn the sails to flee.

Count Seven and Guo Jing watched as the flames from the hold started to reach the deck. Unaware of the Venom's skulduggery, Guo Jing jumped up and cried, "Fire! Fire!"

"That's right," Count Seven said. "It was Viper Ouyang. He set the ship alight on purpose in order to let us burn to death."

Guo Jing looked at his Master blankly. Then, suddenly: "Lotus! We have to save her!"

"Back to the ship," Count Seven said.

Guo Jing heaved at the oars. The large ship had also changed course in order to draw closer. A crowd of snake herders and female servants had gathered on the deck and were shouting for help.

"Lotus!" Count Seven cried, trying to make his voice travel over the din. "Over here! Swim to us!"

It was night and the waves were high, but Lotus was a strong swimmer and there was no other way.

Lotus was overjoyed to hear her *shifu*'s voice. Ignoring the Ouyangs, she rushed to the side of the ship, preparing to hurl herself into the water below. At that moment, she felt something holding her back. A hand around her wrist. It was Viper Ouyang.

"Let go of me!" she shouted, aiming the Emei Needle in her other hand at the Venom's face. But he struck his fist at her, causing her to drop the needle into the roiling waves.

The mainmast and the sails were now aflame. Chaos had broken out among those on board. The ship would sink, any minute. Viper Ouyang knew he had to get onto the boat Count Seven had stolen. "Filthy beggar! I've got the girl!" He lifted Lotus up above his head.

The sea was a scarlet red as the blaze was reflected on its surface. Viper's actions only infuriated Count Seven even more. "He's using her to get on our boat. I'll get her back."

"I'm coming with you!" Guo Jing cried.

"No, you stay on the boat and guard it. You can't let the Venom take it."

"Yes, *Shifu*." Guo pulled hard on the oars again, and, within a few more strokes, they had drawn up alongside the large ship, which, with its sails turned to ash, was now becalmed.

Count Seven kicked the bottom of their craft and flew upward, reaching for the edge of the ship's rail, which he used to haul his body further up, landing with a somersault on the deck.

Viper Ouyang still had Lotus in his grip. "What are you going to do now, you filthy beggar?" he sneered.

"Fight. One thousand blows." Three rapid-fire palms followed.

Viper Ouyang quickly maneuvered Lotus into position as his shield, forcing Count Seven back. Lotus was unable to resist. The vital point on the back of her neck had been locked and she was nothing more than a floppy puppet.

"Have you no shame, Venom? Release the girl and fight me instead."

But he was smarter than that. How could he just release her? His nephew was being pushed back by the flames, so he threw the girl to him and called out, "Get on the boat!"

Gallant caught Lotus and glanced down at Guo Jing. The boat was small—too small. If he jumped down holding the girl, it would capsize. He saw a nearby piece of rope and, with one hand, grabbed it and tied it around what remained of the mast. Then, clutching Lotus, he lowered himself down the side of the ship.

Guo Jing was of course relieved to receive Lotus, but he was so caught up by the fight now in action up on the blazing deck that he failed to notice that her pressure points had been locked. The two martial Masters were launching attacks and counterattacks while jumping around, avoiding falling wood and burning lengths of rope. Count Seven's clothes were still wet from his earlier swim, which gave him a narrow advantage, whereas Viper's robes and hair were already beginning to smolder.

Count Seven took his chance to push Viper back toward the cabin, where the flames were fiercest, just as his hair and clothes were beginning to catch fire in earnest. Viper wanted to jump into the sea, but Count Seven was giving him no opportunity. The slightest lapse in his efforts to hold back the attack might result in injury, if not death. His mind was racing. How could he get out of this?

Count Seven's confidence, meanwhile, was growing. Maybe this time he was going to defeat the Venom of the West. But, at that moment, another thought popped into his head. If he dies now, it will have all been for nothing. I won't get to see him waste his time studying the fake Nine Yin Manual. At this, he laughed.

"Old Venom, today I will show you mercy. Get on the boat."

Viper Ouyang gave him a strange look, but quickly flipped over the edge and into the sea. Just as Count Seven was about to join him, Viper Ouyang called up: "Wait! Now I'm wet too, we can continue the fight, fair and square."

He then reached for a chain that was hanging down the side of the ship and used it to flip himself up onto the deck.

"Excellent! What better time for a fight!"

At that, fists began to fly and the duel was once again in motion.

"Lotus, look how fierce Old Venom is," Guo Jing said, his eyes still glued to the scene in front of them.

But Lotus was unable to answer, her pressure points still locked.

"Should I go up there and help *Shifu*?" he continued. "The ship is about to go down."

Still no answer. Guo Jing turned to look at her, only to find Gallant Ouyang with his hands around her wrists. "Get your hands off her!"

But Gallant had been longing to touch her for so long. How could he let go so quickly? "Make one move," he said with a cold smile, "and I will put my fist through her skull."

Without thinking, Guo Jing swung the oar he was still clutching straight at Gallant's head. Gallant ducked. Guo Jing dropped the oar and sent out two palms, forcing his opponent to let go of Lotus. Gallant cast his eyes around the small boat. It was no place for a fight. With a sweep of his arm, he moved into a Sacred Snake Fist. Guo Jing extended his left arm to block, at which Gallant suddenly bent his elbow and punched Guo Jing on the cheek—hard.

Stars clouded Guo Jing's vision. He momentarily closed his eyes— then, realizing the danger he was in, opened them again, just in time to see a second attack coming his way. He raised his left arm to block it. Again, Gallant's arm bent at an unnatural angle and Guo Jing threw his head back and struck out with his right hand. Usually, sending his body in two opposite directions would have resulted in each counteracting the other, but Guo Jing had studied Competing Hands under Zhou Botong. With his left arm poised, he pushed out with his right, trapping Gallant's arm. Guo Jing twisted and—*crack!* Gallant's bone broke.

Gallant was in fact a fighter on a par with the Quanzhen greats, like Ma Yu and Wang Chuyi, and much more accomplished than Guo Jing. The only thing was, Guo Jing's methods were just so strange. He had never seen anything like it and twice now had been injured because the unorthodox approach had caught him unawares.

Gallant Ouyang fell over, grimacing through the pain. Ignoring him, Guo Jing rushed to Lotus and unlocked her pressure points. Luckily, the combination of Count Seven's attack and Lotus's Hedgehog Chainmail had prevented Viper Ouyang from using the full force of his kung fu when he pressed the point on her neck. Otherwise, Guo Jing would never have been able to release her.

"Quick, *Shifu* needs help!" Lotus cried.

Guo Jing looked up to see his Master and Viper Ouyang engaged in hand-to-hand combat among the rising flames. The air rushed around their rapidly moving fists as the wooden deck bubbled and crackled. Suddenly, with an ear-splitting crack, the ship broke in two. The stern began to vanish into the waves, creating a whirlpool around it. Just as the other half of the ship started to sink, Guo Jing grabbed his oars and rowed the small boat up close.

At that moment, the blazing mainmast broke free and began to fall. Both men jumped back and watched as it landed between them.

Viper Ouyang reached for his Serpent Staff and swung it above the flames. Count Seven pulled out his Dog-Beating Cane and blocked.

Guo Jing rowed closer still, watching in amazement.

There was a saying in the *wulin*: "It takes a hundred days to master the saber, a thousand to master the spear, and ten thousand to master the sword." The sword may be considered the paragon, and yet every master brings their own unique skills and talents whatever weapon they are using, so that, in the end, there is little to separate them in a real fight. Many years ago, the great Masters gathered on Mount Hua in a Duel of Swords, yet this was actually a misnomer; the fighters employed all of the finest martial techniques—in much the same way as the term "classic" was first used for the seminal texts of Confucianism—the five, six, then thirteen classics—but then came to cover other philosophies, such as the *Classic of Mozi*, the *Classic of the Way and Virtue*, etc. Religious texts began to use the term "classic" too, as a translation of the Sanskrit word "sutra."

Count Seven's bamboo cane had been passed down for generations in the Beggar Clan. It was pliable and strong and a foot longer than most swords. A master of external kung fu, he had concentrated on strength when it came to wielding it, but after exploring the full possibilities of his weapon, he matched force with flexibility, which only increased its might many times over.

Viper Ouyang's Serpent Staff was also unique in that it combined the characteristics of the cudgel, the stick and the cane. He was able to execute a bewildering variety of moves with it. The top was carved into the shape of a grinning face with two rows of sharp teeth, like fangs, tipped with poison. The head seemed to dance like a demon about to chomp down on its enemy. A secret button, when pressed, would release darts laced with poison. The head could also be opened to reveal the two tiny snakes, which, now they had recovered from being drained, could wrap themselves around the shaft, spitting poison and writhing in all directions, making them dangerous and unpredictable.

When the two weapons clashed, each had its own advantages. Viper's staff may have been more sophisticated, but beggars are masters of catching snakes. Count Seven's cane danced like summer lightning, parrying each move and scoring hits whenever there was an opening. Viper moved his staff quicker. Count Seven, meanwhile, was yet to display his Dog-Beating skill. Yet both men feared revealing their secrets—one for fear of ridicule, the other for fear of having nothing left to use against his opponents at the next contest on Mount Hua.

Guo Jing stood on his small boat, watching. Several times, he thought of scrambling aboard to help his *shifu*, but it was a close and intense fight. He would not have much to contribute. It would be difficult even to get near them. All he could do was look on, helpless.

CHAPTER TWO

TEN THOUSAND TONS OF ROCK

I

VIPER OUYANG FELT HIMSELF GET HOTTER WITH EACH PASS-
ing second. The deck beneath his feet was cracking and splintering;
the boat was about to sink. Yet, Count Seven Hong's attacks were
as furious as ever. If he did not use one of his special moves now,
he might not come away from the fight alive. He pulled back his
Serpent Staff and struck with his other hand. Count Seven aimed
his bamboo stick at the weapon while blocking with his free hand.

Count Seven watched Viper Ouyang's arm bend and his fist
come corkscrewing toward his right temple, the precise location of
his Great Sun pressure point.

Viper had spent years developing his Sacred Snake Fist repertoire. He had been intending to save it for the second Contest of
Mount Hua. He had not revealed even one of its moves while exchanging over a thousand blows with Count Seven on Peach Blossom Island. Mimicking the writhing of a snake's body, which moves
as if it contains no bones, the arms twist and coil in all directions,
enabling him to land punches even when his opponent believes he
has successfully blocked an attack. Of course, it is not physically

possible for the arms to move like a snake, but the effect of the style was to make it seem that way.

Normally, such a strange and unexpected move would have made it difficult for Count Seven Hong to defend himself. But Gallant Ouyang had already used something similar against Guo Jing in the temple in Baoying, and, though he had prevailed against the Beggar's disciple, in doing so he had revealed his uncle's secret and given Count Seven the chance to spot a vital weakness.

That night, he had not attended the usual feast with Vigor Li and the other beggars, but instead had spent his time contemplating how it could be overcome. And now it delighted him that Old Venom was giving him the chance to test his theory. Forming his hand into a claw, he reached out and caught hold of Viper's fist. His approach was quick and accurate—the perfect way to counter Sacred Snake Fist. It came across as a lucky strike, but in fact it had taken Count Seven many a restless night and thousands of failed attempts to come up with the move. This one technique was sufficient to overcome the entire repertoire. He had doubted it, but now, in the heat of the battle, he could see that its simplicity, speed, and the element of surprise gave him a considerable advantage.

Viper Ouyang was in shock. He had expected his opponent to be rendered helpless, allowing him to move in and make his killer attack. He stumbled backward. At that moment, a cloud of black smoke descended and he disappeared within it.

Count Seven Hong leaped back in surprise. A large sail that had been set ablaze had fallen on top of Viper Ouyang.

In normal circumstances, a falling sail would not have troubled Viper Ouyang. But he had just witnessed the fruits of years of practice and careful training being subdued in an instant. Stupefied by this daunting revelation, he did not move as the large, stiff sail, still attached to the mast, descended upon him. Viper tried to throw it off a few times, but it was too heavy. Despite the danger he was in, his mind was remarkably clear. He tried to raise his Serpent Staff in order to slash through the cloth, but it was trapped beneath the mast.

There it is, he sighed. To the heavens I shall return.

As he relaxed his body to submit to the inevitable, he felt a great weight lifted from him. He opened his eyes and saw that he was no longer covered by the sail. Count Seven had raised the anchor and used it to pull the cloth away. The Old Beggar had no desire to watch his opponent be burned alive.

Viper Ouyang's clothes, hair, and brows were on fire. He jumped up and rolled across the deck, desperately trying to put out the flames. Unfortunately, bad luck rarely comes but once, and, at that moment, the boat lurched to one side, causing the heavy metal chain of the anchor to hurtle toward him.

"*Aiya!*" Count Seven launched himself forward and grabbed the chain, which by now the fire had rendered red hot. His skin crackled and fizzed as it came into contact with the burning metal. Instantly, he cast the chain into the sea. He was about to follow behind it when he felt his back go numb.

I saved Viper, and now he attacks me with his venom? Can it be possible? He turned to find himself face-to-face with a snake, fresh blood dripping from its teeth. Enraged, he threw two palms at Viper Ouyang, who merely stepped aside and watched as Count Seven's hands slammed into the second mast, splitting it in two.

Viper Ouyang was delighted that his surprise attack had succeeded, but Count Seven Hong's thrashing and punching was getting ever more intense and so he slunk back.

"*Shifu! Shifu!*" Guo Jing shouted. He started climbing up onto what remained of the ship.

Suddenly, Count Seven, feeling dizzy, stumbled. Viper Ouyang charged at him and struck his palms at the Beggar's back. One of the snakes had sunk its teeth into the back of Count Seven's neck. Luckily, its normally deadly poison had been depleted only days before in the wager with Zhou Botong. It was enough, however, to scramble Count Seven's wits and leave him unable to summon sufficient internal strength to resist Viper's blow.

He spat blood and collapsed.

Viper Ouyang knew that it was not enough just to defeat a skilled martial artist such as Count Seven Hong. Given a few days of rest, he would be back to cause untold troubles. An attack, once made, had to be decisive.

2

MOMENTS BEFORE, GUO JING HAD PULLED HIMSELF OVER THE side of the crippled ship and was now standing on the deck. His *shifu* was in great danger. He thrust both palms at Viper Ouyang's lower back, in a Twin Dragons Skim the Water. The Venom of the West knew that the boy's martial skills were considerable, yet he paid him little attention at that moment. He blocked with his left hand, and he launched his foot at Count Seven Hong's lower back. Determined to save his Master, Guo Jing leaped up and grabbed Viper's neck, thus exposing his pressure points. With a *pow!* Viper jabbed him below the ribs, knocking him aside.

Viper did not put the full force of his strength behind the blow, but he knew he had the power to kill his opponent if he chose to. Had it not been for Guo Jing's considerable internal strength, he would have suffered great harm. He felt a sharp pain, then a numbness spread through the lower half of his body.

Undeterred, he leaped again and grabbed hold of the Venom's head.

Viper Ouyang was surprised by the boy's rash move; he had expected him to retreat. Now, they both risked being injured. He pulled back his foot before it could meet with Count Seven Hong and bent at the waist to hit out at Guo Jing. He was too close to use any Exploding Toad kung fu or his Sacred Snake Fist. Masters of the *wulin* rarely grappled at such close range.

Within moments, Guo Jing had both hands around Viper Ouyang's throat. Viper flailed his arms behind his back, but did not manage to land a single blow. Guo Jing's grip was tightening, and

Viper Ouyang was struggling to breathe. The Venom thrust his elbow back.

Guo Jing ducked right, released his left hand, slipped it under Viper's armpit and then back onto his neck, and pulled. This was a move known as Camel's Twist, which he had learned from Mongolian wrestling. It owed its name to the fact that, when done effectively, the technique could be used to snap the neck of even a camel. It was brutal and sent an intense pain through Viper's body. Only the most skilled Mongolian wrestlers knew how to counter it. Viper had never come across anything like it, so he suffered the full extent of its power.

Viper flailed once more with his arms, trying to hit back at Guo Jing, who took his chance to let go with his right hand and repeat the move by slipping it under Viper's armpit, grabbing hold of his neck and twisting. Once again, Guo Jing had both hands around Viper's throat, in a move called Breaking Mountain Stranglehold. It was impossible to get out of it without snapping one's neck.

And yet, the Venom of the West was a master of the *wulin*, not some common Mongolian wrestler. Using lightness kung fu, he ducked down and rolled out between Guo Jing's legs.

To have to roll under the legs of a junior fighter like this was humiliating, to be sure, but Viper had been in dire straits. Once on his feet, he immediately launched his left fist at Guo Jing's back. He did not expect, however, that, before his hand met its target, his arm would be stopped dead.

Guo Jing knew his kung fu was no match for his opponent, but a combination of youthful enthusiasm and his knowledge of close-combat fighting and Mongolian wrestling meant that he was managing to keep the Master at bay.

But, before he could press home his advantage, the ship listed violently, knocking the two men off balance and into the flames, setting their hair and clothes alight.

3

LOTUS CAUGHT SIGHT OF COUNT SEVEN HONG'S LIFELESS body slumped over the ship's railings. Was he alive? She could not tell. She looked up to see Guo Jing and Viper Ouyang still fighting without any sign of letup, their clothes now alight. Meanwhile, the Viper's nephew had got to his feet again after the injury he had suffered at Guo Jing's hands. Sensing the acute danger, she had no choice but to lift an oar and swing it in the direction of Gallant Ouyang's head.

Even with a broken arm, Gallant managed to dodge the oar. Then he reached out to grab Lotus's bracelet. Lotus responded by stamping her feet so that the small boat rocked and almost capsized. Gallant was unable to swim, so he let go of Lotus to steady himself. Before the boat had returned to an even keel, Lotus dived into the sea.

Within seconds, she was beside the Viper's ship, which was by now so low in the water that the deck was almost level with the sea. Lotus pulled herself quickly aboard, removed Guo Jing's dagger from her waistband and rushed forward to help him. Guo Jing and Viper Ouyang were twisted into a bundle, rolling around on the deck. At that moment, Viper Ouyang was on top, but Guo Jing had a firm grip on his opponent's shoulders, pinning his arms so there was little he could do to harm the young man.

Lotus cast herself, dagger first, at Viper's back. It was the very blade Qiu Chuji had given Guo Jing's parents, with his name carved on the hilt. It had been in Mercy Mu's possession, but Lotus had swapped it for the dagger with Yang Kang's name on it.

The dagger glanced off Viper's back. Surprised, he twisted violently, spinning so Guo Jing was on top. Lotus bent low and aimed for his head, but Viper once again managed to dodge. Three times she stabbed, and three times he evaded her, so that she plunged the blade into the deck.

A thick plume of black smoke blew over them, stinging Lotus's eyes. She closed them, then felt a pain in her leg and rolled over. Viper Ouyang's heel. She jumped to her feet, only to find her hair had caught fire. She raised the dagger once more, but, as she turned to face the Viper, Guo Jing shouted, "*Shifu!* Save *Shifu* first!"

Lotus ran to Count Seven, picked him up and jumped overboard, into the sea, extinguishing the flames that were consuming his robe.

She moved her *shifu* onto her back and began to swim toward the small boat. Gallant Ouyang watched her approach, raised the oar above his head and called, "Leave the beggar! I'll only let you on board if you come alone."

"Then we can meet in the water," she cried, and she began shaking the boat violently.

It felt as if the boat was about to capsize. Gallant began to panic and gripped the side. "No . . . Don't shake it! It's going to roll!"

Lotus laughed. "Then pull my *shifu* up. Be careful. If you try anything, I'll give you another good drenching."

Gallant Ouyang had no choice but to obey. He grabbed hold of the back of Count Seven's robes and heaved him up with his one good arm.

"I think that's the first noble deed I've seen you do since the moment I met you."

Gallant's heart leaped. He wanted to reply, but he could not find the words.

Just as Lotus was about to turn and climb back onto the burning ship, a deafening rumble echoed all around them. A wall of water was heading their way. She closed her eyes and held her breath, waiting for it to hit, but, when nothing came, she opened her eyes again. She was astonished to see a large whirlpool drawing the ship, Guo Jing and Viper Ouyang into its churning maw.

Her mind went blank. She could not think, she did not feel; it was as if the skies and world around her had all disappeared. She did not know where she was. Suddenly, a rush of water filled her mouth and she felt herself sinking. Only then did her body jolt back into action.

She began kicking her way to the surface. As she broke through to the air, she looked around. All she could see was water, and one lonely boat. Everything else had been swallowed by the waves.

Lotus dived down, kicking herself deeper. She was a powerful swimmer, but the strong current made it difficult to search for Guo Jing. She swam in circles, but there was no trace of him. Viper Ouyang, too, had seemingly gone down with his ship.

She was soon exhausted, but refused to give up. She prayed that the heavens would show mercy and deliver Guo Jing back to her, but the waves rose like mountains on every side. After an hour, she could continue no longer. She would rest for a while on the boat before resuming her search.

Gallant Ouyang reached out and pulled her on board. "My uncle? Did you see him?" He was similarly distraught.

But Lotus was too tired to answer him. Darkness suddenly drew a veil over her eyes, and she fainted.

When, finally, she regained consciousness, it felt as if her body was floating—not in the water, but up in the clouds. The wind and the waves continued to beat against her eardrums. She sat upright and noticed that the boat was moving, carried by the current. How far had they moved from where the ship was swallowed up? She would never find Guo Jing again. The realization made her heart physically hurt, which in turn caused her to faint once again.

Gallant gripped the side of the boat, fearing that the waves would fling him overboard. He did not dare move in case he destabilized the vessel.

Time passed and eventually Lotus awoke. The first thought that came to her was the pointlessness of her existence, now that her beloved was lying on the seabed. She looked across at Gallant Ouyang, his ashen cheeks and frightened expression, and felt nothing but disgust. Am I destined to die alongside this beast? was all she could think. Suddenly, she stood. "Into the water!"

"What?" Gallant replied in alarm.

"Aren't you going to jump? Then I'll capsize the boat."

She began to shift her weight from right to left. The boat lurched more violently with each movement. Gallant began to shout in terror, which only turned Lotus's grief into joy. She rocked the boat harder.

Gallant knew how close the boat was to rolling. He waited until Lotus moved left and threw himself right, his weight canceling out hers. The boat sunk momentarily deeper into the water, but bobbed back up again. Lotus tried twice more, but Gallant continued to counteract her efforts, until the boat began to stabilize.

"Very well, I will make holes in the boat instead. Then we'll see what you do."

She took out the dagger again and moved to the center of the boat. That was when she noticed her Master, lying in the prow. He had neither said anything nor moved a muscle since Guo Jing disappeared into the ocean, so she had completely forgotten about him. A bolt of shock passed through her. She bent over to check his pulse. It was weak, but still there. Relieved, she pulled him into a sitting position. His eyes were screwed tightly shut and his cheeks were white like paper. He no longer clutched at his chest. Pushing aside all thoughts of Gallant, she focused on her Master and unbuttoned his shirt to check his wounds.

At that moment, the boat lurched. "Land! Land!" Gallant Ouyang shouted.

Lotus looked in the direction he was pointing. There, in the distance, was the hazy outline of trees. The boat, however, had stopped moving. It had run aground on a shallow reef.

They were still far from the shoreline, but they could see the seabed. Gallant Ouyang jumped over the gunwale. The water only came up to his belly. He took a few steps, then looked back at Lotus. He returned to the boat.

Count Seven's back bore the bluish-black imprint of a hand. It seemed to have been branded into his skin. Lotus examined it in astonishment. Could the Venom's palm really be so powerful?

At that moment, she noticed two puncture wounds on his

shoulder. Had she not been looking carefully, she would have missed them. She reached over to feel them, but a sharp pain seized her fingertips. She pulled them away. "*Shifu*, how do you feel?"

Count Seven's only answer was a groan.

Lotus turned to Gallant. "Give me the antidote."

Gallant Ouyang threw his hands up in the air. "My uncle has it."

"I don't believe you."

"Then search me." He began to undo his belt to empty his pockets and pouches of all the trinkets stored inside. There was no medicine bottle among them.

"Then you must help me carry *Shifu* onto dry land!"

Together, they each took one arm over their shoulders. Lotus then reached out and took Gallant's free hand, so that Count Seven could sit on their arms. He whimpered, but, wishing to appear brave before Lotus, bore the pain. Slowly, they waded to shore.

Count Seven was shivering violently, and Lotus was growing ever more concerned. Gallant, in contrast, was in a state of ecstasy as he felt her smooth skin in his hand. It was like a dream. He only regretted how quickly they made it to the shore.

Lotus squatted and placed Count Seven on the ground. "Go and drag the boat up onto land," she said to Gallant. "Don't let it be swept out to sea."

Gallant Ouyang did not go; instead, he touched his hand to his lips, as if in a trance. Lotus repeated her instructions, shouting this time, but he merely looked up at her blankly. He had not heard a word she had said.

Fortunately, Lotus was unaware of what he was thinking. She gave him a sideways glance and repeated her instructions a third time.

Gallant returned to the water and dragged the boat to shore. Lotus, meanwhile, had rolled Count Seven onto his back in the grass and was tending to his wounds.

Where are we? Gallant asked himself. He ran up a small hill so that he could assess their surroundings. What he saw was a pleasant surprise. In all directions, as far as the eye could see, the ocean stretched out to the horizon. They had landed on a small, remote island, lush with vegetation, but with no signs of human habitation. But then it hit him. With no food and no shelter, how would they survive? They had been lucky to find it, the heavens had surely arranged it, and he was alone with this beautiful goddess. Apart from the Old Beggar, of course, but he was severely injured. How could he not count this as a blessing? With the right person, even a deserted island like this could be paradise. Should death come quickly, it would still be an ending for which he owed a debt of thanks to the grace of the gods above. His whole body was jittery with the thought.

A pain in his shoulder suddenly reminded him of his broken bone. He approached a nearby tree and broke off two branches, then tore some cloth from his robes and fashioned himself a splint and sling.

Lotus was, at that moment, squeezing the venom from Count Seven's neck. She could not think how else to help him, other than moving him onto a large rock where he might get some rest. Fortunately, the lid to the bottle of Dew of Nine Flowers pills had been screwed securely shut, so no water had got inside. She took out two and fed them to her Master. Then she called over to Gallant: "Go and see where we are and if there is an inn nearby."

"This is an island, there is no inn. We'll be lucky if we find any other people."

Lotus was taken back. "Go and look," she replied.

Excited, he began to run east, using his lightness kung fu. All he could see were trees. There was no evidence of any human activity. He managed to kill two wild hares, however, as he completed his full loop of the island.

"It's deserted," he announced upon his return.

Lotus saw the trace of a smile on his face and felt irritation bubble up inside her. "Deserted? Why are you so happy?"

Gallant did not dare answer, and instead got to work skinning the hares. Lotus reached inside her robes for a tinderbox. It had been wrapped in oil paper, so there was still some tinder that was dry. She lit a fire and roasted the meat. She tossed one toward

Gallant, tore a hind leg from the second and proceeded to feed it to Count Seven.

Count Seven was still feeling faint and confused, but the smell of roasting meat had revived his spirits. He opened his mouth wide, tasted the succulent flesh and then gestured for more. Delighted, Lotus tore off the other leg. Count Seven managed to finish half before he could resist sleep no longer, and, with his mouth still full of succulent flesh, he drifted off.

Lotus ate two mouthfuls before she remembered her poor beloved Guo Jing at rest at the bottom of the sea. The grief was overpowering, and she felt herself choke on the meat. She could stomach no more. The sky was turning dark blue. She found a cave and Gallant helped her to move Count Seven, laying him out carefully on a bed of dry grass. Lotus watched as he fixed bedding for them and settled down next to her.

She drew her dagger. "Get out!"

"Why does it concern you if I sleep in here too? Why are you so fierce?"

Lotus raised her eyebrows. "Are you going?"

"Go to sleep, there's a nice girl. Don't worry. I don't need to leave."

Lotus reached for a lit torch and set fire to the grass bedding under him. Within seconds, it had flared and burned down to ash.

Gallant laughed bitterly. He knew he had no choice but to leave. What if there were poisonous insects or vicious animals? He decided to climb a tree for safety. But he couldn't settle, and shinned up and down at least a dozen times to check on the cave. He could see that the fire at the mouth of the cave was still lit, but Lotus was fast asleep. Still, he could not bring himself to enter. A coward! He had stolen many moments amid the perfume and jade of a lady's private quarters, but he was scared of this particular young woman. In reality, he could overcome her with his one good hand. Count Seven was in a critical condition and would not be able to help her. And yet, still, every time he approached the fire, he ended up shrinking back.

Lotus did not sleep well that night, concerned over Count Seven's health and wary of Gallant returning to the cave. She managed a few hours' sleep just before dawn, during which she dreamed that Count Seven was groaning. She awoke with a start.

"*Shifu*, how are you?"

Count Seven pointed to his mouth and wiggled several of his teeth with his tongue.

Lotus laughed, fetched the leftover roasted hare from the night before and began feeding him. As the meat entered his stomach, he felt his strength return. He pulled himself into a sitting position and regulated his breathing. Lotus did not want to disturb him, so she watched in silence as his cheeks flushed red before once again turning ashen white. The color came and went a few times, until she saw a burst of steam come out of the top of his head. Sweat ran down his forehead like rain and his whole body began to shake.

Suddenly, a shadow passed across the mouth of the cave. Gallant Ouyang had stepped inside to see what was going on.

Lotus knew very well that her Master was calling on his inner strength to heal his injuries. With his life hanging by a thread, any disturbance would break his concentration and put him in real danger.

"Get out," she hissed.

"Let's talk," Gallant Ouyang replied. "We need to come up with a strategy to survive this deserted island. We might be here for a very long time!" He took a few further steps into the cave.

Count Seven Hong opened his eyes only a crack. "Deserted island?"

"*Shifu*, ignore him and concentrate on your kung fu." Lotus turned to Gallant Ouyang. "Come with me. We'll talk outside."

Her answer pleased him no end and he followed her out.

The weather was fine, but the blue skies did nothing to cheer Lotus. She looked out to where the sky met the vast open ocean and saw nothing, save for a few lonely clouds. There was no sign of land.

She walked toward the beach where they had waded ashore the previous day, and where Gallant had deposited their craft.

"Where's the boat?" she said, a tremble in her voice.

"Oh, yes, where is it? The waves must have taken it. What a shame! How terrible!"

One look at his face was enough to tell Lotus that he had pushed the boat out to sea on purpose. How despicable! Guo Jing was dead, and she had no desire to go on living. The boat was probably too flimsy to make it back to the mainland, anyway. But still, she feared she would not be able to keep this scoundrel contained for long enough to allow her Master to heal from his injuries. She stared at Gallant Ouyang, her expression frozen. In her heart, she was thinking of all the possible ways to kill him and save her *shifu*.

Gallant, in turn, looked away in shame.

Lotus jumped up onto a large rock at the water's edge, sat down and gazed out at the sea, clutching her knees.

If I don't try to get close to her now, when will I? Gallant Ouyang thought. He climbed up beside her and sat down close to her. He waited. She did not seem to be angry and did not move further away. He shuffled a bit closer. "Lotus, we could live out our days here. It could be our paradise. I must have done something wonderful in a past life to deserve such happiness!"

Lotus laughed. "There are only three of us on this island. Won't you feel lonely?"

There was something gentle in her tone and it boosted his confidence. "With you by my side, how could I be lonely? And with a few children, even less so."

This made Lotus laugh even harder. "Children? Who is going to have them? I don't know how."

"I'll teach you," Gallant said with a smile, and he reached out to touch her. He felt a warmth in his left hand. Lotus had already placed her hand in his. He felt a rush of blood and his heart started thumping wildly. He was dizzy with happiness.

Lotus removed her hand and gently touched his wrist. "I've heard rumors that you took Mercy Mu's chastity? Is that true?"

"That Mu girl didn't know what was best for her," Gallant said and laughed. "She refused me, and I, Gallant Ouyang, am not a man to force a woman."

"Then the rumors are just talk? She and her sweetheart fought because of them."

"What a pity that her reputation should be thus tainted!" was all Gallant Ouyang offered as a reply.

"What's that?" Lotus said suddenly, pointing out to sea.

Gallant Ouyang looked to where she was pointing. Just then, he felt his wrist tighten and his body go numb. He could not move. Lotus drew her dagger and stabbed in the direction of his abdomen.

Thus immobilized, how could he stop her?

And yet, he had spent a dozen bitter winters training at the summit of White Camel Mount. At the last moment, he managed to launch himself at Lotus's back. She jumped down from the rock, her blade instead scoring a foot-long gash in his leg. Gallant leaped after her. He saw her dagger and laughed. Pain filled his chest. He glanced down to find the front of his robes soaked in blood. The spikes of her Hedgehog Chainmail had torn through his skin.

"We were talking, just now; why did you try to charge at me?" Lotus said. "Well, no matter." With that, she turned and left.

Gallant Ouyang watched her leave in silence, his heart thumping with love and hate, surprise and joy.

4

AS LOTUS WALKED BACK TO THE CAVE, SHE REPROACHED HER-self for having allowed him to escape. It was thanks to her mediocre skills! Once inside, she saw Count Seven asleep and a black pool of blood on the ground.

"*Shifu*, how are you? Any better?"

"Bring me wine," came the reply through shallow breaths.

The request left the young woman feeling anxious; where was

she going to find wine on this deserted island? "I will do my best. Your injuries are not serious, are they, *Shifu*?"

Tears collected in her eyes and a few tumbled down her cheeks. Lotus rarely cried, but, now that she had started, she could not hold it back. Burying her face in Count Seven's chest, she heaved and sobbed. Count Seven stroked her hair and gently patted her on the back. He had spent decades wandering the rivers and lakes, but this was the first time he had consoled a crying maiden. He was not sure what to do. "There, there, little girl," was all he could think to say. "Don't cry, your *shifu* will take care of you. Please don't cry. *Shifu* doesn't want wine anymore."

Presently, the tears stopped, and Lotus looked up to see her Master's clothes were damp from all her crying.

"Oh, why didn't I manage to kill that awful scoundrel?" She then began to relate the story.

Count Seven Hong listened in silence before eventually saying, "*Shifu* can't help you now. That rogue's skills are more advanced than yours. I'm afraid all you've got against him are your wits."

"All *Shifu* needs is a few days' rest, and then you'll be able to take him with one thrust of your palm!" Lotus replied.

"The Venom of the West got me with his deadly venom and his Exploding Toad kung fu. I've had to use all my strength to rid my body of the toxins, but still some remains. Even if I survive, my martial skills will be affected. I will be just like any other old man."

"Nonsense, *Shifu*!"

"My heart still beats, but even an old beggar must recognize when the time comes to look at life philosophically."

He paused, before continuing in a grave tone: "Child, your *shifu* has no choice. I must ask you a favor—a most difficult one! Will you do it?"

"Of course, *Shifu*! Just tell me."

He sighed, then said, "We've not had long together as Master and student; I didn't get to teach you much. But your opponent is skilled, so I must burden you with something of great weight, or I will never find peace."

Count Seven was usually so jovial and lighthearted, so, from the way he hesitated, Lotus knew that, whatever it was he was about to ask of her, it was important.

"*Shifu*, please tell me. You came to Peach Blossom Island for my sake and now you are gravely injured. I will never be able to repay you. I only hope that I am not too young to carry out your request."

"So, you accept?" A glimmer of joy passed across Count Seven Hong's face.

"Yes. Please tell me."

Shakily, Count Seven Hong rose to his feet, cupped his hands and bowed toward the north. "My beggar ancestors," he began, "the clan that you founded has passed into my hands. Unfortunately, I lack the virtue and the talent necessary for the task. Today, great misfortune has befallen me and I have no choice but to pass on my burden. Spirits in the heavens, bless this child so that she might turn calamity into fortuity. This I do for the good of all the Clan." At this, he bowed once more, while Lotus listened in shock.

"Now kneel, child."

Lotus did as she was told and Count Seven raised his bamboo stick, before lowering it into her hands.

"*Shifu*," Lotus began to stutter, "you want me to be the . . . the . . . Chief of the Beggar Clan?"

"Precisely. I am the eighteenth Chief of the Clan, and you shall be the nineteenth. Now, let us thank the ancestors."

Lotus did not dare disobey. Imitating her *shifu's* movements, she cupped her hands and bowed. At that moment, Count Seven spluttered and coughed a globule of phlegm, which landed on Lotus's skirt. *Shifu's* injuries are serious indeed, she said to herself sadly. He is too exhausted even to spit properly. She pretended not to have seen it.

"When it becomes official to the Clan, there will be a disgusting ritual, I am afraid. It will be hard on you."

Lotus smiled. Beggars were all rough and filthy; how could it be avoided?

Count Seven exhaled slowly. His cheeks were white, but it was clear that his heart had been relieved of a heavy rock that had been pressing down upon it. A smile came to his lips. Lotus helped him to lie down.

"Now that you are the chief," he began, "I am nothing but an elder of the Clan. While you must show me respect, you give the orders now. This was the way our ancestors decreed it, so you must obey. And, when you give your instructions, the Clan must obey."

Lotus at once felt anxious. She was stuck on a deserted island, with no way to get back to the mainland. Guo Jing was dead, and she had no desire to live without him, but now her *shifu* had made her chief of all the beggars in the world . . . How was she going to fulfill his wishes? She looked down at Count Seven. Given his condition, she could not reveal these thoughts to him, so she merely nodded.

"On the fifteenth day of the seventh month of this year, the Four Elders of our Clan will gather by the shores of Dongting Lake, in Yuezhou, where they will hear the new chief announced. You need only bring my bamboo cane and they shall understand my intentions. All matters within the Clan are dealt with by the Four Elders. It does pain me, however, to send such a pure and chaste maiden into the arms of a rabble of squalid beggars. Yet, for all their filthy clothes and manners, the beggars are at least pure of heart." He began to laugh, but was soon overcome by a hacking cough. Lotus massaged his back until he stopped.

"I am of no use to anyone now," Count Seven Hong sighed. "Who knows when I will be called on to make my final journey? I'd better start teaching you Dog-Beating Cane, before it's too late."

It was an awful name for a martial-arts technique, Lotus could not help but think. And, besides, she could kill any dog with one punch, so why should she waste her time learning a whole repertoire to achieve the same end? But her Master was very ill indeed, and it was his wish, so she could only comply.

"Becoming the Chief of the Beggar Clan does not require you to change who you are," Count Seven said. "If you like being mischievous, then it is mischievous you must be. This is why we live as beggars, so that we might be free to be ourselves, without restriction. Otherwise, why not become an official or a rich landowner? Or why not Emperor! If you think fighting with the Dog-Beating Cane is beneath you, then just say so!"

Lotus began to laugh. "I am merely wondering what dog could possibly be so fierce that it requires a special weapon and an entire fighting technique to overcome it."

"You are now chief of all the beggars and you must act accordingly. Dressed in your finery and with the airs of a nobleman's daughter, why, of course any dog will happily heel to you. Why would you need to hit it? But that is not the case for us beggars. As the old saying goes, 'A poor man without a staff will be beaten by dogs.' You've never been poor. You don't understand our struggles."

"Aha! *Shifu*, in this, you are mistaken!" Lotus said in delight.

Count Seven Hong looked puzzled.

"Just after Spring Festival this year, I escaped Peach Blossom Island and wandered the country, dressed as a beggar. There were many fierce dogs, but all I had to do was give them a kick and they instantly skulked away."

"And when a dog is particularly fierce, you have to beat it with a staff."

Do such dogs exist? Lotus asked herself. "Oh! I see!" she cried suddenly. "You mean other kinds of villains too!"

"You are clever," Count Seven Hong chuckled. "Unlike . . ." He was about to say Guo Jing, but he stopped himself as a pang of sadness filled his chest.

Lotus understood immediately what he had been about to say, and a well of pain and bitterness flooded her heart. She wanted to wail out loud, but her Master needed her. In many ways, she was the adult in their relationship, and the responsibility of the Clan now lay on her shoulders, so she merely turned her head so that he could not see the wet beads of salt tears falling down her cheeks.

Count Seven knew there was no use in trying to console her—he felt the same sadness, after all—so he drew the conversation back to the history of the technique. "Our ancestors invented the thirty-six moves that make up the repertoire. It is passed only between chiefs of the Clan—no one else is allowed to know. Our third chief greatly surpassed the Clan's founders and expanded its scope. For hundreds of years, now, the chiefs have used these techniques to defeat our toughest enemies."

Lotus's interest was now piqued. "Master," she almost breathed, "why didn't you use it against the Venom of the West when you were fighting him on the ship?"

"This is a most important and sacred repertoire for our Clan, and I had every chance of winning without having to resort to it. Who was to know that Viper Ouyang would be so underhand as to use venom against me, even after I had twice saved his life? He betrayed me."

Lotus could see his mood was sinking. "Master," she said, trying to distract him, "please teach me this great skill so that I might avenge you by killing him."

Count Seven smiled, then reached for a piece of firewood and leaned against the stone wall. He began to recite the instructions, executing each of the thirty-six moves with the stick as he did so. Lotus was of exceptional intelligence, this he knew, and he feared he was not long for this world. The name of the technique may have been coarse, but the movements and transitions were subtle, and, as a whole, it was deserving of its reputation as one of the finest of all the martial systems ever invented. Why else would it have been so jealously guarded by generations of Clan leaders?

And yet, for all her quickness of mind, Lotus was able to remember only the overall structure, but none of the finer details. How could she master such a complex technique in such a short time?

Count Seven paused to catch his breath as the sweat dampened his clothes. "I have not taught you well," he panted. "But that is all I can manage, for now . . ." He groaned, then fell to the ground.

"*Shifu!*" Lotus cried and rushed to prop him up, but his body was cold, his cheeks white and his breath was shallow. It was too late.

These last few days had been full of trials and misfortunes, but, as she lay against her Master's chest, the tears refused to come. She listened to his faint heartbeat and tried to massage his heart to aid his breathing.

Just then, she heard noises from behind. A hand reached out toward her.

She had been too consumed with tending to her Master to notice that Gallant Ouyang had entered the cave, and, when she did, she momentarily forgot that the man behind her was a wolf. "My Master is dying," she said, turning around. "We must save him."

The tears in her eyes and the depth of her despair sent a quiver through Gallant's heart. He bent down to examine the Old Beggar, and the sight of his pale cheeks and rolled-back eyes restored his good mood. He was so close to Lotus that he could feel her breathing and smell her sweet, floral fragrance. A few strands of her hair fluttered, caressing her cheek, and his chest began thumping so hard he could barely contain himself. He reached out and put his arm around her waist.

Taken aback, Lotus struck him and jumped away. Gallant Ouyang had been fearful of Count Seven Hong and thus had not dared to move to claim the young object of his desires, but, now her protector was dying, he was no longer deterred. "I had decided to restrain myself, but you are just too beautiful. Come, kiss me."

He approached her again. Lotus was terrified. She was in greater danger now than she had been in the Prince of Zhao's residence. I have to kill him, or I will never forgive myself. She reached into her robe and took out Guo Jing's dagger.

Smiling, Gallant Ouyang removed his long robe and came two steps closer. Lotus waited for him to take another step. Before his foot could touch the ground, she had thrown herself left.

Gallant followed. Lotus raised her arm. He whipped his robe and flicked the dagger aside. Lotus shot toward the mouth of the cave like an arrow.

But Gallant was faster. Lotus heard the rush of air behind her— his fist was coming for her back. She was wearing her Hedgehog Chainmail and she was not scared to die. In order to attack, she would have to leave herself vulnerable. She turned and jabbed her dagger at his chest.

Gallant had no intention of hurting her—his punch had a feint, nothing but a ruse designed to tire her out. But, with the flash of the blade, he grabbed at her wrist, pivoted and rushed past her, trapping Lotus inside the cave.

Lotus launched a fresh onslaught, fierce and fast, with no thought to her own defense. Gallant was far more accomplished in kung fu than Lotus, but, given his reluctance to cause her any real harm, he found it difficult, at first, to ward off her attack.

Yet, before long, they had exchanged over fifty moves, and Lotus was in trouble. She had learned her kung fu from her father, Gallant from his uncle. Apothecary Huang and Viper Ouyang were peers in the *wulin*, but Lotus was only fifteen and Gallant was in his fourth decade. This amounted to a twenty-year gap between them in training and practice, and that was without taking into consideration the difference in their strength, as governed purely by biology. Lotus was a less diligent student than her opponent. She had learned a few moves from Count Seven, to be sure, but she had not taken the time to truly master them. This all meant that, despite his injury, Gallant had the upper hand.

Suddenly, Lotus pounced forward and threw a handful of needles. Gallant blocked them with a flap of his robe. Lotus followed with a stab at his right shoulder. He tried to strike with his good palm, but the dagger in Lotus's hand twirled, changed directions, and with a *huh!* plunged toward his broken arm.

Lotus grinned, despite the numbing pain pulsing through her wrist. The dagger clattered to the ground.

Gallant had reached out and pressed on her Suspended Bell pressure point, three inches above her left ankle, then the Central Metropolis, seven inches above her right ankle, on the inside of her leg.

Lotus managed two more steps before stumbling and falling. Gallant rushed forward to place his robe beneath her.

"*Aiya*—careful!"

As soon as she hit the ground, Lotus threw more needles at Gallant and tried to propel herself back onto her feet, but, with no feeling in her legs, she fell again.

Gallant reached out to help her up, but Lotus returned the gesture with a punch from her remaining good hand. Her move lacked any strength, however, and Gallant merely laughed as he pressed the pressure point on her wrist.

Lotus coiled into a heap, as if she were a piece of rope. I should have turned the weapon on myself, she lamented. Now, I can't even beg for death.

A darkness descended over her eyes and she fainted.

"Don't be scared," Gallant said in a soothing voice. Just as he reached out a hand to touch her, a cold voice came from behind.

"Do you wish to live? Or die?"

Gallant twisted round and saw Count Seven Hong standing at the entrance to the cave, giving him a cold sideways look. Instantly, he recalled the story his uncle had told him about how Wang Chongyang had jumped out of his coffin and nearly killed him. The Old Beggar was only pretending to be dead; I'm done for. He knew he was no match for the old Master in a fight, so he knelt before him.

"Lotus and I were just playing. Don't be angry, Uncle Hong."

"Scoundrel!" Count Seven spat the word. "Are you going to release her, or shall I?"

Gallant nodded and rushed to press Lotus's pressure points.

"Come back and I will not show the same mercy. Now, go!" With that, Count Seven turned away.

Gallant ran off, disappearing like a puff of vapor.

Lotus came to slowly, as if waking from a dream. Count Seven

Hong could bare the pain no more and collapsed to the ground. Lotus leaped up and rushed to support him. His mouth was full of blood and three of his teeth tumbled from his gums.

A master of his level, Lotus said to herself, and he is reduced to this, losing his teeth in a fall.

Count Seven spat the teeth into his hand. "My poor little choppers, you and I shall never again savor gourmet delights together. I never expected you to be the ones to say goodbye first."

The old man was gravely injured. The venom was still wreaking its havoc and Viper's blow to his back had damaged the vital meridians through which his *qi* flowed. That he was still alive was largely due to the years of kung fu training, but he was so weakened that a stranger would not have guessed he was a martial man at all. He would not even have had the strength to unlock Lotus's pressure points by himself. He looked at her concerned face.

"Don't worry. I may be weak, but I still have my reputation. That foul imp won't be back any time soon."

"True. But where will we get our food?" She was usually sharp-witted, but the shock of events had flustered her, and she could not think straight.

"You're thinking of ways to get food?"

Lotus nodded.

"Help me to the beach and we can sit in the sun."

Count Seven leaned on her shoulder and together they slowly walked toward the sea.

The weather was fine, and the sea stretched without limit, like a sheet of blue satin quivering in a breeze.

If only it were actually made of satin, Lotus thought to herself. So soft, so shiny. So nice to the touch.

The sun warmed their bodies and their spirits.

5

GALLANT OUYANG WAS STANDING SOME DISTANCE AWAY, beside a large rock. He saw them approach and quickly retreated, but they did not follow. So, he stopped to watch.

Gallant was cunning, both Count Seven and Lotus knew that, but he would reveal his weakness eventually. For now, however, they wished to distract themselves, so Count Seven sat on a rock and Lotus broke off a branch to make herself a fishing rod. She peeled the bark from another long stick to use as the line, and took one of her needles out of her robe, bent it and secured it as a hook. She found some small crabs and shrimp to use as bait. The water was teeming with fish and, before long, she pulled up three local mackerel, each weighing around a *jin*. Lotus then wrapped the fish in clay and cooked them slowly—the same method used to make beggar's chicken. Together, Master and pupil filled their bellies.

After they had rested awhile, Count Seven instructed Lotus to perform each of the moves that made up the Dog-Beating repertoire. He sat on the rock and gave her guidance. Lotus was beginning to get to grips with its techniques, its subtle changes and amalgamations.

By sunset, she was hot and dusty from training in the heat, so she removed her outer garments before plunging into the sea. As she felt the rush of water around her, a silly thought struck her: Deep at the bottom of the sea is where the Sea Dragon King lives in his Dragon Palace. Maybe Guo Jing is there and has been united with the beautiful Dragon Princess? A surge of jealousy coursed through her, and her expression turned sullen.

She kept diving down into the water until, suddenly, she felt a pain in her left ankle. She tried to tug it back, but it was caught. Lotus had been playing in the water since she was a young child, so she knew that her foot must be caught in a large clam. She was not alarmed, bending down to feel it with her hand. Wait! It was as big as a table! She had never come across such a large clam in these waters. She reached into the shell with both hands to prise it open. Try as she might, however, she could not make the shells part. The clam gripped harder in response and the pain in her ankle surged. She tried to lift the clam, but it occurred to her that it probably weighed as much as three hundred *jin* and had been growing there for years, cementing itself ever more securely to the reef below. How could she possibly lift it?

Lotus struggled a little longer, but the pain in her foot was becoming unbearable. In her panic, she managed to swallow a few mouthfuls of seawater. I didn't want to live, she suddenly realized. But if I die now, leaving *Shifu* all alone on this island, so that scoundrel can come back and torture him, I will never find peace.

She grabbed a large nearby rock and smashed it against the clam, but its shell was solid, and she could gather little momentum under the waves. After a few attempts, the clam merely tightened its grip once again, and Lotus swallowed yet more seawater.

Then it struck her. She dropped the stone and reached down to scoop up some sand from the seabed. Clams detest sand and small stones more than anything else, she said to herself as she threw it into the mouth of the creature. She felt its grip loosen slightly as it tried to spit out the sand. Instantly, Lotus pulled back her foot, quickly kicked her way to the surface and gasped a lungful of air.

Count Seven had been watching, growing ever more anxious that she had not resurfaced. He had tried to hobble to the water's edge, but he was too weak to go in, so all he could do was stare at the calm surface of the sea, wringing his hands. At that moment, Lotus's head burst up and he could not help but cry out with relief.

Lotus waved to her *shifu* and then dived beneath the surface of the water again. Making sure to plant her feet far away from the clam and not to put her hands near the edges of its shells, she took hold of it and shook it loose from the reef. Treading water, she then pushed the clam toward the beach. Once it was half out of the water, it was too heavy for Lotus to move, so she climbed up onto the shore and took a large rock, using it to beat the thick shell until it was broken into pieces. Only once her anger was sufficiently vented did she look down at the bloody wound on her foot and realize the danger she had been in. She paused as a shiver ran through her.

That evening, they feasted on a delicious meal of sweet, succulent clam.

6

COUNT SEVEN HONG WOKE THE NEXT MORNING TO FIND THAT the pain had eased. He moved the *qi* around his body, noticing how strong the vital points on his chest and stomach felt compared to the day before.

"Ah," he sighed.

Lotus turned. "What's the matter, *Shifu?*"

"A good night's sleep seems to have done wonders."

"It was all that clam," Lotus said with a big smile.

"I don't think clam has any medicinal powers, but it was delicious," Count Seven said and laughed. "Although, I can't deny that my injuries are healed, so perhaps it has its uses, after all."

Lotus laughed, then ran out of the cave and down to the beach to fetch the last bits of clam from the previous day.

In her delight, she had forgotten all about Gallant Ouyang. Just as she was slicing two large chunks of clam flesh, she caught sight of an approaching shadow. Lotus bent down and picked up a piece of shell. Then, without warning, she threw it behind her and leaped toward the water line.

Gallant had spent a day watching them at a distance, observing Count Seven Hong's movements and growing ever more certain that his injuries were grave indeed. The Old Beggar could barely walk.

And yet Gallant was not brave enough to enter the cave. Instead, he approached Lotus.

"Sister, don't go. I just want to talk."

"Well, I clearly don't, and you're respecting that." She pulled a face.

Gallant's face drained of all color. His heart was pounding. He moved two steps closer and smiled. "It's your fault, really. Who gave you permission to be so beautiful? Leaving you alone is quite impossible."

"Well, I don't want to talk to you, and I mean it. There's no point trying to compliment me."

Gallant advanced another step. "I don't believe you," he said with a wolfish grin.

Lotus's face grew darker. "If you come another step closer, my *shifu* will beat you."

"I doubt it," Gallant said and laughed. "Can the Old Beggar even walk? Shall I carry him out here and see?"

Lotus stumbled back a few steps in surprise.

"If you fancy diving again, be my guest. I'll wait here, on the shore. Let's see who lasts longer—you in the water, or me on the beach."

"You are a bully, and you'll never have my affection."

She turned to run, but tripped and fell.

Gallant spluttered with laughter. "The more you resist me, the more I like you." He removed his outer robe and held it up as protection against any needles she might throw, before advancing toward her.

"No closer!" Lotus cried. She struggled to her feet and started running, but tripped again after only a few steps. This time, the fall was harder, and she landed partially in the water before seeming to faint.

This girl is most cunning, Gallant thought. But I'm not so easily fooled. Why would someone of her skill keep falling, let alone faint like that?

He stood watching her for a few minutes. But she lay perfectly still as the tide began to swallow her upper body and head.

Maybe she really did faint? Gallant said to himself, growing more concerned. If I don't save her, the beauty will drown.

He ran toward her and tried to tug at her legs, but, the moment his hand touched her skin, he felt a shock. Her body was stiff. He reached down and took her in his arms, and, just as he hoisted her out of the water, she grabbed his legs and held them tightly.

"Down you go!"

Gallant's footing was unsteady to begin with, so all it took was a sharp tug from Lotus and they both tumbled into the water.

Gallant's martial skills were of no use to him submerged. Despite my caution, the girl tricked me! And now I'm doomed, he thought.

Lotus, on the other hand, was delighted that her ruse had worked. All she had to do was get him into deeper waters and push his head under the surface.

As the water rushed into his mouth, Gallant felt his body spin, as if caught in a whirlpool. He did not know if he was facing up or down. He began thrashing, trying to grab hold of Lotus.

Lotus swam around him, just out of reach.

Gallant Ouyang swallowed a lungful of water and his body grew heavier until his feet sunk down and met the seabed. At the touch of solid ground, he felt his mind clear momentarily. Before his body started to float up again, he grabbed at a rock on the ocean floor and tried to pinpoint the direction of the shore. The water was murky, however.

He felt with his feet and noticed a ridge of higher ground, where the water was shallower. The craggy reef was not easy to navigate, but he moved as quickly as he could across it, using his internal strength, his head still submerged.

Lotus, meanwhile, waited for him to emerge. She dived down to check, only to discover him walking through the water, much to her surprise. She swam up behind him and drew her dagger.

Feeling the water at his back move, Gallant jerked sideways, before urging his body faster through the water. He was rapidly running out of oxygen, so he dropped the large stone and rushed to the surface, gasping for air. The shore was close by, so he dropped back down to the seabed and marched in its direction.

There was no stopping him now, Lotus realized, so she dived down into the water again.

Gallant crawled up onto the beach, his clothes drenched, his hearing muffled and his eyes a blur. He lay on the sand, exhausted, as his stomach convulsed, expelling the seawater until his belly was empty. He panted, the anger swelling inside him. "I'm going to kill that Old Beggar," he spat eventually. "Then we'll see if the girl listens to me!"

They were fine words, but the truth was that Gallant still feared Count Seven. He took a few deep breaths and tried to drive away his fatigue. He snapped a small branch from a nearby tree, with the intention of using it in lieu of his usual folding fan, which he used to strike out at his opponents' pressure points. Then he started walking toward the cave.

He did not approach so as to be visible from the entrance, but circled round to it from the side. He stopped and listened. All was quiet. After waiting some time, he poked his head around the rock and looked inside. Count Seven was sitting cross-legged on the ground, his face turned to the sun. He was meditating and he looked peaceful. There was no hint that he was in pain.

I'll test him, Gallant thought to himself, to see if he can walk.

"Uncle Hong!" he called out. "Help!"

"What?"

"It's Sister Huang. She was chasing a hare and fell down a steep ridge. She's hurt and can't climb up!"

"Run and save her, boy!" Count Seven cried, the shock evident on his face.

So, he can't, Gallant thought with a smile. Otherwise, he would go himself.

He entered the cave, the smile still playing across his lips. "She's been plotting to kill me. How can I save her? You do it."

Count Seven knew at once it was all a ruse. The dirty scoundrel thinks I'm too injured to fight, he thought. This does not bode well!

67

If he was destined to die, he was going to have to take the young man with him. It was the only way. Surreptitiously, he channeled his strength into his right arm and waited for Gallant to approach. But even this small movement sent pain shooting down his back. It felt as if his body was about to break apart.

Gallant grinned and began close in on him. Count Seven sighed quietly, closed his eyes and waited for what was about to come.

LOTUS WATCHED from underwater as Gallant climbed ashore. I won't be able to trick him again so easily, she thought. He'll be on his guard.

She swam a dozen or so meters farther out to sea, rose up to the surface and took a few breaths. Then she turned to her left and sunk back down to safety beneath the waves. From there, she spotted a patch of vegetation by the water's edge, beyond the beach. She was suddenly reminded of Peach Blossom Island and a sadness swept over her. I should find a place for *Shifu* and me to hide, so that villain won't be able to find us, she thought. It was not an inspired plan, but perhaps luck would shine on them and her Master would be able to recover in peace.

She waded ashore, but was careful not to stray too far from the water's edge. If only I had paid more attention to Father's Mysterious Gates and Five Elements instead of always playing, then maybe I would be able to defeat the villain myself. But it was no use thinking that way. Her father had given Gallant Ouyang the map to Peach Blossom Island. He was intelligent enough to be able to decode it.

Lotus was too lost in thought to notice where she was putting her feet. She tripped on a vine and a shower of pebbles fell on her head. She jumped aside. All around her were trees. She stumbled back and into the trunk of a tree, sending another hail of stones down on her shoulders. It was just as well she was wearing her Hedgehog Chainmail.

She looked up into the branches and what she saw gave her a terrible surprise.

Only a few paces behind her rose a sheer cliff, at the top of which was balanced a gigantic boulder, which was trembling above her head. Any slight movement could disrupt its perfect equilibrium and send it crashing down on top of her. It was wrapped in a tangle of vines, one of which extended down the cliff. The same vine she had tripped over. Who knew how many tons the stone weighed, but no doubt it would be enough to turn her into mincemeat.

Carefully, Lotus picked her way through the hanging vines and branches until she was a safe distance from the cliff. No people ever came to this island and there was not a bird in sight. Without anyone passing to yank on the wrong vine, the rock could have been precariously balanced like this for thousands of years, swaying back and forth. All but the gentlest of breezes was blocked by yet taller cliffs and peaks, otherwise a strong wind might have dislodged it by now. No doubt it would remain, trembling like that, for hundreds of thousands of years to come.

Lotus paused. She did not quite dare to go on, and instead turned back to return to her *shifu*. As she walked, a thought came to her: The heavens want this scoundrel dead, too. They are providing the perfect opportunity. Why did it take me so long to realize it? Her body felt lighter and she turned two somersaults in the air.

She hurried back to the cliff and examined the area. The ancient trees would provide a protection of sorts, she only really needed to jump a few feet—five, perhaps—in order to avoid being crushed. Without prior warning, however, even the birds and the squirrels would struggle to escape in time.

Cautiously, she approached the foot of the cliff, and, using her dagger, she found seven or eight vines that were directly connected to the boulder. She then cut away any that were not holding it in place. She held her breath with every slice, moving the blade quickly and steadily, sucking the air deep into her lungs after each one. If she used too much force, she could bring the rock crashing down. By the time she had cut the two dozen or so redundant vines, she was soaked in sweat. She felt more exhausted than she did after a fight. Then she gathered the cut vines into a bundle to make a marker for her return, before looking around her and committing the route to memory. She returned to her Master, whistling a tune as she went.

7

JUST AS LOTUS DREW CLOSE TO THE CAVE, SHE HEARD AN arrogant cackle come from inside.

"You claim to be unparalleled in the *wulin*, and yet I have you, now, in the palm of my hand! Fine—as you are my elder, I will let you have the first three moves. What do you say? Let me see your Dragon-Subduing Palm!"

Oh no, Lotus thought, realizing at once what was going on. "Father! Are you here? And Uncle Ouyang—you've come too!"

Gallant had been just about to strike Count Seven when he heard Lotus outside. His uncle? And the Old Heretic? What were they doing here? Oh, it's the girl, out to trick me again, he thought. Although, as the old man can't move, there's no harm in taking a look, he reasoned. With a flick of his sleeve, he turned and left the cave.

Lotus was waving toward the beach. "Papa! Papa!"

Gallant peered out to sea, but he could see no sign of Apothecary Huang.

"Sister, are you trying to trick me into coming out to play? Looks like you did it again."

"Trick you?" Lotus said with a twinkle in her eye. Then she began to run toward the beach.

"This time, I'm watching you," Gallant called, following her. "I dare you to try dragging me into the water again."

Thanks to his superior lightness kung fu, he was drawing close fast.

Oh no, Lotus said to herself. He might catch me before we get to the cliff.

She kept running, but Ouyang was nearly upon her. At the last moment, Lotus turned left, heading away from the beach.

Gallant Ouyang was actually making sure not to get too close. Instead, he called after Lotus: "Are we playing hide-and-seek?"

Lotus stopped suddenly and said, "There's a tiger up ahead. Keep following me and it'll eat you."

"I'm the tiger and I'm going to eat you."

He leaped toward her, but Lotus dodged, laughed and kept running.

Moments later, they were approaching the cliff.

"Come on!" Lotus called out as she ran faster.

Just as she reached her destination, she saw two figures on the beach. She was curious, but she did not have time to stop and look properly. She spotted the pile of cut vines and ran toward the rock face.

"And the tiger?" Gallant said and laughed. He ran like an arrow toward her. He did not suspect a thing, though it was noticeable that some of the vegetation had been cleared. He charged straight into the vines that remained . . . tugging the rock off balance.

There was a cracking sound and Gallant felt a rush of air press down upon him. He looked up. What he saw frightened him out of his wits. There, hurtling at full speed toward him, was a piece of rock as big as a mountain. The displaced air pushed down on him with such force that he could barely breathe. He tried to jump back, but he slammed into the trunk of a large tree, winding himself, and the force of his body snapped off a branch, which fell and pierced his back. At this critical moment, he felt no pain. He had to get out of the way.

He scrambled toward safety, but, in his panic, he only managed to move about a meter. The fear had petrified him.

At that moment, he felt a hand grab him and pull him back a few feet more.

But it was too late.

CRASH! Gallant howled, the world turned to mist, dust flew.

He had fainted.

Her plan had worked, and she was delighted. The only flaw was that she had not prepared for the deafening sound and the gust of air, which had blown her back to land on her rump. A rain of small stones pelted her head. She bent forward and covered it with her arms, before rolling onto her side. Only once all was quiet again did she open her eyes.

As the dust settled, she saw two figures standing close by.

She rubbed her eyes, as if waking from a dream. There, standing before her, was Viper Ouyang, Venom of the West. The other was her beloved Guo Jing.

Lotus yelped and leaped to her feet. Guo Jing was astounded to see her and he too lurched forward. They were reunited in each other's arms.

In their excitement, both forgot their enemy was nearby.

8

GUO JING AND VIPER OUYANG HAD CONTINUED FIGHTING AS the boat around them went up in flames. Before they realized what was happening, the ship started to sink, drawing them down into the sea with it. As they sank deeper, the pressure grew more intense, and they felt the water forcing its way into their ears and noses. The pain was hard to endure, and they were forced to abandon their struggle against one another as they tried to cover their nostrils and eardrums.

A strong undercurrent was moving in the opposite direction to the surface waves, and, before they knew what was happening, they had been swept away. Guo Jing kicked his way to air, only to discover that the sky was dark and the wreckage of his ship was now very far away indeed.

Guo Jing cried out into the inky blackness. He did not know it, but, at that moment, Lotus was calling out for him too. But, as the waves carried them farther apart, how could they hope to find each other again? Guo Jing kept shouting until he felt something tug at his left leg. A head surfaced. Viper Ouyang. He may have been a master of the *wulin*, but he was not a strong swimmer, so he clutched Guo Jing's leg and refused to let go. Guo Jing tried to kick him away, only to have Viper grab his right leg too.

They wrestled in the water, but quickly began to sink.

"Let go of my legs! I won't leave you," Guo Jing managed to cry out when he resurfaced again.

Viper knew that, if he did not release the boy's legs, they would both drown, so he let go and instead took hold of Guo Jing's right arm. Guo Jing reached out and wedged his hand under Viper's armpit, and together the two men bobbed in the water.

At that moment, a large spar of driftwood came rushing toward them on a wave and crashed into Guo Jing's shoulder.

"Careful!" Viper cried.

Delighted by their luck, Guo Jing seized it. "Quick, hold on! Don't let go."

They had been saved by a length of what had once been the ship's mast.

The two gazed out into the vast expanse of water that surrounded them. There was no sign of any sails. Viper Ouyang had long since lost his Serpent Staff and was feeling queasy with worry. If we encounter any sharks out here, we'll have no choice but to fight like Zhou Botong. I saved him, but who is going to save me?

As they continued to float in the water, shoals of fish swam past. A sharp chop and together they could feast on raw fish.

As the ancients used to say: "Those aboard the same boat must share the same fate." Hours before, they had been fighting; now, they depended on each other for survival. Luckily, they encountered no great danger, and, without their knowing it, the current was carrying them toward the same usually deserted island that Lotus and Count Seven had landed on.

A few days later, they scrambled onto the beach and lay down in the sand, panting as they rested. But, before long, the sound of laughter reached them on the wind. Viper Ouyang jumped to his feet and began to chase after it. Staggered by the coincidence, he caught sight of his nephew. He rushed forward, just as the giant rock was hurtling toward Gallant, and, at the last moment, pulled him far enough out of its path that only his legs were crushed beneath the huge weight. Gallant had fainted before he felt the force hit him.

Viper glanced around anxiously, but could see no other obvious danger, so he began attending to his nephew. He checked his breathing—he was still alive. He tried to push the rock aside, but it refused to budge. He squatted, and, using his Exploding Toad kung fu, pushed with both palms and croaked three times in quick succession. And yet, nothing. He was strong, to be sure, but how could one man alone move some twenty thousand *jin* of rock?

He bent down just as Gallant opened his eyes.

"Uncle!" His voice was weak.

"Keep strong a little longer." Viper pulled the young man's upper body into his arms and tugged, but Gallant screamed and fainted again. He would not be so easily freed, and pulling in this manner would only injure him further. Viper had no shovel and no hoe—there was no way to dig him out. The old man stared, his mind blank.

9

GUO JING TOOK LOTUS'S HAND IN HIS. "WHAT ABOUT OUR *shifu*?"

"Over there," she said, and pointed.

Guo Jing was delighted to hear that their Master was safe, and he was about to suggest they go to see him, when Viper let out a long and terrible wail. Guo Jing could not help but feel moved.

"Let me help you."

"Let's go and see *Shifu*," Lotus said, tugging on his sleeve. "They don't deserve our help!"

Viper Ouyang did not know it had been a trap set up by Lotus.

No one could have placed such a heavy rock at the top of the cliff on purpose. But her words lit a spark of fury inside him, and he was just as startled as Guo Jing to hear that Count Seven was here on the island too. The Old Beggar took a hit to his back *and* he was bitten by one of my snakes, and still he lives? Well, he must be severely weakened, at least. Why should I fear him?

Still holding Lotus by the hand, Guo Jing knelt beside the rock and pretended to push. Then, just as they turned away, he said to Gallant, "Don't worry. I will think of something. Circulate your *qi*, that will protect your heart, and pretend those legs aren't yours. Just forget them."

The young couple left, affectionately clutching one another around the waist. Viper tiptoed behind them, his heart inflamed with rage. If I don't torture these two to the point that they beg for death, why, then my name is not Venom of the West.

Lotus led Guo Jing to the mouth of the cave. Guo Jing ran inside. "*Shifu!*"

Count Seven was leaning back against the rocky inner wall, all color drained from his face, his eyes closed. His encounter with Gallant Ouyang had enraged him and aggravated his injury. Lotus loosened his outer robes, while Guo Jing massaged his hands and feet.

Count Seven opened his eyes to the sight of Guo Jing. "Lad, you're here!" The corners of his mouth pulled upward in a slight smile and his face lit up with delight.

Guo Jing was about to reply when a loud voice came from behind him: "So am I, Old Beggar."

Guo Jing turned quickly and thrust a palm toward the cave opening. Lotus grabbed her Master's bamboo stick and took her place beside Guo Jing.

Viper Ouyang laughed. "Come out, Old Beggar. If you don't, I'll come in."

Guo Jing and Lotus exchanged glances. They were thinking the same thing: he must not be allowed to touch *Shifu*, even if we must pay with our lives.

Viper Ouyang laughed again and leaped up like a monkey. Guo Jing moved to block him with his palm. Viper turned to avoid his strike, brushing past his right side, only to come face-to-face with a stick flying straight at him. It quivered as it split the air, almost as if it was aiming at both his upper and lower body at the same time. A shiver went through his heart. He flicked his hand and swept with a foot to meet whatever was coming his way. And yet, Lotus's bamboo stick plunged straight through his guard, into his abdomen.

Viper Ouyang jumped back in shock and looked her up and down.

It was the first time Lotus had used the Dog-Beating Cane in a fight, and the results left her flushed with pride. He had not been expecting her to possess such skill—indeed, he had never seen anything of the like before. He snorted, leaped forward and aimed for the stick. But Lotus jabbed and hit this way and that, turning it into a blur of dancing green. She was unable to land any blows, but it was enough to confuse the old Master and prevent him from snatching it from her.

"Well done, Lotus!" Guo Jing cried from the sidelines. Then he entered the fray with a palm from the left and a strike from the right. Viper Ouyang roared, crouched and sent two palm strikes in Lotus's direction, whipping up dust from the ground with the force of the thrust. Guo Jing watched in horror. She would be gravely injured if she took either blow head-on, so he leaped toward her and pushed her aside.

Viper Ouyang stepped forward and struck again with both palms. For all his legendary prowess, Count Seven had been unable to prevail against the force behind these moves when they had met, only a few days ago, on Peach Blossom Island. The young couple were forced back until Viper was able to enter the cave. He beat his palm against the stone wall, sending a shower of stones around them. Then he raised his other hand above Count Seven's head and paused, staring down at him.

"My *shifu* saved your life, and yet you threaten him?" Lotus cried. "Have you no shame?"

Viper Ouyang gently pushed Count Seven Hong's chest and felt his muscles shrink back. It was clear that Count Seven's injuries had severely impaired his martial capabilities. Before, his muscles would have rebounded instantaneously against the pressure. Viper was relieved. He grabbed hold of the old man and cried, "Save my nephew and I'll spare your life!"

"The heavens sent that rock down on him, you saw it with your own eyes," Lotus cried. "Who can save him? If you try any more of your tricks, the heavens will find a rock to throw down on you."

Guo Jing watched as, ignoring Lotus, Viper lifted Count Seven by his robes, as if he was going to throw him to the ground. But he felt it was just a threat—he would not really harm Count Seven in this way, surely. And yet, still, he was anxious. "Please, put him down. We'll help your nephew."

Viper was extremely concerned for Gallant and wanted nothing more than to rush to his side. But he kept his face still and, after a moment's hesitation, put Count Seven down.

"We will help you, but we must agree terms."

"What is it the young girl wants?"

"Once we've saved your nephew, and we've settled on this deserted island with our *shifu*, the two of you are never to return to do us harm."

My nephew and I cannot swim, so we will need their help to make it back to the mainland. He nodded. "Fine. As long as you stay on this island, I vow not to come and kill you. Should you leave it, however, I make no promises."

"In that case, we will come for you. My second condition: my father has already betrothed me to Guo Jing. You heard it with your own ears and saw it with your own eyes. Should your nephew harass me again, you two shall be known forever as lower than both pig and dog."

"Fie! Only on this island. Should you leave . . . we'll see."

Lotus smiled. "And the third condition: we agree to help you, but we are not gods. Should the heavens decide to take your nephew, then no man may help him and there shall be no consequences for us."

"If my nephew dies," Viper said, a flash of ire in his eyes, "you three can forget about living. No more nonsense—my nephew needs help now." He then left the cave and ran toward the cliff.

Guo Jing was about to follow when Lotus stopped him. "Brother Jing, when he's trying to move the rock, you hit him in the back. We can be rid of him once and for all."

"But, to strike someone like that? Why, it's dishonorable."

"He poisoned our *shifu*," Lotus said with a hint of displeasure in her voice. "Was that honorable?"

"We must keep our word. First, we save his nephew; then we may seek our revenge."

Lotus smiled and sighed. It was impossible to get Guo Jing to plot in this way. She had spent the last two days believing him to be lying dead at the bottom of the sea, but here they were, reunited, and she was so happy, her heart felt ready to explode. Guo Jing could say or do the most outrageous and unforgivable things and still she would not go against him. No, she would do as he said. His principles were a little tiresome, but they did show he would make a virtuous husband. She smiled again. "Fine. You are the sage; I listen to you."

They ran in the direction of the cliff, the sound of Viper's anguished groans already reaching their ears.

"Hurry!" he called toward them.

They took their positions next to him, all six hands placed on the rock.

"Heave!"

All three pushed as hard as they could. The rock shook slightly before slamming back into position. Gallant responded with a desperate wail and his eyes rolled back.

Viper rushed to his side. The young man's breathing was weak. He had bitten through his tongue due to the pain and his mouth and chin were covered in blood. Even a powerful master of the *wulin* such as Viper was powerless to shift the rock. He was going mad with anguish. By moving it only slightly, he had caused Gallant even more suffering. Viper began to pace up and down, but stopped in his tracks when he felt the ground beneath his feet turn soft. He lifted his foot, only to lose a shoe in the sand.

Viper bent down to retrieve his shoe and froze in shock; the tide was coming in and was now only fifty feet from the rock.

"Young girl, if you want your Master to live, you had better think of a way to save my nephew."

Lotus was already working on a plan. But the rock was so huge and there were only three of them. She had raced through at least ten different ideas, but none were viable.

"If only your Master wasn't injured," Viper said, interrupting her thoughts. "He could have moved it with his considerable external kung fu. Not to mention his palm technique. But now . . ." He threw his hands out in exasperation.

Perhaps it's fate, he found himself thinking. Had the Old Beggar not been injured, he would surely have helped, such is his righteous character. The heavens decreed it: by hurting him, I was as good as killing my boy.

Viper called Gallant his nephew, but in fact the young man was the result of an affair with his sister-in-law. He had always been hard of heart, but now he ached for his own flesh and blood. He turned to see the water was now a few feet closer.

Just then, Gallant cried out to his uncle. "Please, kill me with one blow. I . . . I can't bear it anymore."

Viper removed a sharp dagger from his robes and gritted his teeth. "Just a little longer. You can still live without your legs."

"No, no! Uncle! Use the blade to kill me instead."

"Have all these years of instructions been in vain? Are you so spineless?" Viper was angry now.

Gallant pulled his arms around his chest, shivering from the pain. He was too scared to speak.

Viper looked down at his nephew. The rock was in fact crushing his lower abdomen. Even if his legs were amputated, his chances of survival were slim. He hesitated.

Lotus watched their exchange turn to silence and her heart softened. Suddenly, she remembered how her father used to move large rocks on Peach Blossom Island. "Wait! I have an idea. But there's no guarantee it will work."

"Dear girl, what is it?" Hope had returned to Viper's face. "Your ideas are always excellent."

So, now that I have an idea, he calls me *dear girl*? Lotus thought. She smiled. "Fine, then listen to me. We're going to take some tree bark and wrap it around the rock, like a rope."

"Who will pull?"

"We'll do like we did with the anchor on the boat—"

"Yes," Viper cried, suddenly understanding the plan. "Like a winch!"

Guo Jing listened and, rather than question her, instantly took the dagger from her and began peeling a length of bark from a nearby tree. Viper and Lotus followed his lead. Before long, they had formed a considerable pile.

Just then, Viper looked across at Gallant and cried, "No need!"

"What's the matter?" Lotus said. "Don't you think it will work?"

Viper pointed at his nephew. By now, the tide had risen and submerged the lower half of his body. He would be drowned before they had gathered enough bark, tied it into rope and constructed the winch. Gallant lay still.

"Don't lose hope!" Lotus cried. "Get cutting!"

It was an odd sight to see the tyrant obeying her so meekly, but he went back to cutting bark. Lotus jumped down from her perch high up in the branches and ran over to Gallant. She wedged some stones underneath his back so that his nose and mouth were lifted farther out of the water.

"Miss Huang, thank you," Gallant began in a quiet voice. "If I die, at least I will be content knowing you tried to save me."

"Don't thank me," Lotus said, a wave of regret coming over her. "I set the trap, haven't you realized?"

"Shhh. If my uncle hears you say that, he will never forgive you. I am devoted to you. I have no regrets dying by your hand."

How tiresome, Lotus sighed to herself. But he treats me well—when he isn't trying to take advantage of me.

She returned to the others and began working on the bark. She braided three strips together to form one thin rope, then took six of these to form a thicker rope, before taking several of these and forming a strong cable. Viper and Guo Jing continued to slice bark from the trees for Lotus to weave together.

They worked fast, but the tide came in faster; before the cable was even halfway complete, the water had risen to Gallant's mouth. Soon after, only his nose was left proud of the surface.

Viper jumped down from his branch and looked at the young couple. "You can go," he began, his voice heavy, but his expression surprisingly calm. "I wish to speak with my nephew alone. You tried to save him, and I appreciate it."

Guo Jing saw that it was hopeless, so he climbed down from the tree and left with Lotus. After a few meters, Lotus whispered, "Let's hide behind the rock and listen."

"But whatever he has to say isn't our business. Anyway, he'll notice."

"Once Gallant is dead, he will turn on *Shifu*. We have to be prepared. If the Old Venom sees us, we can just say that we've come to pay our respects."

Guo Jing nodded. They slipped behind some trees, then crept back toward nephew and uncle, and hid behind the rock.

"Go now, boy; I know what is in your heart. You wanted to marry the Old Heretic Huang's daughter, and I will grant you your wish."

Lotus and Guo Jing both listened in surprise. What did he mean by "I will grant you your wish"? Gallant was about to die. What came next was just as bewildering—and enraging. Indeed, it sent shivers down their spines.

"I will kill Miss Huang, so you can be buried together and you will have peace."

Gallant's mouth was already submerged, so he could make no reply.

Lotus squeezed Guo Jing's hand and together they turned away. Neither wanted to watch Viper Ouyang mourn.

"It will be a fight to the death," Guo Jing growled, once they were at a safe distance.

"With him, it is best to use our brains, not our fists," Lotus replied.

"How?"

"I'm still thinking."

As they turned around a corner, they spotted a clump of reeds growing at the foot of the cliff.

Just then, an idea came to her. "I know a way to save his nephew!"

"How?"

Lotus took out a small knife and cut a reed pipe about two feet long. Then she put it between her lips, looked up to the sky and sucked the air through it, like a straw.

"Amazing!" Guo Jing said, clapping his hands. "How did you think of it? Are you going to save him or not?"

"Of course not. If Old Venom wants to kill me, let him. I'm not scared of him! I can run far, far away—he'll never catch me." She paused and thought about the old man's horrible ways. A shiver went through her. Not only was his kung fu exceptional, he was far more intelligent and cunning than his nephew. It would not be so easy to fool him.

Guo Jing merely watched in silence.

Lotus took his hand. "Don't say you want to save a scoundrel like that?" she said softly. "You're worried about me, aren't you? If we were to save him, they wouldn't necessarily repay the kindness."

"You're right. But I'm worried about you, and about *Shifu*. Old Venom commands a sect. What he says contains at least some credibility."

"Fine. Let's save Gallant and take the consequences as they come."

They turned back and approached the rock. As they rounded it, they saw Viper standing in the water, holding his nephew in his arms. He looked up and saw them coming. There was a brutal glint in his eye.

"I told you to leave. What are you doing here?" he cried.

Lotus sat on a nearby stone and laughed. "I've come to see if he's dead yet."

"What does it matter to you if he is dead or alive?"

"If he's already dead, then I'm too late."

Viper Ouyang leaped up. "Dear . . . Dear girl, he's not dead. If you can save him, tell me . . . Tell me how."

Lotus threw the reed pipe to him. "Put this in his mouth, and he might just live."

Grinning, Viper snatched it out of the air and knelt in the water to fit it between his nephew's lips. The water was just starting to cover Gallant's nose and he was down to his last lungfuls of air. He had been able to hear their conversation, however, and so, as soon as the reed was placed in his mouth, he sucked greedily for air. It felt so good that it made him forget the pain in his legs for a moment.

"Quick, let's keep making the ropes," Viper said.

"But, Uncle Ouyang, you're planning to kill me and bury me with your nephew, aren't you?"

Viper was startled. How did she hear that?

"If you kill me," Lotus said with a smile, "who's going to help you the next time you get in trouble?"

Viper Ouyang had no choice but to pretend not to have heard her mockery, and instead he turned his attention back to gathering tree bark.

They worked for more than two hours, weaving together a thick cable, over one hundred meters in length. The water had submerged the bottom half of the rock, and only the tip of Gallant's reed pipe remained above the surface. Viper was uneasy and repeatedly reached into the water to feel for his nephew's pulse.

As they continued, the tide began to recede, slowly revealing Gallant's head again. Lotus measured the rope and called, "We have enough, now! I need four large trunks to act as masts."

Viper Ouyang was skeptical. How could they find the tools on a deserted island to make a winch?

"How?"

"Never you mind. Just find me what I need."

Viper feared the young girl's temper, so he began searching for suitable trees. Once he'd selected them, he crouched and thrust his palms at the lower part of the trunk, in a move from his Exploding Toad repertoire. It took only a few strikes to fell each one. Guo Jing and Lotus watched this fearsome display of internal strength and exchanged glances. Viper then found a long, flat piece of rock. Once again, he gathered his *qi* and shaved the branches from the trunks, before bringing them to Lotus.

Lotus and Guo Jing tied one end of the long cable around three of the trunks, before looping it around the rock and tying it to a nearby pine, several hundred years in age and of such girth that it would take at least four men to stretch their arms around it.

"This tree should be able to take the weight," Lotus said, answering a question no one had asked.

Viper Ouyang nodded.

Lotus instructed them to take another length of their rope and tie the fourth trunk so that they formed a square shape around the rock. They then attached the cable to it.

"How clever, little girl! No one could doubt that you are your father's daughter!"

"I am nothing compared to your nephew," Lotus said and smiled. "Let's begin!"

The three began to pivot the trunks around the old pine. The ropes quickly tightened, and the rock started to rise.

The sun was setting, and half the sky was painted a bright red, its reflection staining the sea. It was a marvelous sight. The tide had long since pulled back, and Gallant was lying in the soft sand, his eyes fixed on the giant rock as it trembled on its upward trajectory. The ropes creaked as Gallant watched in anxious delight.

They had completed one revolution of their giant winch, but the rock had only lifted half an inch. The old pine shook ever so slightly, the strain becoming evident as its needles rained down to carpet the ground around it, and the rope carved a groove into its bark.

Viper was not usually one to call upon the gods for help, for he did not admit to believing in spirits, but at this moment he was praying quietly to himself.

Then the rope snapped and the rock crashed back down upon Gallant with a loud thud. Gallant tried to scream, but no sound came from his lips. The tree trunks spun back, slamming into Lotus and knocking her off her feet. Guo Jing rushed to her side to help her up.

Viper watched, grief overtaking him. No smile graced Lotus's lips anymore.

"Let's tie it back together with another rope, to make it stronger," Guo Jing said.

"There's no way. We give up."

"If only someone could help us," Guo Jing mumbled to himself.

"Huh!" Viper spat. He knew the boy was well intentioned, but, in his grief, he had no patience for such nonsense.

Lotus thought in silence. Then, suddenly, she jumped up and clapped her hands. A smile was spread across her face. "There is someone!"

"Who?" Guo Jing asked.

"The only problem is, Brother Ouyang would have to be patient for another day and wait for the tide to come in again before we could free him."

Viper and Guo Jing looked at her. Was someone going to come with the tide to rescue Gallant?

"We are all tired and hungry. Let's go and find some food," Lotus said.

"Young lady, please explain first," Viper said.

"This time tomorrow, Master Ouyang will be freed from under that rock. I'm afraid I am not at liberty to explain how."

Her confidence appeased Viper's doubts. He did not have a choice. He would stay by his nephew's side and wait.

Guo Jing and Lotus caught a few wild hares and cooked one for Viper and Gallant. They then returned to Count Seven in the cave, where they ate and talked about everything that had happened since they had parted.

Much to Guo Jing's surprise, Lotus explained that she had been the one to set the trap. Viper would not bother them during the night, so they lit a fire at the mouth of the cave to stop any animals entering and then settled down for a full night's sleep.

10

THE NEXT MORNING, GUO JING AWOKE TO SEE A SHADOW hovering at the mouth of the cave. He jumped up, only to realize it was Viper.

"Is Miss Huang awake?"

Lotus pretended to be sound asleep still.

"Not yet," Guo Jing whispered. "What is it?"

"Once she's awake, please ask her to come quickly."

"I will."

"I gave her a glass of One-Hundred-Day Drunken Slumber," Count Seven interjected. "I also pressed her sleep pressure point. She won't be awake for another three months."

Viper stared back at them blankly. Then Count Seven began to howl with laughter. Furious, Viper turned and left.

Lotus sat up and smiled. "If we don't tease Old Venom now, when will we ever get the chance again?"

In no hurry, she brushed her hair and washed her face. She straightened her robes and went out to catch some fish and hares for breakfast. Viper came and went eight more times, as jumpy as an ant in a hot pan.

"Lotus," Guo Jing said eventually, "will there really be help when the tide comes in again?"

"Do you think there will be?"

"No," Guo Jing said, shaking his head.

"Neither do I," Lotus said and laughed.

"So you lied to Old Venom?"

"No, I didn't lie. When the tide comes in, we'll be able to save him."

Guo Jing knew she was always full of schemes, so he did not ask any more. The young couple went down to the beach to collect pretty patterned shells.

Lotus never had other children to play with when she was growing up. The beaches of Peach Blossom Island had been hers alone to explore. Now, with Guo Jing, she felt a joy take hold of her heart. They competed to see who could find the prettiest shells, stuffing their robes as their laughter echoed around the beach.

"Brother Jing," Lotus said suddenly, "your hair is in knots. Let me comb it."

They sat down on a rock. Lotus removed a tiny jade comb, inlaid with gold, from her robes and began to comb Guo Jing's hair.

"How can we be rid of Viper and his nephew, so that the three of us can live on this island in peace? Wouldn't that be wonderful?" Lotus said with a sigh.

"Except that I would miss my mother, and my six mentors."

"Yes, and I father." Lotus was quiet for a while. "I wonder where Mercy is? *Shifu* asked me to take over as chief of the Beggar Clan. I'm starting to miss those beggars a bit, too."

Guo Jing laughed. "Then let's think of a way to get back."

Lotus coiled Guo Jing's hair back into its bun.

"You reminded me so much of my mother while you were combing my hair."

"Then call me Ma," Lotus said with a laugh.

Guo Jing laughed, but did not reply.

Lotus reached out and tickled him under the armpit. "Aren't you going to say it?"

Still laughing, Guo Jing wriggled out of her reach. His hair was already a mess again.

"Fine—don't say it. I don't care. You don't think anyone will ever call me Ma, is that it? Sit down."

Guo Jing obeyed, and Lotus began combing his hair once again, gently brushing the sand away. Her heart was bursting with love. She bent down and kissed the nape of his neck. She recalled the way Guo Jing had watched her use her new Dog-Beating kung fu against Viper Ouyang the previous day and how he had praised her. She would teach him. Seeing Guo Jing's skills improve delighted her even more than bettering her own. As the daughter of the Heretic of the East, she had witnessed many great displays of martial prowess growing up. She was no longer so impressed by great feats in this regard, much as gold and pearls are nothing to the son of a rich man. Except, Dog-Beating kung fu can only be passed to the Chief of the Beggar Clan, she realized.

"Guo Jing, do you want to be the Chief Beggar?"

"But *Shifu* asked you; why are you asking me?"

"I'm a girl. I don't look like the Chief of the Beggar Clan. You would be better. The beggars will be more willing to listen to you than to me; you have such a commanding presence. And, if I don't pass it on to you, I won't be able to teach you Dog-Beating Cane."

"No, no," Guo Jing said, shaking his head. "I can't be the chief. I'm not smart enough to deal with even the smallest of trifles. How could I take on something so important?"

Lotus had to agree. *Shifu* had been in grave peril, he was forced to hand over the chieftainship, but, even so, he must have known that she was of rare intelligence, despite her tender years. He had judged her no less capable than the Clan's Four Elders, and, besides, he had not given her permission to pass on the leadership to another, and certainly not to a simple young man whose only qualification was knowing Dragon-Subduing Palm.

"If you can't, then you can't," Lotus said with a laugh. "But it is a shame you will never learn Dog-Beating Cane."

"As long as you know it, isn't it the same as me knowing it?"

His reply came from his heart, and so touched her that she could not help but say, "When *Shifu* recovers, I will make him chief again. Then . . . Then . . ." She wanted to say, *Then we can become husband and wife*, but somehow the words refused to come out of her mouth. "Do you know how babies are made?"

"Yes."

"Tell me."

"A man and a woman get married and then they have a baby."

"Yes, that much I know. But why do babies only come when they're married?"

"I don't know. Why?"

"Neither do I. I asked my father once, but he said babies tunnel their way out of your armpit."

Guo Jing was about to ask for more details when they heard a loud voice cry, "You'll find out when you're older. The tide is coming in!"

Lotus jumped up. She had not expected Viper to sneak up on them. She may not have known much of the intricacies of what happens between a man and a woman, but she knew that it was shameful to speak of them. Her cheeks flushed red as they ran over to the cliff.

Having spent a day and a night under the rock, Gallant was weaker than ever.

Viper looked at Lotus with a stern expression. "Miss Huang. You said that someone would come with the tide to help. This is not a game."

"My father is most proficient in the ways of Yin Yang and the Five Elements, so it would only be natural for his daughter to have picked some up along the way. No one can compare to the Old Heretic, but I do know a bit about the art of prophesy."

Viper was well acquainted with Apothecary Huang's reputation.

"Is your father coming? Wonderful."

Lotus snorted. "Why would my father bother about a trifle such as this? And once he hears how you hurt my *shifu*, why would he take pity on you? You would never be able to defeat my father and the two of us together. The idea of him coming should not bring you delight."

Viper Ouyang could do nothing but listen to her reproach in silence.

Lotus turned to Guo Jing. "Go and get some more tree trunks. The more the better. Big ones."

Guo Jing nodded and left. Lotus started mending the broken rope with more bark. Viper kept asking if her father was really coming or if it was someone else, but Lotus hummed to herself and did not answer.

Viper was frustrated, but also comforted by the girl's relaxed demeanor, which suggested she had a plan, so he went to help Guo Jing. Guo Jing was using Dragon-Subduing Palm to fell the trees.

The boy's skills are quite extraordinary, Viper thought to himself. And he knows the Nine Yin Manual by heart. Letting him live will only spell disaster. He would have to get rid of him, if his nephew survived or not. He crouched down between two trees, about three foot apart. Then, with a howl, he sent one palm to each and the sturdy trunks snapped.

"Uncle Ouyang," Guo Jing said in amazement, "I wonder how long it would take me to achieve your level of kung fu."

Viper did not reply, but his face was dark. Not in your lifetime, he said to himself.

The two men carried a dozen felled trunks to the foot of the cliff. Viper looked out toward the sea, but the horizon was clear. Not a sail in sight.

"What are you looking for?" Lotus said. "No one's coming."

This surprised Viper. "No one?" he growled.

"This is a deserted island; why would anyone come here?"

Rage boiled so hard in Viper's chest that he could not speak. He felt the strength gathering in his left hand, in preparation for a strike.

Lotus did not look at him directly, but instead turned to Guo Jing. "What's the most you can lift?"

"About four hundred *jin*, I would guess."

"What about a rock that weighs six hundred *jin*?"

"Certainly not."

"What if it was in water?"

"That's it!" Viper cried in delight. Guo Jing still did not understand her plan. "Once the tide comes in, the rock will be lighter," Viper explained.

"And, if we tie it to these trunks," Lotus said, "when they float with the tide, it will be lighter still."

Guo Jing finally understood and clapped his hands.

In order to maximize buoyancy, Viper tied eight large trunks together and then helped Guo Jing connect them to the broken cable from the day before.

Lotus stood watching with a smile as the two men worked steadily for nearly two hours until all the trunks were attached. Now all they had to do was wait for the tide.

LOTUS AND Guo Jing were in the cave with their *shifu* when, later that afternoon, as the sun was setting, Viper came running back to tell them the sea had reached the rock. They made their way to the cliff to wait. As the water reached Gallant's nostrils once more, they looped the rope around the pine again and waded into the water. Together, they began to work the winch.

This time, it felt like they had the strength of an army of men, as the tree trunks rose with the water. After only a few rotations around the pine, Viper held his breath and dived down. Within moments, he had pulled his nephew free and was lifting him to the surface.

Guo Jing cried out with delight. Lotus clapped her hands, momentarily forgetting that she had been the one to lay the trap in the first place.

CHAPTER THREE

ON THE BACK OF A SHARK

I

LOTUS WATCHED AS VIPER OUYANG CARRIED HIS SANDY nephew to the shore. His usually spiteful expression was transformed to one of beaming delight, but he did not utter one word of thanks to either of them. Lotus tugged at Guo Jing's sleeve and together they strolled back toward the cave.

Guo Jing could see the look of concern on Lotus's face. "What are you thinking?" he asked when they were inside with Count Seven again.

"Three things, each of which present us with a grave problem."

"But you're so clever, you always think of a way to solve everything."

Lotus smiled before allowing the frown to wrinkle her brow again ever so slightly.

"The first is of no concern," Count Seven Hong said suddenly. "The second and third, however . . . Indeed, they do present a conundrum."

"But *Shifu*, how do you know what she's thinking?"

"A guess. The first is how to heal my injury. The island houses no doctor, no medicine, never mind a master of internal *neigong* kung fu. But the Old Beggar accepts his fate. Whether I live or die is hardly of import."

"*Shifu*, the Nine Yin Manual," Guo Jing said. "It contains a few passages entitled 'On Treating Wounds.' These explain how to cure internal injuries, although the language is a little odd and I don't understand much. I could recite them for you—I'm sure you can figure them out."

Slowly, Guo Jing began to recite the entire section, since he could not tell, himself, which parts were relevant.

"Enough!" Count Seven said, after listening for a few minutes. "It's of no use to me!"

"Why not?" Lotus asked.

"The Manual speaks of internal injuries, such as rattled blood vessels, damage to the diaphragm, divergent breathing, all different kinds of disturbances to internal strength and how to cure them. While the path to recovery may be long, its methods will lead to considerable improvements. I, however, am suffering the opposite problem. I was bitten by a venomous snake. My injuries are caused by an external trauma. Indeed, more worrying than that, the Venom's Exploding Toad kung fu disrupted the flow of blood around my body."

"Which the Manual is perfect for helping with!" Lotus cried in delight.

Count Seven shook his head. "The Manual's instructions state that one must find a secluded spot, untroubled by adversaries, idle passersby or wild animals. Then, someone well versed in the workings of *qi* places their palms against the palms of the injured party, who in turn should move their *qi* around their body. Should they be lacking in internal strength, the facilitator may transfer some of their own through their palms, thus repairing any damaged blood vessels. This should be done for seven days and seven nights continuously, transporting the *qi* around the body clockwise and anti-clockwise a total of thirty-six times. It is vital, however, that the two do not lose contact via their palms during the process, as otherwise not only will there be no healing effect, on the contrary, they may suffer immediate injury or even death. No intruder or animal must be allowed to interrupt them, else they must accept any such attack without fighting back. This is the most difficult part, rather than the method itself. With Viper and his nephew around, we wouldn't manage a day and a night, never mind seven. Any attempt at healing me and they would be sure to attack."

"So, for seven day and seven nights, how do the two of them empty their bowels?" Guo Jing asked.

"Empty their bowels?" Lotus shook her head, then laughed. "This is an erudite text explaining profound theories of inner strength and *qi*."

Guo Jing grinned.

"If we hurry back to the mainland, we can surely find a secluded spot—or even on Peach Blossom Island," Lotus said. "Nobody would dare disturb you there. Guo Jing will sit with *Shifu* for seven days and seven nights, and I will stand outside with the Dog-Beating Cane and keep guard. No scoundrels, beasts, stray dogs, or poisonous insects will get in. *Shifu*, what about the second and third things that I was thinking about?"

"The second problem Lotus identified is the matter of defending ourselves against the venomous hand of Viper Ouyang," Count Seven continued. "His martial skills are quite extraordinary; the two of you together are no match for him. Which brings me to the third: how we are going to get back to the mainland. Isn't that right, Lotus?"

"Yes, these are our most pressing troubles—most of all, how to defeat Old Venom, or at least stop him from doing evil."

"Engage him in a battle of wits, in short. Old Venom may be cunning, but he is also conceited. He does not ponder things deeply, which means, therefore, it is not so difficult to fool him. But once he discovers deceit, he is quick to seek revenge with swift, savage reprisals."

Guo Jing and Lotus went quiet as they thought about this. Viper, Apothecary Huang, and *Shifu* were all once considered of equal standing in the *wulin*, but, even if her father came to the island, there was no guarantee he could defeat the Old Venom, Lotus realized. Then how could she possibly take him on? Their only hope would be to kill him in one stroke. Tricking him was never going to be enough.

Suddenly, Count Seven felt a sharp pain in his chest and he started to cough violently.

Just as Lotus was helping him to lie down, a shadow blocked the light at the mouth of the cave. Lotus looked up to see Viper Ouyang holding his nephew in his arms.

"Get out! Leave the cave to me and my nephew," he hissed.

Infuriated, Guo Jing leaped to his feet. "My Master lives here!"

"I don't care if the Jade Emperor himself lives here. Everyone has to leave!"

Guo Jing was about to answer him when Lotus pulled at his sleeve. Then she stooped down and helped Count Seven hobble out of the cave.

As they passed Old Venom, Count Seven opened his eyes and smiled. "How terrible, how ferocious!"

Viper's cheeks flushed red. He could have killed Count Seven with one thrust of his palm, but somehow the Old Beggar's righteous air cast a bolt of shame through him. He turned away so as not to see the old man's face. "And bring us some food. Don't try any tricks, or I'll kill all three of you."

The three walked far away from the cave, Guo Jing cursing all the way, while Lotus remained silent, lost in thought.

"*Shifu*," Guo Jing said, "rest here and I will go and find us somewhere suitable to seek shelter."

Lotus helped Count Seven to settle under a large pine tree. Only a few feet from where she was standing, two squirrels scuttled up and down a tree trunk, their big round eyes staring at the two humans as they did so. Amused, Lotus bent down, picked up a pinecone and held it out to them. One of the little creatures approached and sniffed it, before slowly reaching out a paw and grabbing it from her hand. The other squirrel, meanwhile, began to climb along Count Seven's sleeve.

"This island has never seen humans before," Lotus said. "They're not at all scared of us."

At that, the two squirrels ran up the tree. Lotus looked up into the dense tangle of needles and vines. Suddenly, an idea came to her.

"Guo Jing! Come back! We can climb this tree."

Guo Jing stopped and looked back at the tree. It was perfect. They snapped some branches from its nearby neighbors and wedged them between the pine's branches to fashion a platform. Then, standing either side of Count Seven, they put their hands under his armpits and—with a loud "*Hup!*"—they jumped up, depositing him safely in their tree house.

"We're just like birds, living in the treetops," Lotus said in delight. "Let them be beasts, down in that cave."

"Lotus," Guo Jing began, "are we going to take them food?"

"Unless we come up with some ingenious plan, we have no choice," she replied.

Guo Jing looked put out.

Together, they went to the far side of mountain, where they managed to catch a mountain sheep. They then made a fire and roasted it, before pulling the steaming carcass in half. Lotus took once piece and threw it on the ground.

"Pee on it!"

Guo Jing laughed. "They'll be able to tell."

"Don't worry about that, just do it!"

"I can't," Guo Jing said, his cheeks burning.

"Why not?"

"Not with you beside me."

Lotus nearly fell over with laughter.

"Throw me some meat!" Count Seven called from up in the tree. "I'll pee on it."

Laughing, Guo Jing took the meat and jumped up onto the platform. Count Seven drenched the mutton before Guo Jing left to take it to the cave.

"No, wait! Take this one," Lotus called out.

"But that's the clean one," Guo Jing said, scratching his head.

"I know. I want them to eat the clean one."

Guo Jing was confused, but, as usual, he obeyed Lotus without questioning her. In the meantime, Lotus placed the urine-soaked meat beside the fire to smoke, and went to pick some wild fruit.

Count Seven was just as confused. He had been looking forward to eating the succulent roast mutton, but now he had urinated all over their portion.

The meat gave off a mouth-watering aroma, which had wafted all the way inside the cave. Viper Ouyang did not wait for Guo Jing to enter, but stepped outside and grabbed the meat. "Wait—where is the rest of it?" he said suddenly.

Guo Jing gestured behind him with his thumb.

Viper strode over to the old pine tree, snatched the meat from beside the fire and threw the clean piece on the ground. Then he laughed coldly, turned and left.

Guo Jing knew that he must not give anything away, but it was not in his nature to hide what he was thinking. He turned away, so that Viper would not see his face, and waited for him to leave before running to find Lotus.

"How did you know he would come back and swap the meat?" he asked, grinning, as they returned together to their fire.

"My pa used to tell me, 'In artifice there is substance, in substance there is artifice.' Old Venom knew we would play a trick on him, but, in trying to outsmart us, he fell right for it."

Guo Jing listened in awe as he cut the meat into smaller pieces. Then, together, they climbed up into the tree and shared their meal.

"Lotus," Guo Jing said suddenly, as they were still eating. "That really was a wonderful trick you came up with. But it was a risky one."

"Why?"

"What if he hadn't come? Would we have had to eat meat soaked in pee?"

Lotus guffawed, bent over and promptly fell from her perch on the branch. Instantly, she jumped back up, unharmed. "Risky, indeed."

"Silly boy," Count Seven sighed. "Would you really have said no?"

The thought startled him, then he began to shake with laughter until he too tumbled out of the tree.

Viper and his nephew guzzled the mutton. It had a strange smell, to be sure, but they did not suspect a thing. Indeed, they even praised the young girl's cooking skills. She had brought out a slight saltiness in the meat.

2

BEFORE LONG, THE SKIES BEGAN TO DARKEN. GALLANT Ouyang was in pain and he let out a groan.

"Little girl!" Viper said, approaching the pine tree. "Come down!"

Lotus was startled. She had not expected Viper to launch his attack so soon. "What is it?"

"My nephew needs water for his tea. Go and serve him!"

The three sitting in the tree listened in rage.

"Come on, hurry up! What are you waiting for?"

"Let's fight him," Guo Jing whispered.

"You two run beyond the mountain," Count Seven whispered in reply. "Don't worry about me."

Lotus had already thought through their options. Their Master was sure to perish, no matter if they chose to stay and fight or if they fled. Their only option was to try to seek a compromise to protect Count Seven.

"Fine," she said, leaping down from the tree. "I'll go and attend to his wounds."

"Guo, boy," Viper sneered. "You come with me."

Guo Jing swallowed his anger and jumped down.

"Bring me one hundred large tree trunks. Tonight. And if there is but one missing, I will break your leg. Two, and I will break both."

"What do you want all that wood for?" Lotus said. "And how are we going to find it in the dark?"

"You talk too much," Viper hissed. "What does it have to do with you? Go and see to my nephew. If anything happens to him, you will all suffer the bitter consequences."

With a nod, Lotus signaled to Guo Jing to do the best he could and not to do anything rash.

Guo Jing watched as Lotus disappeared with Viper Ouyang into the darkness. Then he dropped to the ground, cupped his head, and hot, angry tears poured from his eyes.

"When I was young," Count Seven said from above, "my grandpa, my pa and I were all enslaved by the Jin. Now that was real hardship."

This startled Guo Jing back to his senses. *Shifu* spent his childhood as a slave and yet he became a master of the martial arts. Surely I must be able to endure this one day of ill-treatment. Guo Jing lit a pine branch, hurried to the far side of the mountain and once again began felling trunks using Dragon-Subduing Palm. Lotus would escape unharmed, he was sure of that, just as she had when they were surrounded in the Zhao Palace. She always managed to get out of any situation, no matter how difficult. He would do his best to complete the task the Viper had given him.

Before long, however, the exertion had exhausted him. His limbs were aching. In an hour, he had managed to fell twenty-one pines. He performed a Dragon in the Field. The tree shook, but nothing more. His chest felt numb. The energy had not flowed out through his palms, but instead traveled back. This was exactly what his Master had warned him about. The eighteen moves that made up Dragon-Subduing Palm required great strength, but it was important that he hold something back in reserve to prevent self-induced injury.

Shocked, he sat down and tried to regulate his breathing. It took an hour before he had the strength to get up and try again, and, even then, his limbs were too weak and fatigued.

Guo Jing knew that forcing himself would cause him yet more harm. But, with no axe to be found on this deserted island, how was he to fell enough trees? He still had at least seventy more to collect, and his legs were about to give way beneath him. Viper's nephew was crushed under that rock, Guo Jing thought. He must hate me to the core. If he wants a hundred trees from me tonight, surely he will just ask me for a thousand tomorrow. How will I ever appease him? We can't beat him in a fight and there is no one on this island to help us.

He sighed. Even if the island weren't deserted, who on this earth could help me? Master Hong is already too weak to fight; we don't even know if he will survive. Lotus's father hates me, and neither the Seven Masters of the Quanzhen Sect nor my six *shifus*, the Heroes of the South, could hope to defeat the Venom of the West, even if they fought together. If only . . . If only my sworn brother Zhou Botong were here . . . But he died jumping into the sea.

The thought of Zhou Botong only made him despise Viper Ouyang even more. His sworn brother, a master of the Nine Yin Manual and the inventor of Competing Hands kung fu, forced to meet his end. The Nine Yin Manual! Competing Hands! The words lit up in his mind like stars twinkling on the horizon in a dark night's sky.

My kung fu may not be accomplished enough to take on the Venom of the West, but the Nine Yin Manual contains many secrets of the martial world. Add to that Zhou Botong's Competing Hands, and my skills will appear to be double what they really are. I will train with Lotus tonight and then we will give the Venom a real scare.

Even so, Guo Jing knew it would be a mighty task, no matter what type of kung fu they used. He stood among the trees, deep in thought. What if I were to ask *Shifu*? He may not be able to fight himself, but he still has all that knowledge; he will be able to point me in the right direction.

He went back to the old pine and explained his thoughts to Count Seven Hong.

"Recite the Nine Yin Manual for me," Count Seven began, "and we will see what of its mighty kung fu you may be able to learn quickly."

Guo Jing began chanting the manual, line by line.

"... Most only know that sitting in quiet contemplation will lead to virtue, but they do not realize the virtuous are also flexible in mind, and cultivate the body twofold, that is, in movement they find stillness, in attack they know peace." As soon as Count Seven heard this, he leaped to his feet.

Guo Jing stopped. "What is it?"

But Count Seven did not answer. Instead, he pondered the lines, before eventually saying, "Can you repeat that last section again?"

Master has found something we can use against Viper! Guo Jing recited the lines again slowly.

Count Seven was nodding. "Indeed. Yes, yes. Carry on."

Guo Jing continued. As he approached the end, he came to the following passage: "*Mahaparas gatekras mahansighra pindaheya jinahuras ghosana . . .*"

The words were nonsense, but he knew that he was reciting them correctly. Count Seven had not understood them then, and he did not understand them now.

"Lad," Count Seven said, shaking his head, "the Nine Yin Manual contains many forms of devastating kung fu, but they cannot be learned in a day and a night."

Guo Jing looked disappointed.

"Go and build a raft from the trunks you have already felled and then get as far away from here as you can. Lotus and I will stay and deal with Old Venom."

"No," Guo Jing said quickly. "How could I leave *Shifu* here?"

Count Seven sighed. "The Venom of the West is scared of Apothecary Huang; he won't do anything to harm Lotus. As for me, I'm just a useless old beggar, now. So, off with you!"

Grieved and indignant, Guo Jing ran with his palm raised straight at a tree.

The sound echoed around the mountain. Count Seven watched in amazement. "What kind of kung fu was that?"

"Why do you ask?"

"You hit it with such force, but the tree didn't even quiver."

Guo Jing felt embarrassed. "All my strength has been used up. My hands are sore. I don't have any power left. I didn't follow *Shifu's* instructions to leave some strength in reserve," he said, after a pause.

"No, no, it was just a little strange, that's all. Do it again. Let me see."

Guo Jing raised his palm and struck the tree again. As before, the sound was deafening but the tree did not move. Suddenly, he realized. "Oh, Brother Zhou taught me. It's one of the seventy-two moves of Luminous Hollow Fist."

"Luminous Hollow Fist? I've never heard of it."

"Brother Zhou was bored and had nothing to do while being held captive on Peach Blossom Island, so he invented it. He taught me the secret in sixteen characters: *kong meng dong song, feng tong rong meng, chong qiong zhong nong, tong yong gong chong.*"

Count Seven looked amused. It sounded like yet more nonsense.

"Let me explain. Each character has its own significance. The fourth character, 'loose', means that the fist must be hollow—that is, lacking strength. The last character, 'worm', refers to the body, which must be soft and supple. The second, 'haze', tells you that the punches must be confused—foolish, even—to render your opponent unsure of their shape. The eighth, 'dream', I think means that you should fight as if in a dream. Why don't I give you a demonstration?"

"I won't be able to see in the dark. But it does sound like there's a logic to it. There's no need to show me, just keep explaining."

Guo Jing began with the first stance, Empty Bowl Filled with Rice, then went on to the second, Empty Cottage Inhabited, narrating the changes and transformations in the use of strength in each move as he went. Zhou Botong's mischievous nature was evident in the witty names he had given them.

By the time Guo Jing had reached the eighteenth move, Count Seven could not help but feel admiration. "That's enough. I know how to deal with Old Venom."

"Using Luminous Hollow Fist? I'm not nearly proficient at it," Guo Jing said.

"I know. But this is a grave situation, so we must at least try. Do you still have the golden dagger Genghis Khan gave you?"

A warm glint of metal flashed in the dark night as Guo Jing removed the dagger from the folds of his robes.

"Use the dagger in combination with Luminous Hollow Fist to fell the trees," Count Seven said.

The blade was only a foot in length. Guo Jing looked at it and hesitated.

"Your weapon is so sharp, it can slice through tree trunks. The blade is perhaps a little thick, but, as long as you follow the principles of empty and loose, the dagger should do the job."

Guo Jing pondered his *shifu's* words. Seeing him hesitate, Count Seven gave him further instructions until finally he understood. He jumped down from the tree and approached a cedar of medium girth. Channeling the techniques Zhou Botong had taught him—light and quick, using force as if without force—he plunged the dagger into its trunk. As it sliced into the tree, he turned in a circle and it fell to the ground. Guo Jing was delighted. He went on to chop another dozen. He would have a hundred before daybreak, after all.

"Boy!" Guo Jing suddenly heard Count Seven call. "Come up here!"

Guo Jing jumped up onto the platform. "It worked. And I don't feel tired."

"We can't be wasting energy, can we?" Count Seven replied.

"Exactly! That's what the *kong meng dong song* means. Brother Zhou spent so long trying to teach me, but I didn't get it."

"This kung fu is for more than merely chopping down trees. And yet, alone, it cannot beat the Venom of the West. You must train once again in the skills described in the Nine Yin Manual if we are to have any chance of overcoming him. Let's think of a plan to buy us time."

Guo Jing nodded, but maintained a respectful silence. When it came to clever plans, he knew he was not much help.

Eventually, Count Seven shook his head. "Nothing's coming

to me. We'll have to ask Lotus to think of something tomorrow. Although, I did have a thought while listening to you recite the Manual. I don't think I am wrong about this. Help me down from the tree; I need to practice."

"But you're not well; how can you train?"

"The Manual said, 'the virtuous cultivate the body twofold, that is, in movement they find stillness, in attack they know peace'. These sentences helped me come to a realization. Come, now, let's get down."

Guo Jing did not understand what the sentences meant, but neither did he wish to defy his *shifu*. Holding his Master in his arms, he gently jumped down from the tree.

Count Seven took several deep breaths, assumed the opening stance and thrust with his right palm. In the darkness, Guo Jing watched him charge forward as if about to fall. He rushed to help, but Count Seven had already stopped.

"I'm fine," he panted.

Moments later, he repeated the move with his left palm. Guo Jing watched him stumble. He was clearly in pain. Several times, Guo Jing wanted to call out to him to stop, but, to his surprise, his Master was growing ever steadier and stronger with each attempt. Before long, the heavy breathing and labored movements had given way to elegant twists of his body and firm, deft footwork. He was making fantastic progress. He finished all eighteen Dragon-Subduing Palms and moved straight into Wayfaring Fist.

Guo Jing waited until he was finished, before crying out, "You're healed!"

"Carry me back up."

Guo Jing wrapped his arms around his Master's middle and jumped up to the platform. "Well done, well done!" He could barely contain his delight.

Count Seven sighed. "Not well done, indeed. It was a fine display, but my kung fu is of no practical use."

Guo Jing was confused.

"After my injury, I took to rest, thinking it the best way to recover," Count Seven explained. "But my kung fu is external in nature, it only improves through sustained movement. I may be out of physical danger, but I will never recover my martial skill."

Guo Jing wanted to comfort his Master, but he did not know what to say. "I'll go back to felling trees," he said at last.

"Lad," Count Seven said suddenly, "I think I have a way to scare Old Venom. Let me know what you think." Count Seven explained his plan.

"Marvelous!" Guo Jing jumped down from the tree at once to prepare.

AT FIRST light the next morning, Viper Ouyang approached their tree and began counting the trunks piled up beside it. Ninety.

"Mongrel! Get down here at once! You still have ten more trees to fetch for me."

Lotus had spent the night by Gallant's side, tending his wounds. The sound of his groans softened even her heart. As the sun had risen, she had watched Viper leave the cave and had followed him. Now, she was worried for her beloved Guo Jing.

Viper waited, but no reply came. The only sound to be heard was the wind gathering speed behind the mountain. It reminded him of people practicing martial arts. Quickly, he followed it to its source. As he reached the top of the mountain, he was surprised to find Count Seven and the young boy locked in combat. Palms flew and kicks soared. It was an intense duel.

Lotus, too, was surprised to see her *shifu* thus recovered and able to fight.

"Boy! Watch out for this!" Count Seven cried and launched a palm. Guo Jing raised a hand to block, but, before they made contact, he flew back and crashed into a tree. It was not an old tree, but its trunk snapped and it fell to the ground.

In fact, it had been a perfectly ordinary palm strike, but it was enough to leave Viper dumbstruck.

"*Shifu!*" Lotus cried out. "Wonderful Splitting Sky Palm!"

"Protect yourself—don't let my palm hurt you!" Count Seven called out.

"Your disciple understands."

Just then, *thwack!* Another palm strike sent Guo Jing flying into another tree. Guo Jing dusted himself off and they repeated the sequence, and, before long, Count Seven's Splitting Sky Palm had felled eight more trees.

"That's ten!" Lotus called out.

Guo Jing was panting heavily. "Your disciple is exhausted."

Count Seven cupped his hands and laughed. "The Nine Yin Manual really is marvelous. I was so weak after my injury, and yet, after just one morning of training, I'm recovered."

Viper watched with suspicion. He bent down to inspect the tree trunks, but what he found only amazed him further. Apart from the inner core, the rest of the trunk had been broken off smoothly—not even a saw could have done it so perfectly. What manner of kung fu must be contained within the Nine Yin Manual? The Old Beggar had been restored. How could he fight three of them at once? There was only one option: he had to start training from the Manual at once.

He gave the three of them a baleful look before rushing back to the cave, where he grabbed the pile of papers wrapped in oil paper, containing Guo Jing's shaky characters, and began reading.

Meanwhile, Count Seven and Guo Jing waited until Viper was long gone before bursting into laughter.

"*Shifu!*" Lotus cried in delight. "The Nine Yin Manual is a true marvel."

Count Seven merely laughed even harder.

Guo Jing ran to her side. "Lotus, we were pretending."

He explained to her how they had done it. Guo Jing had used his blade to cut all but the center of the trees, taking care to leave them standing. Count Seven's palm strikes had carried next to no strength at all, but instead Guo Jing had used his own internal *neigong* to send himself flying backward into the pre-cut trees, toppling them to the ground. Viper Ouyang was not to know that the real work had been done by the dagger and Guo Jing's use of Luminous Hollow Fist.

Lotus laughed, but suddenly stopped, fell silent and then frowned.

"I can walk again," Count Seven said. "That's miracle enough for me. I don't care if it was real or fake martial skill. Lotus, you fear Old Venom will see through our ruse?"

Lotus nodded.

"The question is, can we fool him for any length of time?" Count Seven continued. "And yet, human affairs are never easily anticipated. There is no use worrying unnecessarily. Listen, there is a passage in the Nine Yin Manual that Guo Jing read to me, called 'Transforming Muscles, Forging Bones'. It is most interesting. Why don't we try to practice, seeing as we have nothing else to do?"

His tone was light, but Lotus knew the situation was grave. Their Master would have his reasons for picking this passage.

"Indeed. Please teach us, *Shifu*."

Count Seven asked Guo Jing to repeat the passage two more times, and then, based on what he heard, he gave them instructions before leaving to look for food. When he returned, he lit a fire and cooked them a meal. A few times, the young couple tried to help, but Count Seven would not allow it.

THE DAYS passed quickly, and Guo Jing and Lotus made significant progress with their training. Viper Ouyang, meanwhile, stayed in his cave, studying the Nine Yin Manual. It took all his energy and concentration.

Count Seven Hong turned to Lotus after lunch one day and said, "How was your *shifu*'s roasted goat?"

Lotus merely smiled and shook her head.

"Indeed, I can't stomach it either. You two have finished your first lesson; now, you must relax your muscles, otherwise your *qi* will be stifled, causing you great harm. Lotus, you prepare the meal tonight. Guo Jing and I will make a raft."

"Make a raft?" Guo Jing and Lotus said in unison.

"Why, yes. Don't tell me you were planning to keep Old Venom company on this wretched island forever?"

The young couple were ecstatic and set to work immediately.

The one hundred tree trunks Guo Jing had felled the week before were still piled neatly nearby. They began slicing tree bark and Guo Jing plaited the strands into another rope. But when he tugged on it, it snapped. He had not made it strong enough. He made another, thicker rope, and repeated the action, only for it to break too. Confounded, he stared at the rope, at a loss as to what to do.

Just then, he heard Lotus shouting. He turned to see her running toward them, carrying a goat. She had taken some stones with her to throw at its head, but, without understanding how she had done it, she had overtaken the wild animal in a few steps and scooped it up into her arms. She had moved with such speed, it had taken even her by surprise.

"The Nine Yin Manual is mighty indeed," Count Seven said and smiled. "No wonder so many heroes of the *wulin* are willing to risk their lives to get their hands on it."

"*Shifu*," Lotus breathed with delight, "do you think we can beat Old Venom now?"

Count Seven shook his head. "No, we are still a long way off. You would have to train for another ten years. His Exploding Toad is no laughing matter; no kung fu has been able to overcome it, apart from Yang in Ascendance when combined with Cosmos *neigong*, which only Wang Chongyang knew."

"Another ten years and even then we might not beat him," Lotus said, pouting.

"Well, it's hard to say. I might be underestimating the powers of the kung fu contained within the Nine Yin Manual."

"Be patient, Lotus," Guo Jing said. "It's always good to learn something new."

A few more days passed, and Guo Jing and Lotus were getting to grips with the second part of Transforming Muscles, Forging Bones. The raft was also ready. Together, they wove a sail from yet more tree bark and prepared rations of fresh water and food.

The evening before they planned to set sail, just as they were preparing to go to bed, Lotus suddenly asked, "Aren't we going to say goodbye to them?"

"We will see them again in ten years, to fight," Guo Jing said.

"Exactly!" Lotus exclaimed, clapping her hands. "May the heavens guide those scoundrels back to the mainland and ensure Old Venom lives a long life, so that we might meet again in ten years. Either that, or ensure *Shifu*'s quick recovery, so that we can get it over with in a couple of years' time instead. Yes, that would be even better."

Count Seven woke before sunrise the next morning to sounds coming from the shore.

"Guo Jing! Do you hear that? It's coming from the beach."

Guo Jing jumped down from the tree and ran toward the noise. As soon as he saw what was happening, he charged forward in fury.

By this time, Lotus was fully awake. "Guo Jing! What's happening?"

"Those evil thieves stole our raft!"

Lotus was shocked. By the time she reached the beach, Viper Ouyang had already placed his nephew on the pontoon, raised the sail and, together, they were floating several dozen meters from the shore, out at sea. Guo Jing was about to wade into the water to pursue them when Lotus tugged at his sleeve. "They're already too far out."

"Thank you for the raft!" Viper shouted, then cackled with laughter.

Guo Jing ran to a nearby red sandalwood tree and kicked at it, hard.

Suddenly, Lotus had an idea. "That's it!" She lifted a large rock onto one of the tree's branches and instructed Guo Jing to pull down. "A catapult!"

Guo Jing grinned, braced his feet against the roots and pulled down as hard as he could. The tree was strong but flexible, and the branch bent almost all the way to the ground without breaking. Then Guo Jing let go, and with a loud *swoooooosh!* the rock flew out, landing right beside the raft and causing a large splash.

"What a shame!" Lotus cried, and ran to fetch another rock. Together, they aimed and fired. This time, they hit the floating craft dead on—but they had crafted it so well, it did not break. They launched three more rocks, but each landed with a splash and sunk to the bottom of the sea.

Lotus had another idea, this one even crazier.

"Quick, fire me like a cannonball!"

Guo Jing was startled, unsure if he had understood her correctly.

"Launch me at them. I'll deal with them." She took out her dagger and held it in her hand.

She was a natural swimmer and her lightness kung fu had really improved, so he decided it was most likely safe. "Be careful." Then he pulled down the branch once more.

Lotus sat down carefully and cried, "Fire!"

Guo Jing released the branch and watched as Lotus flew through the air, somersaulting twice before diving gracefully into the water, only a few meters from the raft. It was a marvelous sight to behold. Viper Ouyang and his nephew watched, stupefied. What was she going to do?

Lotus swam down deep, and, instead of resurfacing, approached the raft underwater. As soon as she saw the boat's dark shadow above, she knew she was in the right place.

Viper struck at the water with his oar, but to no avail.

Her dagger between her teeth, Lotus was swimming up to cut the ropes holding the raft together, when a thought struck her, and, instead of sawing them the whole way through, she left them partially intact. That way, the raft would hold until they were farther out, in rougher seas. Then she swam away and resurfaced some distance from the raft, shouting and gasping for breath, pretending to have failed to reach them.

Viper laughed wildly as the sail caught the wind. Before long, they were far, far out at sea.

Guo Jing and Count Seven were waiting for Lotus on the beach, cursing their misfortune. That is, until they saw Lotus's satisfied grin. Lotus explained that the Ouyangs would soon find eternal rest at the bottom of the ocean, and the two men laughed with joy.

"But," Lotus added with a note of vexation, "it does mean we have to start all over again."

Nevertheless, the three ate their breakfast in high spirits, before getting to work cutting down yet more trees. It took them a few days to build a new raft. A southwesterly wind was blowing, so there was no time to lose. They hoisted the sail and set off in a westerly direction. Lotus gazed back at the island as it receded into the distance. "We almost lost our lives, back there, and yet, I feel quite sad to be leaving."

"We can always come back, one day," Guo Jing said.

"Yes!" Lotus cried and clapped her hands. "You've made me a promise. But, first, we need to give it a name. *Shifu*, what do you think?"

"It was the place where you crushed that scoundrel with the rock, so what about Ghost Crushing Island?"

"It's not very elegant," Lotus said and shook her head.

"If it was elegance you wanted, why did you ask an old beggar? It was also the place where we managed to trick Old Venom into consuming my urine, so what about Eat Piss Island?"

Lotus smiled and waved the idea away. She cocked her head and thought. On the horizon, a clutch of ruby clouds were gathering. "Rosy Cloud Island!"

"No, no, far too elegant," Count Seven replied.

Unable to contribute much himself, Guo Jing listened with a smile. He did not care if the island was given an elegant or a vulgar name, but deep down he preferred *Shifu*'s suggestions.

3

TOGETHER, THEY TRAVELED WITH THE WIND FOR TWO DAYS. On the third night, Lotus and Count Seven were sleeping, while Guo Jing was keeping watch, when suddenly he heard a voice carried over the roar of the water.

"Help! Help!" The voice clanged like crashing cymbals as it struggled to make itself heard over the screaming of the wind and the roaring of the waves.

"Old Venom," Count Seven said, sitting up.

They heard him shout once more.

Lotus grabbed her Master's arm. "A ghost!" Her voice trembled.

There was no moon that night and only a mere scattering of stars filled the black sky. A voice emerging from the darkness would be enough to scare anyone.

"Old Venom?" Count Seven cried out. His internal energy had yet to recover, so his voice was quickly swallowed up by the wind.

Guo Jing gathered his *qi* to his diaphragm and called out, "Uncle Ouyang, is that you?"

"Yes, it's me! Help!" The voice sounded faint and distant, now.

"I don't care if it's a man or a ghost, let's get far away!" Lotus said.

"Save him!" Count Seven cried suddenly.

"No, I'm scared!" Lotus cried back.

"It's not a ghost."

"I don't care; we can't save him."

"Helping others in their time of need is one of the principles of the Beggar Clan," Count Seven said. "We represent two generations of Clan leadership. We cannot abandon the customs that have been passed down to us from our ancestors."

"But the custom isn't right," Lotus said. "Viper Ouyang is evil,

and when he passes to the other side and becomes a ghost, he will be an evil spirit. Either way, he doesn't deserve our help."

"We cannot change the customs of the Clan," Count Seven said.

In her heart, Lotus was furious.

"Brother Seven, are you really leaving me to die?"

"Yes!" Lotus cried. "Guo Jing, wait until you have Viper in your sights and then strike him dead with the bamboo cane. You aren't a member of the Beggar Clan; you don't need to live by this ridiculous rule. *Shifu*, the Beggar Clan believes in helping *people* in need, not *devils* in need."

"Striking someone when he's down . . . Is that the righteous behavior of someone who follows the code of *xia*?"

"And yet, striking a devil when he's down . . ."

She gave Guo Jing an anxious look as he steered the raft toward the voice. In the gloom, they managed to make out two figures bobbing in the water. A large piece of timber was floating next to them. They must have been clinging to it since the raft fell apart.

"Insist that he swear never to harm another soul, and then we'll rescue him," Lotus said.

"You know the Old Venom," Count Seven sighed. "He would rather die than admit to being in the wrong. He would never promise to that. Boy, rescue them."

Guo Jing leaned over the side of their craft and grabbed the collar of Gallant's robe. Forgetting how weak he was, Count Seven rushed to help. He held out his hand to Viper Ouyang, who took it. Viper pulled hard and leaped up onto the raft, but, as he did so, he ended up pulling Count Seven into the sea, where he landed with a splash. A heartbeat later, Guo Jing and Lotus jumped after him.

"My *shifu* is so good-hearted as to save you, after all you have done," Lotus growled, as she and Guo Jing lifted Count Seven aboard once more, "and you pull him into the sea?"

Viper knew Count Seven was injured, otherwise there was no way he could have been so easily dislodged. But he himself had been floating in the water for days and his limbs were weak with fatigue.

He was in no position to pursue any advantage. "I . . ." he said, his head held low. "I didn't mean to, Brother Seven. I apologize."

"Fine," Count Seven said with a hearty laugh. "But now you know the extent of my strength, these days."

"Miss," Viper said, turning to Lotus, "do you have anything for us to eat? We haven't eaten in days."

"We only have rations for three. If I give you some, what will we eat?"

"Fine. But please give a little something to my nephew, at least. He's badly injured and won't survive without nourishment."

"I will make you a deal. He may have something, as long as you give my *shifu* the antidote to your snake venom. My *shifu* has not recovered yet."

Viper Ouyang reached into his robes and found two vials. "Look, miss. They have been submerged in water for days; the antidote has been washed away!"

Lotus took them, shook the vials and sniffed. It was indeed seawater. "In that case, give us the method, so that we may make our own, once we land ashore."

"I could tell you anything in order to get my hands on food and water, and you'd have no way of knowing if I was giving you the real recipe or a fake one. But what kind of person would that make Viper Ouyang? Let me be frank. My snakes are the deadliest in the world. One bite is enough to severely injure a hero of the *wulin*. I can give you the recipe for the antidote, but the ingredients are extremely rare, and it takes three winters and three summers for the concoction to be ready. By then, it will be too late. Now that I have told you the truth, it's up to you whether or not I should pay with my life."

Lotus and Guo Jing listened in grudging admiration. To be so cruel, and yet still maintain the dignity befitting his standing in the martial world, even with his life hanging by a thread?

"Lotus," Count Seven said, "he's telling the truth. Our lives lie in the hands of fate. I fear nothing. Give them something to eat."

Lotus's heart was aching. She knew her Master would never recover. Silently, she took a hunk of roasted goat and threw it at Viper, who proceeded to tear it into two chunks, feeding one to his nephew before eating the other himself. The sight reminded Lotus of how they had tricked the two men into eating the urine-soaked meat, back on the island, and she could not help but laugh.

"Too late!"

Viper had no idea what she meant and merely stared back at her, wide-eyed.

"Now that you have injured my *shifu* in this way, Uncle Ouyang," Lotus said coldly, "you will surely be the winner of the next Contest of Mount Hua. May I extend my congratulations."

"Not necessarily," Viper replied. "There is at least one other person who could heal Brother Seven."

Guo Jing and Lotus jumped up at the same time, nearly tipping the raft. "Really!?" they cried in unison.

"Only, this person will be difficult to persuade," Viper said through his chews. "Your *shifu* knows who I mean."

The young couple turned to their Master.

"In which case, why did you mention it?" Count Seven replied with a smile.

"Tell us," Lotus said, tugging her Master's sleeve. "We have to try, at least. I will ask my father—he'll find a way."

Viper Ouyang snorted.

"What are you snorting for?"

But Viper did not answer her.

"He is laughing because you think your father is all powerful," Count Seven said. "The person in question is mighty indeed, but he is of no use. He's a formidable fighter, but even if he were so weak that he couldn't even strangle a chicken, this Old Beggar would never do harm to anyone merely for his own benefit."

"A formidable fighter?" Lotus began hesitantly. "No, wait! Is it King Duan of the South? *Shifu*, let's ask him. How could it possibly harm anyone else?"

"No more questions. Go to sleep! I forbid you from ever bringing this up again. Do you understand?"

Lotus did not reply. She was afraid that Viper might try to steal their food, so she leaned against the bucket containing their supplies and went to sleep.

4

EARLY THE NEXT MORNING, LOTUS AWOKE AND LOOKED OVER at Viper and his nephew. The sight of their pale faces nearly made her jump. Their bodies were swollen from having been in the water so long.

Master is a wonderful man, Lotus thought, but he is rather too righteous. To be so righteous in the face of evil was, in fact, to be evil to righteousness. I hope Guo Jing doesn't decide to copy this aspect of *Shifu's* character. It would be better for him to learn from his father-in-law. This last phrase made her smile: father-in-law!

By late afternoon, a black line had appeared on the horizon. Was it land? Guo Jing was the first to cry out. Before long, it was confirmed. The sea was calm, but the sun was beating down hard on them.

Viper Ouyang suddenly rose to his feet, wobbled and grabbed both Guo Jing and Lotus by the hand. Then, with the tip of his toe, he kicked at one of Count Seven's pressure points. Guo Jing and Lotus tried to get up, but Viper had locked the pressure points on their wrists, rendering each of them numb across half their body in an instant.

"What are you doing?"

Viper grinned, but did not reply.

"Old Venom is arrogant indeed," Count Seven said with a sigh. "He cannot accept the grace of another human being. We saved his life, and yet he can only find peace by killing his saviors. *Aiya*, pity my soft heart. By rescuing him, I have endangered the lives of these two poor youngsters."

"May you never forget it," Viper said. "Also, I own a copy of the

Nine Yin Manual now. If I let the boy live, I will only bring trouble on myself in the future."

The mention of the Manual stirred something in Count Seven. He began to recite confidently . . .

Viper listened in amazement. It sounded familiar, just like one of the many passages he had struggled to make sense of. He was not to know that Count Seven was making it up. Did the Old Beggar understand it? he asked himself. There are so many strange sentences, there must be some key to unlocking its mysteries. If I kill them, I might not find another soul on earth who can understand it, and all I've done to gain possession of this mighty text will be in vain.

"What does it mean?"

Count Seven replied with yet more nonsense. "Guo Jing, you continue!" Though the Old Beggar had heard Guo Jing chant large chunks of the Manual out loud on the island, it would have been impossible for him to memorize it. But he had put on a good show and kept a straight face.

Guo Jing continued with yet more nonsense. Viper Ouyang listened intently.

"Guo Jing, go!" Count Seven cried. Guo Jing pulled his left arm free, struck with his right and kicked out at Viper.

The Venom had been so mesmerized by the recitation that he had loosened his grip on Guo Jing's vital point, allowing him to make his counterattack. Guo Jing had now studied the Manual's Transforming Muscles, Forging Bones chapter as far as the second passage, and, while he had not learned any new moves as such, it had increased his strength by around a fifth. One tug, one slap, one kick—there was nothing new about the movements, but they were charged with a remarkable power. Viper Ouyang was taken by surprise. He had nowhere to retreat to on the small raft. All he could do was raise one hand above his head and try to keep hold of Lotus's wrist with the other.

Guo Jing's fists and palms rained down on him like a storm. If Viper got the chance to use his Exploding Toad kung fu, then all three would be buried out at sea. And yet, the weight of the young man's attack drove Viper back another half a step.

Lotus leaned to the side, preparing to unbalance Old Venom with her shoulder. Sensing the move coming, Viper was amused. Does this little girl think she can hurt me with a bump of her shoulder? Careful you don't rebound into the ocean!

Just then, her shoulder made contact. He did not block or dodge, but stood his ground, feigning disinterest. At that moment, he felt a needle-sharp pain grip his chest. She was wearing Hedgehog Chainmail! He was already on the edge of the raft, so he could not back away. Assaulted by a thicket of sharp spikes, he let go of her wrist and flung her aside.

Lotus had no way to stop herself falling off the raft and plunging into the water, but Guo Jing reached behind him and grabbed her, his other hand still on the attack. Lotus pulled out her dagger and threw herself into the fray.

Viper was balanced near the edge of the raft, salt water splashing his legs. But, no matter how hard they pressed, the young fighters could not force him over the side.

He was the stronger, more experienced fighter, and his powers were superior to those of the young couple combined, but he had been weakened by the days he had spent floating in the water. Lotus was armed with a dagger and protected by her Hedgehog Chainmail, which was enough to make him cautious. In addition, Guo Jing had now studied the Eighteen Dragon-Subduing Palms, the seventy-two stances that made up Luminous Hollow Fist, Zhou Botong's Competing Hands kung fu and, most recently, the passages from Transforming Muscles, Forging Bones.

Viper could feel the strength gradually returning to his palms and, as the fight wore on, Guo Jing and Lotus began to notice the change in him. Count Seven was watching anxiously. As their fists danced, Viper's left leg flew out, sending with it a gust of air. Lotus was forced to somersault out of the way and into the water.

Guo Jing was feeling the strain, but Lotus swam under the raft and climbed up on the other side, blade aimed at Viper's back. This pincer movement put them on an equal footing once more.

The only way for us to defeat him, Lotus was thinking as she fought, is to take the fight underwater.

She sliced her dagger through the bark rope, sending the sail fluttering down. No longer propelled by the wind, the raft bobbed on the waves. Lotus then wrapped the rigging several times around Count Seven's body and then around one of the tree trunks that made up the raft, securing him with two tight knots.

Guo Jing was flagging. He had managed to block three successive attacks, but the fourth forced him onto the back foot. Viper redoubled his efforts, pushing Guo Jing back even farther. He tried to counter with a Leap from the Abyss, but was yet again pushed back until he found his feet in mid-air. Not letting nerves cloud his mind, he kicked with both feet before splashing into the water.

Taking advantage of the violent swaying of the raft, Lotus leaped into the water, and together the young fighters pushed and pulled at the raft in an attempt to capsize it. Gallant would drown and Viper would struggle to match them in the water. But they would have to dispose of Old Venom quickly before saving their Master.

Viper understood their intentions. He raised his foot close to Count Seven's head and cried, "Rock the raft and I will kick him!"

Lotus had a backup plan, however. Taking a deep lungful of air, she dived underneath the raft and began hacking through the ropes that held it together. She had calculated that, after the Ouyangs had drowned, the three of them could float to the shore clutching the wreckage.

The raft let out a loud cracking sound as it broke in two. Gallant was on one half, Viper and Count Seven on the other. Viper reached out and pulled his nephew toward him. Then he peered into the sea, waiting for Lotus to approach, so that he could grab her.

Lotus could see Viper's outline from below the surface of the water. Aware that his counterattack would be fierce, she decided not to cut any more ropes. Instead, she swam some distance from the raft, took another deep breath and dived back down to wait for an opportunity to make the next move.

They both waited. Suddenly, the sea became calm, its surface twinkling in the sunshine. Their surroundings were peaceful, but their hearts raged with murderous intent.

If the raft splits . . . Lotus was thinking.

As soon as she comes up for air, I'm going to slap the water. The vibration alone will kill her, Viper was thinking. With her out of the way, the boy and the Old Beggar won't cause me any bother.

They waited, unblinking.

Suddenly, Gallant pointed beyond the port side. "A boat! A boat!"

Count Seven and Guo Jing turned to see a large junk with a dragon at its bow, sails raised, fast approaching them. Moments later, someone appeared at the front. He was tall and wearing a crimson *kasaya*. Lama Supreme Wisdom? Gallant Ouyang wondered. As the boat drew closer, his suspicions were confirmed. Quickly, he informed his uncle.

Viper Ouyang gathered the *qi* to his diaphragm and cried, "Over here! We are friends!"

Lotus was unaware of the developments above water. Guo Jing, however, knew they were in trouble. He ducked down under the surface, pulled at her arm and signaled that Viper had backup. Lotus could not understand what he was trying to tell her. But, whatever it was, it had to be bad. She gestured to Guo Jing that he should go back and distract Viper while she cut the rest of the ropes.

Guo Jing was acutely aware that he was at a disadvantage—all the more so, now that he was in the water and Viper was on the raft. His life was at risk, but he had no choice but to try. He gathered the strength into his arms and shot upward.

"Ha!" Viper Ouyang slapped his palms against the water just as Guo Jing's hands were rushing to the surface. The two forces collided, propelling the raft upward and—*crraaaccckkkkkkkk!*—it broke in two. Lotus must have cut the ropes just in time.

Lotus dived back down and was just about to leap up to stab

Viper Ouyang when she caught sight of Guo Jing sinking motionless to the bottom of the sea. She swam quickly to his aid, grabbed his arm and pulled him away some distance before resurfacing. Guo Jing's eyes were screwed shut, his cheeks pale and his lips blue. He was unconscious.

Meanwhile, the junk had drawn close to Viper and lowered a small rescue boat. Its crew rowed over and fished Viper, Gallant, and Count Seven out of the water.

"Guo Jing!" Lotus cried his name three times, but he did not respond. The ship might be hostile, but she had no choice. She hooked her arm around Guo Jing's head and pulled him toward the rescue boat.

The men pulled Guo Jing aboard and then held their hands out to Lotus, but, instead of taking them, she placed her left hand on the edge of the small boat and leaped up like a flying fish, startling the men inside.

Only moments previously, Guo Jing had felt a force surge through his body and had almost immediately passed out. Luckily, the force traveled straight through him, without rebounding internally. Now, he awoke to find his cheek pressed against Lotus's chest. They were on a small boat. He took a few deep breaths and was relieved to discover that he had sustained no internal injuries. He looked up at Lotus and smiled. She replied with a grin as the fear melted from her heart. Only then did she look around to see who else was with them in the vessel.

The answer was not a happy one: eight men, including five she had encountered in the Zhao residence, in the Jin capital, only a few months before. A short, stocky man, known as Butcher of a Thousand Hands Tiger Peng; one with a shiny bald head, called Dragon King Hector Sha; a man with three cysts on his head, whose name was Browbeater Hou, or the Three-Horned Dragon; and, sitting behind them, the Ginseng Immortal Graybeard Liang, and Lama Supreme Wisdom Lobsang Choden Rinpoche. The other three she had never seen before.

Guo Jing and I have made great improvements in our kung fu, she said to herself. If I am forced to fight Tiger Peng or any of the others one-on-one, I might not win, but Guo Jing surely would. But Viper Ouyang is here, and there are so many of them. We are in danger.

5

THE CREW AND PASSENGERS OF THE JUNK HAD BEEN AMAZED to hear Viper Ouyang calling from the raft. Now, the presence of Guo Jing and Lotus only compounded their surprise.

Viper carried his nephew, while Guo Jing and Lotus supported Count Seven, and together they all climbed on board the junk.

Before long, a man appeared at the door of the main cabin to welcome them. He was dressed in a resplendent embroidered robe, and a neat beard graced his handsome face. His eyes met Guo Jing's and the two men looked at each other in stunned silence. It was the Sixth Prince of the Jin, Wanyan Honglie.

After escaping the Liu ancestral temple in Baoying, fearing that Guo Jing would follow him, Wanyan Honglie had decided not to return north. And, when he came across Tiger Peng, Browbeater Hou and the others, he led them south, instead, to steal the book of General Yue's last writings from his tomb.

Meanwhile, the Mongolians had launched a large-scale military attack against the Jin. The capital, Yanjing, had been under siege for months, and the surrounding sixteen prefectures had already fallen into Mongolian hands. As each day passed, the situation was growing more and more critical. Wanyan Honglie was fearful for his Empire—he had seen with his own eyes how agile and brave the Mongolians were. The Jin army outnumbered them, and yet they were being defeated in every battle. He could think of no way out, other than to recover General Yue Fei's book, unlock the secrets of his battle strategies contained within it and use them to force the Mongols to retreat.

Wanyan Honglie and his band had moved south with caution, so as to avoid discovery by the Song. They had decided that traveling by sea would be safest. They could come ashore on the coast of Zhejiang and secretly make their way inland, to Lin'an, to find the book.

Before setting sail, Wanyan Honglie had tried to find Gallant Ouyang, thinking that he would make a useful ally. But, after searching in vain for some time, he decided to leave without him. Little did he expect to come across him out here, at sea, accompanied by Guo Jing. Had his secret plan been leaked?

Guo Jing, meanwhile, was seething. This was the man who had killed his father. His eyes burned with hatred, so much so that he barely registered the others gathered on board this ship.

Just then, someone began to emerge from the cabin behind Wanyan Honglie, before quickly slipping back inside and closing the door. Lotus had seen enough, however. Yang Kang.

"Uncle," Gallant said, breaking the silence. "This is the Sixth Prince of the Jin. He is a great supporter of virtue and skill."

Viper cupped his hands as a sign of respect.

Wanyan Honglie was not aware of just how formidable Viper Ouyang's reputation in the *wulin* was. He had an arrogant air, but, for the sake of his friendship with Gallant Ouyang, the Sixth Prince returned the gesture.

Tiger Peng, Hector Sha, and the others bowed at the mention of his name.

"For many years, Elder Ouyang has held the title of the Supreme Master of the *Wulin*, claimed at the summit of Mount Hua," one of them said. "It is our pleasure to make your acquaintance."

Viper Ouyang bowed hurriedly in a halfhearted gesture of courtesy.

Only Lama Supreme Wisdom had not heard of the Venom of the West. He pressed his palms together and said nothing.

Wanyan Honglie observed that Hector Sha and the others were united in genuine admiration, which was unusual, considering their otherwise conceited behavior. They almost seemed to fear this new-comer, and their flattery was like nothing he had heard from them before. This strange man, with his swollen limbs and disheveled appearance, was no ordinary stranger. Intrigued, he chimed in with some words of respect.

Graybeard Liang's thoughts were elsewhere. This young man, Guo Jing, had drunk the precious magic blood of his prize snake, the result of many years of special care and attention. He was still furious. And yet, Guo Jing was accompanied by the man he feared most in this world, Count Seven Hong. Despite the fury bubbling in his breast, he kept a smile on his face, bowed and said, "Your humble servant, Graybeard Liang, offers Chief Hong my best wishes."

The others were startled. Was the Beggar of the North here, too? What were the chances of finding two of the greatest men of the *wulin* together on a raft, out at sea? They were about pay their respects when Count Seven let out a loud roar of laughter.

"This old beggar has been having the rottenest luck. I've been bitten half to death by the most vicious creature. There's no need to be so formal!"

Everyone was shocked. He was injured! Nothing to fear, then. They all looked at Viper Ouyang to gauge his reaction.

Viper's plan had been to get rid of Count Seven as soon as possible, so that his wretched actions would not be made known throughout the *wulin*. Then he would force Guo Jing to explain the more difficult passages of the Nine Yin Manual, before killing him, too. As for Lotus, she could not be allowed to live, no matter what his nephew felt for her. And yet, he could not do the deed himself. Her father would never rest in his quest for vengeance. No, he would have to make someone else kill her, in order to avoid the blame. But, now they had come aboard the Sixth Prince's ship, they would not be able to escape, at least.

He turned to Wanyan Honglie. "These three are most cunning, with passable kung fu. May I ask the Prince to guard them closely?"

Graybeard Liang was pleased. He shouldered past Hector Sha

and grabbed Guo Jing's hand. Guo Jing twisted his wrist and slapped Liang's shoulder with a Dragon in the Field. The unexpected force behind the move took the old Master by surprise and he stumbled back two steps.

Tiger Peng and Graybeard Liang were constantly vying for the Sixth Prince's approval. Anything that might give them the upper hand was a cause for celebration, and watching the old Ginseng Codger stumble secretly delighted his rival. Seeing his chance, Tiger Peng stepped forward to block Count Seven Hong and the others.

Graybeard Liang had run past Hector Sha in order to avoid Guo Jing's Haughty Dragon Repents. He would be unable to counter it head-on, hence he planned a sideways assault. Little did he know that, in the months that had passed since their last meeting, Guo Jing had progressed beyond this one move. Guo Jing did not give chase, however, so Graybeard leaped up and launched the move which marked the pinnacle of all his years of training: Liaodong Wild Fox Fist. He was determined to kill the young man for humiliating him just now, as well as for killing his prize snake.

The move had been inspired by a journey up the Mountain of Eternal Snow, looking for ginseng. There, he had encountered a hunting dog and a wild fox fighting in the snow. The fox was sly, it jumped from side to side, avoiding the dog's razor-sharp claws and fangs. Graybeard had watched as the fox leaped up high, and suddenly he was inspired. Instead of gathering ginseng, he decided to build himself a hut on the mountain and contemplate the animal's movements over a period of several months. And that was how Wild Fox Fist was born.

It encompassed four fundamental principles: *ling, shan, pu, die.* That is, alertness, timely avoidance, pouncing, and tumbling. So far, it had proved effective against even his strongest opponents. It caused in them confusion, as they could not ascertain if he was moving in or fading back, or shifting left or right. This gave him the chance to make surprise attacks.

This time, he would not let himself underestimate his opponent.

He launched his signature move straight at Guo Jing, ducking first, then pouncing mid-fall.

How odd, Guo Jing thought. He had never seen anything like it. Lotus makes use of a lot of feigned moves in her Cascading Peach Blossom Palm—perhaps as many as five or eight to every genuine strike—but this old man is all feint and no thrust. What strange technique is this?

But Count Seven's advice came back to him. No matter what style of kung fu he was faced with, he should respond with Dragon-Subduing Palm.

The others watched and secretly shook their heads. The old Ginseng Codger was a master, the head of his own sect of martial arts. Why was he constantly dodging and feinting? Did he not dare make a proper attack on a young man who was by every martial measure his inferior?

Within a few moves, the strength of Guo Jing's palm had pushed Old Liang back to the edge of the vessel. Graybeard Liang realized that his Wild Fox Fist would not lead him to victory, but it was too late to think of another technique. He was surrounded by the boy's palms. He had no space to work a counterattack.

"Lower!" Count Seven's voice floated above the roaring wind.

Guo Jing launched into a Dragons Tussle in the Wild, sweeping with his left arm.

Old Liang cried out and tumbled over the railing.

Stunned, everyone rushed to the side and peered down. At that moment, they heard a long cackle from out at sea. Suddenly, Old Liang flew up and landed on his back on the deck, where he lay motionless.

The onlookers were astounded. Had the water sent him bouncing back? They crowded round and peered down at the water, only to catch sight of an old man, his long, white hair and long, white beard catching the wind as he crested the waves. They looked closer: he was sitting on the back of a shark! Together, man and shark rode the waves with the speed of a horse galloping across dry land.

Guo Jing was surprised, but delighted. "Brother Zhou! Over here!"

The man riding the shark was none other than the Hoary Urchin, Zhou Botong.

Zhou responded with a cheer and then punched the shark close to its right eye. The animal instantly turned left and drew up beside the boat.

"Brother Guo? Is that you? How are you, boy? There's a large whale up ahead. I've been chasing it all day and all night. I'm getting close. See you later!"

"Brother Zhou!" Guo Jing cried out anxiously. "Come aboard! We are being bullied by a whole crowd of bad men!"

"Is that so?" The Urchin was most displeased. He reached into the shark's mouth and tugged, his other hand clutching the side of the ship. Suddenly, man and shark flew up and over the heads of the onlookers, before landing on the deck. "Who dares bully my little brother?"

Every one of the fighters on board had seen some strange things in their time, but this bearded man's appearance was stranger still. They were stunned into silence. Even Count Seven and Viper Ouyang were stupefied.

Zhou Botong spotted Lotus. "What are you doing here?"

"Why wouldn't I be here?" Lotus said with a smile. "I had a feeling you would appear today, so I was waiting. Teach me how to ride a shark!"

"Very well, my child," Zhou Botong said, and he laughed.

"But first, get rid of all these scoundrels," she said.

Zhou Botong surveyed the crowd gathered on the deck. His eyes came to rest on Viper Ouyang. "I was wondering who would dare be so brazen. I should have known it would be you."

"A man who does not keep his word, no matter how much he tries to hide away, will always be a laughing stock to the heroes of this world," Viper Ouyang said coldly.

"Indeed. A man can do as he pleases, but, if his words are worth no more than a fart, people won't know if they came from his mouth or his backside. Actually, I was looking for you. We have a score to settle, so it is quite wonderful to see you. Old Beggar, you are our witness, stand up and say a few words. Make it official."

Count Seven smiled from where he was lying on the deck.

"Old Venom has encountered many troubles," Lotus began. "My Master must have saved him at least nine times. And yet, he has the heart of a wolf. He has shown only cruelty in the face of such kindness, locking my Master's pressure points."

Count Seven had saved Viper Ouyang only three times, in fact, but Lotus could be forgiven for her exaggeration. And it would have been a weak argument to point it out, so Viper Ouyang could only glare at her in furious silence.

Zhou Botong leaned down and tried to release Count Seven by rubbing his Pool at the Bend point, located in the crook of his arm, and the Gushing Spring, on the sole of his foot.

"It's no use, Old Urchin," Count Seven breathed.

Viper Ouyang had locked his pressure points using an unusual method. The only people who knew how to unlock them were the Venom himself and Apothecary Huang.

"Go on, try to release him, Urchin," Viper said with a sneer.

Lotus recognized the method, but did not know how to unlock it.

"Huh, what is so clever about that? My father knows this Bone-Piercing Pressure Lock."

Viper was amazed to hear the girl name the technique, but he ignored her and instead turned to Zhou Botong. "We had a bet and you lost. It appears you are the one talking out of your Zhou Bottom."

"Pheeeew!" Zhou cried and pinched his nose. "What a stink! Remind me, what was our bet?"

"Everyone gathered here is a master of the *wulin*. Well, except the Guo boy and the young girl. Let me relate the events and those gathered here can be our judges."

"Indeed, indeed. Tell us, Master Ouyang," Tiger Peng said.

"The man standing before you is Zhou Botong, Master Zhou of

the Quanzhen Sect," Viper began. "He is known across the rivers and lakes as the Hoary Urchin, and claims Qiu Chuji, Wang Chuyi, and the other Immortals as his martial nephews."

Zhou Botong had spent the last decade or so detained on Peach Blossom Island. Before that, he had not accomplished anything of note in the field of martial arts; he had been too busy making mischief. His name carried no special resonance in the *jianghu*, but the sight of him riding a shark and flipping it up onto the deck before them was enough to make the fighters gathered that day pay attention. A muttering rippled from lip to lip.

Tiger Peng recalled his upcoming meeting at the Tower of Mist and Rain in Jiaxing, which was scheduled to take place during the Moon Festival, in the eighth lunar month of the year. If the Quanzhen Sect were going to have the help of this strange man, things were going to be tougher than he had thought. He began to feel apprehensive.

"Brother Zhou, here, was stranded among a school of sharks, so I rescued him. I told him that I could kill all of them with the most meager effort on my part, and Brother Zhou did not believe me. So, we made a bet. Isn't that right, Brother Zhou?"

"Indeed, absolutely true." Zhou Botong nodded. "Now, tell them what we bet."

"I was just coming to that! I said that, if I lost, he could determine my punishment. And if I refused, I would jump into the sea and be food for the sharks. If he lost, the same would apply. Wasn't it thus, Brother Zhou?"

"Yes, yes." Zhou Botong nodded again. "Then what happened?"

"What happened? You lost, that's what happened."

This time, Zhou Botong shook his head vigorously. "No, upon my word! You were the one who lost, not me."

This made Viper Ouyang furious. "A great man can distinguish right from wrong! Are you denying your own words? If I was the one who lost, why did you jump into the sea?"

"Yes, that is true." Zhou Botong sighed. "I did indeed admit defeat. But who would have thought it? As I plunged into the water, the heavens sent me a gift. Only then did I realize that it was the Old Venom who had been defeated, and that it was I, the Hoary Urchin, who had prevailed."

"What gift?" Viper, Count Seven, and Lotus cried in unison.

The Urchin bent down and grabbed the stick wedged inside the shark's mouth, then raised the animal's head and said, "This fine shark. I'm sure you remember, Old Venom. Your beloved nephew jammed this stick in its mouth, isn't that right?"

Gallant had indeed come up with the wicked plan to starve the shark to death by forcing its mouth open so it could not eat. Viper Ouyang had seen him do it with his own eyes. The wound at the side of its jaw, caused by Gallant's fish hook, was also more than apparent. It was, indeed, the very same animal they had returned to the sea.

"And?" he said.

Zhou Botong clapped his hands. "Which means you lost! Our bet was that you would kill every last one of the sharks, but this fine beast was lucky enough to be given a lifeline by your dear nephew. It couldn't eat the poisoned sharks, and thus survived. So, you must concede, therefore, that I am the winner." He burst out laughing.

Viper's face went dark, but he did not reply.

"Big Brother," Guo Jing interrupted, "where have you been, these last few days? I was so sad."

"I was amusing myself," the Urchin replied with a grin. "Not long after I jumped into the water, I spotted this fellow on the surface, in great pain. 'Old shark,' I said, 'misery loves company!' I then leaped up onto its back. It dived down to the seabed. All I could do was draw a deep breath, clutch its neck and kick its belly until it resurfaced. I barely had time to draw another breath before it dived down again. We carried on like this for the best part of a day, until it finally admitted defeat and was tamed. If I told it to go right, it went right. If I wanted it to leap out of the water, it was too scared to do the opposite."

He patted the shark gently on the head, inordinately pleased with himself.

Of all his audience, it was Lotus who felt the most admiration for the Hoary Urchin. "I've spent so many years swimming in the sea, why have I never thought of such a trick?" she said, her eyes shining. "How stupid of me!"

"Their teeth are as sharp as knives," Zhou Botong answered. "If it didn't have a stick in its mouth, it would be impossible."

"You've been riding this shark for days, now?" Lotus said.

"Indeed. We've become quite a team at catching fish. We chase them as soon as we spot them, then I either punch or slap the little things. For every ten we catch, I only get to eat one. This old fellow gets the rest."

Lotus gently stroked the shark's belly. "You drop the fish into its mouth? Doesn't it need to chew?"

"Oh, he just swallows them whole. He only really lets me ride him because I feed him. On one occasion, we were chasing the most humongous cuttlefish . . ."

Lotus and the Urchin were so absorbed in their conversation, they had forgotten all about the others. Viper was muttering to himself, trying to come up with a plan. Eventually, Zhou remembered him and called out, "So, Old Venom, do you admit defeat?"

With the others as his witness, how could go back on his word? "And so what if I lost?"

"Hmm, then I must think of your punishment. You said that I was talking farts, before. Very well. Give us a fart at once! Let everyone smell it."

Such a mundane request irritated Lotus. For the average person, it would be difficult, but for someone practiced in *neigong* inner strength? All they had to do was circulate their breathing around their body. A trifle. The thought that the cunning snake might get away with it all so easily was too much to bear. "No, no, first make him unlock my Master's vital points!" she cried.

"See?" Zhou Botong called out in delight. "Your farts frighten the young lady. Fine—this time, you get away with it. Tend to the Old Beggar instead. He is your equal in skill and it is only your cunning that enabled you to prevail against him. Once he is better, you can fight him again. This time, the Old Urchin will judge who the winner is."

Viper Ouyang knew that Count Seven's injuries were permanent. He was not afraid of retaliation. But he was concerned that Zhou Botong might come up with a stranger, more difficult request. The others looked on as he hesitated. He could not go back on his word. He bent down and, with the force of his palm, released Count Seven from the lock on his pressure points. Lotus and Guo Jing rushed forward to help their Master to his feet.

Zhou Botong looked again at the people gathered on the deck. "The thing that really gives me the shivers is the rank urine smell of the mutton eaten by these northern barbarians. Let down the small boat so that the four of us can go ashore."

The Hoary Urchin's fighting techniques were decidedly strange— Viper had known this since witnessing his fight with Apothecary Huang. He was not entirely assured of his own victory, therefore. He would wait until he had absorbed the Nine Yin Manual. Then he would return and settle the score. In any case, he now had the excuse of having lost their bet. It would be better to be rid of him, for now.

"Very well, you have been most fortunate. As you won the bet, we shall do as you say." Turning to Wanyan Honglie, he said, "Prince, please set down a boat to take these four passengers ashore."

Wanyan Honglie hesitated. What if they reveal my secret mission? he thought.

Lama Supreme Wisdom had been watching coldly. Viper Ouyang's bedraggled appearance filled his heart with contempt. And so easily he accepts that lying scoundrel Zhou Botong's word? The coward. The Venom of the West was surely undeserving of his reputation. Nothing the lama had seen suggested that he was any more accomplished than any of the other masters gathered on this boat. Noticing Wanyan Honglie's moment of hesitation, he took two steps forward. "Had we met on the raft, then surely we would do as Mr. Ouyang says. But we are on a Jin ship now, and it is the Prince who gives the orders."

This caught the attention of the others and they looked at Viper to gauge his reaction.

Viper looked the monk up and down with an icy gaze. Then he raised his eyes to the heavens and said, "Is the Venerable Monk trying to make life difficult for an old man?"

"I wouldn't dare. I arrived in the Central Plains ignorant and friendless. Today is the first time I have ever heard Sir Ouyang's great name. What ill will could I have toward—?"

Before he could finish, Viper had taken a step forward, feigned with his left hand and grabbed the monk with his right. Within moments, the monk's large frame had been spun around and was now hanging upside down.

It had all happened so fast that all the others saw was a flash of the monk's red vestments.

The monk was more than a head taller than everyone else on the boat, so, even if Viper had held him upright, with his arm extended at full length, Lama Supreme Wisdom's feet would have trailed the boards. By flipping him upside down and grasping his neck like he was holding aloft a lump of meat, Viper kept his head four feet above the deck.

The lama kicked and roared curses. The others had seen him take on Wang Chuyi at the Zhao residence, so they knew him to be a considerable fighter. The sight of his legs flailing, his arms hanging limp by his ears as if they had been broken, was shocking.

With his eyes still raised to the sky, Viper Ouyang began to speak. "Today was the first time you heard my name? You look upon me, an old man, with scorn, is that right?"

Lama Supreme Wisdom was both scared and angry. He tried to redistribute his *qi* a few times and struggle free, without success. Tiger Peng and the others watched in amazement.

"You may scorn me," Viper continued, "but I refuse to lower

myself to your level in front of the Honorable Prince. You wish to keep the Old Urchin, Master Zhou, and the Divine Vagrant Nine Fingers, Master Hong, on the ship with you. Ha! Are you going to rely on your mediocre skills to overcome them? You are indeed ignorant and friendless, but you are also unaware of your own limitations. Let me show you. Old Urchin, take this!"

Before anyone could see what was happening, the lama was sailing through the air like a cloud, toward the starboard side of the ship. As soon as he left Viper's grip, Lama Supreme Wisdom felt free. He tried to straighten his body and perform a Flipping Carp in order to right himself. But a sudden pain shot through his neck. He tried to strike back with a Secret Blade Mudra, but his arms were numb. He felt his body continue on its course, and, before he could do anything, Zhou Botong had received him.

Wanyan Honglie understood the danger the lama was in. No one could accuse Viper Ouyang of not having warned him. "Master Zhou," he called. "No more games. I will lower a boat for you and your three friends."

"Wonderful," Zhou Botong replied. "You have a go. To you!"

He mimicked Viper's push of his palm and sent the monk's weighty mass flying toward the Prince.

Wanyan Honglie had some grounding in the martial arts, of course, but his skills were for the most part limited to using a spear or a bow and arrow on horseback. How was he going to stop the momentum of the monk flying toward him? If it did not kill him, he would certainly be injured.

Hector Sha saw the danger the Sixth Prince was in and placed himself in front of Wanyan Honglie, in a display of Shape Changing kung fu. If he struck the lama with his palm, he might cause him serious injury. He preferred to grab the back of his neck, just as Viper Ouyang and Zhou Botong had, and place him on his feet.

He had forgotten one crucial detail, however. His martial skills were meager next to theirs. Viper Ouyang and Zhou Botong had made it all look so effortless. He leaped up, intending to grab the lama, only to feel a burning sensation flow through his hand as soon as his fingers made contact with the back of the monk's neck. If he did not take steps to protect his wrist, it would snap. He pulled back, straight into a Bone-Piercing Awl.

As he was being thrown between the Venom and the Urchin, Lama Supreme Wisdom's blood had been forced backward through his veins. He felt dizzy, and fury swelled inside him. As he sailed through the air, he gathered his *qi*, made a mudra by touching his index finger and thumb together, and released it as soon as he felt Hector Sha's touch.

They were fairly well matched as fighters, but the lama had caught Hector Sha off guard, forcing him to stumble back. The lama, meanwhile, crashed belly first onto the deck. He spun and jumped quickly to his feet, however, only to realize who it was that had just hit him. Hector Sha! So, even you, you filthy traitor, are out to get me! He roared and pounced.

Tiger Peng could see the misunderstanding playing out. "Reverend, please!" he cried, as he cast himself between them. "Brother Sha's intentions were good."

While all this had been going on, the small boat had been lowered. Zhou Botong had removed the stick from the shark's mouth and hurled the beast back into the water, breaking the stick in two with his other hand. Realizing it was free, the shark dived deep in order to look for food.

"Guo Jing, next time, we can ride with Brother Zhou. Maybe even have a race!" Lotus said with a broad smile.

"I'll be the umpire!" Zhou Botong cried out, clapping his hands.

Wanyan Honglie watched as they climbed aboard, but his thoughts were focused on Viper Ouyang. He could be useful in stealing the last writings of Yue Fei. He took the lama's hand and pulled him toward the Venom. "Come, now, gentlemen, we are all friends. Reverend was merely jesting. It was all just a game!"

Viper Ouyang smiled and extended a hand. But Lama Supreme Wisdom was still aggrieved. You are only good at catching your opponent off guard, he said to himself. I have trained for decades in Five Finger Blade; am I not your equal? He reached out to take the Venom's hand, but secretly gathered his energy to it. Just as he was about to squeeze down hard, he suddenly jumped up. His hand stung, as if he had clenched an ingot of red-hot steel. Viper Ouyang merely gave a faint smile. The lama looked down at his hand, but saw no sign of injury. Damn this old scoundrel and his demonic sorcery.

Viper Ouyang glanced across at the Ginseng Codger, Graybeard Liang, who was still lying prostrate on the deck. He went over to examine him, unlocking his pressure points. From now on, Viper Ouyang would be the leader of this ragtag bunch of fighters. Wanyan Honglie, meanwhile, gave orders for a feast to be prepared in honor of the Venom and his nephew.

6

THE MEN ATE AND DRANK, AND THE SIXTH PRINCE EXPLAINED his plan to travel to Lin'an to seize the last writings of General Yue Fei. Would Master Ouyang do him the honor of assisting him in this mission?

Viper Ouyang had, in fact, already been acquainted with the plan by his nephew, but the request insulted him. Who do you think I am? Do you imagine that I, the Venom of the West, would submit to you? And yet, General Yue Fei's kung fu skills were almost as legendary as his military prowess. Perhaps these writings contain the key to his learning? If I agree to help him, then maybe I can get something out of it, too.

And so it was: every man scheming for himself. Wanyan Honglie was the mantis hunting the cicada, unaware of the finch lying in wait behind him. One side bathed the other in flattery and received soft words of compliance in return.

Graybeard Liang was doing his best to liven the feast, keeping the wine flowing. Only Gallant Ouyang, still recovering from his injuries, abstained from drinking. After a few mouthfuls of food, he asked to be carried to bed.

As the festivities continued, Viper Ouyang's countenance suddenly grew dark. His cup hovered by his mouth, but he did not drink. Had someone offended him? The others were startled and anxious. Just as the Sixth Prince was about to ask him what the matter was, Viper interrupted him: "Listen!"

They all froze. But all they could hear was the sound of the waves.

"Can't you hear it? A flute."

Viper was right. A halting tune from a flute was just about audible over the ocean's song. But they would never have noticed it had he not pointed it out.

Viper Ouyang walked to the bow and let out a long, loud whistle. The others followed him.

The sky was already black, and the moon had just risen beyond the horizon. In the distance, a dark green blob was slowly coming into focus: three sails. A ship was slicing through the waves toward them. Was the music coming from the ship? But it was still so far away.

Viper Ouyang cried out to the sailors to turn the ship to face the oncoming vessel. Now, they were approaching each other. In time, a man became visible at the prow. He was wearing a long, emerald green robe, and, indeed, he carried a flute in one hand.

"Brother Ouyang!" he cried. "Have you seen my daughter?"

"With a temper like hers, I wouldn't dare go near her!" Viper replied.

The boats were now only meters apart, but still nobody saw how or when the other man leaped. There was a quick green blur, and then, there he was, standing on their deck.

Yet another warrior to recruit to his cause, Wanyan Honglie thought.

"Your name, sir?" he said, stepping forward. "We are most honored to have you join us."

It was a particularly modest tone for a prince of the Jin to take, but the man glanced at his Jurchen robes, gave him a contemptuous look and proceeded to ignore him.

"Brother Huang, let me introduce you to the Sixth Prince of the Great Jin." Viper Ouyang then turned to Wanyan Honglie. "This is the Lord of Peach Blossom Island, the most accomplished martial fighter across the *wulin*. He is unparalleled."

Tiger Peng and the others shuffled back in astonishment. They had found out only after the event that the girl they had encountered in the Zhao Palace was Lotus Huang. And Lotus's father had a reputation for being formidable—fierce, even. Twice Foul Dark Wind were originally his disciples, after all, and they had terrorized the *wulin*. The thought that they had offended his daughter made them shake with fear. No one said a word.

Apothecary Huang knew that his daughter must have run away to look for Guo Jing. He had been angry, at first. But, after a few days passed, he began to worry. She might find him on the special boat he had built, and then they would both end up at the bottom of the sea. Unable to contain himself any longer, he had set sail in search of her.

He knew that Guo Jing and his companions were heading in the direction of the mainland, so he set out west. But it was no easy task to find one boat on such a vast and boundless sea. Apothecary Huang may have been able to call on extraordinary talent and knowledge, but still he could not find her. He decided to gather his inner strength and play his flute in the hope that his daughter might hear his song carried far over the waves. Little did he know he would come across Viper Ouyang instead.

Apothecary Huang had never met the others, nor did he know who they were, but an introduction to a prince of the Jin was enough to make him want to turn and leave at once.

"Please excuse me; I must continue the search for my daughter. My apologies for not staying." Then he turned.

Yet another rude, arrogant man, Lama Supreme Wisdom thought.

He had heard Viper Ouyang's introduction, but could there really be so many exceptional men of the *wulin*? It was more likely that they were versed in witchcraft and demonic sorcery. Maybe he could trick this newcomer?

"Is your daughter of about sixteen years of age?" he said in a loud voice.

Apothecary Huang paused, then turned, a smile spread across his face. "Yes. Have you seen her?"

"I did see a young lady," the lama replied coldly. "She was dead."

"What?" His heart froze and his voice trembled.

"About three days ago. Her body was floating in the sea. She was dressed all in white and wore a golden ring in her hair. Oh, she must have been pretty when she was still alive. What a shame. Her body was swollen by the water."

Exactly the outfit Lotus had been wearing when he last saw her. Apothecary Huang's mind was a muddle, his limbs shook and his cheeks drained of all color. "Is this really true?"

Everybody had watched Lotus board the small boat, only moments before. The lama was clearly taking pleasure in this deception, but even the sight of Apothecary Huang's agonized features was not enough to make them speak up.

"There were three other corpses," the lama continued. "One of a young man with thick eyebrows and big, round eyes. Another was an old beggar, who carried a dark red calabash on his back, and the third was an old man with long hair and a wispy beard." He was, of course, describing Guo Jing, Count Seven Hong, and Zhou Botong.

Apothecary Huang was completely taken in. He looked at Viper Ouyang and thought, If you knew about my daughter, why didn't you say?

Viper Ouyang noticed his expression and the mounting grief in his eyes. Here was a man intent on revenge. "I only just came aboard," he began quickly. "This is the first time I've met these people. This young woman's body—it needn't be your daughter's." He sighed, then continued. "She is such a good girl. If she really has passed on at such a young age, it would be a tragedy indeed. If my nephew were to find out, he would die of a broken heart." It was a clever speech, pushing the blame from his shoulders without causing it to land elsewhere.

Apothecary Huang's heart sank. He liked nothing more than to take indiscriminate revenge—otherwise, why did he break the legs of his other disciples and cast them from the island, when it was Twice Foul Dark Wind who stole the Nine Yin Manual from him?

His chest felt like ice, but his blood was boiling over. His reaction had been just the same when his beloved wife passed away, all those years ago. His hands shook and his cheeks alternated between pasty white and crimson red.

The others watched in silence, fear coursing through their hearts. Viper Ouyang, too, was nervous. He prepared himself by gathering his *qi* to his abdomen.

The deck was still—until a burst of laughter broke the silence, loud and carefree, like the roar of a dragon.

Apothecary Huang's reaction surprised them. They watched as he raised his face toward the sky and laughed madly, louder and louder. His laughter sent a chill through the air, which only intensified as the seeming mirth gave way to heaving sobs. His grief was fierce. The sight of him moved the others almost to tears.

Only Viper Ouyang was familiar with the Heretic's wild mood swings, where he could shift between singing and sobbing in seconds. He did not find the display so remarkable. And yet, he could not help but hope that such crying might cause the old man an injury. In ancient times, the poet Ruan Ji cried for his dead mother until he vomited blood. The Heretic followed the customs of old more than he knew. What a shame that I lost my iron zither when our ship sank, Viper Ouyang said to himself, or I could play now, stoking his grief until it causes him real harm. Then, when the time comes for the second Contest of Mount Hua, I will have already defeated one of my opponents. Ah, what a pity to lose such an opportunity!

Apothecary Huang cried for a while longer, before lifting his jade flute and thumping it against the edge of the boat. Then he began to sing:

> *God, who grants life,*
> *why make us guess how long it lasts?*
> *Some may live until their heads are crowned white,*
> *while others do not survive the womb.*
> *The last tragedy not yet passed*
> *and a new one is upon me.*
> *The flower withers, burned dry*
> *like dawn's dew.*
> *The departed cannot be pursued*
> *but the emotions arrive swift and relentless.*
> *With skies so far away, so far above,*
> *to whom may I empty the sorrow that fills my breast?*

At that moment, the flute cracked in two.

Lama Supreme Wisdom rushed forward and blocked him. "You laugh and cry like a madman."

"Reverend," Wanyan Honglie started, "please don't—"

Apothecary Huang's right hand shot out and grabbed the back of the lama's neck. He then spun the lama's body one hundred and eighty degrees, so that he was upside down, before throwing him head first at the deck, crashing his shiny bald pate through the wooden boards.

Lama Supreme Wisdom's weakest point was in his neck. All three Masters—Viper Ouyang, Zhou Botong, and Apothecary Huang—had seen that instantly.

Huang started to sing once more:

> *Skies eternal earth enduring,*
> *man lives but how long?*
> *Past and future do not feel it,*
> *yet everything has Time bestowed.*

And, with an emerald blur, he was back on his boat, where he swung the rudder and sailed away.

Unsure if he was alive or dead, the others rushed to help Lama Supreme Wisdom. They heard a grunt coming from below deck, and, a moment later, a cabin door opened and out came a young man with rosy red lips and white teeth. He bore a jade crown on his head. It was Wanyan Honglie's son, Yang Kang.

After the unfortunate disagreement with Mercy Mu, he had recalled his father's promise of infinite wealth. He had made contact with Jin officials in the north and, with their help, located his father not long afterward, joining him on his journey south. As soon as he saw Guo Jing and Lotus climb aboard, he had slipped down below deck, too scared to come out, and watched the events unfold through a crack in the door. He had remained below during the feasting, listening to their conversations, fearful that Viper Ouyang was an associate of Guo Jing. Only now, after Apothecary Huang's departure, did he dare to make a reappearance.

Despite the force of the move and his weak neck, Lama Supreme Wisdom's strong skull had spared him from serious injury. He was merely a little dizzy. Placing both hands on the deck, he concentrated his qi and, with one push, popped himself out of the hole and landed back on his feet.

The others glanced at each other in amazement. It was a funny sight, but they felt it would be inappropriate to laugh. Instead, they all looked away in awkward amusement.

Wanyan Honglie broke the silence. "Son, come and meet Master Ouyang."

Yang Kang dropped to his knees and kowtowed four times. It was quite out of character and the others watched in surprise.

In fact, Yang Kang had been impressed by Lama Supreme Wisdom, back at the Zhao residence, but, having watched three martial Masters cast him around as if playing with a baby, he recalled the humiliation he had felt when held captive at Roaming Cloud Manor by Lake Tai, and the fear that Guo Jing and Lotus might have discovered him helping Wanyan Honglie evade them at the Liu ancestral temple in Baoying. He was acutely aware of the shortcomings in his own martial training, whereas the man standing before him was truly a great. "Father, I wish to call this great man Master."

Wanyan Honglie was most pleased. He stepped toward Viper Ouyang and made a quick bow. "My son is fond of the martial arts, but he is yet to find himself a suitable *shifu*. If sir would deign to honor the request and bestow instructions upon the boy, father and son, princes both, would be most grateful."

Who would not want to take the boy as their disciple? thought the others. But Viper Ouyang made a perfunctory gesture of respect by cupping his hands and nodding, before saying, "There is a rule in my school of martial training that a master may only take one disciple. And I already have one: my nephew. I am, therefore, not at liberty to take another. May I beg for the Prince's forgiveness."

Wanyan Honglie did not press him further. Instead, he ordered his men to bring out more food and wine. But Yang Kang was bitterly disappointed.

"I do not deserve to call myself Master to the young Prince," Viper Ouyang said with a smile. "But I can give you a few tips. We can talk later."

Yang Kang had seen Gallant Ouyang's many concubines at the Zhao residence. They had supposedly been trained by Gallant himself, but, as they were not considered proper disciples, their kung fu was mediocre at best. Yang Kang was not enthused by Viper's offer, but he obliged the old man with some polite words of gratitude. He did not know that the man's nephew was nothing compared to his uncle in terms of learning and skill, and that a few words of advice from the senior Ouyang would be enough to boost his powers and his prestige no end in martial circles.

Viper Ouyang sensed the young man's lack of enthusiasm, however, so decided not to mention the matter again.

As they feasted, conversation turned to Apothecary Huang's rudeness and arrogance. Lama Supreme Wisdom had done well to fool him.

"Who would have thought that a master of the *wulin* could have that little vixen as a daughter!" Browbeater Hou said. He turned to study the lama's bald head. After staring at it for a while, his gaze shifted down to the rolls of fat at the back of his neck. Suddenly, he reached to seize his own and cried, "Brother! The three of them were using some sort of grabbing technique. What was that?"

"Keep quiet!" Hector Sha shushed him.

Lama Supreme Wisdom could not restrain himself any longer. He reached out and grabbed Browbeater Hou's three horns. Browbeater Hou shrank back and slid under the table. The crowd jeered and clapped.

Browbeater Hou struggled back to his chair and turned to Viper. "Master Ouyang, you are so accomplished! Can you teach me how to grab the back of someone's neck?"

Viper Ouyang smiled, but did not answer. The lama glared at Browbeater Hou, but the latter merely turned to Hector Sha and asked, "Brother, what was Apothecary Huang singing through his tears?"

Hector Sha did not know what to say. "Who knows? It was just the gibbering of a madman."

"They were poems written by Cao Zhi during the period of the Three Kingdoms," Yang Kang explained. "Two verses lamenting the death of his daughter. Some live long lives, others die before they are born. Why is God so unfair? The heavens are too distant, they do not hear his grief, even if he climbs onto his throne. The pain is so deep that he will soon follow her to the grave."

"Truly, the young Prince is a scholar," Browbeater Hou said. "We are merely rough men of the *wulin*. What do we know?"

7

APOTHECARY HUANG'S HEART WAS OVERFLOWING WITH GRIEF and rage. Pointing at the sky, he cursed the heavens, the earth, the ghosts and the gods for such unjust treatment, for such cruel fate. Then he commanded his boatman to head for land.

Once ashore, anger took hold again. He looked up to the sky and shouted, "Who killed my Lotus? Who killed my Lotus?"

The Guo boy. It was him. If it had not been for him, she would never have gone aboard the boat. But he too perished. Upon whom can I vent my anger?

At once, he recalled Guo Jing's *shifus*, the Six Freaks of the South. They are the ones who have killed my Lotus! Lotus would never have met this boy if it had not been for them. I will cut their legs off, one by one!

Anger gave way to sorrow. He arrived at a small town and stopped to eat, his mind still fixated on how he would find the Six Freaks. They are not great masters, but they do carry a certain reputation, he thought. There must be something that sets them apart. Maybe just a bag of tricks. If I pay a simple visit to their homes, chances are they won't be there. I must go in the dead of night, take them by surprise. Their families, young and old, must all pay—I will kill them all.

With large strides, he walked in a northerly direction toward Jiaxing.

CHAPTER FOUR

TROUBLE IN THE PALACE

I

COUNT SEVEN, ZHOU BOTONG, GUO JING, AND LOTUS TOOK
the small boat west. Guo Jing sat at the stern with the oar, while Lotus interrogated Zhou about riding the shark. The Old Urchin came
up with ever more elaborate suggestions as to how they could catch
another such beast, in order to amuse the young woman.

Guo Jing looked across at Count Seven and noticed that his
cheeks were pale. "How are you feeling, *Shifu?*"

Count Seven was panting heavily, but did not reply. His pressure points had been unlocked, technically, but his internal injuries
were still troubling him. Lotus gave him a few Dew of Nine Flowers
pills, which helped with the pain somewhat, but his breathing was
still strained. Lotus had received the pills as a present from Zephyr
Lu, who had lovingly filled up the ceramic bottle, screwed the lid
firmly shut and wrapped it in oil paper so they would not be ruined
by water.

Unaware of the feelings of those around him, the Old Urchin
was shouting about how they absolutely had to jump into the water
and catch some fish. Lotus cast him a glance to tell him to be quiet

and stop vexing Count Seven. But Zhou Botong was oblivious and kept rambling on.

"But you don't have any bait," Lotus said, knitting her brow.

The Urchin was as childish as his name suggested, but he was unaffected by having someone his junior chastise him in this way. "I know!" he said and paused, before crying out, "I know! Brother Guo, I'll hold your hand and you lower your upper half into the sea."

Guo Jing instantly agreed, out of respect for his elder.

"No!" Lotus cried. "Don't listen. He wants to use you as the bait to catch a shark!"

"Exactly!" Zhou Botong cried, clapping his hands. "When it comes near, I'll give it a good knock to the head and pull it up. You won't get hurt. Or, you hold my hand and I'll attract the shark."

"The boat is so small—why are you two causing such trouble? You'll capsize us."

"If only!" Zhou Botong cried. "Then we could have fun in the water."

"And what about Master Hong? Don't you care if he survives?"

Zhou Botong scratched his cheek, at a loss for words. He paused, then said, "I don't understand what's so extraordinary about the Old Venom. You're a man of experience. How could you be so careless as to leave yourself on the receiving end of a beating?"

"If you say another word of this nonsense, the three of us will stop speaking to you for three days and three nights," Lotus retorted.

Zhou Botong stuck out his tongue, but was finally quiet. Instead, he took the oars from Guo Jing and began to row with force.

The shoreline had appeared close, but it was almost dusk before they landed. That night, they slept on the beach. By the next morning, Count Seven's condition was worse still. Guo Jing began to cry.

"Even if I were to live another hundred years, I would still have to die one day. Boy, I have only one wish remaining. With my last breath, I would like to ask you three to do something for me."

"Tell us, *Shifu*," Lotus said, with tears in her eyes.

"I never liked that Old Venom," Zhou Botong interrupted. "I will get revenge on the snake for you. I'll kill him."

Count Seven smiled weakly. "Revenge is a waste of a dying man's last wish. All I ask is to have one last bowl of Contrast of the Five Treasures, just like they make in the imperial kitchens."

A last meal!

"That's easy, *Shifu*," Lotus replied. "We're not far from Lin'an. I'll sneak into the Imperial Palace and steal a few pots. You can eat to your heart's delight!"

"I'd like to try some, too," Zhou Botong said.

Lotus gave him a sharp look. "What do you know about good food?"

"It won't be easy to find," Count Seven said. "I hid in the palace kitchens for three months and tried it only once. But the memory of those delicious flavors . . . Why, it's enough to make me drool."

"I know!" Zhou Botong cried. "We'll capture the Emperor's chef and force him to make it for you."

"Not a bad idea," Lotus said.

The Old Urchin felt very pleased with himself.

"No," Count Seven said firmly, shaking his head. "It is a complex recipe that requires particular kitchen implements, a charcoal fire and specific chinaware. Not one bit can be missing, otherwise it won't taste right. We have to go to the palace."

He could see the doubt on their faces.

"It will be a most valuable experience," he urged.

Guo Jing hoisted his Master onto his back and, together, they set off northward.

2

UPON REACHING THE FIRST SMALL TOWN, LOTUS SOLD SOME jewelry and purchased a small mule and cart, so that Count Seven might rest and recover.

Lotus and Guo Jing agreed in hushed tones that it would be best to return their Master to Peach Blossom Island, where they, or

Apothecary Huang, could take care of him. There, in a locked underground chamber, concealed according to the principles of the Five Elements and Eight Trigrams, which governed the entire design of the island, he could be cured. Their only fear was that, if Lotus's father caught sight of Guo Jing, he might hound him about the Nine Yin Manual. Were they to get into a fight, it would only agitate their Master. Perhaps it would be better if he were to recover in Lin'an, after all.

Guo Jing worried that his six *shifus* would go to Peach Blossom Island to look for him. The quicker he could reunite with them, the better—then he could go with Lotus to meet her father. It would be better to have Zhou Botong with them; he could explain the whole funny story about the Manual and clear up the sorry misunderstanding. Then Count Seven Hong would be able to rest properly on the island. And yet . . . Zhou Botong was so unpredictable. What if he somehow made Apothecary Huang even more angry? It would not be easy to get him to stick to the plan.

Before the end of the first day, they had crossed the Qiantang River and were on the outskirts of Lin'an. The evening mist clung to everything around them, blanketing the scene so that they could barely discern the outline of the metropolis in front of them. A lone crow cried through the fog. They decided not to go any farther, but rather to look for lodgings in a nearby inn. In the distance, where the water curved around a mighty bend, there was a cluster of a dozen or so houses.

"Over there. We can spend the night in that lovely village," Lotus said.

"What's so lovely about it?" Zhou Botong said glumly.

"It looks like something out of a painting."

"So what?"

Lotus stared back at him blankly, unsure how she should answer.

"A rather ugly painting. As if the Hoary Urchin had painted it himself," Zhou Botong said.

"If you're asking the heavens to create a landscape just like your random scribblings, I'm sure they could manage that too," Lotus said with a smile.

"I wouldn't be so sure. Why don't I draw something and you ask the heavens to oblige?"

"Fine. You've said you don't want to stay here, so why don't you go? The three of us aren't moving."

"Why would I leave without you?"

By the time they had finished this silly exchange, they had reached the village.

The village was, in fact, no more than a desolate, run-down collection of buildings, with the flag of a tavern fluttering in its eastern corner. They stopped in front of it and observed the thick layer of dust that covered the two tables standing outside, under the eaves.

"Hi!" Zhou Botong called out.

A young woman of about twenty emerged from the doorway. Her hair was uncombed, but held up with a hairpin made from a twig of bramble. She met the visitors with wide, blank eyes.

Lotus ordered food and wine, but the girl shook her head.

"You don't have food or wine? What kind of inn is this?" Zhou Botong said.

The girl shook her head again. "I don't know."

"What a silly girl," he replied.

The girl grinned. "Yes, my name is Silly Girl."

At this, they all laughed.

Lotus stepped inside and went to look at the kitchen. Everything was covered in dust and cobwebs. There was some leftover rice in one of the pots, and a broken mat covered a bed. A shiver went through her.

"Do you live here alone?" she said, upon her return.

The silly girl smiled and nodded.

"What about your mother?"

"Dead!" She rubbed her eyes, as if pretending to cry.

"Your father, then?"

The young woman shook her head. Her cheeks were dirty, and

her long nails were black with mud. Who knew how many months she had gone without washing?

We couldn't eat any food she made, anyhow, Lotus thought.

"Do you have any rice?"

The young woman nodded and carried out a large pot that was half filled with the cheapest unpolished rice.

Lotus began washing the rice, while Guo Jing went to look for provisions, returning with two fish and a chicken from another house, at the western edge of the village.

By the time the meal was ready, it was already dark. Lotus brought out the food and placed it on the tables outside, before going in search of an oil lamp, but the young woman merely shook her head. She did not have one.

Lotus collected some firewood and lit a fire in the hearth, then went in search of some bowls and chopsticks. She opened a cupboard door and a foul stench assailed her nose. Taking a burning log from the fire, she gazed inside and saw seven or eight chipped bowls. Scattered around them were a dozen dead cockroaches.

Guo Jing reached in and took the bowls.

"Wash them first, then snap a few twigs into chopsticks," Lotus instructed.

Guo Jing nodded and left. Lotus reached for the last bowl and was surprised to find that it felt cold. Colder than normal. She tried to grab it, but it refused to move, as if nailed to the shelf. Afraid to break it by yanking too hard, she tried one more time, gently, before giving up. Could it have been in there so long that the dirt had glued it stuck? She looked more carefully and discovered it was covered in rust. The bowl was made of metal.

Lotus chuckled to herself. She had seen rice bowls made of gold, silver and jade, but never in her life had she seen one made of steel. She gave it another tug, but still it would not move. She was intrigued. Given her strength, surely the shelf would crack, at the very least? Maybe it, too, was made of steel? She tapped it with her middle finger, only to find that it was indeed made of metal.

Her curiosity piqued, she pulled with all her strength. Still, nothing. She tried turning it right, then left, and felt it loosen somewhat. She tried again—harder, this time—and the bowl moved. She heard a cracking sound, and then the two sides of the cupboard opened to reveal a large, dark opening. This was the source of the sour smell, strong enough to turn her stomach.

Lotus cried out and quickly leaped to one side. The sound drew Guo Jing and Zhou Botong. Together, they peered inside. What is this place? Is the girl just pretending to be a fool?

She passed her makeshift torch to Guo Jing, approached the young woman and reached for her wrist. The woman, in turn, shook herself free and sent a palm at Lotus's shoulder.

Something told Lotus her intentions were not good, but the move was straight out of the same school of martial arts that she had herself trained in, and this surprised her. She made a hook with her left and grabbed with her right. Since she had learned the Transforming Muscles, Forging Bones chapter of the Nine Yin Manual, her speed and strength had improved immeasurably.

"*Ow!*" The young woman cried out as her arm was hit, but she followed with two moves in quick succession. They exchanged a few more blows. Lotus was astonished to watch her opponent perform Jade Ripple Palm, one of the basic techniques of Peach Blossom Island kung fu. Lotus held back, hoping to goad the young woman into revealing more about where she had studied. But it soon became apparent that she only knew these six or seven basic moves, in much the same way that Guo Jing had fought Graybeard Liang with only Haughty Dragon Repents. She was not as strong as Guo Jing, of course, and she had no variation in her technique.

They were all astonished to find a poor, filthy girl in an abandoned inn out here in this benighted village able to fight Lotus for more than ten moves.

Zhou Botong, of course, found the whole thing amusing. The girl kept crying out "*Aiya!*" as she felt the force of Lotus's swift and unrelenting attack.

"Lotus!" the Urchin cried out eventually. "Be gentle. Let me fight her instead." Having noticed that she did not seem to mind Count Seven and Guo Jing calling her by her first name, he had long since abandoned any sense of caution or feelings of propriety that might have encouraged him to call her Miss Huang.

Guo Jing's thoughts had turned to the idea that the girl might have friends nearby, watching and waiting to attack. He stuck close to Count Seven.

Lotus struck the girl on the shoulder and her left arm hung limp. At this point, Lotus decided to show mercy. "Kneel and I will spare you."

"Only if you kneel too!" the girl replied, swishing her palm in another display of Jade Ripple Palm. Lotus could see that it was the very same technique as taught on Peach Blossom Island, but the wave-like motion of her hand lacked finesse. Lotus's suspicions only grew deeper.

"How do you know Jade Ripple Palm? Who is your Master?"

The young woman smiled. "You can't beat me!"

Lotus raised her left, struck right, jabbed with her left elbow and dipped her right shoulder, all feigned attacks, before sending both hands curving out. This too was an empty attack, but it provided cover for a swift kick. This one was real. As the young woman fell to the ground, she cried out, "A nasty trick!" She scrambled to her feet. "That didn't count! Let's go again."

Lotus would not let her stand, and instead leaped forward, pushing her down. She tore a piece of cloth from the girl's robes and quickly tied her hands behind her back. "I think I just beat you."

"You tricked me!" she kept calling out in reply.

Seeing that Lotus had the girl under control, Guo Jing went outside and jumped up onto the roof. He looked around them, but saw no sign of any other people. He dropped back down and went round the back of the building. The inn stood apart from the other buildings in the village. There was no one else around. He was flooded with relief.

155

He walked back inside, only to find Lotus holding a dagger before the girl's face. "Who is your Master? Tell me, or I'll kill you." She jabbed the dagger closer as she spoke.

By the light of the candle, it was possible to see a smile trace across the girl's face. It was not bravery or defiance. No, it was a stupid smile, as if she was unaware of the danger she was in. Did she think Lotus was just playing? Lotus repeated her question, but the girl laughed and said, "If you kill me, I'll kill you back!"

Lotus raised an eyebrow. "This girl really is a fool. Let's go and look inside. Brother Zhou, you look after *Shifu* and keep an eye on her. Come on, Guo Jing."

Zhou Botong waved his hands in protest. "No, I'm going with you."

"I don't want you to come," Lotus said firmly.

Despite his seniority in age and martial capabilities, Zhou Botong did not dare defy the young woman. "That's fine, miss. You decide."

Lotus smiled and nodded. Zhou Botong found two pine branches, lit the ends and waved them in the entrance to the dark hole. The smell from inside was overwhelming. Lotus took one of the smoldering branches and threw it into the darkness. They heard a clatter as it struck a wall on the far side and crashed to the ground. The space was quite small, as it turned out.

Holding up the other torch, she peered inside. All was still, there was no trace of any movement. Unable to help himself, Zhou Botong slipped past Lotus and went inside. Cautiously, Lotus followed behind. The room was cramped.

"I've been tricked!" Zhou Botong cried out. "Not fun!"

Lotus gasped. There, on the ground, lay a skeleton. It was lying face up, its clothes half disintegrated. The ribs were in full view, and two of them had been broken. There was another skeleton in the far corner. It was slumped over an iron chest, a long blade standing tall between its ribs, having penetrated the chest's lid.

Zhou Botong looked around the small, dirty room and appeared unconcerned by the corpses. He waited impatiently as Lotus examined them more closely, but he was too scared to interrupt, lest he anger her. After a while, however, his impatience got the better of him and he asked gently, "Miss Lotus, fine maiden, may I go outside?"

"Fine. Get Guo Jing for me."

The Old Urchin happily retreated and said to Guo Jing, "Come, it's most interesting in there." He did not want to be called back in to keep Lotus company.

Guo Jing entered the darkness. Lotus raised her torch to show him the skeletons. "How do you think they died?"

"Looks like this one died in a surprise attack while trying to open the chest," he said, pointing to the one in the corner. "The other one has two broken ribs, so he was probably attacked by someone with considerable internal strength. A palm attack."

"Yes, but there are some things that don't make sense."

"Like what?"

"The fool out there was using Jade Ripple Palm, a technique from Peach Blossom Island. She only knew six, maybe seven of the moves, but, while she was clumsy in her execution, she clearly knew the theory. Why did these two die here, in this room? What's their connection to her?"

"Let's ask the girl." Having frequently been referred to as a fool, slow and worse, he refused to use the words against her.

"The girl really is a fool—I don't think we will get any sense out of her. Maybe we can make our own investigations, based on the evidence we find here," Lotus suggested. She lifted her torch again and noticed something shiny close to the chest. She picked it up and examined it. It was a small gold plaque, inlaid with a piece of agate the size of a thumbnail. She turned it over. There was an inscription on the back: *Bestowed by Imperial Decree upon the Loyal and Great Master of the Martial Arts responsible for defending our Great State, Shi Yanming.*

"If it belonged to him, this was a man of great rank," Lotus said.

"A high-ranking official, dying here? That's strange," Guo Jing said.

Lotus went back to the other skeleton, where she noticed something sticking out from between its ribs. She used the end of her torch to prod it, and it fell in a cloud of dust, which died down to reveal a round, flat sheet of metal. She gasped as she picked it up.

Guo Jing looked down at the object in her hand. "Wow."

"You know what this is?"

"Yes, I do," Guo Jing said. "It's an Eight Trigram throwing disc, belonging to the head of Roaming Cloud Manor, Squire Lu."

"It's an Eight Trigram throwing disc, to be sure, but it doesn't necessarily belong to him."

"You're right. The clothes on the bodies have disintegrated. They must have been here for at least ten years."

Lotus did not reply. She was thinking. Suddenly, an idea came to her. She approached the body in the corner, pulled out the blade from the lid and approached the torchlight. There was a character engraved on the blade: *Qu.*

"The one lying on the ground is my martial brother, Tempest Qu."

"Oh," Guo Jing said, unsure what to say next.

"Brother Lu said that Brother Qu was still alive. But, all this time, he was lying here, dead. Guo Jing . . . look at his legs."

Guo Jing bent down. "They were both broken. Was it your father who did this?"

Lotus nodded. "Tempest Qu. My father once said that, of all his disciples, it was Brother Qu who had the strongest technique. He was a talented writer, too. He was the one who studied the most with my father . . ." At that, she ran out of the room. Guo Jing hurried after her.

Lotus ran to the young woman. "Is your last name Qu?"

The girl giggled, but did not reply.

"Miss," Guo Jing tried, more gently, "what is your family name?"

"Family name?" She giggled. "Family name!"

"Hey!" Zhou Botong called out, interrupting them. "I'm hungry!"

"Yes," Lotus said. "We need to eat." She untied the young woman's hands and invited her to eat with them. Unabashed, the young woman smiled and held out her hands to take the bowl.

Lotus told Count Seven about all that she had found in the room. "It looks like some official by the name of Shi killed Brother Qu," Count Seven concluded. "Just before he died, he threw the weapon and killed his assailant."

"Yes, it seems so," Lotus agreed.

Then she presented the blade and the Eight Trigram disc to the young woman. "Whose are these?"

The girl's expression suddenly changed. She tilted her head, as if she was trying to recall something. Then, suddenly, her face turned blank. She shook her head, took the blade and refused to give it back.

"She's seen this before," Lotus said. "But it must have been a long time ago. She doesn't seem to remember where."

After they had finished eating, Lotus settled Count Seven to sleep. Then she and Guo Jing went back into the hidden room to examine the scene further. The key to the mystery would be found in the chest. Carefully, they removed the skeleton on top of it and opened the lid. It had not been locked and was easy to lift.

They held up the torch and peered down. The chest gleamed and shone with pearls, jade and all kinds of other expensive treasures.

Guo Jing was surprised, but only Lotus realized the true value of the objects inside. This collection went far beyond that of her father's. She reached for a handful of pearls and let them pour through her fingers, making a delightful tinkling as they clinked against the other rare items inside.

"There must be quite a story behind all these different treasures. If father were here, he could tell us the origins of each piece." She lifted each one, explaining to Guo Jing what they were. This one is a jade belt loop, this one is a case made out of rhino hide, this is a cup made from agate, a jadeite dish. And so on.

Guo Jing had grown up in the desert, and never in his life had he seen riches like this. People put so much effort into making and collecting these trinkets, but what were they for?

Lotus reached into the chest again and dug down until her fingers touched a piece of solid wood. There was another layer beneath. She pushed away the jewelry to reveal a series of rings, into which she inserted her fingers and lifted the board. The bottom layer contained old objects made of green oxidized copper. She had heard her father describe the history of bronzeware, so she recognized the traditional three-legged Shang dynasty ritual cauldron, decorated with a dragon pattern, as well as the wine vessel from the same era, not to mention the various-shaped vessels characteristic of the Zhou. Her knowledge was scanty at best, but she knew that, if the top layer was worth a fortune, these items were priceless.

At that moment, she realized there was another layer to the chest. She removed the board covering it, only to discover a collection of scrolls. Together, Guo Jing and Lotus unrolled each one. To her amazement, she realized she was looking at the master of Buddhist art Wu Daozi's *God Sending a Son*. The next was the Tang painter Han Gan's *Herding Horses*. Together, they unfurled a majestic work by Li Yu, the last Emperor of the Southern Tang, entitled *Man Crossing a Secluded River*. There were more than twenty scrolls and each one was a treasure by one of China's most famous artists. There were several examples of both calligraphy and painting by Emperor Huizong. Some were by contemporary masters, including painter-in-attendance at the Imperial Court, Liang Kai.

After unrolling a dozen or so, Lotus wished to see no more. She returned the items to the chest, closed the lid and sat down on top, hugging her knees. *Father has been collecting all his life, and yet he has nothing like the treasures in this chest. How did Brother Qu get hold of such priceless pieces? And why did he keep them here?* She could think of no reasonable explanation.

Guo Jing watched her in silence, not daring to interrupt her thoughts.

"Hey!" Zhou Botong's voice came from outside. "Come out! It's time to visit the Emperor for some of that Contrast of the Five Treasures!"

"This evening?" Guo Jing asked.

"The sooner, the better. I'm not getting any stronger," Count Seven called back.

"*Shifu*, don't listen to the Old Urchin's nonsense," Lotus replied. "We can't possibly go tonight. We can enter the city tomorrow morning. Any more ridiculous ideas from him and he won't be coming with us to the palace."

"Huh!" Zhou Botong snorted. "Once again, I'm to blame," he said, falling into a sulk.

3

THAT NIGHT, THE FOUR OF THEM SLEPT ON STRAW BEDS LAID out on the floor. Early the next morning, Lotus and Guo Jing got up to make breakfast, which they ate with the young woman. Lotus turned the iron bowl to close the cabinet doors, and returned the broken tableware to the shelf. The young girl watched on indifferently as she played with the blade. Lotus gave her a piece of silver, which she took and then tossed onto the table.

"If you get hungry, use that to buy yourself some rice and meat," Lotus suggested.

The young girl just grinned back at her.

A sadness was creeping into Lotus's heart. She must be related to Brother Qu—if not by blood, at least by the bonds of master and disciple. He had definitely taught her those half a dozen moves of Jade Ripple Palm, even if she had not practiced them with care. Had she been this way since birth, or was some traumatic experience, some terrible shock to blame? Lotus was tempted to ask around the village, but Zhou Botong urged them on, and so the four of them climbed up onto the cart and headed for the city of Lin'an.

Lin'an was the largest city in the world, at the time. When the Song court was forced south, it chose the city as the Empire's new capital, bringing all kinds of people and goods from far afield, causing it to flourish even more.

Together, Lotus and the others entered by the East Gate, from where they headed straight for the main entrance to the Imperial Palace.

Count Seven stayed on the cart while the others went to look around. They saw golden nails banged into scarlet doors, painted columns, engraved beams, copper tiles on the roof, and sculptures of flying dragons and soaring phoenixes in all their splendor.

"Wonderful!" Zhou Botong cried, before striding toward the door.

The guards had been watching the old man and the young couple, clutching their weapons. Now, they strode forward to arrest the troublemakers.

Zhou Botong loved to make mischief and he was itching to fight with the sturdy men in their glinting armor.

"Come, let's go!" Lotus cried.

"Why?" Zhou Botong said, staring at her wide-eyed. "What harm can these babies do to the Old Urchin?"

"Guo Jing," Lotus continued, "let's go. The Old Urchin always does as he pleases. We'll ignore him."

Back on the cart, she lashed the whip and the mule lurched forward, pulling them westward. Guo Jing followed behind.

Concerned that he might be about to miss out on something interesting, Zhou Botong ran after them.

Taking them for simple villagers on their first visit to the city, the guards laughed and did not give chase.

Lotus drove the cart to a quiet part of the city and checked they had not been followed, before stopping at last.

"Why didn't we try to get into the palace? Those sacks of rice wouldn't have stopped us!" Zhou Botong said.

"Are we here for a fight, or are we after the food? Our presence

TROUBLE IN THE PALACE

would cause chaos in the palace, and then do you think the chef would calmly agree to make some Contrast of the Five Treasures for *Shifu*?"

"Capturing intruders has nothing to do with the palace chefs," Zhou Botong said.

Lotus was momentarily stumped by this logic, but she did not want to admit it. "There's nothing stopping a chef from catching an intruder," she said hesitantly.

Now it was Zhou Botong's turn to be silenced. "Fine," he said eventually. "Let's say I was wrong."

"What do you mean, 'Let's say'? You were wrong from the start," Lotus retorted.

"Fine, have it your way. Let's say no more about it." Turning to Guo Jing, he said, "Boy, don't be fooled—all women are fiendish. That is why the Old Urchin lives by the motto, 'Never take a wife'!"

Lotus laughed at this. "Brother Guo is a good man. I would never be fiendish toward him."

"Does that mean I'm not a good man?" the Urchin replied.

"You tell me," Lotus said with a smile. "I rather think the reason you aren't married is that no woman can stand your constant troublemaking. Or, what do you say? What's the real reason you don't have a wife?"

Zhou Botong cocked his head, but could not think of a reasonable answer. His cheeks flushed red, then white. Worry spread across his face. Lotus had rarely seen such a serious expression on his face and it took her by surprise.

"Let's find an inn and go back to the palace tonight," Guo Jing suggested.

"Good idea!" Lotus said. "And I will prepare some dishes for you, *Shifu*, as an appetizer. The real feast is coming tonight."

Count Seven clapped his hands in delight.

They found a small place called the Brocade Mansion, where they settled, and, true to her word, Lotus pulled together three dishes and a soup for her Master. The aroma filled the inn and the other guests were soon asking the innkeeper if there was a famous chef in the kitchen.

Zhou Botong, meanwhile, was still stewing over Lotus's comment that, rather than not wanting a wife, he was unable to find one. He refused to join them. Used to his childish ways, the others merely laughed and ignored him.

After the meal, Count Seven lay down to rest. Guo Jing asked if the Urchin wanted to join him for a walk outside, but the old man was still sulking and would not answer.

"Look after our *shifu*, then," Lotus said lightly. "We'll be back soon, with presents."

The Hoary Urchin's face lit up. "Promise?"

"When a word bolts, no horse can chase it down."

4

WHEN LOTUS LEFT PEACH BLOSSOM ISLAND IN THE SPRING to go north, she had passed through Lin'an. She had not dared stay longer than a day, back then, as it was too close to home and she feared her father might find her. This time, the days were long and her mind was unburdened. Hand in hand, she and Guo Jing made their way to the beautiful West Lake.

Lotus glanced across at Guo Jing and noticed the look of melancholy on his face. He was worrying about their Master's health. "*Shifu* mentioned that there is someone who can cure him," Lotus began, "but he wouldn't let me ask who. From his tone, I'd guess that it's King Duan of Dali. We are many thousands of miles from Dali, but somehow we've got to find him and beg him to save our Master."

"That's wonderful! Do you think we can manage it?"

"I was trying to find a way to ask *Shifu* while we were eating, but he sensed what I was getting at and clammed up. I'll get it out of him eventually."

Guo Jing knew full well how talented Lotus was at such tasks, and so felt greatly relieved.

As they talked, they came to Broken Bridge, one of the lake's most famous beauty spots. They crossed to its midpoint and looked down at the lotus flowers beneath. Nearby stood a charming little drinking house. "Let's have a cup of wine and admire the flowers," Lotus suggested.

"Yes, let's."

They entered and sat down. The owner brought them wine and a series of delicious dishes, and their hearts felt light. Lotus looked across to the windows on the eastern side and spotted a beautiful screen, covered in a jade-colored gauze. She approached to get a closer look and saw that, beneath the thin layer of material, a poem had been inscribed in the wood. It was called "Wind Enters Pines":

> Spring money wasted on blossoming bosoms
> and drunken days by the lake.
> Riding my white colt, I look up and see
> a tavern door
> apricot scent layered with drums
> a swing in the poplar's shade.
> Maidens caressed by the warm breeze,
> petals pressing on their hair.
> Boats painted in the setting sun.
> What feelings that linger must be left for
> morrow's fun,
> when looking for new jeweled flowers
> drunken we will return.

"It's a good poem," Lotus said.

Guo Jing asked her to explain what it meant. The more he heard, the angrier he became. "We are in the capital, the heart of the Great Song, and yet the government officials spend their days drinking and admiring flowers. Don't they care about what's happening to our country?"

"Indeed. They are shameless."

"Huh!" came a voice behind them. "What do you two know? What nonsense."

They turned to find a man of about forty, dressed in scholars' robes and wearing a sneer.

Guo Jing clasped his hands and bowed. "May I humbly apologize? Please enlighten us."

"The poem is by Yu Guobao, a student of the Imperial College during the Chunxi period. Emperor Gaozong came to this very inn, read it and praised it highly. That very same day, he granted Yu a government position, which is every scholar's dream. And here you two are, making a mockery of it!"

"The innkeeper keeps it covered with this green gauze because the Emperor once saw it?" Lotus asked.

The man sniggered. "Ha! Is that what you think? Come here and look carefully at this line. Can you see two of the characters have been changed?"

Guo Jing leaned in close and saw that "drunken we will return" had once been "carrying wine we will return."

"The Emperor commented that this line was somewhat shallow—wretched, even—so he took his brush and changed it. Truly, his was a wisdom and intelligence sent from the heavens. He turned iron into gold." The man nodded in a self-satisfied manner.

Guo Jing, however, was furious. "This is the same Emperor who instructed Qin Hui to kill General Yue Fei!" His leg flew up and smashed the screen. Then he grabbed the man, dragged him forward and, with a splash, dumped him head first in a vat of wine.

Lotus laughed. "I have my own suggestion: 'When looking for new mischief, in the barrel he was turned.'"

The man's head popped out over the rim. "But it doesn't fit the rhythm," he said matter-of-factly.

"And, as for the title," Lotus continued, "instead of 'Wind Enters

Pines,' I suggest 'Man Enters Barrel.'" At this, she reached out and pushed his head back under, then flipped their table over with a loud crash. The customers and the innkeeper dashed for the door.

Guo Jing and Lotus were now on the rampage. They broke the ceramic wine vats, pots, and cauldrons. Guo Jing then launched into a move from Dragon-Subduing Palm, unleashing all his strength on one of the supporting columns, causing the roof to collapse. Within moments, the building had been transformed into a pile of rubble.

Laughing, the young couple held hands and walked away. No one knew who they were or where they had come from, and certainly they did not dare to follow them to find out.

"That felt good," Guo Jing said with a smile. "I got all the anger off my chest."

"We must break anything that does not please us," Lotus replied. "Indeed!"

The truth was, since leaving Peach Blossom Island, they had been through many tribulations. They had been reunited, but their Master was gravely injured and the thought that he might not recover pressed heavy on their hearts. This moment of wanton destruction had provided a brief outlet for their frustrations.

Together, they walked along the shore of the lake. Dotted everywhere were poems—on rocks, on trees, on pavilions and on walls. They spoke of sightseers bidding farewell to the majestic scenery, or else young men professing their love. Guo Jing could not claim to understand their precise meanings, but all the talk of wind, flowers, snow, and the moon affected him. "We wouldn't be able to smash all these, even if we had a thousand fists. Lotus, you've read so many books. What's it all for?"

"There *are* good poems," Lotus said with a laugh.

"I still think studying how to kick and punch is more useful," Guo Jing said, shaking his head.

They continued walking until they reached the pavilion at Flying Peak. A sign carved in wood, in Han Shizhong's calligraphy, read: *Pavilion of the Emerald Hills.* Guo Jing had heard of Han Shizhong,

the great general who had fought the Jin. Delighted, he ran inside, where he saw a stone stela, upon which was carved another poem:

> In uniform beclad in years of dust
> I take in the perfume
> of the Emerald Hills.
> Never could I tire of such beauty
> but the moon and the hooves urge me on.

It, too, seemed to have been written by the general.

"This is a fine poem," Guo Jing declared. In fact, he had no idea if it was fine or not, but, if the general had written it and it contained phrases like "uniform beclad in years of dust" and words like "hooves," it had to be good.

"That's a poem by General Yue Fei," Lotus said.

"How do you know that?" Guo Jing asked in surprise.

"My father told me the story. During the eleventh winter of the Shaoxing period, General Yue Fei was killed by Chancellor Qin Hui. Han Shizhong built this pavilion the following spring and carved this poem in his memory. Unfortunately, Qin Hui was still a very powerful man, so Han could not openly acknowledge that the pavilion had been built for the General."

Guo Jing traced his fingers across the carved characters, lost in thought. Suddenly, Lotus tugged on his sleeve and pulled him toward some bushes behind the wooden structure. As they crouched down out of sight, they heard the footsteps of people entering the pavilion.

"Han Shizhong was a hero, of course. His wife, Liang Hongyu, may have started out as a courtesan, but she beat the drum during battle and helped her husband to victory, so she's a true heroine, too."

Guo Jing thought that he recognized the voice, but he could not place it. Then, another man spoke.

"Both Yue Fei and Han Shizhong were heroes, but the Emperor wanted them dead and stripped of their military titles. Yue Fei's killers had no choice but to follow orders. No one can stand against the might of the Emperor."

Yang Kang! Guo Jing was startled by the realization. What was he doing here? Just then, another voice: Venom of the West, Viper Ouyang.

"That is correct. With muddle-heads in power at the Song court now, too, what use are heroes?"

"But, if a wise ruler occupies the throne, then a great man like Master Ouyang would help him immensely in achieving his ambitions." The first voice again.

Guo Jing realized suddenly who it was. The man who had killed his father: the Sixth Prince of the Jin, Wanyan Honglie.

The three men exchanged a few more words and then left, laughing. Guo Jing waited until they were long gone before asking, "What are they doing in Lin'an? Why is Brother Yang with them?"

"Huh!" Lotus snorted. "I knew from the first moment I saw him that this brother of yours was up to no good. You said he was descended from a hero. Well, you have been deceived. Now you know who he really is. If he truly were a good man, he would never associate with such scoundrels."

"I don't understand," Guo Jing replied.

Lotus went on to tell Guo Jing all she had heard at the Hall of Perfumed Snow in the Zhao residence. "Wanyan Honglie brought together Tiger Peng and the others in order to steal the last writings of General Yue Fei. Perhaps they have traced them to Lin'an. If they succeed, then the lowly subjects of the Great Song will suffer untold calamity."

"They cannot be allowed to succeed," Guo Jing said with a shiver.

"But now they have the Venom of the West with them."

"Are you frightened?"

"Aren't you?"

"Of course, I'm scared of the Venom. But we have to . . . No matter how scared we are, we can't ignore it."

"If you're in, so am I," Lotus said with a smile.

"Then let's follow them."

5

THEY HAD BEEN TOO SLOW TO GIVE CHASE, AND, WITHOUT any indication of which direction the three men had taken, they were forced to search the city at random. But, with such a large area to cover and the streets so crowded, how could they possibly find them? They walked all afternoon and, as the sky was turning dark, they arrived at the Wulin Park, in front of the main theater and entertainment district of the city. Lotus spotted a shop, the entrance of which was festooned with masks, their features vivid and colorful. Amused, she remembered her promise to buy Zhou Botong a present. She spent five silver coins on ten masks that represented the demon vanquisher Zhong Kui, the divine Judge of the Underworld, the Kitchen God, the Earth God, and other divine soldiers, ghosts and supernatural beings.

As the shopkeeper was wrapping them, the delicious aroma of freshly cooked food came wafting in from the restaurant next door.

"What place is that next door?" Lotus asked.

"Your first time here, is it?" the shopkeeper said with a smile. "Otherwise, you'd know. That is Premium Scholars Inn, one of the most famous establishments in the city. Their food is the best in all the Empire. You can't leave without having tried it."

As soon as the package was ready, Lotus pulled Guo Jing to the entrance of the inn. The building was brightly painted in red and green, and lanterns embellished with jasmine flowers hung from the eaves. The interior was richly decorated. They were greeted by a waiter, who led them down a corridor into a private room set out with the finest tableware. Lotus ordered some dishes and then the waiter left.

Guo Jing looked out into the corridor and, by the candlelight, saw a line of ten or so richly dressed women waiting outside. He was about to ask what they were doing, when, suddenly, Wanyan Honglie's voice came booming from the room next door: "Wonderful! Let's invite them to sing to us while we drink!"

Guo Jing and Lotus exchanged glances. Just as they had stopped searching, they had found them.

A waiter called out. An exceptionally beautiful woman stood up and began to beat a rhythm with a pair of ivory clappers. Then, she sang. Lotus strained to make out the words:

> "The Yangtze flows down to
> the three Wus,
> where the Qiantang River has flourished
> since ancient times.
> Smokey willows painted bridges,
> screens and curtains emerald-green,
> a hundred thousand cottages scattered all
> around.
> Cloud-crested trees stand along the banks
> where furious waves churn snowdrifts,
> until the river reaches out of sight.
> Pearls and gems laid out on stands
> to compete with silks and satins.
> Lakes and peaks praise each other
> as the autumn osmanthus flowers
> greet lotus uncoiling for miles.
> Tunes play from the northwest by day,
> while water chestnut songs interrupt the night
> and fishermen smile at maidens
> collecting lotus pods.
> A thousand banners raised as you arrive

drunken on horseback, you hear flute and drum,
sing praises to the pinky clouds
of a scenery that reminds you of days of old
that you will extol to the court on your return."

Guo Jing did not understand a word of what was being sung, but he did enjoy the gentle rhythm of the ivory clappers and the rise and fall of the flute accompaniment.

"Wonderful!"

"Bravo!"

Wanyan Honglie and Yang Kang declared their praise loudly as soon as the song finished. The woman thanked them profusely and left, along with the musicians. The Sixth Prince must have rewarded them handsomely.

"Boy, did you know that the song we just enjoyed was written by Liu Yong and is called 'Gazing at the Tide'? It has great significance for us Jin."

"No, I didn't. Please tell me more, Father."

Guo Jing and Lotus exchanged glances. Did he call him "Father"? And with such affection? Guo Jing was furious. He wanted nothing more than to go in there, grab him by the throat and demand an explanation.

"As our Empire was beginning to prosper, Our Majesty Emperor Wanyan Liang read this poem by Liu Yong, which praised the beauty and wonder of West Lake. For this reason, he dispatched an envoy south, along with a master painter, who painted the scenery of Lin'an and added Our Majesty riding a horse inside the city walls, at the summit of Mount Wu. Our Majesty then added the following poem:

"Ten thousand miles of road, united by brush,
How can a separate court be named in the south?
I will lead a million soldiers to West Lake,
and alone claim the peak of Mount Wu."

"What heroic ambition!" Yang Kang said.

Enraged, Guo Jing clenched his fist so hard his fingers cracked.

Wanyan Honglie merely sighed, however, and continued, "Our Majesty Emperor Wanyan Liang never realized his vision of sending an army south and taking command of Mount Wu, but it is something we, his children and grandchildren, bear with us and have made real. He once wrote a poem on a fan that went like this: 'With the hilt firmly in my grasp, a cool breeze will engulf the world.' That was the extent of his ambition!"

"With the hilt firmly in my grasp, a cool breeze will engulf the world," Yang Kang repeated.

Viper Ouyang laughed. "One day, the Sixth Prince will stand on top of Mount Wu."

"I do hope so," Wanyan Honglie said quietly. "But there are many eyes and ears about, so let us drink instead." And, with that, conversation turned to the local scenery and customs they had observed as they traveled.

"They sound a bit too comfortable," Lotus whispered. Together, she and Guo Jing slipped out of the dining room and into the yard at the rear of the complex. With a wave of a torch, Lotus set fire to the wooden buildings that surrounded the courtyard.

Within moments, the flames had climbed high and people began pouring outside.

"Fire!"

"We need water!"

Copper gongs were sounding all around.

"Quick, to the front, or we'll lose them," Lotus said.

"Tonight, we must kill that villain Wanyan Honglie!"

"Only after we've made sure *Shifu* has had his fill from the palace kitchens. Then we can get the Old Urchin to fight the Venom of the West, while we deal with the other two."

"Good idea."

They made their way through the crowd to the front of the inn, just as Wanyan Honglie, Viper Ouyang and Yang Kang emerged. They followed the three men at a distance, along long streets and winding alleys, toward the city's western market, where they entered the Crown and Seal Inn.

Lotus and Guo Jing waited outside, until eventually concluding that the party must be staying there.

"Let's get the Old Urchin and bring him back here," Lotus suggested, and with that they set off in the direction of the Brocade Mansion.

6

AS THEY APPROACHED THE INN, THEY COULD HEAR ZHOU Botong's voice. He was shouting. Fear surged through Guo Jing as the thought hit him: perhaps their *shifu's* condition had taken a turn for the worse. He rushed forward, only to see Zhou Botong squatting on the ground outside the inn, squabbling with a group of half a dozen young boys. They had been betting who could throw coins the farthest, but one of them was refusing to pay up. As soon as the Urchin caught sight of Lotus, however, he quickly abandoned the fray and went inside.

Once inside, Lotus presented him with the masks. He was delighted and began trying them on, playing the Judge of the Underworld one minute and a demon the next.

Lotus told him of their plan and Zhou Botong quickly agreed. "Have no fear—these fists of mine will make short work of the Venom! I have two techniques I can use."

Lotus recalled the fight on Peach Blossom Island. Afraid that he might reveal moves from the Nine Yin Manual, Zhou Botong had tied his hands and thus had been injured by her father. "The Venom of the West is a bad man. Your martial brother, Master Wang Chongyang, once fought him, so it wouldn't be going against his last decree to use some moves from the Nine Yin Manual."

"No, I can't," Zhou Botong said, looking at her intensely. "I've trained hard for many years; I don't need the Manual."

Count Seven, meanwhile, was still dreaming of the food inside the palace. Waiting until evening was proving arduous. But, at the second watch that night, Guo Jing hoisted his Master onto his back and the four made their way across the rooftops of the city.

The palace towered above the surrounding buildings, and its glazed roof tiles sparkled, making it easy to spot. Before long, they had leaped over the walls and were inside.

Within the complex, guards patrolled the grounds and gardens. But, using their lightness kung fu—under the guidance of Count Seven Hong's whispered instructions—they were able to make straight for the kitchens, located behind the Six Ministries Mount and east of the Radiance Hall, where the imperial family took their meals. The private chambers in which the Emperor conducted official business were adjacent, patrolled by personal attendants, eunuchs and guards. The Emperor had already retired for the night and the kitchen staff had left. As they entered, they were greeted by lit torches, however. Several young palace eunuchs were sleeping on the floor.

Guo Jing helped Count Seven into position on one of the roof beams, while Lotus and Zhou Botong searched the cupboards for food. Before long, they were feasting.

"Old Beggar," Zhou Botong said with a shake of his head, "this food is nothing compared to Lotus's cooking. I have no idea why you insisted on us coming."

"I want to eat Contrast of the Five Treasures. Tomorrow, we'll capture the chef and force him to make it. Then you'll see."

"I still think Lotus is a better cook."

Lotus smiled. She knew it was his way of thanking her for the gift.

"I'll stay here and wait for the chef," Count Seven said. "Since you're already bored, why don't you and Guo Jing leave the palace? Lotus can stay and keep me company. You can come back tomorrow night to collect us."

Zhou Botong reached for the city bodhisattva mask and laughed. "No, I'll stay. I'm going to wear this tomorrow and scare the old Emperor. You two young 'uns keep your eyes on Old Venom. Don't let him get his hands on Yue Fei's book."

"Good idea," Count Seven said. "Go now. But be careful."

Lotus and Guo Jing gave him their word.

"But don't fight him!" Zhou Botong said. "Leave him to me. Tomorrow, I'll get him."

"Of course we won't," Lotus said. "We could never beat him."

Together, the young couple slipped out of the imperial kitchens and through two halls. Suddenly, a cool breeze hit their skin and the faintest sound of trickling water met their ears. A sweet perfume wafted past on the night air. It was as if the palace had transformed into a remote mountaintop.

There must be a flowering garden nearby, Lotus deduced, filled with the most marvelous and exotic specimens. She had to see it. Taking Guo Jing's hand, she pulled him in the direction of the scent. Gradually, the sound of running water grew louder, and they were soon winding among tall pines and bristling thickets of bamboo. Flowers bordered the path and, to the sides, the ground rose into man-made miniature mountains. A beautiful stillness reigned.

Lotus marveled at the scene. The landscaping may not have been as intricate as her father's gardens on Peach Blossom Island, but the plants were more beautiful. They kept walking until they came across a waterfall that tumbled down like the finest woven silk and gathered in a pool, from which an overflow stream carried the water on elsewhere.

Red lotus flowers dotted the surface of the pool, and to one side of it stood an ornate building with the characters *Hall of Wintry Jade* carved above the threshold. Lotus approached and peered inside. The steps leading up to the entrance were festooned in jasmine, musk vine, hibiscus, osmanthus, and scarlet banana—all fragrant, summer-flowering plants. Orchids and scented prayer beads hung on the back wall inside, and musk melon, lotus root, loquat, and other fresh fruits had been placed on a table in the middle. A fan had been dropped in a chair. This must be where the Emperor cooled down from the day's searing heat, before bed.

"The Emperor certainly knows the good things in life," Guo Jing said.

"Why don't you have a try?" Lotus said, and with a chuckle she pulled Guo Jing down onto the bamboo chaise longue. She then brought him fruit, knelt beside him and said, "Your Majesty, please enjoy."

Guo Jing selected a loquat and laughed. "Please stand."

"An Emperor would never say that. It's far too polite."

"Hark!" A voice interrupted their game. "Who goes there?"

Startled, they scrambled out of the pavilion and hid behind a miniature mountain, listening as the footsteps grew louder. Two sets, but they could hear that the men approaching were not martial-arts practitioners.

The guards ran up to the pavilion, brandishing their sabers, but found nothing.

"A ghost," one of the men said, laughing.

"I've been seeing things for days," the other man replied, as he walked back outside.

Lotus smiled and took Guo Jing by the hand. At that moment, they heard a "Hey!" and then another. The two guards gasped and fell, their pressure points locked. Had Brother Zhou come to cause trouble?

"According to the map of the palace, the building next to the waterfall is the Hall of Wintry Jade. That's where we're headed." It was Wanyan Honglie.

Lotus and Guo Jing dived back down into their hiding place. Shocked, they did not dare make a sound. They peered out and, by the faint flicker of starlight, they saw shadows move across the front of the hall. Viper Ouyang, Tiger Peng, Hector Sha, Lama Supreme Wisdom, Graybeard Liang, and Browbeater Hou.

What are they doing here? Have they too come to steal food from the kitchens?

"I examined the letters Yue Fei left behind, as well as the documents from the Gaozong and Xiaozong reigns. According to what I could work out, the secret writings should be buried fifteen paces east of the Hall of Wintry Jade."

Their eyes followed his finger east. Fifteen paces . . . was the waterfall.

"Just how he hid a book inside a waterfall is anyone's guess. But that's where it is, according to the documents."

Hector Sha's skills in water were renowned. "Let me look," he said, and, without waiting for any further instruction, he dived straight into the pool. The others waited, watching, until he re-emerged. They rushed forward to meet him.

"Your Majesty, behind the waterfall there's a cave with a locked door."

"It must be inside there!" Wanyan Honglie exclaimed with delight. "I'm afraid that I will have to ask you kind gentlemen to help me open that door."

Keen to show their willingness to serve, the men held their weapons high and ran straight for the waterfall. Only Viper Ouyang stayed by Wanyan Honglie's side. Such an errand was beneath him.

Hector Sha pushed to the front and ducked under the stream. A rush of air hit his face. An enemy attack? He dodged, but someone grabbed his left wrist and pushed him back out, under the waterfall, into Graybeard Liang. Luckily, neither man was injured.

The others looked on in surprise, but Hector Sha was determined to go back. Placing his hands over his face, he entered the waterfall. And, sure enough, another punch came from behind the sheet of water. Blocking with his left fist, he sent out his right. Before he could see who it was, Graybeard had joined him.

A stick swept at shin height, crashing into Graybeard Liang and knocking him off his feet and into the waterfall. Water pounded at his chest, while the stick struck at the soles of his feet, sending him shooting out into the pool.

Moments later, Hector Sha followed.

Dismissing the voice in his head telling him that, if his martial brother was so easily defeated, he would stand little chance, the Three-Horned Dragon, Browbeater Hou, stepped forward. No, he would try. He could see underwater. With a roar, he charged through the curtain of water.

Aware that the situation was precarious, Tiger Peng was just about to rush into the fray when something black and shiny flew over his head, before crashing to the ground. Browbeater Hou cried out. Tiger Peng rushed to his side.

"Shhh, brother, what happened?"

"Damn it! My backside has been broken into four."

Tiger Peng could not help but be amused, despite his astonishment. "Is that even possible?" he asked, reaching out and stroking Browbeater's buttocks. He could only feel two, but he did not dare make a closer inspection. "Who are they?"

"How would I know?" Browbeater huffed in irritation. "I keep getting knocked back out as soon as I go in!"

Lama Supreme Wisdom's red robes fluttered in the starlight as he strode toward the waterfall, before plunging through it. The others listened as his cries rose above the noise of rushing water. It sounded like an intense fight.

Through the curtain of water, they could just about make out the silhouettes of a man and a woman. They exchanged glances. The man was fighting with his fists, the woman with a stick. Then came the monk's roar; he too had been severely dealt with.

"What's that idiot monk doing?" Wanyan Honglie hissed, his brow knitted. "His shouting will attract more guards. Then how will we get the book?"

Just then, a flutter of red came flying out of the waterfall and splashed through the surface of the pond. This was followed by the two copper cymbals the monk had been using as weapons. Afraid that the sound of them landing would alert the guards, Tiger Peng rushed forward to catch them.

A curse from behind the waterfall. Then, a large body.

As the monk came crashing to earth, he managed to steady himself and land on his feet, thus avoiding the same buttock-splitting fate as Browbeater Hou.

"It's the boy and the girl from the boat."

7

LOTUS AND GUO JING LISTENED AS WANYAN HONGLIE GAVE the order to bring him the book. If he were to get his hands on Yue Fei's strategies, the Jin army could use them to invade the south, to disastrous effect. They may have been scared of Viper Ouyang, but they would never have forgiven themselves if they had stood by and done nothing to prevent such a disaster for the common people.

Lotus had first thought of scaring them off, but Guo Jing could see they did not have time for such a plan. Instead, he pulled Lotus with him behind the waterfall. From there, they could ambush the Old Venom. Luckily, the roar of the waterfall ensured that no one heard them slip through it.

They were surprised to find how easily they had repelled Hector Sha and the others. The Transforming Muscles, Forging Bones chapter of the Nine Yin Manual was exceeding all expectations. Lotus was using all the various and fantastic permutations of Dog-Beating Cane, rendering Hector Sha and Lama Supreme Wisdom confused and helpless. This enabled Guo Jing to supply the coup de grâce with his palms.

They knew, however, that, once the others were dispatched, Viper Ouyang would step forward, and there was no way they could defeat him.

"Let's go, and shout as we leave," Lotus said. "That way, the guards will come and drive them off."

"Good idea! You raise the alarm. I'm going to stay."

"But you mustn't fight Old Venom."

"I won't. Go!"

Just as Lotus was about to slip out and scurry away, they heard a snort, followed by a burst of energy that came blasting through the waterfall. Rather than attempting to block it, they jumped aside.

Thwang!

Viper Ouyang had used his Exploding Toad kung fu to send a wave of energy through the cascading water, to crash against the metal door. Water splashed Lotus and Guo Jing where they watched, in astonishment.

Lotus had been struck in the back. Her breathing became labored and her vision blurry. She managed to regain focus, then rushed outside.

"Assassin in the palace! There's an assassin in the palace!"

The nearby guards were awoken with a start. Lotus jumped onto a rooftop and watched the men spring into action. Then she started grabbing tiles and throwing them—*Bing! Bing! Bang! Bang!*—down below.

"Let's get the girl," Tiger Peng snarled, and launched himself in pursuit of her, using his lightness kung fu. Graybeard Liang leaped up onto a nearby rooftop, trying to block her way.

Wanyan Honglie remained calm, however. He turned to Yang Kang and said, "Son, go with Master Ouyang and get the book."

Viper Ouyang was crouching behind the waterfall. With a grunt, he pushed out another wave of energy and blasted the door inward.

Just as he was about to enter, a shadow flew at him from the side, palm first, in a Dragon Soars in the Sky. In the darkness, he could not make out who it was, but he could tell from the move that it was Guo Jing.

This is my chance to capture the boy and get him to explain the Nine Yin Manual to me, Viper said to himself as he dodged the palm and grabbed at Guo Jing's back.

Guo Jing was determined to stop Viper from getting inside. If he could hold him off for just a few moments longer, it would be long enough for the guards to arrive, and even a martial master of the Venom's caliber would be forced to flee. But Viper appeared to be trying to capture him, rather than hurt him. He brushed Ouyang's hand away with his left and attacked with his right, using Luminous Hollow Fist. This technique may have offered less in terms of strength than the Dragon-Subduing Palms, but it made up for it in its light, swift feints and turns.

"Excellent!" Viper cried, dipping his shoulder and reaching out for Guo Jing's. His movements brought with them a gust of energy like a thunderclap.

Viper Ouyang had spent his time on the deserted island studying the pages Guo Jing had written out for him, but, the more he practiced, the more it felt that something was not right. It never occurred to him that it had been deliberately scrambled. Instead, he had taken its impenetrability for profundity, judging that the manual's teachings required time to be understood. Later, when on the raft, he had heard Count Seven chant some strange language, and he wondered if it might be the key to unlocking the Manual's secrets. Furthermore, Guo Jing's martial skills had improved. It surprised him that the boy had been able to unlock the Manual's powers, when thus far they had eluded him, but he was also pleased, assuming that, now he had his hands on the text, he would, in time, become unassailable.

He had fought Lotus and Guo Jing on the raft and had been close to losing both his life and his reputation. But, now he was in control, he could study the boy's moves in order to help crack the Manual. He would unravel the mystery, blow by blow. In truth, he did not care if he managed to get hold of Yue Fei's writings. His heart was intent on mastering the martial lessons of the Nine Yin Manual.

The lanterns were now lit, and guards were flooding this area of the palace grounds. Yang Kang had followed Viper Ouyang behind the waterfall. He was growing increasingly anxious as the guards gathered, but their attention was taken up by Tiger Peng and

Graybeard Liang chasing Lotus across the rooftops. Indeed, they did not realize there was another fight unfolding. Wanyan Honglie knew it would not be long until they were discovered, however. "Quickly!" he cried, waving his hands, unable to stop himself.

"Worry not, Your Highness—I will go in again," Lama Supreme Wisdom announced. With a flick of his left palm, he entered the waterfall.

By now, the bright lights of the lanterns had penetrated the sheet of water, and the lama was able to make out Viper Ouyang and Guo Jing exchanging blows at the entrance to the cave. Yang Kang was trying to sneak around them. But how could he make it past the furious tempest being whipped up by their fast-moving palms?

The lama could stand to watch no more. The situation outside was in the balance, and here was the Venom of the West, indulging in a fight with the boy!

"Let me help, Master Ouyang!"

"Don't come any closer!" came Viper's reply.

Even now, you want to play the hero? The grand martial Master?

He crouched and then launched himself at Guo Jing's left side, aiming for his Great Sun point.

Viper Ouyang was furious. He grabbed the back of the lama's neck and tossed him aside.

This only provoked the lama further. He began shouting and cursing, but the water poured down over his face, into his mouth, and drowned out the words before they were fully formed.

Wanyan Honglie watched the lama fall back, as if riding clouds, until his body sailed into a large flower pot in front of the pavilion, smashing it into little pieces. Thus alerted, the guards came running. The Sixth Prince gathered his robes and slipped behind the waterfall.

The ground was slippery, and, moments later, he lost his footing and crashed to the ground. Yang Kang rushed to help him up. Wan-yan Honglie glanced quickly around the cave, assessing the situation.

"Master Ouyang," he cried, "can you get rid of the boy?"

It was a considered tactic. If he begged or ordered, Viper Ouyang might ignore him. A gentle prod, framed as a question, would be more effective, he judged. And he was right.

"Of course I can." Viper squatted, then jumped up with a grunt, both hands extended, in a perfect display of Exploding Toad.

Toads spend long periods hibernating in the mud, building up the nutrients in their body and storing their strength. Once out of the mud, they do not need to eat much. Viper Ouyang's Exploding Toad kung fu followed a similar principle: the greatest part of the work came in gathering the strength before the move. Once launched, it was nigh on impossible to stop, even for those with far greater inner strength. The move was the result of a lifelong cultivation of qi, and not even Count Seven or Apothecary Huang would be able to block it, so what hope did Guo Jing have?

Viper Ouyang had observed the subtleties and exquisite variations in Guo Jing's Luminous Hollow Fist and assumed that this must result from the teachings contained within the Nine Yin Manual. He desired nothing more than to see the moves up close so that he might imbibe as much as he could. Unfortunately, not only had they been interrupted by Wanyan Honglie, but the Sixth Prince had also questioned his skills, thus provoking him into using his most vicious move. Yet Guo Jing was useful to him, he did not want to harm the boy, so he decided at the last moment to pull it back.

Guo Jing, however, was determined to safeguard Yue Fei's writing, even if it cost him his life. He realized that calling on guards to help him would be of little use—how could they hope to overwhelm a master of the *wulin* and his associates? He watched as Viper Ouyang came flying toward him. It was a ferocious move, he could tell, and he would not be able to block it. With a tap of both feet, he flew up into the air, making sure to land so that he was still blocking the mouth of the cave.

He heard a crash and felt a shudder as rocks and sand fell around him. Viper Ouyang had smashed into the cave wall.

"Excellent!" Viper called out, and, riding on the force of the last move, launched straight into a second.

Guo Jing felt a rush of air swallow him. He knew he was in serious danger now. He launched into Thunder Rocks a Hundred Miles, one of the most powerful moves in the Dragon-Subduing Palm repertoire. This time, he was choosing to meet firm with firm. For a moment, they were both perfectly still. But a moment was long enough for Guo Jing to sense that his inner strength was no match for Viper's. He would be defeated; there was no other way.

Wanyan Honglie watched the two men fight, leap, and dodge. One leaped up, another crouched down, until suddenly they were both stiff, like corpses. Not even their hands trembled. It was as if they had stopped breathing. A strange sight indeed.

Guo Jing was drenched in sweat, and Viper Ouyang could see the fight would result in injury for the young man if it continued. He considered yielding, and indeed softened his stance, but, as soon as he did so, Guo Jing leaned in with as yet untapped strength and pressed against his chest. The move surprised him, even if he was strong enough to avoid injury. The boy had great strength in his palms for such a raw fighter. Viper took a deep breath and launched a counterattack. If he added just a little force, he would be able to knock the boy off his feet or even kill him. But this youth was the key to accessing the profound erudition contained within the pages of the Nine Yin Manual. He would instead wait for the young man to exhaust his powers, and then he would capture him, unharmed.

Wanyan Honglie and Yang Kang watched, wondering how long the two men would continue their fight. For all they knew, only moments had passed, but, as the lamplight brightened on the other side of the waterfall and the cries of the guards grew louder, it felt as though they had been waiting for a very long time indeed.

Suddenly, they heard a loud noise, and two guards burst through the sheet of water. Yang Kang leaped up and punched his fingers through their skulls. Nine Yin Skeleton Claw. The stench of blood assailed their nostrils. Yang Kang drew a dagger from his boot and launched himself at Guo Jing's abdomen.

Already occupied with holding back the Venom, Guo Jing had

no way to defend himself. Either he be undone by Viper's Exploding Toad kung fu, or by the dagger. A sharp pain surged from his flank, his breath caught and all he could do was punch down at Yang Kang's hand.

Guo Jing's fist struck Yang Kang's wrist, almost cracking the bone. Yang Kang quickly pulled back, but his dagger had already half-penetrated Guo Jing's flesh. At precisely this moment, the force of the Exploding Toad made itself felt against Guo Jing's chest, and, with barely a grunt, he fell to the ground.

"What a pity," Viper Ouyang muttered, realizing that he had hurt the boy. He would most probably never recover. The Venom turned away. It would be better to go looking for Yue Fei's writings. He glared at Yang Kang. You have done me great harm, he thought. Then he strode into the cave. Wanyan Honglie and Yang Kang followed.

The palace guards came rushing forward. Without turning, Viper reached behind him, grabbed them one by one as they came at him, and threw them aside.

Yang Kang, meanwhile, waved his torch around the cave and examined it. It was covered in a thick layer of dust. It seemed as if no one had entered in a very long time. A small stone table occupied the center of the space, on top of which had been placed a square marble box. A piece of paper had been pasted over the seal. Other than these two items, the cave was empty.

Yang Kang edged closer, to take a better look. The characters written on the paper were too faded for him to make out.

"It must be in there," Wanyan Honglie announced.

Yang Kang grinned and reached for the box. At that moment, Viper gently shunted the boy aside with his shoulder, causing him to stumble and then fall. To Yang Kang's surprise, Viper then took the box.

"Well done, we have it! Everyone out!" Wanyan Honglie cried.

Viper led the three men out of the cave.

Yang Kang saw Guo Jing's lifeless, bloodied body lying just outside the entrance. A brief moment of remorse came over him. "It's your fault for meddling where you're not wanted," he muttered under his breath. "We may be sworn brothers, but you have brought this on yourself."

Remembering his dagger was still lodged in Guo Jing's flesh, he stooped down to retrieve it, just as a figure appeared on the other side of the veil of water.

"Guo Jing! Where are you?"

Yang Kang recognized the voice: Lotus. Startled, he jumped over Guo Jing's body and ran out the opposite side of the waterfall to catch up with Viper Ouyang.

8

LOTUS HAD BEEN RUNNING ACROSS THE ROOFTOPS, PURSUED by Tiger Peng and Graybeard Liang, but, as soon as the guards started to arrive, the two men retreated to the waterfall to wait with the others for Wanyan Honglie to emerge. Together, they had killed a few more guards that had tried to enter while Viper Ouyang was inside the cave.

Worried, Lotus returned to look for Guo Jing. She ventured into the darkness and called his name, but received no answer. She lit a torch in order to see better. Glancing down at her feet, she saw him. Covered in blood. The sight was a jolt to her system. Her hands shook so badly she dropped the torch. It clattered to the floor and went out.

Yet more guards were approaching now, calling to each other to catch the intruder. They were scared by the sight of so many fallen comrades, but they had to make a display of their loyalty to the imperial family.

Lotus knelt down and took Guo Jing in her arms. His hands were still warm, she was relieved to discover. She called his name, but he did not answer. She would have to carry him. Quietly, she picked him up and slipped out through the waterfall, then up and down the other side of the miniature mountain.

By this time, the sheer number of lanterns surrounding the pavilion made it as bright as if the sun had been high in the sky. By the look of it, every guard in the palace complex had arrived on the scene. Lotus was quick, but not even she could get past so many of them undetected. Someone caught sight of her, and the cry went up.

You useless pustules, you should be chasing the real villains, not me, she thought to herself.

Gritting her teeth with the weight, she started running as fast as she could. A few of the guards trained in martial arts gave chase, so she threw a handful of needles behind her. *Aiya!* The other guards heard the cries and did not dare follow. Instead, they watched helplessly as, still carrying Guo Jing, she jumped over the palace walls and out into the city.

The palace was in a tumult. Was it a coup? Someone trying to usurp the imperial throne? Officials inciting a rebellion? The imperial army was as frightened as the guards, but no one knew what was happening. For the rest of the night, there was no rest inside the palace walls. At daybreak, they sent out cavalry to search the city. They managed to round up a considerable number of "rebels" and "assassins," only to discover that they were merely petty thieves and had not been involved in the previous night's disturbances. They could not return with nothing to show for their efforts, however. They had no choice but to fabricate some confessions and execute a few of the delinquents before returning to the palace to report their findings, thus saving their own necks.

Once clear of the palace walls, Lotus ran without knowing where she was going. She picked her way through the city at random, hoping to throw off any potential pursuers. At last, certain she was not being followed, she turned into a small, dark alley, where she reached to feel for Guo Jing's breath. He was breathing, luckily, but she had lost her torch in the palace and it was too dark to examine the extent of his wounds. The city gates were closed at this hour, but she was worried that he would not make it through the night if she did not carry him to safety, so she began to trace the length of the city walls, looking for an opening. Eventually, she found a narrow gap, allowing her to squeeze through and rush to the run-down inn in the desolate village outside Lin'an. No one would think of searching for the intruders to the palace in that forgotten place.

She shunted the door open and, gasping for breath, placed Guo Jing down. She then took a seat. Before she could get her breath back, however, she was up again, lighting a fire. She took a torch from the blaze and approached Guo Jing.

What she saw shocked her even more than discovering him injured, back in the palace.

Guo Jing's eyes were screwed tight shut, his cheeks were blanched and his breathing labored. Lotus had seen him injured before, but never as badly as this. It felt as if her heart was beating in her throat. She stood over him, clutching the torch, overwhelmed by the extent of his wounds.

At that moment, a hand reached out and took the torch from her. Lotus turned slowly. It was the Qu girl.

Lotus took a few deep breaths. Having another person by her side gave her courage, but, just as she was about to examine Guo Jing's wounds more closely, the light from the torch caught on something dark protruding from his abdomen. It was the ebony hilt of a dagger.

A sudden calm descended over her. Gently, she pulled away the clothes around the dagger to reveal his skin. The blood around the weapon had coagulated. The blade was sunk a few inches into his flesh. Would pulling it out kill him instantly? But the longer she waited, the harder it would be to save him. She clenched her jaw, reached out, then pulled her hand back. She repeated this sequence several times. What should she do?

The Qu girl was becoming impatient. After Lotus pulled back a fourth time, she reached out, grabbed the hilt and yanked the blade free. Guo Jing and Lotus yelped. But the girl merely laughed.

Blood began pouring forth from the wound, like a freshwater spring. The girl was still laughing, and Lotus's shock turned to anger. She struck out with her palm and the girl tumbled into a somersault. Then Lotus grabbed some cloth and pressed it against Guo Jing's abdomen to stanch the flow.

Dropped in their scuffle, the torch went out and all was black. Furious, the girl aimed a kick at Lotus, who did not move, allowing it to connect with her leg. Scared that Lotus might retaliate, the Qu girl ran out.

Outside, she waited and listened. All she could hear were Lotus's quiet sobs. She fetched another torch, lit it and approached. "Did I hurt you?"

The pain as the dagger had been pulled out was enough to wake Guo Jing. He looked up and, in the dim torchlight, saw Lotus kneeling beside him. "The General's writings . . . Did . . . they get them?"

Lotus was overcome with relief at hearing him speak. But, given his condition, she did not dare tell him the truth. "Don't worry, they didn't get their hands on them . . ." But, seeing her hands covered in blood, she felt a lump in her throat choke off the words.

"Why are you crying?" he asked her.

"I'm not crying," Lotus said with forced brightness.

"She is crying," the Qu girl interrupted. "Look. Her face is covered in tears."

"Don't worry, Lotus. The Nine Yin Manual has a whole section on how to treat injuries like mine. I won't die."

These words were like a shaft of light penetrating the darkness. Lotus's eyes twinkled. She turned to the girl and took her hand. "Sister, did I hurt you, just now?"

But the Qu girl was still absorbed by the question of Lotus's tears. "You were crying. Admit it."

Lotus smiled. "Yes, I was crying. You didn't cry. That makes you better than me."

The praise delighted the girl.

Guo Jing, meanwhile, was trying to move the *qi* around his body, but the pain was unbearable. Lotus had made up her mind. She took out one of her steel needles and began to insert it at various pressure points above and below the wound, both to stave the flow of blood and to reduce the pain. Then she cleaned the wound, sprinkled some blood-clotting powder on it and wrapped it in a bandage. She also gave him a Dew of Nine Flowers pill to relieve what remained of the pain.

"I've been lucky," Guo Jing began. "The dagger may have gone deep, but . . . but . . . it didn't hit any organs. I won't die. I think Viper's Exploding Toad could have done more damage. But he didn't use all his strength. I think I will get better. Only, I might have to trouble you for seven days and seven nights."

"Seven years would be no burden if it saves you. You know I'll do it happily."

A sugary rush filled his heart, making his head feel light. He paused for a few moments to calm himself before speaking again: "It's just a pity that the Venom and his nephew were there on the island when *Shifu* was injured. I could have helped him, instead of worrying about them all the time. He wouldn't be . . . permanently affected, like he is now."

"We'll use the same method for you as the one you described on the island?"

"Yes. First, we must find somewhere quiet. Then, we must circulate our *qi* together, just as the Manual describes. We place our palms together and your internal energy will help to heal me." At this point, Guo Jing paused to catch his breath before continuing. "The only hard part is that during each circulation we must keep our palms touching for seven whole days and seven whole nights. Our inner energy, our breathing must become as one. We can talk, but we cannot have anyone else interrupt us. And we most definitely cannot get up to leave. If someone does come . . ."

It was much like the meditative process that was used for cultivating inner strength, Lotus realized. It had to be done uninterrupted, otherwise the heart and mind would become unsettled and all martial powers would be drained, resulting in serious injury, if not death. That was why martial artists would look for secluded spots at the top of mountains or in the wilderness, or else would lock their doors and not come out. Some even enlisted the help of a strong friend, in case things went wrong.

But where can we find such a quiet place? Lotus thought. I am the only one who can help. We cannot rely on this foolish girl to guard us from any external interference. Indeed, there is more risk that she will interrupt us herself. If only Brother Zhou were back. But then he would hardly be capable of sustaining seven days and seven nights of concentration. If I cannot guarantee success, I might bring more damage upon dear Guo Jing. What should I do?

Lotus was quiet for a moment, lost in thought. Then an idea hit her. Of course! We can hide in the secret room. Cyclone Mei managed to practice her dark arts by herself. And she too hid in a secret, underground chamber.

Dawn was breaking. The Qu girl went to the kitchen to make some congee.

"Guo Jing," Lotus whispered. "Wait here. I'm going to buy supplies and, when I come back, we can start at once."

In the hot weather, rice and cooked dishes would spoil, even if left in the dark room, so she went to buy one hundred *jin* of watermelon. The farmer helped deliver the load to the inn, where they were placed in a heap on the floor. "We are proud of our watermelon, here, in Ox Village," he said, taking the money. "They are crisp and sweet. One taste and you will surely agree, young miss."

Ox Village? Lotus's heart skipped a beat. This is where Guo Jing's family came from. He must not find out, not until he is stronger. She made a brief reply and escorted the farmer back outside.

When Lotus went to check on Guo Jing, he was sleeping. She checked his bandage, which was still clean.

She approached the cupboard and twisted the metal bowl to open the doors to the secret chamber. Then she started carrying the melons inside, one by one. The only thing that remained was to work out what to do with the girl. Lotus explained to her repeatedly that she must not let anyone know they were there, no matter what was happening outside. Whatever she did, she must not call for them.

The young woman did not understand, but she could detect the seriousness with which the instructions were being given, so she nodded a firm promise. "You want to eat your watermelon in peace, in case someone steals them, and, once you have finished, you'll come out again. I understand. Silly girl won't tell."

"Silly girl won't tell. Good girl," Lotus said. "If you tell, silly girl will be a bad girl."

"Silly girl won't tell. Silly girl is a good girl," she insisted.

Lotus proceeded to feed Guo Jing a bowl of congee, and then she too filled her stomach, before helping him hobble into the dark chamber. As she was about to close the door, Lotus looked up and saw the girl's blank expression. She was watching without comprehension.

"Silly girl won't tell."

Lotus felt a pang in her heart. What a foolish young girl. What if, the first person she sees, she says, "They're in the secret room, eating watermelons. Silly girl won't tell"? The only way to make sure we are safe is to kill her.

Lotus had grown up under a father who cared little for traditional ideas of justice, good and evil. The girl had some kind of close relationship to her martial brother, Tempest Qu, she knew this, but she was also a real and present danger. If there were ten of these silly girls, she would kill them all.

She took the dagger from Guo Jing's belt and stepped back into the room.

CHAPTER FIVE

IN THE SECRET CHAMBER

I

LOTUS ONLY MANAGED TWO STEPS BEFORE TURNING TO glance back at Guo Jing. She was met with a look of suspicion. It was as if he had read the murderous intent on her face.

Killing her isn't essential, Lotus thought. And Guo Jing would be very upset with me. This got her thinking. It would be no simple matter to make amends. He might not just be upset with me; he might hate me forever. Maybe he won't say anything for years, decades, but instead carry the feeling in his heart. No, it's not worth it. We'll just have to take the risk.

She closed the door again and looked around the chamber. In the western corner, there was a small skylight of only a foot square, allowing light to filter through. The paper window pane was caked in dust, but it did at least mean they could just about see around them. The air holes were clogged, so Lotus cleaned them with the tip of the dagger. The small, stuffy chamber was filled with a foul, musty smell, but, considering the danger they were in, it was the best they could do.

Guo Jing leaned against the wall and smiled. "This is perfect. Only . . . we are joined by two dead bodies. Does that scare you?"

In her heart, Lotus did feel a little afraid, but she was determined not to show it. "One was my martial brother; he won't harm me. The other was a good-for-nothing official. I wouldn't have been scared of him when he was alive, let alone as a ghost." She proceeded to move the skeletons into the northern corner of the room, setting them down side by side. Then she spread out the rice straw that had come with the watermelons and laid a dozen or so of them in a circle on top of it. "What do you think?"

"Excellent. We can start."

Lotus led him over to the straw and sat him down. She then settled down to his left and crossed her legs. She looked up and spotted a small hole in the wall, the size of a coin. She peered through and, to her delight, discovered a mirror on the other side, which reflected a view of the room beyond. Whoever built this secret chamber had planned it carefully. They could see what was going on outside, even when hiding inside. Unfortunately, the mirror too was covered in a thick layer of dust. She wrapped a handkerchief around her finger, poked it through the hole and rubbed it clean.

The Qu girl was sitting on the floor, throwing stones. Her lips were moving, but Lotus could not make out what she was saying. She placed her ear to the hole; now, she could hear. The girl was singing a lullaby. Lotus found it funny at first, but, the longer she listened, the more her heart stirred. Had the girl's mother sung the same song for her when she was a baby? If my mother . . . hadn't died so young, maybe she would have sung it for me, too. Her eyes were wet.

"What's the matter?" Guo Jing said. "Don't be upset—I'll recover."

Lotus quickly wiped her eyes. "Come, teach me how to do this."

Guo Jing dutifully began reciting the relevant section of the Nine Yin Manual once again.

There was a saying in the *wulin:* "Before you punch, you must first learn to take a punch." That was the most fundamental thing for any student—how to stop yourself from getting seriously injured. This could involve sophisticated techniques to aid recovery, including the unlocking of pressure points, the setting of broken bones or the drawing of poison from wounds. But the chapter "On Treating Wounds" in the Nine Yin Manual was aimed at masters of the martial arts and focused on the restorative power of deep-breathing exercises. It assumed any reader would already know how to deal with external injuries like fractures and cuts.

Lotus only needed to hear the passage once to memorize it. There were, however, several sections in which the meaning was unclear and needed to be discussed. Luckily, what Guo Jing lacked in intelligence, he made up for in years of practice in the principles of Quanzhen kung fu, so, together, they were able to make out most of it.

Lotus reached out her right palm and connected with Guo Jing's left. Together, they started to move the *qi* around their bodies, just as the Manual described. The injured party used their breathing to dislodge any blockages, while the accomplice added their own *qi* when needed.

Four hours later, having managed several full circulations, they separated their palms for a short rest. Lotus took up the dagger and cut one of the watermelons into slices, feeding some to Guo Jing and then to herself. Then they began again. After a few hours, Guo Jing began to feel the tightness in his chest ease. Lotus's warm *qi* began to flow through his veins and pressure points. The pain in his abdomen also started to let up. The techniques described in the Manual were truly amazing. He would follow them to the letter.

By the time they took their third break, the light coming through the small skylight was noticeably dimmer. Outside, the sun was setting, and already Guo Jing's chest was feeling less constricted. Lotus, meanwhile, was also feeling invigorated.

They chatted briefly, but, just as they were about to start up again, they heard the pounding of footsteps, which stopped outside the inn door. Then came the sound of several people bursting inside.

"Bring us food! We're starving!"

Guo Jing and Lotus looked at each other in shock. They recognized the gruff voice. It was Hector Sha.

Lotus got up quickly and peered through the small hole. Not only could she see Hector Sha, but also Wanyan Honglie, Yang Kang, Viper Ouyang, Tiger Peng . . . They were all there.

Hector Sha slapped his hand down on the table, but no one came. Where was the girl?

Graybeard Liang reappeared after looking through the different rooms. "The place is abandoned," he said, frowning.

Hector Sha volunteered to go into the village and buy food. Viper Ouyang had already spread out some straw in a corner; now, he carried his nephew over, so that he might rest and recover.

"Those palace guards may be useless," Tiger Peng began, "but their heinous influence seems to extend in every direction. We haven't eaten all day. Your Majesty, you're from the north, and yet you knew about this isolated village and could lead us here. Such knowledge really is remarkable."

Yet Wanyan Honglie did not look in the least pleased to receive this compliment. He sighed briefly before speaking. "I first came here nineteen years ago."

Everyone noticed the pained look on his face. It puzzled them, for they did not know that this was where Charity Bao had saved his life. The village was as desolate now as it had been then. But he would never again see that beautiful girl dressed in plain green robes, with a hairpin in her hair, who had fed him chicken soup.

At this point, Hector Sha returned with wine and food. Tiger Peng poured a draft for everyone and then turned to Wanyan Honglie. "Your Majesty, the Sixth Prince, today you succeeded in obtaining General Yue Fei's last writings—surely a sign, if ever there was one, that the Great Jin will soon triumph over the world, bringing ten thousand lands under your dominion. May we all offer our sincerest congratulations!" He raised his cup, then swallowed its contents in one.

His voice had been so loud that even Guo Jing could hear him, through the wall. General Yue's writings have fallen into their hands? The shock went through him, undoing the effects of the day's training in an instant. Lotus could feel her palm trembling. She could sense that he had heard everything and that the news had affected his *qi*. If she did not act, he could come to great danger. She leaned closer and put her lips to his ear.

"They may have got hold of it, but we can always steal it back. Your second *shifu* Quick Hands Zhu Cong could steal ten books, if he wanted," she whispered.

Indeed, Guo Jing thought. He closed his eyes and shut out the voices on the other side of the wall.

Lotus once again put her eye to the spyhole. This time, she saw Wanyan Honglie raise his cup and drink from it. "You have all worked hard to secure this victory, but, above all, Master Ouyang must be praised for his role. Had he not dealt with the Guo boy, it would have been much more difficult."

Viper Ouyang's laugh clanged like crashing cymbals. Guo Jing heard it and a shiver shot through his heart.

Heavens above, please protect us, Lotus thought. Don't let the Venom start plucking his devil's zither, or else Guo Jing's life will be in grave danger.

"There is no way the Song army will find us here," Viper Ouyang said. "I confess, I am curious about these writings of the General. Why don't we all take a look?"

He removed the marble box from his robes and placed it on the table. If the writings did indeed contain passages relating to the martial arts, he would take them for himself. If they were concerned merely with military strategy, then he would have no use for them and would happily let Wanyan Honglie take them.

Everyone gathered round. Lotus was also watching. What can I do? It would be better to destroy it completely than let it fall into the hands of these traitors.

"I have made a comprehensive analysis of the General's poetry,"

Wanyan Honglie began, "as well as official documents and records from previous dynasties as relating to the construction of imperial palaces, which is how I came to deduce its location, fifteen steps east of the Hall of Wintry Jade. I was proved right. I do not believe anyone in the Song court was aware of the treasure hidden in their palace. Therefore, I don't think they will have realized what the commotion last night was about."

He was clearly proud of himself, and the men gathered in the inn understood that this was their opportunity to heap yet more praise on the Prince.

"Son," the Sixth Prince continued, twisting his mustache, "open the box."

Yang Kang stepped forward, ripped the paper that covered the seal, and opened the lid. Everyone crowded forward and peered inside. Immediately, their faces fell, and no one dared to speak.

The box was empty.

Lotus could not see inside it, but she understood just from their expressions. She watched in great amusement.

Wanyan Honglie reached out to clutch the edge of the table, sat down and placed his head in his hands. All this time spent making plans, deciphering texts—all of which suggested the writings would be in that box. How can they have suddenly disappeared?

Just then, a smile broke across his face. He took the box and went out to the courtyard, where he threw it against the stone slabs, breaking it into hundreds of small pieces.

He thinks there is a secret compartment, Lotus thought at once. She wished she could see, but she could not risk going outside. Moments later, however, she had her answer, as Wanyan Honglie entered, his face as glum as before.

"There was a secret part to the box. But it too was empty," he said as he sat down.

The others took turns offering their ideas. Lotus listened to their outrageous summations and could not help but feel amused. She related the events to Guo Jing, who was relieved to hear that the Prince did not have the writings, after all.

Not that these traitors will give up so easily, Lotus thought. They will go back to the palace tonight. Lotus and Guo Jing's *shifu*, Count Seven Hong, was still inside and he could be implicated. The Hoary Urchin was there to protect him, but he was erratic and could not be trusted to deal with things in the right way.

"We can go back to the palace tonight and keep looking." Just as she had guessed. It was Viper Ouyang who was first to make this suggestion.

"Not tonight," Wanyan Honglie replied. "The palace will be on alert, after the disturbance we made."

"We can't avoid the guards, that much is true," Viper continued, "but why worry about them? His Majesty and the young Prince can rest here, along with my nephew."

Wanyan Honglie cupped his hands. "Master is most kind. I will remain here, awaiting your good news."

At this, everyone spread out straw and lay down to sleep.

2

AFTER A MERE TWO HOURS OF SLEEP, VIPER OUYANG WOKE the men and together they set off in the direction of the city.

Wanyan Honglie, meanwhile, tossed and turned. Around midnight, he heard the sound of the rising tide along the Qiantang River. A dog started barking at the other end of the village. It sounded like wails of distress, which only added to his anxiety.

Hours later, he heard footsteps outside. Someone was coming. He sat up and drew his sword. Yang Kang was already at the door, waiting. A pool of moonlight collected on the floor. The door opened and in stepped a bedraggled young woman.

She had been out in the forest all this time. The sight of people sleeping in her room did not trouble her. Instead, she walked over to where the firewood was piled up, found a patch of floor to lie down on and was soon snoring loudly.

A simple country girl, Yang Kang thought. He smiled and went back to sleep. Wanyan Honglie's mind, however, was racing. He got up, took a candle from his bag and lit it. Then he took out a book and started flipping through its pages.

Lotus saw the light through the small hole in the wall. She leaned in to take a look, but all she could see was a moth dancing around the candle. Suddenly, it threw itself into the flame, scorching its wings, before falling onto the tabletop. Wanyan Honglie picked it up. "If only Lady Bao were here, she would make you right again." He then removed a small silver knife from inside his robes, as well as a bottle of herbs, and stroked them affectionately.

Lotus tapped Guo Jing on the shoulder and then moved aside so that he might take a look. Guo Jing watched, rage swelling in his chest. He vaguely recognized the blade and the bottle as belonging to Yang Kang's mother, Charity Bao. He had seen her using them when she was tending to the injured rabbit in the Zhao residence.

"Nineteen years ago," Wanyan Honglie began to murmur. "In this very village." He rose to his feet with a sigh, picked up the candle and went outside.

The implication of what he had just heard hit Guo Jing hard. Could this be his true home? Ox Village? He pressed his lips to Lotus's ear to ask her. Lotus merely nodded. Guo Jing felt his blood bubble and his body shake.

As Lotus's right palm was still touching Guo Jing's left, she could sense the agitation in his *qi*. This was dangerous. She reached for his other palm and together they started to try to calm his beating heart.

After what felt like a long time, a shaft of light flickered through the hole as they heard Wanyan Honglie sigh and enter the inn once again. By now, Guo Jing's heart and mind were at peace. He peered out.

Wanyan Honglie was sitting in the candlelight, as if in a trance, clutching several pieces of broken tile and brick in his hands.

This traitor is only ten steps away, Guo Jing was thinking. All I would need to do to kill him is throw my dagger.

He drew from his waistband the golden blade Genghis Khan had given him, and whispered to Lotus, "Open the door."

"No!" Lotus hissed. "Killing him may be easy, but then our hiding place will be revealed."

"But I don't know where he will be in six days and six nights," he replied with a tremble in his voice.

Lotus knew he would not be easily persuaded, so she leaned close to his ear and whispered, "Both your mother and I want you alive."

Guo Jing slowly nodded and replaced the dagger in its sheath. He then pressed his eye to the hole once more. Wanyan Honglie was asleep, slumped over the table. At that moment, he saw someone rise from the bed of straw. Light fell on their profile, but it was difficult to make out who it was by way of the dusty mirror. Guo Jing watched as the figure walked over to Wanyan Honglie, took the silver knife and medicine bottle, examined them and then placed them gently back on the table. The figure turned to face Guo Jing, and that was when he saw who it was. Yang Kang.

Now is your chance to avenge the death of your parents, Guo Jing said to himself, willing Yang Kang to hear his thoughts. Stab him. Then you will never have to breathe the same air ever again. You won't get another chance like this. The Old Venom and the others will return soon.

He watched anxiously to see if his sworn brother would make a move. But, after replacing the items on the table, Yang Kang blew out the candle. For a moment, all was black, until Guo Jing gradually managed to make out some vague shapes by what remained of the moonlight. He watched as Yang Kang removed his robe and draped it over Wanyan Honglie's shoulders. This only infuriated Guo Jing even more. He could not bear to watch. How could Yang Kang treat the man who killed his parents with such tenderness?

"There, there," Lotus whispered. "Once you're better, we can chase these traitors to the ends of the earth. He is no Viper Ouyang, after all. He isn't going to be that hard to kill."

Guo Jing nodded and they went back to their practice.

Before long, dawn arrived and the sound of roosters crowing filled the air. They had now circulated their *qi* seven times in total and were feeling more at ease.

"One day gone!" Lotus said with a smile, holding up her index finger.

"And a dangerous one at that," Guo Jing said quietly. "If it weren't for you, I wouldn't have kept my focus and surely would have made things worse."

"We have six more days and six more nights left. You did promise to obey my instructions."

"I always obey you," Guo Jing said with a silent laugh.

Lotus cocked her head. "Is that so?"

At that moment, a shaft of light came piercing through the skylight, casting her cheeks in a pinkish morning glow. Suddenly, her palms felt warm and tender. Something stirred in Guo Jing's chest, but he chased the thought away, though his cheeks were already flushed a dark crimson.

Guo Jing had never had such thoughts in all the time they had spent together, and they shocked him. Silently, he rebuked himself.

Lotus noticed his blushing cheeks and she too felt something was different. "What's the matter?"

"I've been very bad. I . . . I . . . had a thought." His voice was quiet.

"What thought?"

"It's gone now."

"What was it?" Lotus pressed.

"I thought of taking you in my arms. Of kissing you."

A warm feeling like syrup flowed inside her, and now her cheeks too were red. She looked so bashful, and even lovelier than usual.

Lotus lowered her gaze and did not reply.

"Lotus, are you angry? I know that having such a thought makes me just as bad as Gallant Ouyang."

Lotus looked up and smiled. "I'm not angry," she said gently. "I was thinking that, one day, you'll do just that—take me in your arms and kiss me—because I will be your wife."

Her reply filled his heart with joy, but he could not speak.

"Was it so awful to think of kissing me?" Lotus continued, softly.

At that moment, the sound of footsteps outside interrupted them and two men came bursting into the inn.

"Damn it! I told you . . . I told you there were ghosts, but you . . . wouldn't believe me!" It was Browbeater Hou. He was so agitated, he could barely speak.

Hector Sha replied, "Ghosts? What are you talking about? That was a man of the *wulin*!"

Lotus peered out and saw Browbeater's face covered in blood, while Hector's robes were ripped. They must have been in a fight.

Rudely awakened, Wanyan Honglie and Yang Kang looked up at the two men in surprise. They began to ask questions.

"It was a ghost, I'm certain," Browbeater Hou began. "He cut my ears off!"

His cheeks were indeed covered in blood. Wanyan Honglie looked closer and was astonished to see that he had no ears.

"A ghost? Don't you know how ridiculous you sound?" Hector Sha shook his head.

Browbeater Hou feared his martial brother, but he was insistent. "I saw him with my own eyes! His were blue, and he had a red beard, just like the divine Judge of the Underworld. He said, 'Waaaaaa!' I turned, he grabbed my neck and, the next thing I knew, my ears were sliced right off! He looked just like the Judge in the temple—how could it not be him?"

Hector Sha had managed only three moves against the Judge before his clothes were ripped to shreds, and thus he knew this was a master of the *wulin*, not a ghost. But his strange appearance was still a puzzle.

The four men continued to speculate, and even went as far as to ask Gallant Ouyang, who was still recovering from his injuries in the corner. But nobody had a sensible explanation to offer.

As the others were talking, Lama Supreme Wisdom, Tiger Peng, and Graybeard Liang arrived back, one after the other. The lama's hands had been chained behind his back and Tiger Peng's cheeks were swollen black and blue. But, of all of them, Graybeard Liang's appearance was the most amusing: every last white hair on his head had been plucked out, leaving his scalp clean and shiny, like a monk's. Why, it was almost as shiny as Hector Sha's.

After entering the Imperial Palace, they had spread out to search for General Yue's book. But they had all encountered what seemed to be ghosts, though each was different. One fought with the Messenger of Death, one with the divine Judge of the Underworld, and one with the Earth God.

Graybeard Liang stroked his smooth scalp and cursed every goddess in heaven. The shackles dug into the monk's flesh. Tiger Peng silently worked on releasing the lama from his chains, scraping his hands and wrists bloody from the effort.

They all exchanged glances, but no one spoke. They had encountered a master fighter, that was clear, but the humiliation was too much to bear. Browbeater Hou continued to insist it was a ghost, and the others had no heart to argue with him.

There was a long pause until Wanyan Honglie spoke. "Why hasn't Master Ouyang returned? Maybe he too encountered one of these creatures."

"Master Ouyang's abilities are unparalleled throughout the *wulin*," Yang Kang said. "He wouldn't be defeated by a phantom."

This only made the others feel even more aggrieved.

Lotus, meanwhile, was regarding the scene with amusement. *Those masks I bought for Brother Zhou turned out to be more useful than I ever imagined. I wonder if he came across the Venom.*

At that moment, she felt Guo Jing's internal energy pulse through her palms, so she turned her attention back to him.

Tiger Peng and the others were hungry after a night of fighting, so they began to chop firewood, and some went to buy rice. When breakfast was ready, Browbeater Hou went to the cupboard to find some bowls. He reached for the metal one, but of course it was stuck down. "A ghost!" he cried, tugging at it with all his internal strength.

Lotus understood at once what was happening. They could not allow anyone to find them. Guo Jing's life depended on it. But what could they do?

As she was trying to think of a plan, she heard Hector Sha scolding his martial brother again. But Browbeater Hou ref̲ ̲ admit he was wrong. "Fine—you try to move ̲ ̲"

Hector Sha grasped the bo̲ ̲uck. Tiger Peng then approached to̲ ̲

"Looks like there's a secret ̲ ̲ it left or right."

They did not have much time̲ ̲ Jing and took Count Seven's ba̲ ̲ whispered to Guo Jing that he w̲ ̲ way, they could disconnect their p̲ ̲aker even than someone with no martial-a̲ ̲e could not fight these men. The realization that deatn was near for both of them turned Lotus's heart cold.

Looking around in vain for another way out, she glanced into the corner of the room and spotted the skeletons. That was it! She ran over and picked out the two skulls. Then she collected a watermelon and pressed the skulls into it.

Seconds later, a creaking sound. The metal door opened.

Lotus placed her creation on top of her head and covered her face with her hair.

Hector Sha appeared in the doorway and was greeted by the most frightful two-headed monster imaginable.

The others peered inside from behind him. Browbeater Hou screamed, turned and ran outside. The others followed. Only Gallant Ouyang remained on his straw bed, unable to move.

Lotus sighed and closed the door. A smile crept over her face, but she did not dare hope they would be left alone for long. These were the best fighters of the *jianghu;* they would be back. The Hoary Urchin had done the heavy work; without his antics at the palace, she could not have fooled them so easily.

Lotus was still racking her brains for a solution to their predicament when she heard the door to the inn open. She grabbed the dagger and placed the bamboo cane by her side. If anyone tried to enter again, she would throw the blade in their face.

She waited.

"Hello! Innkeeper?" The voice was delicate and sweet.

Surprised, Lotus ran to the hole and peered through. There, she saw a lady dressed in finely embroidered brocade, her hair decorated with jewels. She was clearly the daughter of a very wealthy family, but she had her back to the mirror, so Lotus could not see her face.

"Innkeeper! Innkeeper!" she tried again.

Where do I know that voice from? Lotus thought. Before she had time to search her memory, the woman turned. Miss Cheng from Baoying! What is she doing here?

3

THE QU GIRL HAD BARELY STIRRED DURING THE COMMOTION earlier, keeping her eyes firmly closed throughout, but now she opened them and crawled out of her straw bed in the corner.

"Ah, there you are," Miss Cheng said. "I would like something to eat. My warmest thanks."

The girl shook her head, as if to say that she had nothing to offer her. But then the smell of freshly made rice wafted into her nostrils. She scuttled over to the pot and lifted the lid. Delighted, she grabbed two bowls and filled one for Miss Cheng and the other for herself. Miss Cheng peered into the bowl: no accompaniments, and, worst of all, the rice was the cheapest unpolished kind. She tried a few mouthfuls before placing it on the table. The girl, meanwhile, finished her third bowl before patting herself contentedly on the stomach.

"Excuse me, miss," Miss Cheng began. "May I ask where we are? How far is it to Ox Village?"

"Ox Village?" the girl repeated. "You're in Ox Village. But I couldn't say how far away it is."

Miss Cheng's cheeks flushed red. She lowered her gaze and fiddled with her waist belt. There was a pause before she spoke again: "This is Ox Village. Then, may I ask . . . do you know . . . someone called . . . ?"

But the girl did not wait for the young woman to finish. Instead, she merely shook her head and ran outside.

Lotus, who had been listening to the whole exchange, wondered who Miss Cheng was looking for. Then it hit her. Miss Cheng was a disciple of one of the Seven Quanzhen Immortals, Sun Bu'er, who was the only woman among them and wife of Scarlet Sun Ma Yu. Miss Cheng must have received an order from the Sect to find Qiu Chuji's protégé, Yang Kang.

Lotus watched her. She was sitting upright, straightening her clothes and fiddling with the pearls in her hair. Her cheeks were rosy and she was smiling just a little, but Lotus could not imagine what she was thinking. She was captivating.

Just then, footsteps, followed by the door opening once more.

It was a tall man with a forceful stride. "Innkeeper!"

Another familiar face! Ox Village seemed to attract everyone she knew, Lotus reflected. Guo Jing's hometown had wonderful feng shui.

The young man who had just walked in was none other than Laurel Lu, master of Roaming Cloud Manor.

He glanced around and was startled to see a beautiful young woman sitting at one of the tables. "Innkeeper!" he called again.

Emerald Cheng looked up at the handsome young man, blushed and turned away.

What is such a dazzling young lady doing here, all by herself? he thought to himself. He walked over to the kitchen, but saw no one. His stomach was aching, so he served himself a bowl of rice and turned to the young woman. "Do excuse me; I am very hungry. I hope miss won't mind."

Emerald smiled without looking up. "It's not mine," she replied quietly. "Please eat, sir."

Laurel Lu ate two bowls, then bowed by way of thanks. "Do excuse me," he began again, "but does miss know how far we are from Ox Village?"

Emerald and Lotus were both equally surprised, not to mention delighted, by his question. Another person looking for Ox Village!

"Why, this *is* Ox Village," Emerald replied, blushing even harder and fiddling with her gown.

"Excellent! And may I trouble the young miss again? I am looking for a certain man, in particular."

Emerald was about to reply that she did not know anyone in the village, but changed her mind at the last moment. "Who is sir looking for?"

"He goes by the name of Guo. Master Guo Jing, to be precise. Do you know which house is his? Or if he might be at home?"

Once again, Emerald and Lotus had the same reaction. Why was he looking for Guo Jing? Emerald did not reply, averting her gaze instead, her cheeks now an almost impossible shade of red.

Judging by Emerald's reaction, Lotus was almost positive that she was in love with Guo Jing—he had saved her in Baoying, after all. But this did not make Lotus feel jealous, for three reasons. She was young, she had an open mind, and—most importantly—she knew Guo Jing was of constant heart. On the contrary, it rather pleased her another woman had such strong feelings for her betrothed.

Lotus was correct, of course. Vigor Li of the Beggar Clan had tried to come to Emerald Cheng's aid while Gallant Ouyang held her captive, but he had been no match for the scoundrel. Had Guo Jing and Lotus not intervened, she would have been disgraced.

Guo Jing was not only a skilled fighter, but also upright and honest by nature. Emerald was the daughter of an extremely wealthy family and thus had never been allowed out of the women's quarters of the family complex. She had barely seen a young man before and was just starting to take an interest in the opposite sex.

After her rescue, Emerald Cheng's days were filled with thoughts of Guo Jing, until, one day, she gathered her courage and left. She knew a little kung fu, but she was almost completely ignorant of the different schools and styles of the *wulin*. All she knew was that Guo Jing came from Ox Village, on the outskirts of Lin'an.

Though she had traveled alone, her journey had passed without incident. She wore her standing clearly in her clothes and bearing, and so those with ignoble intentions let her be. She asked the way as she went, and, in the last village, she found out that she was close. But, when the inn girl confirmed that she was at last in Ox Village, all thoughts of what to do tumbled out of her mind. She had come hundreds of *li*, and yet now she found herself hoping that Guo Jing was not home. I will go to his house under the cover of darkness tonight, look from the outside, and then I will go home, she said to herself. I cannot let him know I have come looking for him. It would be too great a humiliation. At precisely that moment, Laurel Lu had stepped through the door. When he mentioned Guo Jing's name, she wondered if he had read her heart. She paused, then stood up, as if to leave.

Just then, a face—a hideous face—popped through the door, before instantly disappearing. Emerald stumbled backward. The face reappeared.

"Two-headed demon, the Three-Horned Dragon challenges you to a fight! Come outside into the daylight!"

Laurel and Emerald had no idea what was happening.

"They are back," Lotus whispered to Guo Jing. Master Lu and Miss Cheng were not skilled enough fighters to take on Tiger Peng and the others alone. And, should Lotus and Guo Jing come out of hiding to help them, they would still be in danger. She went over the possibilities in her mind, but could not think of a good plan. If it did come to a fight, of course, it would buy her and Guo Jing some time.

Tiger Peng and the others had assumed that the melon demon Lotus had played was part of the band of ghosts and spirits that had chased them the night before. And yet, despite being the only one who really believed they had been spirits rather than masters of the *wulin*, Browbeater Hou was now the only one who dared come back. He was a simpleminded fellow.

These evil demons are stripped of all their powers during daylight, he reasoned. And yet they dare roam the *jianghu*, making trouble? I'm not scared. Once I drive them away, the others will finally give me the respect I deserve.

So he had returned, albeit with some lingering trepidation in his heart. He stuck his head round the door and was surprised to see a young man and a young woman sitting in the middle of the room. Has the demon transformed into two human forms? This is not good. Old Hou, you had better tread carefully.

Laurel and Emerald were baffled, meanwhile. He must be mad. So they decided to ignore him.

Browbeater Hou continued to curse and rave outside, but the demon did not appear. It was clearly afraid of the blazing sun, which was beating down on his scalp. Yet, he was too scared to charge inside the inn and drag the creature outside. So he waited.

Then he remembered spirits were afraid of dirt and contamination. He turned on his heel and left.

There were several stores of manure dotted around the village, including a sizable one right next to the inn. He removed his outer robe and proceeded to scoop a large pile of animal feces into it. Then he went back to the inn.

He peered through the window and saw that Miss Cheng and Master Lu were still seated inside. Now armed, he felt emboldened. "Brave demon! Reveal yourself!" he cried, running for the door with a pitchfork in his left hand and a large piece of dung in his right.

Emerald and Laurel were startled by the madman's reappearance, and by the pungent smell of feces that accompanied him.

Browbeater Hou's eyes darted between the two young people. In human form, men are the most aggressive, he said to himself, but, when it comes to spirits, it's the women one has to watch out for! So, he threw the dung straight at Miss Cheng.

Emerald yelped and ducked. Laurel had already reached for a bench and swung it at the oncoming excrement. With a dull splat, the manure sprayed in all directions, covering the young man. He gasped, trying not to vomit.

"Two-headed demon, unmask yourself!" Raising his pitchfork, Hou charged at Miss Cheng. The attack was quick and fierce.

By now, both Emerald and Laurel could see that this was a man of the *wulin*, not some local lunatic.

To Laurel, Miss Cheng looked to be a delicate daughter of a nobleman, frail and tender, like a flower stalk that could be snapped in the wind. So, he blocked once more with the bench.

"Who are you, sir?"

Browbeater Hou ignored the young man's question and instead jabbed three times with the fork. Laurel parried each thrust with the unwieldy bench, repeating the question as he did so.

Browbeater Hou was puzzled. The demon certainly knew some kung fu, and yet he was using a different style from the one he'd employed the night before. The reason must be his dung attack. "You're asking for my name so you can put a curse on me—admit it, demon! I won't fall for it!"

He had been about to say, "Master Hou won't fall for it!" but stopped himself at the last moment. He intensified his onslaught, the clang of his fork echoing around the small inn.

Laurel's skills were inferior to his opponent, and his only weapon was the large bench. He had a saber hanging from his belt, but found no opportunity to draw it. Each exchange pushed him farther back, until he had his back to the wall, covering the hole through which Lotus was watching.

Browbeater Hou lunged, Laurel Lu ducked sideways, and the metal prongs sunk into the wall, less than a foot from where Lotus was crouching on the other side. Before Browbeater Hou could pull it free, Laurel Lu made to bring the bench down on the old man's head. Hou kicked at Laurel's hand and followed up with a punch. The bench fell and Laurel ducked for cover.

Browbeater Hou yanked the fork from the wall.

The situation was critical. Emerald jumped forward, pulled the saber from Laurel's belt and handed it to him.

"Why, thank you!" Her intervention was a welcome surprise.

Just then, the glint of the oncoming fork caught Laurel's eye. He parried, inches from his chest. Sparks flew. The fork passed by his side, but he felt a pain in his chest. The madman was formidable, but Laurel felt more confident now that he had his saber.

The men continued to fight, their feet slipping in the manure, which by now covered the entire floor.

Browbeater Hou had entered the fight with one eye on the door, in case he needed to escape, but, the more blows they exchanged, the more he understood that the demon was not capable of defeating him. His trick with the dung had worked. He pressed on, putting more power behind his attacks. Laurel Lu was struggling to block them.

Emerald Cheng had retreated to a corner to watch, afraid of getting her clothes soiled. But now she feared the handsome young man was in grave danger. She hesitated, then drew a sword from her pack.

"Young gentleman! I . . . will help. Please excuse me!"

She was polite in the extreme—who apologized for helping?— though she did not wait for a reply before plunging her sword toward Browbeater Hou's chest.

Having studied under Sage of Tranquility, Sun Bu'er, she used the Quanzhen Sect's sword technique. But her excessive courtesy had given Browbeater Hou prior warning. Besides, he had been expecting the female incarnation of the demon to attack the whole time. Laurel Lu, however, was pleasantly surprised once more. She was quick—his heart throbbed with admiration. His own movements had become erratic and he was drenched in sweat, but her intervention gave him new strength.

Browbeater Hou had been dreading the female demon's attack, but, while she was proficient with the sword, there was no real force behind the thrusts. Furthermore, she was noticeably nervous. She had probably not been a demon for long—she was unpracticed. Relieved, he intensified his moves. He knew he had the upper hand, now.

Lotus, meanwhile, was watching anxiously. Miss Cheng and Master Lu were bound to lose, but she could not leave Guo Jing's side. Had she been able to help, she would have outsmarted the Three-Horned Dragon without much effort.

"Miss!" Laurel Lu cried. "Step back, don't put yourself in danger!"

Miss Cheng was grateful for his concern, but she could see that he would not prevail alone. She shook her head and continued to fight.

Laurel Lu changed his tactics. "What kind of hero fights a defenseless young woman!" he cried at Browbeater Hou. "Let me fight you, man to man, and leave the young maiden out of it!"

By this stage, Browbeater Hou had begun to suspect these two might not be incarnations of the demon, after all. But the young miss was dazzling. Why would he let her go?

"But Miss Demon is the greater prize!" he cried, launching his fork at Miss Cheng. He did not put his full force behind the move, however, since he had no wish to injure her.

"Miss, you must leave!" Laurel Lu cried. "I, Master Lu, am most grateful for your assistance thus far, but it's too dangerous."

"Master Lu? Is that your name?" Emerald asked, almost in a whisper.

"Indeed! And what is the young miss called?" Laurel Lu asked, just about managing to keep Browbeater Hou's pitchfork at bay. "To which school do you belong?"

"My *shifu* goes by the name of Sun Bu'er, the Sage of Tranquility," Miss Cheng said. "My . . . my . . ." She could not bear the embarrassment of telling him her name.

"Miss, I'll block him, you run! As long as I'm still alive, I will find you. Many thanks again for your help!"

Emerald blushed. "Sir . . ."

She turned to Browbeater Hou. "You, madman! You mustn't hurt this young gentleman. Did you not hear me? My *shifu* is the Sage of Tranquility of the Quanzhen Sect. She is on her way!"

The Seven Masters of the Quanzhen were acclaimed throughout the *wulin*, and, indeed, Browbeater Hou had not forgotten the day the Iron Foot Immortal, Jade Sun Wang Chuyi, had intimidated him and his comrades at the Palace of Zhao. Miss Cheng's words sent a shiver through him. "Even if all the Quanzhen Masters come to your aid, I will butcher each and every one of them!"

"Who is that, talking such nonsense?" A voice boomed from outside.

The three of them leaped back in shock. Laurel pulled Emerald into his arms and raised his saber in case Browbeater Hou launched a fresh attack.

He glanced up to see a young Taoist standing in the doorway, dressed in the characteristic robes and hat. His features were delicate and his eyes twinkled. In his hand, he carried a horsetail whisk.

"Who wants to butcher the Seven Masters of the Quanzhen Sect?"

"Me. What of it?" Browbeater Hou said, clutching the pitchfork and stuffing his other hand into his waistband.

"Very well. Let me see you try." *Swish.* The whisk came straight for Hou's face.

Guo Jing had just finished another round of breathing, and scrambled to his feet to join Lotus at the hole.

"Is he also one of the priests of the Quanzhen?" she asked.

Guo Jing recognized him at once: Harmony Yin. Disciple of Qiu Chuji. He had challenged Guo Jing to a secret fight in Mongolia, two years before, defeating Guo Jing with ease. Guo Jing conveyed the whole story to Lotus in a whisper.

After witnessing the first few exchanges between the young Taoist and Browbeater Hou, Lotus shook her head. "He won't defeat the Three-Horned Dragon."

Laurel Lu had reached the same conclusion, stepping forward to join the fight once more. Harmony Yin's skills had developed somewhat since his encounter with Guo Jing, but the two young men could only just match Browbeater Hou when fighting together.

Laurel's touch had left Emerald breathless and her heart was beating madly. Despite the intensity of the fight, only a few feet away, she was in a trance, caressing her hand where the young man had held it—until a loud clanking broke her reverie.

"Miss! Watch out!" Laurel Lu cried.

Browbeater's fork was coming right at her. Laurel blocked it with his saber and Emerald blushed. This was no time for daydreaming.

Emerald had not studied much kung fu, but a third pair of hands made it difficult for Browbeater Hou to block their combined attacks. Harmony Yin's whisk danced in front of his eyes, distracting him for the briefest of moments, long enough for Laurel Lu's saber to slice into his leg.

"Damn your ancestors for eighteen generations back!"

The wound slowed him. He tried to block with his fork, but Harmony Yin's whisk wrapped itself around it. They both pulled back at the same time, but Browbeater Hou was the stronger and he pulled the whisk out of Harmony Yin's hand.

Emerald lunged with her sword in a Shake the Milky Way, piercing his right shoulder. Browbeater Hou dropped his fork in agony. Harmony Yin swept his leg in a horizontal kick, knocking Hou to the ground. Laurel Lu then pounced on Browbeater Hou and, using his leather belt, tied his hands behind his back.

"You cannot even defeat one disciple of the Quanzhen Sect; how are you going to take on all seven Masters?" Harmony Yin sneered.

Browbeater Hou cursed. Three against one was no heroic victory!

Harmony Yin tore a strip of cloth from Browbeater Hou's clothing and stuffed it into the prisoner's mouth. The Three-Horned Dragon's cheeks burned with red-hot fury, but he could not say anything in reply.

Harmony Yin turned to Miss Cheng and bowed. "Elder Martial Sister, you are the disciple of Elder Sun? I greet you with sincere respect."

Emerald bowed in return. "Brother, may I ask which of my martial uncles is your Master?"

"I am the disciple of Eternal Spring," he replied.

This being the first time Emerald had left her home, she had never met the other six Quanzhen Masters, but her *shifu* had of course explained who they were, and that, of all of them, Eternal Spring was the bravest and most honorable, not to mention the best fighter. "Then you are my elder," she said quietly. "My family name is Cheng. You must address me as your younger sister."

Her shy, girlish manner amused him. He then turned to Laurel Lu to introduce himself. Laurel repaid the courtesy without revealing who his father was.

"This madman can certainly fight. I wonder who he is. Whatever we do, we must not release him," Harmony Yin said.

"Let me dispatch him," Laurel said.

As the leader of the pirates of Lake Tai, he would have no qualms about killing their prisoner. For Emerald, however, the idea was unthinkable. "Oh, no, don't kill him!"

Harmony Yin smiled. "No, we have no reason to kill him; that wouldn't be right." Then he turned to Miss Cheng. "Little sister, have you been here long?"

"No, I just arrived," she said, blushing.

Harmony Yin regarded the two of them. He could sense that there was something between them. I should leave them be, he decided. "My *shifu* ordered me to go to Ox Village to find someone and give them a message. I must take my leave. But I am sure our paths will cross again!" He cupped his hands and turned to go.

The redness in Miss Cheng's cheeks only intensified. "Brother Yin, who is it that you are looking for?"

Harmony Yin hesitated. Miss Cheng belongs to the Quanzhen Sect, and she travels with Master Lu. I suppose it will do no harm to tell them. "I am looking for a friend by the name of Guo," he said at last.

Everyone, on both sides of the wall, was stunned.

"Is his given name Jing?" Laurel Lu asked.

"Indeed, it is. Does Brother Lu also know Guo Jing?"

"I am looking for the very same Uncle Guo."

"Uncle Guo?" Both Harmony Yin and Miss Cheng were surprised by the term of address.

"My father is of the same martial generation, so I must call him Uncle." Laurel's father, Zephyr Lu, was a disciple of Lotus's father, and Guo Jing was betrothed to the young lady, so technically the young couple were of the same generation as Laurel's father.

Emerald was silent, but her heart was troubled.

"Have you seen him? Where is he?" Harmony Yin asked.

"I have only just arrived. I was about to make inquiries when this madman attacked us for no reason," Laurel Lu replied.

"Excellent. Then we will look for him together."

The three young people made for the door.

Lotus and Guo Jing exchanged puzzled glances.

"They're leaving," Guo Jing said. "Lotus, open the door and call to them."

"What would be the point? It must be something urgent, and you cannot attend to anything until you have made your recovery. Your attention must not be diverted from this task."

"You're right. It must be important, though. Can't you think of something? A way to resolve this?"

"I will not open the door, even if the sky should fall on our heads," Lotus said firmly.

4

BEFORE LONG, HOWEVER, THE THREE WERE BACK.

"Not one person in the whole village knows where he is. This can't be good," Laurel Lu said.

"I wonder what matter is of such importance to send you here to look for him," Harmony Yin replied. "May we know?"

Laurel Lu was unwilling to say, but Miss Cheng's expectant expression was somehow hard to resist. "It's a long story. Let me first clean the floor of this manure, and then I will tell you."

They could find neither broom nor dustpan in the inn, so they went to fetch some branches and, together, they cleaned up the mess. Then they sat down to talk.

Just as Laurel Lu was about to begin, Emerald suddenly interrupted. "Wait!" She approached Browbeater Hou and cut two more pieces of cloth from his clothes. "He mustn't hear."

"Miss Cheng is most attentive," Laurel Lu said. "We don't know who this madman is. He must not be allowed to hear our discussion."

Lotus was amused. *That there are two of us on this side of the wall is perhaps difficult to spot, but Gallant Ouyang has been listening from his corner this whole time. For all your attentiveness, have any of you noticed?*

This was Emerald's first time away from home, and Harmony Yin had a reckless streak, like his master, and was young and inexperienced with it. It did not occur to any of them that there might be further danger lurking in this small, isolated inn.

As Emerald bent down to stuff the cloth into Browbeater Hou's ears, she noticed for the first time that they had been cut off. She was startled at first, but proceeded to push the material into the inner canal, then turned and smiled at Laurel Lu. "You may talk now."

"*Aiya*," he sighed. "Where do I start? I, too, am seeking Uncle Guo. By rights, I shouldn't be. In fact, I should really be doing the opposite. And yet, I must find him."

"How odd," Harmony Yin said.

"Indeed, it is," Laurel Lu conceded. "But it's not so much Uncle Guo I'm looking for, but rather his six *shifus*."

"The Six Freaks of the South!" Harmony Yin exclaimed, thumping the table.

"The very same."

"In that case, I think you have come over the same matter as me, concerning the same person. Why don't we each write down the name and let Sister Cheng determine if we're here on the same errand?"

Emerald smiled. "Good idea! Turn your backs to each other and write."

Harmony Yin and Laurel Lu each took up a twig and scratched a name in the dirt floor.

"Sister Cheng, did we write the same name?" Harmony Yin asked.

Emerald glanced at what each young man had written, before answering, "Brother Yin, you are wrong. You each wrote something different."

"Is that so?" he said, getting to his feet.

"You wrote *Apothecary Huang*," Emerald said, "and he drew a picture of a peach blossom."

They are both looking for Guo Jing because of my father, Lotus said to herself, in shock.

"Brother Yin wrote down the name of the Grandmaster of my school of kung fu," Laurel Lu said. "I did not dare write his name."

"Your Grandmaster?" Harmony Yin was surprised by this. "Apothecary Huang is the Lord of Peach Blossom Island, isn't he?"

"Ah, I see," Miss Cheng said.

"If Brother Lu is a disciple of Peach Blossom Island, then you cannot be looking for the Six Freaks for any favorable reason."

"That is not true," Laurel Lu replied.

Harmony Yin noticed the reticence in his voice, now. "If Brother Lu does not consider me a friend, then you needn't say any more," he said coldly. "I shall take my leave."

"Brother Yin, wait! I am in trouble and I need your help."

Harmony Yin liked nothing more than being needed. "Fine. Then tell me what is wrong."

"Brother Yin, you are a student of the Quanzhen Sect. You know that, if someone is in danger, it's a man's moral duty, according to the code of *xia*, that he must warn that person. But what if your own Master was out to harm an innocent party? Would you still owe it to them to warn them? Even if it meant going against your Master?"

"Indeed!" Harmony Yin cried and slapped his thigh. "You are a disciple of Peach Blossom Island, so this matter puts you in a rather difficult position. Tell me more."

"If I do nothing, I am being dishonorable. If I intervene, I am betraying my Master. There is something I would like to ask of Brother Yin, but I dare not."

Harmony Yin had worked out what it was Laurel Lu wanted him to do, but if the young man would not open his mouth to ask him, there was nothing he could do to help. He scratched his head, an awkward expression on his face.

Just then, Emerald had an idea. There was a habit among young women, whereby, if one among them was too shy to say what she was thinking, her mother or sister, for example, would ask her questions, to which she could reply by nodding or shaking her head. It was not the most direct method, but it did usually allow for the young girl to say what was on her mind. The mother might ask, for example, "Are you in love with Third Brother Zhang?" To which the girl would shake her head. "Is it Fourth Brother Li?" Again, the same response. "Cousin Wang?" Then she would hang her head and make no reply, which would mean yes.

"Brother Yin," Miss Cheng said, "you must ask Brother Lu questions. If the answer is yes, he will nod his head. If the answer is no, he will shake it. That way, no one can accuse him of betraying his Master."

"An excellent idea!" Harmony Yin exclaimed. "Brother Lu, let me first explain why I am here. My *shifu*, Eternal Spring, happened to hear that the Lord of Peach Blossom Island has taken against the Six Freaks and has vowed to kill them and their families. My *shifu* set out at once to Jiaxing to deliver the warning, but the Freaks were not to be found. He then went to visit each of their families in turn, but could not find a single one of them. This made him furious, so he set off north. Since then, I have had no news. Are you familiar with these matters?"

Laurel Lu nodded.

"I think Apothecary Huang is pursuing the Freaks northward. It is true that, at first, there was some animosity between my *shifu* and the Freaks, but this has all been resolved. Indeed, my Master admires greatly their dedication to helping those in need. And furthermore, in this particular matter, he considers them blameless. The Seven Masters of the Quanzhen Sect happened to be meeting down here among the rivers and lakes when they heard of the danger, and so they have spread out to look for the Freaks. For their own sake, Guo Jing's *shifus* would do well to hide somewhere, so that your Grandmaster cannot find them. Do you agree that this would be the best plan?"

Laurel Lu nodded his head vigorously.

Guo Jing kept his promise to go to Peach Blossom Island, so what score does Father have to settle with the Six Freaks? Lotus asked herself. She could not know about Lama Supreme Wisdom's lie that she had died at sea, and that Apothecary Huang blamed Guo Jing's Masters.

"As he could not find the Freaks," Harmony Yin continued, "my *shifu* thought of Guo Jing. Ox Village is where his parents lived, so my Master guessed that he might have returned here, and sent me to look for him. My Master thought he would know where his six *shifus* are. Did you come on the same errand?"

Once again, Laurel Lu nodded.

"And yet, he doesn't appear to be here. My *shifu* is most fond of the Six Freaks and is distressed by his failure to find them. His one comfort is the possibility that the Lord of Peach Blossom Island is struggling to find them too. Is it in relation to this matter that you need my help?"

Another nod.

"Then please explain in full, Brother Lu. I will do my best to help."

Laurel Lu looked back at the young Taoist with an awkward expression.

"Brother Yin," Miss Cheng said with a smile. "You forget, Brother Lu cannot speak freely."

"You're right," he said, smiling back at her. "Brother Lu, do you want me to wait here for Guo Jing?"

Laurel Lu shook his head.

"Do you want me to go looking for the Six Freaks and Guo Jing?"

Again, he shook his head.

"I know! You want me to spread word throughout the *wulin*. That way, before long, the news will reach the ears of the Six Freaks."

Yet again, Laurel Lu shook his head.

Harmony Yin presented the young man with another half a dozen guesses, but none was right. Miss Cheng offered two of her own, but she too was unsuccessful. Lotus listened, similarly confounded.

"Miss Cheng, you try to get it out of him," Harmony Yin said eventually. "I can't stand these riddles. I'm going for a walk. I'll be back in a few hours." With that, he left.

Laurel and Emerald now believed themselves to be alone, save for Browbeater Hou. Miss Cheng looked away shyly; Laurel did not move. She stole a glance at him, only to catch his eye. They both looked away. Miss Cheng's cheeks blushed even redder and she fiddled with the silk ribbons on the end of her sword's hilt.

Laurel Lu rose to his feet and walked over to the hearth, above which was painted an image of the Kitchen God.

"Kitchen God, my heart is heavy, but I cannot unburden myself. So I must tell you, and hope that, in your divine wisdom, you might bless me with the answer."

Very clever, Miss Cheng thought. She raised her head slightly, so that she might hear better.

"My name is Laurel Lu, son of Squire Lu of Roaming Cloud Manor, by the shores of Lake Tai. My father goes by the name of Zephyr, and he is a disciple of Lord Huang of Peach Blossom Island. A few days ago, Grandmaster Huang arrived at my home and announced that he was looking for the Six Freaks. He wishes to enact a bloody revenge on them and their families. He commanded my father and my martial aunt, Cyclone Mei, to find their whereabouts. Mistress Mei bears a deep hatred of the Freaks, so she accepted the order gladly. But not my father. He considers the Freaks patriots and heroes, and he does not believe killing would be a righteous deed. Indeed, my father has developed a friendship with a disciple of the Freaks, my martial uncle, Guo Jing. The situation is most difficult for my father. That night, he looked up to the sky and confessed his concerns to the heavens. He said he was considering sending me to find the Freaks, to warn them, but such an order would be a betrayal of his Master. Luckily, I was standing nearby and heard every word. My filial obligations are stronger than the loyalty I owe my Grandmaster. This is why I decided to set out on this journey."

The fact that he was copying his father's method of overcoming his dilemma did not escape Lotus or Miss Cheng.

"The Six Freaks are nowhere to be found, and neither is their disciple, Martial Uncle Guo, who is betrothed to my Grandmaster's daughter—"

At this, Emerald gasped. She covered her mouth quickly. She had yearned for Guo Jing day and night, thought herself to be in love, but, after having met Laurel Lu, she realized that her feelings had been nothing more than a childish infatuation. Laurel Lu was handsome, distinguished and superior to Guo Jing in every way. She was shocked to hear of Lotus and Guo Jing's relationship, but the news did not leave her heartbroken. In fact, she felt relieved. She recalled that they had seemed close in Baoying. Now, it did not matter. Her heart had already found a new home.

Laurel Lu had heard her gasp. He wanted to turn and look, but he forced himself not to. *If I acknowledge that she is listening, I will have to stop talking. Father did not look over at me when I overheard him. My words are for the Kitchen God, it is not my fault if she is eavesdropping.*

"I hope to find my Martial Uncle Guo and his betrothed," he continued, "so that together they might beseech Grandmaster Huang. Lord Huang has a hot temper, but he loves his daughter and his son-in-law, so he would never kill his son-in-law's *shifus*. Yet, from the way my father was talking, it sounds as if Martial Uncle Guo and Martial Aunt Huang may have met with danger. Only, it would be improper to ask him."

How could Father know about Guo Jing's injury? Lotus thought. *It was not possible. He must have heard that we were stranded on the island.*

"Brother Yin is kind and Miss Cheng is extremely intelligent and amiable"—Emerald's heart was thumping at this mention of her name—"but the contents of my heart are too strange for her to be able to guess. The Six Heroes of the South are heroes. Their kung fu may not be of the same level as Grandmaster Huang, but wouldn't asking them to take precautions be insulting them? Suggesting they are afraid of death? If they were to hear of the threat, I fear they would go looking for the Grandmaster rather than running away! And would I not have caused them more harm, therefore?"

Lotus nodded. Laurel Lu certainly understood the way that heroes of the *jianghu* thought.

"The Seven Masters of the Quanzhen Sect are righteous and deserving of their reputation," he continued. "Not to mention being extremely skilled fighters. Were Brother Yin and Miss Cheng to beg their Masters to intervene, Grandmaster Huang would certainly listen. Surely there is no reason for Grandmaster Huang to carry such a deep animosity toward the Six Heroes of the South. Mostly likely, it is all a misunderstanding—the Six Heroes must have said something to displease him. If someone were to act as mediator, the issue could be resolved. Kitchen God, my dilemma is this: I have an idea as to how to resolve it, but I cannot tell anyone. In your great wisdom and power, please help me to find a way."

Then he cupped his hands and bowed several times before the painting.

Emerald decided she must find Harmony Yin, but, just as she was about to head for the door, she heard Laurel Lu speak once more: "Kitchen God, if the Seven Masters of the Quanzhen Sect would be willing to help in this matter, it would be a deed befitting their reputation. I only hope that they will be courteous and not risk offending the Grandmaster, for, if another wave of fury were to come before the first has passed, all efforts will have been in vain. That is my confession in full."

Emerald smiled. Now, let me take care of this, she said to herself.

5

EMERALD CHENG LEFT THE INN AND STARTED TO WALK around the village, looking for Harmony Yin. But she could find no trace of him. Just as she was about to turn back, she heard someone hiss, "Sister Cheng!" It was him, peering out from around a corner.

"There you are!" Emerald cried.

Harmony Yin gestured for her to be quiet, then pointed west as he approached. "I have seen some suspicious characters," he whispered. "Carrying weapons."

"They're probably just passing through," Emerald replied, distracted by thoughts of all that Laurel Lu had said.

But Harmony's expression was grave. "They moved quickly, and they are trained in the martial arts. We must be careful."

He had, of course, spotted Tiger Peng and the others. They had waited for Browbeater Hou, but, as he did not return, they realized he must be in danger. Yet, whoever it was pretending to be a demon in the palace was an accomplished fighter and no one was eager to confront him again. While they were deciding what to do, they spotted the young Taoist and quickly hid.

Harmony Yin waited, but, as all was quiet up ahead, he decided to investigate, only to find no trace of them.

Emerald related all that she had heard from Laurel.

"So that's what he wanted? We would never have been able to guess!" Harmony Yin said with a smile. "Sister Cheng, if you go and ask Mistress Sun, the Sage of Tranquility, I will approach my *shifu*. As long as they all act together, what task is beyond their abilities?"

"But they must be careful not to make things worse," Miss Cheng said. She explained Laurel Lu's concerns.

"Huh—who is this Apothecary Huang? Are his martial skills really greater than that of the Seven Masters?"

Emerald wanted to remind him not to be too arrogant, but the severity of his expression stopped her.

Instead, they went back to the inn together.

"Brother, I must take my leave," Laurel Lu said as soon as they crossed the threshold. "If you are ever passing Lake Tai, do please visit us at Roaming Cloud Manor and stay a few days."

Emerald was devastated that he should be leaving so soon. How could she reveal her feelings to him?

Harmony Yin turned to face the Kitchen God. "Master Kitchen God, the Quanzhen Sect is indeed most willing to aid all those in need. No injustice in the *jianghu* goes unnoticed or ignored by the Seven Masters."

Laurel Lu knew that Harmony Yin was speaking to him, so he too turned to the painting. "Kitchen God, I pray only that you will give your blessing so that this matter might be resolved peacefully. I will be forever in debt to the heroes who reach out their hand to help."

"Master Kitchen God, please do not worry. The might of the

Seven Masters makes the world tremble. As long as they are willing, there is nothing they cannot accomplish."

This startled Laurel Lu. How were they going to persuade Apothecary Huang if their plan was to pit their might against him?

"Kitchen God, you know my Grandmaster does as he pleases and has little regard for rank or hierarchy. Should they speak to him as friends and equals, he can be persuaded. But he will heed no man's command."

"Kitchen God, why should the Seven Masters fear anyone? This matter has nothing to do with them. Should they be provoked, however, it matters not if the offending party is the Lord of Peach Blossom Island or of Cherry Blossom Island, the Seven Masters will surely teach them a lesson!"

Anger was rising in Laurel Lu's chest. "Kitchen God, please ignore all that I have said to you today. If we are to be belittled, then we don't want help."

Emerald Cheng was listening in distress. She wanted to intervene, but the two young men seemed unwilling to yield even an inch.

"Kitchen God," Harmony Yin said eventually, "the Quanzhen are the greatest of the orthodox Taoist sects. All others are heretics. No matter how accomplished they may be, how can the heretical win over the orthodox?"

"Kitchen God, the Quanzhen Sect's reputation reaches far and wide, and is certainly deserved for many in its ranks. But this does not mean that they do not claim some disciples that are truly arrogant and boastful."

"How dare you insult me!" Harmony Yin struck his palm against one corner of the stove, and the stove partially collapsed.

Bang! Laurel Lu struck the other corner. "How dare I? I insult only those who deserve it!"

Harmony Yin could see that Laurel Lu's kung fu was no match for his. "Fine. Let us see who is truly deserving of insult."

Laurel Lu knew that he was unlikely to prevail, but, now that he had climbed onto the tiger's back, it was going to be difficult to get down. He drew his saber and nodded. "I am honored to take on your most accomplished Quanzhen fighting technique."

Tears were now pouring down Emerald Cheng's cheeks. She wanted to throw herself between them, but she was too afraid. Harmony Yin drew his horsetail whisk, and within moments the fight had begun.

Laurel Lu did not hope for victory, only to avoid a humiliating defeat. Using the Arhat Saber technique taught to him by Reverend Withered Wood, he immediately adopted a defensive stance.

Harmony Yin attacked head-on, but was surprised by his opponent's saber skills. He might have been somewhat reckless in his assessment—a suspicion that was confirmed when he nearly lost his left arm. His heart trembling, he concentrated and parried. This was a key tenet of his school's style: the calming of the mind, to be slow in step but quick in hand.

For the last month, Laurel Lu had been receiving instruction from his father and had made considerable progress, but his skills were negligible in comparison to those of one of Eternal Spring's disciples.

Following the fight through the small hole in the wall, Lotus watched Harmony Yin gradually gain the advantage, and silently cursed. That little Taoist insulted my father. If it wasn't for Guo Jing's injury, I'd teach him a few heresies from Peach Blossom Island.

She watched as Laurel Lu repeated the saber strike and Harmony Yin blocked it with ease before twisting past the blade and aiming for Laurel's elbow. Laurel's arm went numb and he dropped his weapon. Unrelenting, Harmony Yin aimed his whisk at the young man's face and cried, "This is Quanzhen's fighting technique. Don't forget it!"

The whisk was made of horsehair mixed with silver threads. Were they to make contact with Laurel's face, they would be certain to draw blood.

Laurel Lu ducked, but heard Harmony correct the whisk's course.

Then, suddenly, a tender voice: "Brother Yin!"

Emerald Cheng's sword blocked the whisk. Laurel Lu leaped back and reached for his saber.

"Sister Cheng, you would choose an outsider against your own school? Why, then, the lovers can fight me together."

"You . . ." Emerald Cheng's cheeks blazed red.

Harmony Yin flashed his whisk, forcing her back. Laurel Lu sprang forward with his saber. It could have been two against one, but Emerald Cheng did not want to fight a martial brother, so she withdrew.

"Come, now, he cannot defeat me on his own!" Harmony Yin cried.

Lotus watched in amusement. Just then, there was a noise at the door. In walked Tiger Peng, Hector Sha, and the others, followed by Wanyan Honglie and Yang Kang. They had waited for Browbeater Hou's return, but Hector Sha had grown increasingly worried, and had ventured back alone, at first. The last thing he had expected was to encounter two young men fighting, so he went back and gathered the others.

The two young men noticed the Sixth Prince's retinue and instantly stopped fighting. They inquired as to who they were, but Hector Sha stepped forward and grabbed both by the wrist. Tiger Peng, meanwhile, untied the leather belt around Browbeater Hou's hands.

Browbeater Hou was furious. With the cloth still in his mouth, he roared and threw himself at Emerald Cheng, attacking her with his palms. She withdrew. Browbeater Hou followed, flailing his fists, his face swollen and blue.

"Stop!" Tiger Peng called. "Let's talk."

But Browbeater Hou's ears were blocked with cloth. He could not hear a thing.

Hector Sha had locked the pressure point on Laurel Lu's wrist, paralyzing him down one side. But Browbeater Hou was like a crazed tiger and Emerald Cheng was in danger. A burst of strength came surging through Lu from nowhere. He threw Hector Sha aside and leaped at Browbeater Hou.

But, just at the last moment, Tiger Peng intercepted him and sent the young man crashing to the floor. He then pounced on him, grabbed him by the back of the neck and lifted him up like a prize. "Who are you? Are you the one who was pretending to be a demon?"

Suddenly, the door let out a long creak as it was slowly opened. Everyone turned, but there was no one in the doorway. A shiver went through them all.

A head appeared: a young woman with disheveled hair.

"Help!" cried Lama Supreme Wisdom.

"A she-devil!"

Tiger Peng saw at once that she was nothing more than an ordinary peasant girl. "Come in," he said.

The young woman walked in. She giggled and stuck out her tongue. "So many people."

Graybeard Liang had been the one to call her a she-devil, but now he too saw that she was in fact an ordinary, wretched girl with tattered clothes, and most probably a fool. Embarrassment at his first reaction now turned to fury. "Who are you?" He jumped forward and made to grab her arm.

She stepped back, flipped her hand and retaliated with a Jade Ripple Palm. Her execution may not have been refined, but it was a perfectly respectable example of kung fu. Graybeard Liang was caught by surprise, and the strike hit the back of his hand with a loud slap.

This only made the old man even more furious. He rushed at her with both fists raised. "You merely play the fool!"

The young girl took another step back, then pointed at his shiny pate and laughed.

This caught everyone by surprise, not least Graybeard Liang, who stopped dead for a few moments. Then he launched himself at her. The girl raised her hands while retreating. Knowing she was in danger, she turned and tried to escape. But the Ginseng Codger was in no mood to be generous. He stretched out his leg to block, while striking with his elbow, then fist. The girl felt a sharp pain to her nose and the room started spinning.

"Sister, eating the watermelon! Come out and help me!"

Lotus froze. I should have killed her while I had the chance, she thought. She is going to be the death of us. Just then, she heard the faintest snort, barely audible. Her heart leaped in delight. Papa has come! She leaned closer to look through the hole and saw Apothecary Huang, dressed in a mask made of human skin, standing at the door to the courtyard.

Nobody else had noticed him arrive. He stood, still as a tree trunk. At last, the others turned to look, and shuddered. His face was not green, he bore no fangs, he was neither fierce nor ugly. But it was clear to all that this face did not belong to a living being.

Apothecary Huang had witnessed the whole brief exchange between the young girl and Graybeard Liang, and he could tell at once that she had been trained in the martial arts of Peach Blossom Island.

"Young miss, who is your Master? Where is he?"

The girl shook her head. The sight of this strange face had struck her dumb. Then, suddenly, she clapped her hands and laughed.

Apothecary Huang frowned. She had to have some connection to Peach Blossom Island, and he would never let the disciple of a disciple be bullied. He had even come to Cyclone Mei's defense when she was mistreated by Guo Jing. "Silly girl, why didn't you strike back when that old man hit you?"

The men gathered had not realized who this was, until he opened his mouth. Wanyan Honglie, Yang Kang, and Tiger Peng recognized his voice at once. Was this the man they had encountered in the palace, the night before? Tiger Peng wondered. If so, there was no way they could overcome him. They would have to use Sun Tzu's thirty-sixth strategy: if all else fails, run.

"I can't hit him," the girl said.

"Says who?" Apothecary Huang replied. "If he hits your nose, you hit his nose. If he hits you once, you hit him three times."

"All right!" It had not occurred to her that there was a mismatch in their skills. "If you hit my nose, I must hit your nose. If you hit me once, I must hit you three times." At that, she sent her fist toward Graybeard Liang's nose.

The Ginseng Codger moved to block, but instantly felt the Pool at the Bend pressure point at his elbow go numb. His forearm froze. *Thump!* The girl hit him squarely in the face.

"Number two!" she cried, and punched again.

Graybeard Liang bent his knees, his back straight and chest pulled in, and reached out in a move from his famous Grapple and Lock technique. He was aiming to dislocate the girl's shoulder, but, just as his fingers made contact, his arm again went numb. *Thump!* Another blow to the nose. This time, his head was thrown back and he was rocked onto his heels, seething with fury.

The others watched in amazement. How had she done it? Tiger Peng was an expert in secret projectiles; he was the only one who heard the faint swish that told him Apothecary Huang was throwing the tiniest of needles at Graybeard Liang's pressure points. And yet, he never saw the great Master's arm move.

Apothecary Huang was in fact flicking his finger from inside his sleeve, sending the needles through the fabric of his robe. It was an invisible and almost inaudible attack. Who could possibly defend themselves against it?

"Three!"

With both arms locked, Graybeard Liang watched as the girl's fist hurtled toward his face once more. He tried to step back, but, at that moment, the White Ocean point on the inside of his right leg went numb. A spark danced before his eyes, he felt a pain in them, and they began to brim with tears. This last punch to his nose had also hit the pressure point in his tear ducts. To be seen crying would be even more humiliating than defeat. He tried to wipe away the tears, but his arm would not move. Two fat drops rolled down his cheeks.

"Oh, don't cry!" the young girl said. "I promise I won't hit you anymore."

These words were worse than the blows to his nose. Unable to bear it, Graybeard Liang bent forward and vomited a mouthful of blood.

"Sir, who are you?" he said, looking up at Apothecary Huang. "Using such tricks, is that the behavior of a Master?"

"Who are you to demand my name?" Apothecary Huang replied. Then he turned to address all the men gathered. "All of you, go!"

Apothecary Huang's order came as a relief. Nobody watching had any desire to join the fight. Tiger Peng was the first to leave, but, as he approached the door, he saw the great Master was blocking the way out. He stopped dead.

"I told you all to leave, and yet you're still here. Are you asking me to kill you?"

Tiger Peng had heard all about Apothecary Huang's strange moods. He wanted nothing more than to do as the Master said. So, he turned to the others and cried, "The great Master has instructed us to go. Let's go."

By now, Browbeater had removed the cloth from his mouth. He ran straight at Apothecary Huang. "Let me pass!" he snarled.

"Who are you to demand that I move aside?" he said firmly. "You may crawl between my legs. If you want to live, that is."

The men looked at each other in dismay. This man was humiliating them. Yet they were all considered accomplished fighters. Together, they might just be able to overcome him.

Browbeater Hou launched himself at Apothecary Huang, but suddenly he found himself up in the air and felt a hand pulling at his left arm.

Crrraaaack! Browbeater Hou's arm was pulled clean from his body. Apothecary Huang tossed man and arm aside. Browbeater Hou fainted instantly from the pain, as blood poured onto the floor.

Apothecary Huang glanced up at the ceiling, seemingly indifferent. The others were horrified, the color draining instantly from their cheeks.

Slowly, Huang's eyes swept over each of the men, one by one. Hector Sha, Tiger Peng—they had all killed plenty of men in their time, but they shuddered under Huang's cold gaze. Goose bumps prickled their skin.

"Are you leaving or not?" Apothecary Huang roared.

Any thoughts of fighting back turned to dust. Tiger Peng hung his head and crawled out beneath Huang's legs. Hector Sha released Harmony Yin and Laurel Lu and scrambled through next, dragging Browbeater Hou behind him. Yang Kang helped Wanyan Honglie, followed by Graybeard Liang and Lama Supreme Wisdom.

As soon as they were outside, they ran like startled rats. Not one of them dared to glance over their shoulder as they fled.

CHAPTER SIX

A DESOLATED INN
IN A DESOLATED VILLAGE

I

"LAUREL, YOU AND THE YOUNG LADY MAY STAY," APOTHECARY Huang ordered.

Laurel Lu had of course recognized his Grandmaster, but, as he was dressed in the mask, he had not greeted him properly when he first entered the inn. Now, he bowed four times.

Harmony Yin also bowed. "Disciple of Eternal Spring of the Quanzhen Sect, Harmony Yin is honored to meet you, sir."

"I did not ask you to stay. Why are you still here?"

Apothecary Huang's tone took him aback. "I am a student of Eternal Spring—I am not a criminal."

"What do I care if you are a member of the Quanzhen Sect?" Huang grabbed the corner of a nearby table, pulled a chunk of wood from it and, without the slightest movement of his arm or hand, threw it at Harmony Yin. The young man tried to block with his whisk, only to realize at the last moment that the projectile was hurtling at him with the might of a metal staff. He felt the gush of air. As he tried desperately to evade it, his whisk swung round and hit him at the side of his lips at the same time as the wooden block. The pain was sharp. There was also something in his mouth. He spat and looked down into his bloody palm, only to find a few of his teeth. Shocked and frightened, he said no more.

"I am Apothecary Huang. Or you could call me the Black Apothecary. Now, tell me: what does the Quanzhen Sect want?"

Harmony Yin and Emerald Cheng were stunned.

Laurel Lu was similarly surprised. Perhaps the Grandmaster heard me fight with the Taoist, he thought. But what if he heard what I told the Kitchen God, too? The thought brought him out in a cold sweat. And what about Father . . . ?

Rubbing his cheek, Harmony Yin mustered the strength to speak through the pain. "You are a master of the *wulin*, and yet your behavior is so capricious? The Six Heroes of the South are just that—heroes. Why do you harass them? Had my *shifu* not sent out a warning, would you have killed them already?"

"So, that's why I've not been able to find them," Apothecary Huang snarled. "You stinky Taoists have been meddling in business that does not concern you."

"If you desire to kill me, then do so!" Harmony Yin cried in agitation. "I am not afraid of you."

"Did you enjoy cursing me behind my back?" Apothecary Huang said coldly.

"I am not afraid to curse you to your face, you demon! You freak!"

Ever since he had first gained fame throughout the *wulin*, no one had ever dared insult Apothecary Huang directly in this manner. This young Taoist was the most unbridled, offensive man he had come across in more than a decade. Even after watching the way Apothecary Huang had dealt with Browbeater Hou, he dared to speak to him like this? Huang could not help but admire the young man's courage. It reminded him of himself, in his younger years. "Keep going, if you dare," he said, taking a step closer to the Taoist.

"I'm not scared, you monster!"

He will never get out of this alive, Laurel Lu thought. I must intervene.

"You brazen swine! How dare you insult my Grandmaster!" Laurel raised his saber and aimed it at Harmony Yin's shoulder. If he injured Harmony Yin first, perhaps Apothecary Huang's fury might abate long enough to allow the young Taoist to escape.

Harmony Yin leaped aside and then cried, "I am not scared of death, so I will curse until I am satisfied!"

Laurel Lu hefted his saber once more, just as Emerald Cheng raised her sword and shouted, "I, too, am a disciple of the Quanzhen. If you would kill him, then kill us both!"

This took Harmony Yin by surprise. "Excellent, Sister Cheng!"

They stood shoulder to shoulder, facing Apothecary Huang. Laurel Lu could no longer risk attacking Yin, for fear of hurting the lady.

"You certainly have guts and integrity—I admire these qualities in a man. I, Apothecary Huang, am indeed a demon and a heretic. You are not wrong, there. Besides, your *shifu* is my junior, so how could I lower myself to fight with you? Be off with you!" He reached out, grabbed the young man by the front of his robes and flung him outside.

As Harmony Yin flew through the air, he had time to imagine how hard a landing he faced. But—who would have guessed it?— he alighted perfectly, with both feet touching the ground at the same moment. Apothecary Huang must have thrown him in such a way as to ensure he would not be injured.

That was close! Harmony Yin thought to himself, in a daze. The old freak has been merciful. However much courage Yin had shown up to now, he was not going to go back inside that inn. With a stroke of his swollen cheek, he turned and left.

Emerald Cheng sheathed her sword and started for the door.

"Wait," said Apothecary Huang. He reached up and removed the mask. "Will you consent to be this young man's wife?" he said, pointing at Laurel Lu.

Emerald Cheng's snowy-white cheeks flushed a crimson red.

"Your martial brother was correct," Apothecary Huang continued. "I am a heretic, but who doesn't know that? People even call me the Heretic of the East. The thing I hate most in this world is hypocritical social conventions, especially the words of false sages. They are mere tools for duping idiots. Generation after generation falls into their trap, taking their nonsense for truths. It's laughable, really. I, Apothecary Huang, do not subscribe to such falsehoods. People may call me a demon and a heretic, and yet I have probably caused less injury to others than those bastards who talk day and night about righteousness and morality!"

Emerald Cheng's heart was beating wildly, but she said nothing. What did he want with her?

"Tell me," he continued. "You would like to marry my disciple's son, isn't that so? I like those with guts and backbone. That little Taoist cursed me behind my back, but, if he had knelt before me, polite and sniveling, I would have killed him. You defended him, despite the danger, which shows character. You would make a good match for this young man. Come on, answer me!"

Emerald Cheng wanted to say yes with all her heart, but she would not have dared to tell her own parents, let alone a stranger she was only meeting for the first time—and certainly not while Laurel Lu was standing beside them. Her cheeks flushed pink, like petals of a rose.

Laurel Lu hung his head.

Apothecary Huang's thoughts turned to Lotus and he sighed. "If you are both in love, I will give your union my blessing. But even parents cannot decide who their children should marry." Had he agreed to his beloved daughter's betrothal to Guo Jing, she would not be lying at the bottom of the ocean. The realization vexed him. "Laurel—speak up, boy—do you want to marry this young lady?"

"Grandmaster," he began with a stammer, "my only fear is that I am not good enough—"

"Not good enough!" Apothecary Huang interrupted. "As the son of my disciple, you are worthy of the Emperor's daughter!"

Laurel Lu could see that his Grandmaster's mood would worsen if he hesitated any longer. "I am most willing."

A rush of warmth filled Emerald Cheng's heart.

"Excellent," the Heretic said, turning to address her. "And what about you, miss?"

Without looking up, she answered, "My father must decide."

"Your father? Never mind him, nor the matchmaker. Let me make the decision. If your father doesn't like it, he can challenge me to a duel."

"Father only knows how to use a brush and abacus," Emerald Cheng said, a smile creeping across her lips. "He doesn't know any kung fu."

Apothecary Huang considered this for a moment. "Then we can battle with brush and abacus, that is fine with me! There is no one on this earth better at doing calculations than me. And can your father's calligraphy compare to mine? Now, give me your answer, girl. Will you marry him?"

Emerald Cheng was silent.

"Then it's a no. Very well, it is your choice. Old heretic that I am, I always keep my word. I never allow anyone to go back on a decision."

Emerald Cheng stole a glance at Laurel Lu and saw the anxiety on his face. Father adores me, she thought to herself. If I ask Auntie to talk to him and arrange for a matchmaker, Father will say yes. Why do I feel so flustered?

"Laurel," Apothecary Huang suddenly cried and rose to his feet, "you're coming with me. We are going to find the Six Freaks of the South. If you utter so much as a single word to this young lady ever again, I will cut out both your tongues."

Laurel Lu knew full well that his Grandmaster was capable of such an act. He turned to Emerald Cheng and bowed. "Miss, I am but a mediocre fighter, without talent or education. I live a wandering life and would not be an acceptable match for you. But I feel that fate has brought us together today . . ."

"There is no need to be humble, young sir. I ... I am not ..." Emerald Cheng trailed off.

The young man's heart skipped a beat. If only he could make her answer with a nod or a shake of her head. "Miss," he whispered, "if the man standing before you does not please you, please shake your head." The blood was pumping so violently through his body that he could barely look at her.

But Emerald Cheng did not move. Sensing a sliver of hope, Laurel Lu smiled and said, "If miss is willing to marry me, please nod."

But Emerald Cheng did not move.

Apothecary Huang was losing patience. "You neither shake nor nod your head. What does that mean?"

"If I do not shake my head," Emerald Cheng began hesitantly, "then it means ... I nod my head." The words were spoken so quietly that only Apothecary Huang, whose hearing was enhanced by years of *neigong* training, could make them out.

He threw back his head and guffawed. "Wang Chongyang is a brave and valiant man. Who would have thought that he would end up with such a meek disciple! How funny. You both belong to the best schools in the *wulin;* it is a suitable match. Come, come, let me make it official today."

The two young people looked up at Apothecary Huang in amazement.

"Where's that girl, the fool?" he continued. "I want to ask her who her *shifu* is."

But the Qu girl was nowhere to be seen.

"Well, well, there is no hurry, I suppose. Laurel, you will marry Miss Cheng, here, today?"

"I am most grateful for my Grandmaster's magnanimity," Laurel Lu began, "but to marry in this lowly inn seems a little hasty ..."

"You are a disciple of Peach Blossom Island. Don't tell me you abide by such ridiculous societal conventions? Come, now, you two, let me see you bow to the heavens." His tone was austere, and they did not dare go against him. Emerald Cheng knew she had no choice. Gracefully, she knelt before him.

"Now, bow to the earth . . . And your Grandmaster . . . Excellent. Excellent! And now, to each other."

Lotus and Guo Jing watched the pageant as Apothecary Huang barked his orders. They were surprised, to be sure, but also amused.

"Excellent. Now, go and get the candles for your first night together as man and wife," Apothecary Huang continued.

Stunned, Laurel Lu stared back at him. "Grandmaster!"

"What? You have already made your promises to the heavens and the earth. All that awaits, now, is the bridal chamber. You're both fighters of the *wulin;* you're not expecting brocade sheets, are you? This crumbling inn isn't good enough?"

This silenced the young man. In fact, his heart was pounding with anticipation. He promptly left and went to find a pair of red candles, some wine and a chicken. Then, together, the young couple prepared a meal for their Grandmaster.

2

APOTHECARY HUANG FELL INTO A LONG SILENCE. HIS thoughts had turned to his daughter. Lotus watched and knew that he was thinking about her. Several times, she nearly threw open the door, but she was afraid he might force her to accompany him back to Peach Blossom Island. Besides, she could see no way her beloved could survive the encounter. These thoughts drove her hand away from the door.

Laurel and Emerald, meanwhile, glanced at their Grandmaster and then at each other. Their cheeks were flushed red with a mixture of happiness and embarrassment.

Gallant Ouyang was listening from his bed of straw. His stomach ached from hunger, and he barely dared to breathe for fear of attracting attention.

Gradually, the sky darkened. Emerald's heart was nearly beating out of her chest.

"Where's that silly girl?" she heard Apothecary Huang mutter. "Why hasn't she come back? Those traitors better not be giving her any trouble." Then he turned to Laurel Lu. "Why don't you light the candles now?"

"Yes, sir," Laurel Lu replied. He struck a flint and the wick flickered. There, by candlelight, he gazed at Sister Cheng's wisps of hair as they caressed her temples. Her cheeks were as white as fresh snow and, in her expression, he sensed a pleasing bashfulness. Words failed him. The insects outside hummed and the evening breeze blew through the bamboo thicket. Was this all real?

Apothecary Huang moved a wooden bench outside into the courtyard and lay down on it. Before long, his gentle snores filled the room. The young couple were frozen, they hardly dared move. They stayed like this until the candle burned down and, with a puff, the flame was out.

One of them ventured to speak, and, in the darkness, they sought each other out with their words. Lotus leaned in closer, trying to hear what they were saying. Suddenly, she felt Guo Jing's body tremble beside her. His breathing was quick. His *qi* had branched, she guessed, and quickly she gathered her inner energy to come to his aid.

After some time, his breathing began to return to normal, and once again she turned her attention to the couple on the other side of the wall. A shaft of moonlight had burst through the window. Laurel and Emerald were sitting side by side on one of the benches.

"Do you know what day it is today?" she heard Emerald whisper.

"The happiest of our lives," Laurel replied.

"Of course," Emerald said. "Today is the second day of the seventh lunar month," she continued. "My third aunt's birthday, on my mother's side."

Laurel smiled. "You must have a large family," he said. "How do you remember all those birthdays?"

Your wife comes from a large Baoying clan, Lotus thought. Aunts, uncles, nephews and nieces . . . It would wear you out trying to remember all those birthdays, Master of Roaming Cloud Manor.

Her thoughts drifted. If today was the second day of the seventh month, she realized, Guo Jing would need until the seventh to recover. The Beggar Clan was due to meet in Yuezhou on the fifteenth. Somehow, the timing was tight.

Just then, she heard a loud whistle from outside, followed by laughter and then the shaking of the roof tiles above.

"Old Venom!" Zhou Botong! "You have chased the Urchin all day and night from Lin'an to Jiaxing and back again, and still you cannot catch me. Victory is surely mine. What else is there to compete over?"

From Lin'an to Jiaxing and back, Lotus said to herself in astonishment. That's over five hundred *li* in the space of a day and a night!

"I will chase you to the ends of the earth," Viper's voice replied.

"Then let us have a competition. Who can run the fastest, and the longest? No breaks for eating, sleeping . . . not even shitting!"

"Why not? Let us see who will be the first to collapse from exhaustion."

"Old Venom, I said no shitting."

She heard the two men laughing in the distance. It sounded as if they were already a hundred feet hence.

Laurel Lu and Emerald Cheng looked at each other in shock, then joined hands and cautiously made their way toward the door.

If the Urchin and Old Venom are holding a martial contest, then her father would want to watch, Lotus thought to herself.

Sure enough, Laurel Lu said, "What about Grandmaster?"

"Over there," Emerald said, and pointed. "Three figures. The last one looks like your Grandmaster."

"Yes. Oh, they're already so far away. I wonder who the other two are? What a shame we will never know."

The Hoary Urchin is one thing, Lotus said to herself, but I wouldn't desire a meeting with Old Venom.

Laurel and Emerald assumed they were alone now, and their inhibitions began to melt away. Laurel placed his arm around his wife's waist and whispered, "My dear, what is your given name?"

"Guess," she replied with a smile.

"Little Kitten? Or else Little Puppy?"

"No," she said, and laughed. "My name is Caterpillar."

"Then I must hunt you down, Caterpillar!"

Emerald wriggled free and leaped over the table. Laurel laughed and gave chase. Giggling, they ran hither and thither around the inn.

The stars in the sky provided only the dimmest light, so Lotus was unable to see the young couple clearly, but their laughter was loud enough.

"Do you think he will manage to catch Sister Cheng?" Guo Jing whispered suddenly in Lotus's ear.

"Of course," she replied with a gentle chuckle.

"And then what?"

Lotus's heart skipped a beat. She did not know how to answer him. At that moment, the young couple collapsed onto one of the benches, Emerald locked in Laurel's arms. They started murmuring to one another.

Guo Jing's left hand was touching Lotus's right. She could feel his palm growing hotter, his body shaking from side to side. Fear for him gripped her heart. "Guo Jing, what's happening? Let's stop."

The laughter, the beautiful young maiden by his side. These devilish thoughts were dangerous to one who had suffered such injuries, especially while practicing Nine Yin breathing techniques. His blood was nearly at boiling point. He turned and reached for her shoulder. The feel of his burning palm and the rush of his hot breath startled Lotus.

"Be careful, Guo Jing," she breathed. "Steady your *qi*."

"I can't . . ." he panted. He was visibly shaken. "I . . . I . . ." He moved as if to stand.

"No, stay still!"

Guo Jing forced himself to stay seated and fought to control his breathing. But it felt as if his chest was about to burst. "Lotus, help me," he pleaded. Once more, he made as if to stand.

"Sit! If you move, I will lock your pressure points."

"Yes, do it. I can't control myself."

But if she sealed his points, Lotus realized, she would also be blocking his *qi*, and the last two days would be wasted. And yet, in this state, he was in mortal danger. She gritted her teeth and made a circle with her left arm, in a display of Orchid Touch technique. Then she struck at his Camphor Gate pressure point, located on the left side of his eleventh rib.

Just as her finger made contact, however, one of his muscles contracted, deflecting her touch. She tried again, but the same thing happened. When she reached to try once more, he grabbed her wrist.

Lotus looked into Guo Jing's eyes, now just visible in the first dawn light. They were bloodshot and red, as if on fire. He gripped her wrist tighter and seemed to mumble something incomprehensible. It was as if he had gone mad. Scared, Lotus jabbed her shoulder against his arm. The spikes of her Hedgehog Chainmail pricked his skin, and the pain sent a shock wave through him.

Just then, a rooster crowed. His mind was suddenly clear, as though he'd been struck by lightning. He dropped Lotus's wrist and looked back at her. His embarrassment was obvious.

Lotus saw beads of sweat pouring down his forehead. His cheeks were pale, and he looked exhausted. But she knew that he was safe.

"Guo Jing, we've already managed two days and two nights."

Slap! Guo Jing struck his cheek. "Stupid!" He was about to hit himself again, but Lotus stopped him and smiled.

"All is well. Remember Old Urchin? With all his years of training, he still couldn't resist my father's flute. You? You're injured. Don't blame yourself."

In the heat of the moment, they had forgotten to lower their voices. Laurel and Emerald were aware only of each other in their lovers' confusion, so they heard nothing.

But Gallant Ouyang, still lying in the corner, had picked up on it. Had he even recognized the young Huang girl's voice? He listened attentively, but there was no sound now.

As both legs had been crushed by the giant rock, he shifted his weight onto his hands and managed to "walk" himself out of his hiding place.

3

LAUREL AND EMERALD WERE SITTING SIDE BY SIDE ON A bench, his left arm draped over her shoulder. Just then, they heard a rustling from the area around the pile of firewood. They turned, only to see a man walking across the room on his hands. They jumped to their feet and drew their weapons.

Gallant Ouyang's weak state had only been made worse by the hours of hunger he had endured. The glint of a blade dazzled him, and he collapsed onto his stomach. Laurel Lu instantly registered the paleness of his cheeks. He rushed forward and helped the injured man up onto the bench, where he could lean against the table.

At that moment, Emerald let out a gasp of recognition. It was the awful man who had kidnapped her in Baoying.

Laurel could not miss the fear in her eyes. "Don't worry, his legs are broken."

"He's a bad man. I know him," Emerald replied.

Surprised, Laurel turned to look at the injured man just as he came to.

"Rice. I'm starving."

Emerald observed how sunken his cheeks had become. His eyes were dull. This was not the same man who had insulted and attacked her. Her heart was moved, perhaps because she was in love, and so she went to the kitchen to fetch him a bowl of rice.

Gallant ate it and immediately asked for another one. Upon finishing the second bowl, he felt his strength returning. He looked at

Miss Cheng and felt a stirring in his loins. But then he remembered Lotus. "Where is Miss Huang?"

"Which Miss Huang?" Laurel asked.

"The daughter of the Lord of Peach Blossom Island, Apothecary Huang."

"Do you know my martial elder personally? I heard she is no longer of this world," Laurel said.

"Don't lie to me," Gallant sneered. "I just heard her speak." He placed his left hand against the table and suddenly flipped himself over it. The injury to his right arm already felt better.

Continuing on his hands, he circled the room. The voice had come from the eastern side, but there was no door to be found. There must be a hidden chamber, accessed from the cupboard, he surmised. He pulled the table toward it and then flipped himself up on top. From there, he opened the door. He was disappointed, however. Far from finding a secret passage, he saw only a few dirty shelves. Indeed, it was intolerably filthy. He looked carefully, and saw some handprints in the dust. And some more on a metal bowl. He reached out and grabbed it, but it was stuck. He tried twisting it loose, only for a door inside the cupboard to creak open.

Inside, Lotus and Guo Jing were sitting cross-legged, facing each other.

The sight of the young man with Lotus dampened his joy. In fact, he felt intensely jealous. "Are you training in here?" he said, after a short pause.

Lotus had been watching his movements and had known that they were soon going to be discovered. As the door to the cupboard was opened, she whispered in Guo Jing's ear: "I'll draw him in, you kill him with your Dragon-Subduing Palm."

"I don't have the strength."

Just as Lotus had been about to reply, the door to their secret chamber began to open.

Panicked, Lotus tried to come up with a plan. How can I get him to leave us alone, so that we might have another five days and nights?

Gallant Ouyang was normally wary of Guo Jing, but the young man's pale cheeks reminded him of his uncle's words in the Imperial Palace. If he ever found the boy in a weakened state, he should use Exploding Toad kung fu. If that did not kill him, it would at least leave him severely injured.

"Sister," he said, "why don't you come out? The air is very stuffy; you don't want to sit in there for any length of time." He reached out to take her sleeve.

With a whoosh, Lotus brought her stick down toward his head. It was one of the deadliest moves in all of Dog-Beating Cane technique and she had employed it with devastating speed. The rush of air as it came toward him was enough to force Gallant to move aside. But the staff was suddenly coming at him in a horizontal sweep. Startled, Gallant somersaulted over the table.

Had she been better positioned, Lotus could have followed with a Jab the Dog's Buttocks. It would have been a deadly move, but tricky to launch while sitting cross-legged, and she was unwilling to risk leaving Guo Jing alone.

Laurel and Emerald, meanwhile, watched in astonishment. By the time they realized who the two people inside were, Lotus had already launched her attack on Gallant.

Gallant spun out of his somersault and was heading toward the ground when he reached out, pushed both hands against the floor and rebounded back onto the table. Then he made a grab for Lotus.

Lotus had nowhere to go, and she was mindful that she could not exert too much inner strength herself, for fear of hurting Guo Jing. Even with no legs, Gallant was a stronger fighter than her. She was in trouble.

Laurel and Emerald drew their weapons and launched themselves at Gallant. He merely laughed, however, and struck out at Guo Jing's face with his palm. Unable to defend himself, Guo Jing closed his eyes and waited.

Lotus blocked with her staff; Gallant flipped his hand and

grabbed the end of it. Lotus was no match for his strength, and so she was pulled with it. Fearing that her palm would lose contact with Guo Jing's, she let go of the Dog-Beating Cane. Instead, she reached into her robes, pulled out one of her throwing needles and hurled it at him.

He threw himself back, bending at the waist so that he was almost lying across the tabletop.

Laurel regarded him as if he was a piece of meat laid out for sacrifice. He raised his saber high and aimed at his neck. Gallant rolled right. The blade bit deep into the wood. Just then, Laurel heard the swish of another needle above his head. Suddenly, his back went numb. He was paralyzed down one side of his body, and someone was holding him, from behind, by the arm.

Emerald ran forward to help.

"Excellent!" cried Gallant as he grabbed the front of her robes.

Emerald swung her blade at his hand, jumping back at the same time, leaving a scrap of fabric in his grasp. Afraid, she nearly let go of her weapon. The blood drained from her cheeks and she retreated to the corner.

Still keeping hold of Laurel Lu, Gallant took a seat at the table and turned toward the cupboard. The door to the secret chamber was, once more, closed. A shudder went through him as he thought of how close Lotus's needle had come. The young girl was not an easy opponent. But he could toy with the Cheng girl loudly enough for Lotus and Guo Jing to overhear. They would be unable to concentrate on their practice, and he might be able to draw Lotus out into a less defensible position.

He turned to Emerald Cheng. "Miss Cheng, do you want this young man to live, or die?"

With her husband still in this man's grip, she knew it would be unwise to act rashly. "He has done you no wrong. Please, let him go. There is no acrimony between you. Were you not hungry, just a moment ago? Did I not bring you rice to eat?"

At this, Gallant laughed. "Two bowls of rice? Is that sufficient payment for a life? I'm sure you disciples of the Quanzhen Sect never imagined having to beg a hero from another school for mercy."

"He . . . He is a disciple of Peach Blossom Island. Don't hurt him."

"Who instructed him to come at me with his saber? Had I not been so quick, I would no longer have a head upon my neck. Don't threaten me with Peach Blossom Island. Lord Huang is my father-in-law."

Emerald stared back at him. She did not know if he was lying. "Then you are his martial elder. Let him go and he will plead your forgiveness."

"Ha! Since when was anything in life that easy? If you want me to let him go, you must first do as I tell you."

There was no mistaking the lascivious smirk on his face. His intentions were surely villainous. Emerald lowered her gaze and did not reply.

"Watch!" Gallant cried, then smashed his palm down on the corner of the table, cutting a piece from it as neatly as if he had used an axe.

Emerald was stunned. Not even my *shifu* is capable of something like that, she thought.

Gallant had been training under his uncle since he was a small boy, so it was no wonder that his martial skills had surpassed those of the Sage of Tranquility, who had only started her practice in adulthood.

Emerald's frightened expression boosted Gallant's confidence further. "You must do exactly as I say. Otherwise, I will perform the same move, but on his neck." Then he swung his palm in the air.

Emerald shivered and gasped.

"What do you say?"

Emerald nodded, reluctantly.

"Excellent. That's a good girl. Now, go over there and close the door."

Emerald did not move.

"What? You are not obeying?" His tone was furious.

Emerald trembled. She had no choice. She rose to her feet and went to close the door.

"You two were joined in matrimony last night, I witnessed it all. It was your wedding night, and yet neither of you undressed. I have never heard of such a couple in all my life. If you don't know how to be a good bride, let me teach you. Take off your clothes. All of them. If you leave so much as one thread of silk, I will send your husband to meet the heavens, and you will be known as a wanton young widow!"

Laurel was perfectly still. He was so furious, it felt as if his eyes might pop out of their sockets. He wanted to tell Emerald to run and not worry about him, but he could not make his lips move.

4

WHEN GALLANT HAD GRABBED LAUREL, LOTUS HAD TAKEN the opportunity to pull the door to their chamber shut. Then she took out her dagger and waited. She listened in astonishment to what was going on in the next room. Had Gallant really asked Emerald to remove her clothing? She was indignant, and yet, she could not help but admit that there was something amusing about the situation. Such was her childish nature. She hated Gallant Ouyang, to be sure, but she was also curious to know whether the chaste Miss Cheng would strip naked.

"Where's the shame in taking your clothes off?" she heard Gallant say. "Were you not naked when you came from your mother's belly? What matters most to you? Your husband, or your pride?"

Emerald paused, then said, "Kill him, then!"

This was the last thing Gallant had been expecting her to say, and it took him by surprise. Then he saw her lift her sword to her neck. Quickly, he threw a Bone-Piercing Awl, knocking the blade to the ground.

Emerald was bending down to retrieve her sword when she heard a knock at the door.

"Innkeeper! Innkeeper!"

A woman's voice. Emerald sighed with relief. Maybe she can help. She grabbed her weapon and then leaped to open the door.

There, in the doorway, was a young woman in white. Her head was wrapped in white cloth and she had a sword attached at her waist. Her face was thin and pallid, but she was striking nonetheless.

"Please, come in," Emerald said quickly, hoping that, whoever she was, she had come to save them.

The young woman regarded Emerald's fine features, expensive clothes and the weapon in her hand, and was clearly surprised that she would happen upon such a person in a run-down inn, in a desolate village such as this.

"I have two coffins with me outside. May I bring them in?"

Emerald had no objections. Indeed, she would have let her bring in a hundred, perhaps even a thousand coffins. "Excellent," she said, instead.

Excellent? What an odd response, thought the young woman in white. Ordinarily, it was considered taboo to have coffins inside. Never mind. She turned and waved. Eight young men started to bring the black coffins inside.

The woman in white then turned and was surprised to see Gallant Ouyang. Instantly, her hand dropped to the hilt of her saber.

Gallant laughed. "It is our destiny to be together again. There's no avoiding it when the heavens have decided it must be so. It would be a great insult for us not to obey their command."

The woman in white was, of course, Mercy Mu, who had been captured by Gallant Ouyang in the past. After she parted with Yang Kang in Baoying, she cut her hair as a statement of her sorrow, before remembering that she had a duty to bring the bodies of Ironheart Yang and his wife back home. They must be buried together in Ox Village. Once her task was completed, she would devote her life to the Buddhist scriptures.

She had never set foot in Ox Village before and she found it almost entirely abandoned. The houses were barely standing. She had spotted the lone inn and decided to make inquiries there.

The last person she expected to see was Gallant Ouyang.

Was this finely dressed young woman his captive? Mercy had been hidden away in the coffin the day Gallant had attacked Miss Cheng, so they had never set eyes on each other. She could just as easily be one of his concubines. Mercy drew her sword.

A flutter of robes. A shadow flickered overhead.

Mercy jabbed her blade upward, but Gallant grasped it between his finger and thumb and pulled it, still in mid-air. He then reached for her wrist. Mercy tried to let go of her sword, but, in the split second before she could do so, her body was pulled up, landing alongside Gallant on top of the coffin that was now halfway through the door.

The four men carrying the coffin cried out and it crashed to the ground, landing on three of the men's feet.

Gallant pressed Mercy to his chest, while waving his dagger at the men. They screamed, before scrambling over the coffin and out of the door. The remaining men dropped the other coffin, and they too made a hasty escape, with no thought for the money owed them.

Now free from Gallant's grip, Laurel had fallen to the ground. Emerald rushed to help him to his feet. She had no idea what was happening, but she was determined to get out of the inn as fast as possible.

Still clutching Mercy, Gallant leaped toward the table. He grabbed Emerald by the belt and swept her into his grip, before locking both women's pressure points. He sat on the bench and cried, "Miss Huang! You must join us!"

5

AT THAT MOMENT, A SHADOW CROSSED THE COURTYARD OUT-side and, just as suddenly, a gentleman appeared at the door. It was Yang Kang.

He had fled Ox Village with the others, angry and humiliated by their treatment at the hands of Apothecary Huang. Nobody spoke of the shaming experience. Yang Kang had decided that, if he wanted revenge, he must first find Viper Ouyang, who was yet to return from the Imperial Palace.

He explained his thoughts to his father, Wanyan Honglie, and came back alone, stopping to watch and wait in the forest on the outskirts of the village.

That night, Zhou Botong, Viper Ouyang, and Apothecary Huang had come and gone so fast that Yang Kang had not been able to discern the meaning of their movements in the dark. Early the next morning, he watched as Mercy Mu arrived with the coffins. His heart thumping with excitement, he followed her to the inn and saw her go inside.

Shortly afterward, the porters came running from the building. What was happening in there? He approached silently and peered through a crack in the door. Apothecary Huang was nowhere to be seen, but he did catch sight of Mercy Mu in Gallant Ouyang's arms.

Gallant Ouyang saw the young man and called out, "Your Majesty. You're back!"

Yang Kang nodded.

Gallant noticed the strange look in his eyes and tried to comfort him. "All those years ago, Han Xin also humiliated himself by having to crawl between someone's legs. But great men do not break with a bit of bending and stretching. Wait for my uncle to return; he can exact retribution on Apothecary Huang on your behalf."

Once more, Yang Kang nodded. His gaze was fixed on Mercy Mu.

Gallant Ouyang smiled. "What do you say, young Prince—they are both beauties, are they not?"

Again, Yang Kang nodded. Gallant had not been present at the Duel for a Maiden, when the Prince and Mercy had first met, and therefore knew nothing of the connection between them.

At first, Yang Kang had not thought much of Mercy. But he had noticed her devotion to him and could not help but be moved by it. She was excessively charming and he had every intention of fulfilling his promise to wed her. To see her in Gallant's dastardly arms made his heart swell with hatred and jealousy, but somehow he managed to maintain his composure.

"There was a wedding here, last night," Gallant said with a smirk. "There is wine and chicken in the kitchen. Could I trouble the Prince to fetch it? I would like to drink a toast with you. These two beauties will then strip and dance for you."

"Wonderful," Yang Kang replied, and smiled.

Mercy had been secretly pleased to see Yang Kang, but when he failed to pay her any attention, fury began to boil within her. Now, as he went along with Gallant's plan to humiliate her, her heart turned to ice. As soon as she was free from Gallant's grip, she would slit her throat in front of the heartless Prince. Then, finally, she would escape the cruel indignities of this world.

She watched as he went to the kitchen, returned with the food and sat next to Gallant. Gallant poured two cups of wine and held them to Emerald and Mercy's mouths. "Drink first; it will help you with your performance."

Both young women were furious, but, with their acupressure points sealed, they were unable to turn away. They were each forced to swallow half a cup.

"Master Ouyang, I do admire your martial skills," Yang Kang began. "Let me toast your prowess before we enjoy the dancing."

Gallant received the cup from Yang Kang and downed its contents in one gulp. He then released the two women's pressure points, before casually placing his hands over the ones on their backs. "If you do as I say, you won't get hurt. In fact, I will make you very happy!" Then he turned to Yang Kang. "Your Majesty, I guarantee you will enjoy the performance. Choose one!"

"Why, thank you," Yang Kang replied.

Mercy pointed toward the coffins. "Yang Kang, do you know who lies inside those coffins?"

Yang Kang turned and saw that, on one coffin, a red piece of paper had been affixed, bearing the words, *Here lies Ironheart Yang, a loyal patriot of the Great Song.* A rush of cold blood entered his heart, but his face betrayed not a trace of it.

"Master Ouyang," he said, seemingly ignoring Mercy's question, "will you hold them tight? I would like to see who has the smallest feet—she will be my choice."

"Very clever!" Gallant said, and laughed. "I think this one has the smaller feet." He stroked Emerald on the chin. "I have a rather special talent. I need only look at a girl's face to know her body intimately, from head to toe."

"How impressive! May I bow to you and call you Master, so that you might teach me this special skill?" As he spoke, he bent down under the table.

Both Emerald and Mercy had secretly devised the same plan. As soon as he touched their feet, they would kick at the Great Sun point, on his temple.

"Master Ouyang," Yang Kang called from under the table, "have another cup, and then I will tell you if you guessed correctly."

"All right!" He reached for another cup with both hands.

Yang Kang glanced up from beneath the table and saw Gallant drinking, his head thrown back. Just then, he reached into his robes for the broken spearhead. Gathering all his strength to his arm, he thrust the point into Gallant's stomach, plunging it five inches into his flesh. Then he rolled back out from underneath the table.

Something had happened—Lotus, Mercy, Laurel, and Emerald all knew it, but they did not know exactly what. Gallant pushed the bench from under Mercy and Emerald, and threw his wine cup at the Prince. Yang Kang ducked, and the cup smashed into hundreds of small pieces. Gallant must have thrown it with extreme force.

Yang Kang rolled toward the door, but the coffins were blocking his way. He flipped onto his feet and saw Gallant standing on his hands, on top of the bench, his chest bent forward. He wore a strange smirk on his face, and his eyes were fixed on Yang Kang. Yang Kang felt a shiver go through him. He wanted nothing more than to escape, but his feet were rooted to the spot.

"I have been wandering for half my life, and yet, I am destined to die by the hand of a mere boy?" Gallant sneered. "Tell me, Prince, why did you kill me?"

Yang Kang leaped. Mid-air, he felt a gust of air behind him. A hand that felt cold, like a metal hook, caught him by the neck, forcing him to land next to Gallant on the bench.

"Won't you answer my question? You wish me to die in ignorance?" Gallant pressed again.

Gallant locked the pressure point on the back of Yang Kang's neck, paralyzing him. He would not get out of this alive.

"Very well," Yang Kang said with a cold smile. "I'll tell you. Do you know who she is?" he said, pointing at Mercy.

Gallant turned to the young woman, who was poised to strike with a dagger. Mercy was reluctant to intervene lest she accidentally hurt Yang Kang. Her face bore the same expression of concern that Emerald had shown for Laurel.

Gallant suddenly realized, and laughed. "She . . . She . . ." he began, but was cut off by a bout of coughing.

"We are betrothed. You have harassed her repeatedly. You tell me: should I let you go?"

"Indeed," Gallant managed to say, smiling. "Then we are going to hell together." With another splutter of coughing, he raised his palm as if to strike the top of Yang Kang's skull.

Mercy yelped and charged.

Yang Kang had closed his eyes, waiting for Gallant's strike. But nothing happened. He opened his eyes. Gallant's palm was still raised and ready, but his other hand had relaxed its grip on Yang Kang's neck. Yang Kang took his chance and leaped free.

Gallant collapsed on top of the coffin. He was no longer breathing.

Yang Kang and Mercy exchanged a glance before rushing toward each other. They held hands and stared at each other in silence. Neither knew where to start. They looked down at Gallant, fear still lodged in their hearts.

Emerald unlocked Laurel's pressure point and helped him to his feet. Laurel knew that Yang Kang was an envoy of the Jin. He had killed Gallant Ouyang, and therefore Laurel owed him a debt, but he could not treat an enemy of the Song as a friend. He cupped his hands and nodded, then took Emerald by the hand and left.

It had been the most extraordinary few hours, and they had only narrowly escaped death. Under the circumstances, it was only natural that they forgot Lotus and Guo Jing were sitting in the next room.

Yang Kang and Mercy's reunification pleased Lotus. He had saved Mercy from a terrible fate. Guo Jing, too, was surprised to see his sworn brother act so honorably. He exchanged glances with Lotus and they both smiled.

"I have brought the bodies of your parents home," they heard Mercy say to Yang Kang.

"I should have done that. What trouble you must have been through."

Mercy did not want to look back, so she focused on burial preparations for Ironheart Yang and his wife, Charity Bao.

Yang Kang reached down and pulled the spearhead from Gallant's abdomen. "We must bury him quickly. If his uncle finds out what happened, he will chase us to the ends of the earth."

Immediately, the young couple began to dig a hole behind the inn. Then they went into the village to find some people to help them carry the two coffins back to where the Yang cottage had once stood. It had been so many years since Ironheart Yang left the village that all those who remembered him had long since died. But the villagers were obliging and asked no questions.

By the time they had finished burying their dead, darkness had already swept across the sky. That night, Mercy slept in the home of one of the villagers, while Yang Kang bedded down at the inn.

6

EARLY THE NEXT MORNING, MERCY RETURNED TO THE INN.
As she approached, she could see Yang Kang pacing about inside,
stamping his feet and mumbling to himself. She went in and asked
him what the matter was.

"I should never have let those two go, yesterday. I should have
killed them. Who knows where they have got to by now."

"Why?" Mercy asked, a little frightened.

"They saw me kill Gallant Ouyang. What if they tell someone?"

Mercy frowned. "Real men are brave and get things done. You
shouldn't have killed him if you were going to worry so much."

Yang Kang did not reply. He was too busy trying to think of
how he might find Laurel and Emerald and silence them forever.

"His uncle may be terrifying," Mercy began, "but we can go into
hiding."

"My dear Mercy . . . I have another idea. I could make his uncle
my master."

This caught Mercy's attention.

"The idea first came to me a while ago. But his school of martial
arts has a very strict rule: only one student per generation. Now that
his disciple is dead, however, he might consider taking me on." He
seemed very proud of himself for coming up with this plan.

A cold shiver ran through Mercy's heart. "So, the reason you
killed him," she said with a tremble in her voice, "was not to save
me. You had another purpose, all along."

"You are too suspicious," Yang Kang said, and laughed. "I would
do anything for you. Why, I would let myself be crushed into a
thousand pieces."

"We can talk more about this later. What is your plan for the here
and now? Are you willing to declare your allegiance to the Great

263

Song? Or are you still determined to follow our enemy in the name of money and power?"

Her beauty was bewitching. But it displeased him to hear her articulate his inner thoughts. "Money? Power? Huh. What money and power do I possess? Yanjing has fallen to the Mongolians. The Jurchens have been defeated in battle after battle. The Great Jin will soon be no more."

The more he spoke, the more furious Mercy became. "The Jin's downfall is our dearest wish," she said sternly, "and yet you lament it? So what if the Great Jin is no more? Do you consider yourself Jurchen?"

"Why are we talking about this? I have missed you bitterly ever since you left." He approached her slowly and took her hand.

These words softened her, and she let him pull her gently closer. Her cheeks glowed a soft pink.

Yang Kang was about to put his arm around her when, suddenly, the screeching of birds filled the air. He rushed outside, looked up and saw a pair of white condors flying above. Yang Kang had seen another pair just like them the day his father, Wanyan Honglie, led the team of soldiers to kill Tolui. What were they doing here?

Mercy joined him outside. The birds were now circling above them.

There, under the shade of a nearby tree, they saw her. A young woman was sitting astride a magnificent horse, looking straight at them. She was dressed in Mongolian attire, wearing leather riding boots and carrying a whip. A bow was slung over her shoulder and a leather quiver hung from her belt.

The condors continued to screech a while longer, before flying off again, following the road out of the village. Before long, however, they were back, accompanied by the beating of hooves.

A cloud of dust rose on the horizon, out of which three riders emerged.

The birds are leading horses to the girl, Yang Kang thought.

A loud swishing sound caught their attention. An arrow. Yang

Kang and Mercy watched as the Mongolian girl drew one of hers from the quiver and shot it up into the sky. The three riders heard it, whooped and spurred their horses on faster.

The girl kicked her horse and rode in the direction of the approaching riders. Once they had drawn to within ten meters of each other, they jumped from their saddles, joined hands in mid-air and landed together on the ground.

With such horsemanship, it is no wonder the Jin are being defeated by the Mongolians, Yang Kang thought. Even their young women are expert riders. As the new arrivals left their mounts in the courtyard and made for the inn door, Yang Kang led Mercy to the kitchen, where they could listen to what unfolded without being seen.

7

LOTUS AND GUO JING HAD HEARD THE SCREECHING OF CON-
dors and the pounding of hooves from inside the secret chamber. Moments later, they heard voices, as several people entered the inn.

Guo Jing sat up in surprise. How did she get here? How wonderful!

The Mongolian girl was none other than Khojin, the daughter of Genghis Khan to whom he had been betrothed. The other three riders were Tolui, Jebe, and Boroqul.

Lotus could not understand them, of course, but Guo Jing listened to their laughing and joking, his face green one moment and white the next. His initial delight quickly gave way to anxiety. My heart belongs to Lotus; I can't marry Khojin. But, if she has followed me all this way, how can I turn my back on a promise? What should I do?

"Guo Jing," Lotus whispered, "who is she? What are they saying? Why do you look so pale?"

Many times, Guo Jing had meant to tell Lotus, but every time the words had got as far as his lips, he had swallowed them back down again. Now she was asking him straight out, he could no longer conceal the truth from her. "She is the daughter of the Great Khan of the Mongolians. And we are promised to one another."

Shock registered on Lotus's face, and tears filled her eyes. "You . . . You . . . You're promised to each other? Why didn't you tell me?"

"I wanted to tell you, but I didn't want to upset you. And some-times, well, I even forgot about it myself."

"She will be your wife one day. How could you forget such a thing?"

Guo Jing did not know how to answer this. "In my heart, I have always regarded her as a sister. I don't want to marry her."

A flicker of hope registered on her face.

"The Great Khan decided it," he went on. "I wasn't upset at the time, but neither did the thought please me. I merely thought, What-ever the Great Khan decides must be right. But, Lotus, how can I marry a woman who is not you? If I cannot marry you, I cannot go on living."

"Then what should we do?"

"I don't know."

Lotus sighed. "As long as you are true to me in your heart, then I don't mind if you marry her." She paused a moment, then continued, "Actually, don't marry her. I can't bear the idea of you and another woman together from morning till night, and I'm no good at con-trolling my temper. I might stick a blade in her heart, and then you would curse me till the end of your days. Let us not talk about this anymore. Concentrate on what they are saying."

Guo Jing pressed his ear to the small hole and heard Tolui and Khojin talking about all that had happened since they had left. It seemed that, after Lotus and Guo Jing took to the sea, the white condors had circled in the wind and rain looking for them. But, with nowhere to rest, they had given up and returned to land. They then flew north to find their other master, Khojin.

Khojin had been surprised by their return. She noticed one of the condors had a piece of cloth tied to one foot, upon which was scratched two Chinese characters. Unable to read this foreign script, she took it to some Han Chinese who were fighting alongside the Mongolians, and they translated the message for her: *HELP.* Concerned, she immediately rode south.

By this time, her father was fighting against the Jin. Each day brought new battles on both sides of the Great Wall. With the Great Khan's attention fixed on the enemy, it was easy for her to slip away.

The condors understood their master's intention and led her south. By day, they would fly ahead several hundred *li*, looking for Guo Jing, before returning and guiding Khojin on. This they did until they reached Lin'an, where, instead of finding Guo Jing, they came across Khojin's brother, Tolui, instead.

Tolui had continued his journey to Lin'an after Guo Jing had rescued him from Wanyan Honglie's attack in Baoying, to carry out his father's misson of convincing the Song to join forces with the Mongolians in an attack against the Jin. But the Song officials were at last enjoying peace and prosperity in their new capital, and they feared entering into yet more hostilities with the Jurchen forces. Every day of peace was a gift from the heavens above and the earth below. Why would they risk pulling the tiger's tail? The Song court barely deigned to receive him officially, and Tolui was housed in the guesthouse—an insult, indeed. It was pure luck that the Jin Prince had been captured by the Masters of Roaming Cloud Manor at Lake Tai, else Wanyan Kang would have delivered the order to the Song to kill Tolui.

News followed that the Mongolians were advancing at speed and that the Jin capital, Yanjing, had fallen. These tidings compelled the Song officials to change their attitude to Tolui, and he was suddenly addressed as the Fourth Prince of Mongolia. They flattered him and fawned on him. They even agreed to an alliance against the Jin. If they could win back what they had lost at the hands of the northern invaders, at little cost to themselves, then why not?

The ministers and officials rushed to prepare the agreement, but Tolui still smarted at their initial treatment of him. He signed it, nevertheless, and on the same day returned north. He was sent off with great fanfare, but Tolui had no stomach for their hollow rituals, and instead spurred his horse and galloped into the distance.

He had yet to make it beyond the outskirts of the city, however, when he spotted a pair of fine, white condors in the sky. Guo Jing is here!

To his surprise, however, he was instead greeted by his very own sister, Khojin.

"Have you seen your *anda*?" she asked, now, cutting off her brother's story.

Before Tolui could answer, a noise came from outside. The clanging of metal. Horses' hooves.

The Song escort, courteous to a fault, had finally caught up with him.

Yang Kang watched in silence from his hiding place. The Song men were carrying a large banner, upon which had been painted the words: *WISHING THE FOURTH PRINCE OF MONGOLIA A SAFE RETURN NORTH.*

A disquieting thought seized Yang Kang. Before he was captured on Lake Tai, he too had been regarded as an honored envoy. But, now, he was nobody. He had enjoyed the gilded life of royalty, lauded to the skies and waited on hand and foot. It was not easily relinquished.

Mercy Mu watched him coldly. She saw the wistful look on his face and, though she did not know what he was thinking, she could not easily forget that he had so willingly lived among the enemy, even after he had learned of his true heritage.

The leading officer of the Song escort entered the inn and bowed before Tolui. They exchanged a few words. Then the officer went outside again and cried to his men: "Go to each house and ask if they know the whereabouts of a gentleman named Guo Jing!"

The soldiers spread out at once. Before long, the sounds of clucking chickens and barking dogs filled the village. Men shouted. Women cried. Having failed to obtain the information they were looking for, the soldiers had started helping themselves to the villagers' belongings. How else were they to penalize them for their reticence?

From the kitchen where he and Mercy had taken shelter, Yang Kang watched the scene play out before them and an idea struck him. If the Song soldiers used this opportunity to steal from their own people, would it really be a betrayal if he befriended the Mongolians? *I will go with the Fourth Prince north, and, on the way, I will kill him. It shouldn't be too difficult. Genghis Khan will assume it to be the work of the Song, and their alliance will be shattered before it has truly begun. It will be a great favor to the Jin.*

He turned to Mercy and said, "Wait here." Then he went into the main room of the inn. The leading Song officer barked at him and tried to halt him with a hand. Yang Kang merely tossed him into a wall. The officer collapsed in a heap and lay still.

Tolui and Khojin were startled. Yang Kang now took up a position in the center of the room. He took the broken spearhead from his robes and raised it above his head, before bowing and placing it on the table. "Brother Guo Jing, Brother Guo Jing," he wailed. "What a miserable way to die. I will avenge you, Brother Guo Jing."

Neither Tolui nor Khojin understood Chinese, but they did understand Guo Jing's name. They turned to the Song officer, who was groggily getting back to his feet, and asked him to translate the young stranger's words.

Through tears, Yang Kang spoke: "I am the sworn brother of Guo Jing. A bastard killed him with this spearhead. A Song soldier. I think it came as an order from Chancellor Shi Miyuan."

The Song officer dutifully translated. Brother and sister listened, their faces falling. The other Mongolian riders, Jebe and Boroqul, recalled their friendship with the young Chinese boy who had grown up among them, and together they wept.

Yang Kang reminded them of how Guo Jing had defeated the Jin soldiers at Baoying, saving Tolui and the others in the process. At this, Tolui was fully convinced by the stranger's tale. How had their friend died and who had done the deed? Yang Kang told them his sworn brother was killed by a Song official by the name of Justice Duan. He knew the bastard's whereabouts and he was in fact on his way to seek revenge. It would be a difficult task to complete without help. He spoke with such feeling that the others had no doubt he was telling the truth.

Guo Jing listened from the secret chamber in deep frustration. He watched as Khojin drew her sword and held it to her neck.

"Sister!" Tolui rushed forward and grabbed the weapon. "You mustn't kill yourself. We must avenge Brother Guo's death instead."

It's working, Yang Kang thought with delight. He lowered his head and blinked out yet more tears. At that moment, he caught sight of the bamboo stick that Gallant had snatched from Lotus, lying on the ground. It was dark green and shone like crystal, a most unusual object. He went to retrieve it. Lotus watched in horror, but there was nothing she could do.

The soldiers returned with food and wine, though they found the Mongolians in no mood to eat. Instead, they urged Yang Kang to lead them to Guo Jing's killer. Yang Kang nodded and, still holding the bamboo staff, moved toward the door. He turned back and called to Mercy to join them, but she stayed put. This was not an opportunity Yang Kang could pass up, so he decided to leave without her. Affairs of the heart could wait.

8

"DIDN'T HE KILL JUSTICE DUAN AT ROAMING CLOUD MANOR?" Guo Jing whispered to Lotus.

"I don't understand it either. Wasn't he the one who stabbed you at the waterfall? He's a devious and wicked young man. What does he want?"

Just then, they heard a voice outside: "*Unbridled heart I am not weighed, by either shame or glory* . . . Ah! Miss Mu! What brings you here?" It was Eternal Spring Qiu Chuji.

Mercy had come outside to see if the soldiers had left. Before she could reply, Yang Kang appeared in the doorway. At once, he spotted his *shifu*. His heart started thumping wildly. There was nowhere for him to hide—they had been brought face-to-face. He had no choice but to kowtow and greet Qiu Chuji with customary deference.

Beside his Master stood Scarlet Sun Ma Yu, Jade Sun Wang Chuyi, the Sage of Tranquility Sun Bu'er, and another of Qiu Chuji's disciples, Harmony Yin.

After having had most of his teeth knocked out by Apothecary Huang the previous day, Harmony Yin had rushed back to Lin'an to report back to his Master. Qiu Chuji had listened in shock and anger; he wanted nothing more than to go and find the Lord of Peach Blossom Island at once. But Ma Yu had tried to dissuade him.

"Many years ago, Old Huang shared the same honor as our late Master," Qiu Chuji said. "Among us, only our martial brother Wang Chuyi has had the pleasure of meeting him, when they fought at Mount Hua. I have long admired the man and have no desire to fight him."

"I have heard that Apothecary Huang is of strange temperament," Ma Yu said. "And you can be quite rash and prone to outbursts yourself. I doubt that a meeting between you would go well. May I remind you that he spared Harmony's life. There was no obligation to do so."

But Qiu Chuji was insistent, and Ma Yu could not stop him. It just so happened, however, that all seven Masters of the Quanzhen Sect were in or around Lin'an, so letters were sent out summoning them to meet in Ox Village the next day.

9

THE SEVEN MASTERS WERE QUICK TO REALIZE THAT, DESPITE their considerable prowess, they would find in Apothecary Huang a formidable opponent. They had to be careful. Ma Yu, Qiu Chuji, Wang Chuyi, Sun Bu'er, and Harmony Yin would enter the village first, while Tan Chuduan, Liu Chuxuan, and Hao Datong waited on the outskirts.

Yet they found no sign of Apothecary Huang. Instead, they were greeted outside the inn by Yang Kang and Mercy Mu.

Qiu Chuji watched his disciple kowtow, then snorted and turned away.

"Master," Harmony Yin spoke, "this *is* where the Lord of Peach Blossom Island attacked me."

Ma Yu had scolded them for referring to him as the Old Heretic, so now they were all careful to use the more respectful title.

"All seven disciples of the Quanzhen Sect have come to pay their respects to Lord Huang," Qiu Chuji cried, his voice echoing around the courtyard.

"The Masters have come to the wrong place," Yang Kang said. "He's not here."

"What a shame." Qiu Chuji's tone was exasperated, and he even stamped his foot a little in annoyance. "What are you doing here?" he said finally, to his student.

Yang Kang was too scared to reply.

Khojin, meanwhile, was staring hard at Ma Yu. Suddenly, she ran forward. "You're the uncle with the three buns who helped me capture the white condors! They've grown up to be so big!" she said, stretching out her arms. She whistled and two huge white birds suddenly came into view and landed next to her.

"You too have come south," Ma Yu said with a smile.

"Sir, Guo Jing has been killed. You must avenge him!"

Ma Yu's body twitched. He translated what the young girl had said into Chinese. Qiu Chuji and Wang Chuyi were visibly shocked. They bombarded her with questions, but she merely pointed at Yang Kang. "He saw it happen with his own eyes—ask him."

Yang Kang had not known that Khojin knew Ma Yu. Now, he was scared to say too much, in case his story aroused suspicion, dashing his hopes of tricking the Mongolians. And yet, he could not lie to his Master and martial uncles. He turned to Tolui and

Khojin and said, "Go ahead and wait for me outside the village. I need a few moments to speak with the Taoists."

Tolui listened as the Song officer translated what Yang Kang had said. He then nodded and led Khojin out of the village and on to the road north.

"Who killed Guo Jing?" Qiu Chuji barked. "Come on! Tell us."

Yang Kang paused for a moment to think. *I was the one who killed him, but what should I say?* Then it hit him. He could place the blame onto a master of the *wulin*, someone with the power and skill to kill Qiu Chuji in a fight. That way, his dilemma would be resolved.

"The Lord of Peach Blossom Island."

Apothecary Huang was known to be searching for the Six Freaks of the South, so it made perfect sense that he had killed their disciple. This explanation aroused no suspicion.

Qiu Chuji cursed the Old Heretic under his breath and swore that he would have revenge. Ma Yu and Wang Chuyi, in contrast, nursed their sadness in silence.

Just then, laughter echoed in the distance. A different voice followed, harsh like clashing cymbals, and then another, this one softer. They were some distance away, but everyone heard them clearly. Three men, on the outskirts of the village.

"That was Martial Uncle Zhou!" Ma Yu exclaimed in delight. "He's still alive!"

Three whistles came from the east. It sounded as if they were getting progressively farther away.

"The other two appear to be chasing Uncle Zhou," Wang Chuyi said.

"They must have excellent lightness kung fu, if they're able to keep up," Ma Yu said, a concerned look on his face. "I wonder who they could be. And why are they chasing him?" He shook his head.

The four Quanzhen Masters strained their ears as the voices faded into the distance.

"Perhaps Brother Tan and the others have managed to catch up and provide assistance," Sun Bu'er said hopefully.

"I doubt it," Qiu Chuji countered. "If only Unlce Zhou knew we were here, he might come back this way."

Lotus listened in amusement. My father and Old Venom are merely playing with the Urchin, not fighting. If they were, do you really think a gang of stinking cow muzzles like you would be a match for them?

She had listened with displeasure to Qiu Chuji's cursing of her father. And yet, she did not mind so much that Yang Kang had falsely accused him of killing Guo Jing, if only because her beloved was sitting beside her at that very moment.

Ma Yu gestured for everyone to go inside and sit down.

Qiu Chuji turned to his student and said suddenly, "Are we to call you Yang Kang, or Wanyan Kang, these days?"

Yang Kang saw the glint in his Master's eyes and noticed his jaw twitch with menace. If he said the wrong thing, he could be killed.

"Had it not been for the illumination of my Master and martial uncles Ma and Wang, I would have still believed myself to be Jurchen, and thus be a traitor to my own blood. Now, I go by the name Yang, of course. Last night, Sister Mu and I gave my mother and father the burial they deserve."

This pleased Qiu Chuji and his expression instantly became softer. Wang Chuyi's displeasure at Yang Kang's treatment of Mercy dissipated too, as he assumed the young man had resolved to honor his promise.

Yang Kang held out the broken spearhead he had used to kill Gallant Ouyang. "This is all that is left of my late father's belongings. I treasure it."

Qiu Chuji took it and stroked his fingers along the blade's edge. His heart was filled with sorrow. He sighed and said, "Nineteen years ago, I happened across your father and his friend, your uncle Skyfury Guo. The years have passed and now both have been returned to dust. It pains me to know that they are gone. That I was unable to save your parents will be my life's great regret."

Guo Jing listened, his heart overflowing with grief. Reverend

Qiu still remembers my father, and yet I never got to see his face. At least Brother Yang got to meet his real father.

Qiu Chuji then returned the conversation to Guo Jing's supposed death, and Yang Kang could only continue to weave his web of lies. The three Quanzhen elders sighed as he spoke.

Yang Kang, meanwhile, was distracted by the thought that he had to catch up with Tolui and Khojin.

Wang Chuyi studied the young man, then looked over at Mercy Mu. "Are you two married?" he asked.

"Not yet," Yang Kang replied.

"You had better make the arrangements soon. Brother Qiu, how should it be handled?"

Lotus and Guo Jing exchanged glances. Were they about to witness yet another wedding?

Sister Mu is not as mild-mannered as Miss Cheng, Lotus thought. She might insist on a rematch, another Duel for the Maiden. This should be interesting.

"Let Master decide," she heard Yang Kang say, the delight clear in his voice.

"On one condition," Mercy Mu spoke up.

Qiu Chuji smiled faintly and said, "Please."

"The traitor Wanyan Honglie killed my adoptive father and Yang Kang's real father, Ironheart Yang. Before we can be married, Yang Kang must avenge his death."

"Excellent!" Qiu Chuji cried, and clapped his hands. "I couldn't have said it better myself. A perfect plan, wouldn't you agree, boy?"

Yang Kang hesitated. How should he answer?

Just then, a loud, gravelly voice came to their ears from outside. Someone was singing the lyrics to "Fallen Lotus Flower." They heard a high-pitched voice rasp in response, "Master, lady, take mercy on a poor beggar!"

Mercy listened. She thought the voice sounded familiar. She turned to see two beggars standing on the doorstep. One was fat, the other short and thin. Indeed, the second was so small, the first looked to be three times his size. There was something unusual in the way they held themselves. Indeed, they were so distinctive that Mercy instantly knew who they were. She had tended to their wounds at the age of thirteen. Count Seven Hong had spent three days teaching her a few tricks because she was of such tender heart.

She was about to rush forward to greet them when she noticed that they were staring at the bamboo staff in Yang Kang's hand. They looked at each other and nodded. They approached the young man, crossed their arms over their chests and bowed.

Ma Yu and the others noticed how brawny the beggars were beneath their rags, and that each carried eight hemp sacks on their back. Senior members of the Beggar Clan. They were men of rank; why did they show Yang Kang such respect?

The smaller one began, "We heard some among us say that the Clan chief's cane had been spotted in Lin'an. It is our honor to see it here. I wonder, what became of our old chief, Count Seven Hong?"

Yang Kang understood nothing. "Mmm," he replied, trying to hide his ignorance.

The men were taken aback, but remained respectful, such was the power bestowed by the Dog-Beating Cane upon whoever carried it.

"It is not long now until we gather at Yuezhou. Elders Lu and Jian headed west not seven days ago," the larger of the beggars said.

Yang Kang was even more confused. "Mmm," he said again.

"We have been delayed for some days, looking for the cane," the thin beggar continued. "We must hurry. If sir would care to start the journey today, we humbly offer our services to accompany you all the way."

Yang Kang saw his chance to get away from Qiu Chuji. He kowtowed before the Quanzhen Masters. "Humbly I beg the forgiveness of my elders, but I have an important matter to deal with."

Was Yang Kang connected to the Beggar Clan? They were the biggest secret society in the whole Empire, and their chief, Count

Seven Hong, commanded a reputation equal to that of their late Master. This being the case, they could not possibly detain the young man and it would be impolite to ask the beggars any questions. As was the custom in the rivers and lakes, they merely paid the two men their respects.

The beggars were equally humble in their conduct toward the Quanzhen Masters. And, when Mercy Mu reminded them of how she had helped them, all those years ago, she too was invited to travel with Yang Kang.

Together, the four of them took their leave.

Qiu Chuji had observed his disciple's courteous treatment of Ironheart Yang's adopted daughter and his anger toward him subsided. Had this young man not been the son of a true patriot, he might have crippled him, such had been his fury. But perhaps the Duel for a Maiden had turned out well, after all. Perhaps the young man had learned his lesson and had renounced the riches of a life in the Jin court in favor of his father's good name. Was it possible that all those years of guidance on his part had not been in vain? He had to admit that the respectful way in which these two members of the Beggar Clan had spoken to him and his brothers did reflect well on the Quanzhen Sect. Indeed, his anger was giving way to something akin to pleasure. Gently, he twirled his long beard and watched as the young couple left.

10

THAT EVENING, THEY SLEPT AT THE INN AS THEY WAITED FOR the other masters of the Quanzhen Sect to join them. When there was no news for the whole of the next day, they began to feel anxious.

Just as midnight was drawing near, they heard a whistle from the edge of the village.

"Brother Hao is back!" Sun Bu'er said.

Ma Yu replied with his own, low-pitched whistle. Before long, a shadow flitted across the doorway and Hao Datong appeared.

This was the first time Lotus had ever laid eyes on Master Hao. She pressed her eye to the hole. It was the fifth day of the seventh month, and a new moon illuminated him. He was broad and tall, and carried himself with the air of a high-ranking official. The sleeves of his Taoist robes were cut short at the elbows. It was an unusual style, nothing like the clothing worn by the other Quanzhen Masters. In fact, Hao Datong had been the son of the wealthiest family in Shandong's Ninghai prefecture. He was highly educated and had made money from divination before joining their Master, Wang Chongyang, in his cave in the mountains. Wang Chongyang had taken off his own robe, torn the sleeves short and presented it to Hao. "Worry not for its lack of sleeves," he had said. "You will complete them yourself." Making use of the similarity between the word for *sleeve* in Chinese and the word for *teaching*, his meaning was that, no matter how intensely the master gave his instructions, it was up to the disciple to achieve the Way. Hao Datong had worn short sleeves ever since, in order to honor his Master.

"How is Master Zhou?" Qiu Chuji broke in impatiently. "Is he fighting, or is he clowning around?"

"I am ashamed to admit that I didn't manage to catch up with them," Hao Datong said, shaking his head. "I gave chase for some seven or eight *li* before I lost sight of them. Masters Tan and Liu were ahead of me, however. I carried on searching for them for a whole day and a night, but, alas, I could not find them anywhere."

"Brother Hao is tired," Ma Yu said. "Sit and rest."

Hao Datong positioned himself on the floor and crossed his legs. Then he began to circulate his *qi*.

"On my way back, I encountered six people by the Temple of the King of Zhou, who seemed to fit the description, given by Master Qiu, of the Six Freaks of the South. I approached them and discovered that my instincts were correct. They are on their way back from Peach Blossom Island."

"The Freaks are most courageous," Qiu Chuji said. "They went to Peach Blossom Island? No wonder we couldn't find them."

"Their leader, Great Hero Ke Zhen'e, said that they had offered to accompany their disciple Guo Jing to Peach Blossom Island to seek Apothecary Huang. But they could not find the young man so they went by themselves, only to find, to their surprise, that Huang was not there."

"They took a great risk! Indeed, they were very lucky the Heretic could not be found."

Guo Jing was relieved to hear his Masters were unharmed. By now, he and Lotus had been circulating their *qi* for five days and five nights, and he was almost completely recovered.

During the second watch of the sixth night, another whistle was heard from the east of the village.

"Brother Liu is back," Qiu Chuji said.

Moments later, Liu Chuxuan appeared outside, accompanied by an old man with long hair and a long beard. The old man was dressed in a short shirt made from arrowroot-cloth, and a simple pair of hemp shoes, and, in his hand, he carried a large cattail-leaf fan. He was smiling and talking as they entered. He glanced at the five Quanzhen Masters and nodded in their direction, as if greeting any ordinary man in the market.

"This is Master Qiu," Liu Chuxuan began, "also known as the Iron Palm Water Glider. We are most fortunate to come across him today."

Lotus had to hold back her laughter as she nudged Guo Jing with her elbow. Guo Jing grinned at her. They were both waiting to see what Qiu Qianren's latest swindle was going to be.

The Quanzhen Masters knew of Qiu Qianren, of course; he was well-known and respected throughout the *wulin*, so they addressed him with the customary courtesy. Qiu Qianren's tone, in contrast, was gruff and self-important.

"Has sir seen Master Zhou Botong?" Qiu Chuji asked, after a while.

"The Hoary Urchin? Apothecary Huang killed him years ago."

Shock ran through the room.

"How can that be?" Liu Chuxuan exclaimed. "I saw him only the day before yesterday. He was running so fast that I couldn't catch up with him."

This stumped Qiu Qianren, and all he could do was smile. His mind was spinning, trying to find an explanation.

"Brother Liu, did you get a good look at the two men who were chasing Master Zhou?" Qiu Chuji interrupted.

"One was dressed in white, the other in a long, dark green robe. They ran at great speed. I managed to glimpse the face of the one in green, and it was most curious indeed. Like that of a corpse."

Qiu Qianren had met Apothecary Huang at Roaming Cloud Manor, where he had been wearing green robes and a mask made of human skin. In fact, he had not known at the time that it was Apothecary Huang, but it all made sense now. "That's right! The one who killed the Urchin was dressed in long green robes. Apothecary Huang. Who else could have managed it? I was too late to stop it. *Aiya*, it was a most miserable death."

Qiu Qianren was known for his excellent kung fu skills, but the Quanzhen Masters were unaware of his other reputation as the most brazen swindler in all of the south. They were deeply aggrieved. Qiu Chuji slammed his hand against a table and decried Apothecary Huang in the most colorful terms.

Lotus was seething. Not because Qiu Qianren had started this silly rumor, but because Qiu Chuji was so quick to curse her father—and with such terrible fury.

"Brother Tan is faster than me; perhaps he caught up with them and saw how Master Zhou was killed?" Liu Chuxuan said.

"Brother Tan is yet to return," Sun Bu'er began. "I only fear that he too has suffered at the hands of that old villain . . ." Her voice trailed off, her expression grim.

Qiu Chuji drew his sword. "We must have our revenge!" he cried.

Afraid they might come across Master Zhou and his lie would be revealed, Qiu Qianren quickly added, "Apothecary Huang knows you are all here. He might arrive at any moment. The Old Heretic is evil, and I simply cannot allow his crimes to go unpunished a moment longer. Wait for me here."

As Qiu Qianren was their senior, they knew it would be inappropriate to defy the old Master's words. Also, they might miss the scoundrel if they went out looking for him. It would be better to wait for him here and conserve their energy.

Grateful, they bowed to Qiu Qianren and sent him on his way.

"Don't worry," Qiu Qianren said, with a wave of his hand, as he left. "I will bring the Old Heretic to justice, you will see!" At that, he drew the sword from his waist and, with a grunt, thrust it at his own belly.

The others cried out as the blade entered the old man's flesh. Qiu Qianren merely smiled, however.

"No blade can harm me. If the Old Heretic comes for you, don't fight him, lest you all be injured. Wait for me to return, and I will deal with him."

"We must avenge our martial uncle," Qiu Chuji replied, bristling.

Qiu Qianren sighed. "Fate, too, has decided it must be thus. But, if it is revenge you want, there is one thing you must remember."

"Please, enlighten us, sir," Ma Yu said.

Qiu Qianren's expression became very grave indeed. "If you see the Old Heretic, you must kill him at once. Do not bother trying to speak or reason with him, else you will lose your chance forever. This is very important!"

At this, he turned, the sword still stuck in his belly.

The others watched in amazement. In all their years, none of them had ever seen a blade enter the flesh in this way and yet cause no harm. The old man must have reached a level of martial skill none of them had witnessed before.

What they did not know, however, was that it was just another of Qiu Qianren's tricks. The sword was, in fact, made up of three sections. As soon as even the lightest of forces was applied to the tip of the blade, the first and second sections would retract into the third, which would, in turn, disappear into a seam in his waistband. To any onlooker, it appeared as though the blade had plunged into his abdomen.

And the reason for his tricks? Wanyan Honglie had employed him to sow enmity among the heroes of the south, so that, when the Jin made their attack, they would be too busy fighting among themselves to unite against a common enemy.

For the rest of that day, the Quanzhen Masters were restless. They could barely eat, and instead sat on the floor of the inn, practicing their breathing. Only Harmony Yin was able to sleep.

At around midnight, they heard the faintest sound of whistling coming from the northern end of the village. They jumped up. Within moments, they heard people outside.

"The enemy!" Ma Yu cried. "They have been chasing Brother Tan. Be careful, everyone."

Guo Jing was into his last night of breathing exercises; his internal and external injuries were almost healed. Not only that, but both he and Lotus had made great strides when it came to their *neigong* strength. These last hours were crucial. Lotus, however, was worried. If that is Papa outside, there will be a fight. But I am in no position to go out there and tell them the truth. What if my father injures the Quanzhen Masters? I am not so fond of them myself, but Guo Jing is devoted to Elder Ma, in particular. It will take a lot for him to resist helping them; he will feel it is his duty. And, if he does, all these days of training will be wasted. Indeed, if he cuts it short before completing all thirty-six revolutions, his life will be in danger.

"Guo Jing," she whispered, "promise me that, whatever happens, you won't go out. Not until we're done."

Guo Jing nodded, but it was plain to see he was deeply conflicted.

"Brother Tan!" Qiu Chuji called outside. "Assume the Heavenly Northern Dipper!"

Guo Jing's heart leaped. The Northern Dipper. Those words appeared several times in the Nine Yin Manual. It was an essential component in reaching the highest levels of martial learning. The textual explanation, however, was obscure, to say the least. Guo Jing had not understood it himself. He peered through the hole to watch.

Bang! The door flew open and the figure of a Taoist priest appeared in its place. His left foot just made it over the threshold before he was suddenly pulled back out again.

Qiu Chuji and Wang Chuyi leaped forward, sleeves fluttering, palms raised.

Thwack! Their palms struck the attacker. The two Quanzhen Masters jolted back, as did their opponent.

Tan Chuduan stepped into the room.

By the light of the moon, they took in his appearance. His hair was disheveled and two blotches of blood decorated his face. The long sword in his right hand had been snapped in half. He looked terrible.

He walked into the center of the room and, without saying anything, sat down and crossed his legs. His martial brothers immediately took up their positions.

II

"REVEREND TAN." A WOMAN'S VOICE FROM OUTSIDE suddenly broke through the darkness. "Had it not been for your Brother Ma's presence, I would have delivered you to the heavens already. Why did you lead me here? Whose palms did I just encounter? Tell this old blind woman."

Despite the intense heat of the still summer's night, her raspy voice sent chills down the Taoists' backs. Silence descended, disturbed only by the constant hum of insects outside.

Suddenly, an awful cracking sound was heard. Guo Jing recognized it at once: Cyclone Mei's joints. She was about to attack.

"*Some spend years in isolation,*" a soft voice began. It was Ma Yu. His tone was soothing.

"*Cultivating only unkempt hair and eccentricity,*" another voice added. Guo Jing looked across at the Quanzhen's Second Master, Tan Chuduan. The muscles on his face were taut and his eyebrows thick and bushy. His body was similarly robust and athletic. He had worked as a blacksmith in his native Shandong before joining the Taoist sect and assuming the name Eternal Truth.

Their Third Master was, by contrast, thin and small. He reminded Guo Jing of a monkey. This was Eternal Life Liu Chuxuan. He took up the next lines: "*Double Sun sits in the Crab Apple Pavilion.*" He was slight in stature, but his voice was surprisingly resonant.

"*As the Spirit Immortal's boat floats on lotus leaves,*" Qiu Chuji continued.

"*To the empty shell belongs all matter,*" Wang Chuyi added.

"*Some men see before they are born.*" This was Infinite Peace Hao Datong.

"*Laughing, I leave home and am free,*" Sun Bu'er said, before Ma Yu finished the poem: "*As in West Lake the clouds are reflected and the Moon hangs high above me.*"

Cyclone Mei listened. Each voice was propelled by an incredible burst of *qi*. Are all seven Quanzhen Masters here? she asked herself, in shock. They can't be. Ma Yu is here, to be sure, but the other voices do not sound right.

Cyclone Mei had last encountered the Quanzhen Masters on top of a desolate cliff on the Mongolian steppe. Or, at least, that is what she thought. In fact, she had overheard Ma Yu and the Six Freaks pretending to be the Seven Immortals of the Quanzhen Sect.

"Reverend Ma," she called out. "Are you still well? It has been some time since we last met." Cyclone Mei may have had a reputation for cruelty, but she could not deny that Ma Yu had shown her mercy back in Mongolia.

Unable to find Zhou Botong, Tan Chuduan had given up on his search. On his way back to the inn, however, he came across Cyclone Mei. He knew that Twice Foul Dark Wind had turned to evil, but he was unaware of Hurricane Chen's death and that Cyclone Mei had been accepted back to Peach Blossom Island. He ran straight at her and attacked, only to find that he was no match for her. Luckily, Cyclone Mei had realized that he was a member of the Quanzhen Sect and refrained from hurting him, out of respect for Ma Yu. Instead, she let him go, and followed him to Ox Village.

"Why, I am very well, thank you!" Ma Yu exclaimed. "The Quanzhen Sect and Peach Blossom Island bear each other no ill will. Is your honored Master on his way?"

"Are you expecting my *shifu*?" Cyclone Mei replied, somewhat startled by his question.

"Vixen!" Qiu Chuji suddenly interjected. "Bring him to us, so that we might show him the almighty strength of the Quanzhen!"

"Who are you?" she snarled.

"My name is Qiu Chuji. Surely you have heard of me, harlot?"

The blind woman howled and cast herself in the direction of Qiu Chuji's voice. She held her left palm in defense, her right hand shaped in a claw.

How would Qiu Chuji hold off her attack? Guo Jing watched with bated breath. But the Taoist did not move, and remained seated on the floor. Oh no, Guo Jing just had time to say to himself, as Cyclone Mei's claw flew straight at Qiu Chuji's head.

Just then, Liu Chuxuan and Wang Chuyi sent out their palms, one from each side. Cyclone Mei swiped at both and blocked. But little did she realize that the two men had harnessed their internal strength in a complementary fashion, yin and yang, creating a force that sent her body up like a cannonball. She struck down with her right hand and flipped into a backward somersault, landing back at the threshold to the inn.

She was in shock. Whoever these men were, they were far more accomplished than the Taoists of the Quanzhen Sect. "Count Seven Hong? King Duan?" she cried out.

Qiu Chuji laughed. "Count Seven Hong? King Duan? We are the Masters of the Quanzhen."

This confused Cyclone Mei. If Master Tan had not been her match, how could his martial brothers be so much more powerful? Could there be such a gulf in skill within one school?

Guo Jing was also puzzled. Masters Liu and Wang were excellent fighters, to be sure, but how could they overcome Cyclone Mei so easily? The only masters he knew that should be capable of such a feat were Zhou Botong, Count Seven Hong, Apothecary Huang, and Viper Ouyang.

Cyclone Mei feared only her own Master. The more she was challenged, the more reckless she became. Ma Yu had been courteous and respectful. But Qiu Chuji had just been told that Apothecary Huang had killed Zhou Botong and Guo Jing. His hatred of Peach Blossom Island and all who belonged to it was lodged deep in his bones.

Cyclone Mei knew that she was outmatched, here, but she would not give up. She hesitated only a moment, before reaching into her robes and pulling out her White Python whip.

"Reverend Ma! Forgive me!"

"You flatter me," he replied.

"Draw your weapons!"

"There are seven of us," Wang Chuyi began, "and only one of you. And, on top of that, you are blind. The Quanzhen Sect cannot possibly use weapons against you—that would be a dishonor. We shall remain sitting. You may attack!"

"You will take my Python whip sitting?"

"You will die tonight, witch!" Qiu Chuji snarled. "Or are we here merely to exchange pleasantries?"

Cyclone Mei snorted. She flicked her wrist and her weapon uncoiled as if in slow motion. Its barbs sailed gracefully through the air.

Lotus was listening. Cyclone Mei's Python whip was notorious. How could the Quanzhen Masters take it sitting down? She pulled Guo Jing aside and pressed her eye against the hole.

The Quanzhen Masters were indeed sitting perfectly still. The Heavenly Northern Dipper! That was what Reverend Qiu had said, wasn't it?

Her father was an expert in the study of the stars. She had spent many a night sitting in her father's lap as he explained to her the constellations in the night sky. She looked again at where the Taoists were sitting, and immediately she understood.

Ma Yu assumed the Heavenly Pivot position, Tan Chuxuan the Heavenly Jade, Liu Chuxuan the Heavenly Pearl, and Qiu Chuji the Heavenly Power, thus together forming the head of the constellation. Wang Chuyi took the Jade Scales, Hao Datong the Manifest Sun, and Sun Bu'er the Shimmering Rays. These made up the handle of the Dipper.

Of all the stars that made up the Northern Dipper, the Heavenly Power was the dimmest. Yet it also connected the head with the handle, and was therefore the most important. Being the strongest fighter, Qiu Chuji took this position. In the handle, Wang Chuyi was most vital to the overall formation.

A flick of Cyclone Mei's wrist sent the whip unfurling in the direction of Sun Bu'er. The Sage of Tranquility had time to move out of the way, but she did not even try. Lotus followed the movement of the whip's silver barbs. As her eyes shifted onto Sun Bu'er, she noticed a skull embroidered on her robes. It looked like something Cyclone Mei would wear! But the Quanzhen were Taoism's greatest orthodox sect. What she did not know was that Wang Chongyang had drawn Sun Bu'er a skull when she became his disciple. It was supposed to remind her that life was short, death could come quick, and that all humans would one day be no more than dust and bones. The only way out of this cycle was to cultivate the Way. Sun Bu'er had the image sewn onto her clothes to remind her of her late Master and his wise counsel.

Just as the barbs reached to within a couple of inches of Sun Bu'er's embroidered skull, causing the air to shriek as they tore through it, they suddenly lurched back, as if startled. Quick as an arrow, the whip recoiled.

Indeed, it was so quick that Cyclone Mei felt only a tremble in her hand and a rush of air at her cheek. She ducked. The barbs flew over her head, gently brushing her hair.

That was close! She panted, flicked her wrist to bring the whip back under her control, then launched it again. This time, it lashed at Ma Yu and Qiu Chuji. Neither moved. Instead, Tan Chuduan and Wang Chuyi raised their hands and blocked.

Lotus watched the fight unfold. The Quanzhen Masters were each knocking the whip away with one hand, while they kept the other placed firmly on the shoulder of the person next to them. Then she realized: this was the same technique of passing *qi* between them that she and Guo Jing had been using for the last seven days and seven nights. They were combining the strength of seven into one. How could Cyclone Mei possibly prevail?

The Heavenly Northern Dipper was the Quanzhen's most accomplished and mysterious formation, and had been developed by their Master, Wang Chongyang. It combined the strength of all seven Masters, while allowing for infinite variations, making it perfect for battle. When an opponent launched an assault, the individual who was being attacked could remain still, relying on the other Quanzhen disciples to fend it off.

Panic was rising in Cyclone Mei. She could feel that her whip was being forced into a diminishing circle of movement, and, before long, she found herself unable to pull it back. If she were to let go, she might escape unharmed. But that would mean surrendering her weapon. How could she? It had taken her years of training to be able to fight with it like this.

She hesitated, and, in those moments, lost her chance. Now, the Northern Dipper formation was on the move, all seven stars in the constellation as one. Only the member in the Heavenly Power position could stop it. And it was too late for Cyclone Mei to retreat.

Liu Chuxuan's palm met the whip. Cyclone Mei was yanked forward. *Pang!* The walls shook. Tiles crashed to the floor in a cloud of dust.

Had she let go of the whip sooner, Cyclone could have escaped. But now she had been pulled closer in. She sent her palms out on both sides and met the force of Sun Bu'er and Wang Chuyi. Ma Yu and Hao Datong attacked from behind, forcing her to stumble yet another step forward. Somehow, she regained her footing, shrieking and kicking, knocking them back again.

"Excellent!" Qiu Chuji cried.

Qiu and Liu Chuxuan struck—one from the front, one from behind. Before Cyclone could plant her right foot, her left was kicking out at both men's palms. As she landed, however, she was sent forward yet another step. This drew her deeper into the formation. Her only hope of escape was to knock one of the masters out of position.

Lotus's heart was beating fast. By the light of the moon, she watched Cyclone Mei's long hair flapped like wings as she fought back. Her limbs leaped and pounced like tigers clawing at their prey.

The Quanzhen Masters remained in their sitting positions as they hit back at Cyclone Mei, never letting her out of the formation.

Cyclone Mei tried her Nine Yin Skeleton Claw and Heartbreaker Palm, but to no avail. Frustrated, she let out a strange and terrible wail.

The Quanzhen were now in a position where they could easily kill her, but they held back.

Now, at last, Lotus understood: They are using the fight to practice the formation! There were not many in the *wulin* who could resist it for so long. They are going to tire her to death.

She was only half right, however. They were indeed practicing, but they were Taoists. They did not believe in needless killing.

Lotus did not hold Cyclone Mei in high regard, but there was something affecting about seeing her being humiliated like this. Indeed, Lotus was starting to feel angry. Disgusted, she moved aside to let Guo Jing watch instead. Still, the sound of rushing air told her when the fight was intensifying and when it was abating. There was no sign of it coming to an end.

Guo Jing was puzzled. Why were the Quanzhen fighting while sitting down?

"It is called the Heavenly Northern Dipper formation," Lotus whispered. "It connects their inner strength. Do you see?"

Yes, the second part of the Nine Yin Manual made frequent mention of the Northern Dipper. He had memorized it, but had no idea of its meaning. Watching the Seven Masters, he understood. The more he saw, the more excited he became, and he started to scramble to his feet.

Lotus yanked him back before their palms lost contact. Guo Jing sat down again, and together they trembled in shock at how close they had come. And yet, he could not contain himself. He pressed his eye to the hole once more. The essence of the method was more or less clear to him, but he still did not know how to use it. The author of the Nine Yin Manual had been an expert in the Taoist canon. Wang Chongyang had developed the Heavenly Northern Dipper independently, but they were both rooted in the same ideas. The variations that Guo Jing was observing, therefore, corresponded more or less exactly with the descriptions in the Manual.

Cyclone Mei was in danger, he could tell, but the Quanzhen were also tiring.

Just then, a voice came from the door: "Brother Huang, do you want to go first, or shall I?"

It was Viper Ouyang! How long had he been outside? The Seven Masters were just as startled; they turned and saw two men standing side by side in the doorway, one wearing a long, dark green robe, while the other was dressed in white. It was the two men who had been seen chasing the Hoary Urchin the previous night.

Together, the Quanzhen Masters made a low whistling noise, stopped fighting and stood up.

"What a sight!" Apothecary Huang cried. "Seven Taoist dogs pitted against my one disciple. Brother Ouyang, if I were to teach them a lesson, would you think me a tyrant?"

"They were the ones to insult you first," Viper replied with a smile. "If you don't show them the error of their ways, they might never know the might of Peach Blossom Island."

Wang Chuyi had met the Heretic of the East and the Venom of the West at the summit of Mount Hua, all those years ago. He was about to step forward and greet them, when Apothecary Huang's palm suddenly came at him. Wang Chuyi staggered back, but he was too slow. With a loud slap, it connected with his cheek, and he fell.

"Resume formation!" Qiu Chuji cried.

Thwack, thwack, thwack, thwack!

Tan, Liu, Hao, and Sun were all struck.

Only Qiu Chuji spotted the smudge of dark green approach. He saw the palm sail toward him. Qiu Chuji flicked his sleeve, aiming for Apothecary Huang's chest.

Apothecary Huang felt a sharp pain. He had underestimated Qiu Chuji's strength. He placed one hand to his chest and grabbed Qiu Chuji's sleeve with the other, tugging and ripping it. Ma Yu and Wang Chuyi hit out, but Apothecary Huang had already leaped behind Hao Datong and kicked him, sending him rolling into a somersault.

Lotus had reclaimed her position at the hole. Her father's magnificent display pleased her no end. Were she not aware that Guo Jing still needed a few more hours before his recovery was complete, she would have jumped up and clapped.

"Wang Chongyang took these carbuncles for his disciples?" Viper Ouyang scoffed.

Qiu Chuji had never suffered such a humiliation in all his years in the *wulin*. "Return to your positions!" he kept shouting. But Apothecary Huang had already swept into a series of more than half a dozen quick-fire attacks. The Quanzhen Masters were struggling to hold him back and could not resume the formation. Instead, they drew their swords.

Two loud cracks echoed around the small inn. Huang had snapped Ma and Tan's weapons and cast them to the ground.

Qiu Chuji and Wang Chuyi continued to deploy the Quanzhen Sect's special sword technique, their power building. Apothecary Huang concentrated and launched his counterattack.

Ma Yu, meanwhile, ran back to his position and sent out a palm. This allowed the other six to scramble into formation.

With the Heavenly Northern Dipper re-formed, the dynamics of the fight quickly changed. Heavenly Power and Jade Scales attacked head-on, Heavenly Pearl and Manifest Sun sent out palms from left and right, while Shimmering Rays and Heavenly Jade circled round from behind.

Apothecary Huang struck out in all four directions at once.

"Brother Ouyang," he cried out, "I didn't know Wang Chong-yang had such skills to pass on!" He knew he was in danger. The Quanzhen Masters each possessed immense power, and, when it was combined together, they were truly formidable. Apothecary Huang moved into his Cascading Peach Blossom Palm technique. His body spun gracefully as his hands danced through the air.

When Papa taught me Cascading Peach Blossom Palm, Lotus thought, he only explained to me the principle of five feints to one solid strike, or seven feints to one strike. He said it could be used to lure one's enemy into danger. I didn't realize the feints could be used to hurt or cause harm.

Lotus watched with bated breath, as did Viper Ouyang. He had had no idea Apothecary Huang possessed such levels of skill.

Cyclone Mei listened to the rush of moving air, enraptured, but also terrified.

"Huh!"

Then came a thud.

Harmony Yin had made himself dizzy trying to follow the fight, and was now lying passed out on the floor.

The Quanzhen Masters held their positions. One mistake and they would all be killed, bringing about the demise of the best part of their Sect.

Apothecary Huang, meanwhile, regretted not having delivered the decisive blow, only moments before. He had only his own merciful nature to blame, and now victory would not come easy. But he could not be allowed to lose. Each side was riding the tiger, there was no way down, now.

The roosters began to crow as the sun climbed above the horizon, casting its light into the dim room. Apothecary Huang had used thirteen different kung fu techniques and yet still he had not found a way to prevail.

Inside the secret chamber, Guo Jing and Lotus were coming to the end of their seven days and seven nights of breathing practice. Guo Jing was at peace, despite the earth-shattering fight still in progress on the other side of the wall. His eyes were closed as he focused on the movement of his *qi*, starting in his Tail Bone Gate at the sacrum, moving up to his kidneys and his spine, through two more passes to the Heavenly Pillar and the Jade Pillow, and finally to the Hundred Convergences at the crown of his head. There, it paused for a moment, before descending down his face to the Divine Courtyard, then on to the Magpie Bridge on the palate of his mouth, moving slowly through his chest, until it arrived at the Elixir Field in his lower abdomen, thus completing the thirty-sixth revolution of his breath.

Lotus observed his flushed cheeks. With a smile, she turned back to the spyhole, only to be startled by what she saw.

Slowly, her father's feet were moving through the positions of the Eight Trigrams. Lotus knew this was his last resort and most powerful move, one that he did not use lightly. This was a decisive moment that would have stark consequences—a matter of life and death.

The Quanzhen Masters gathered all their strength. Their robes were wet with sweat as they let out one united, almighty howl from the depths of their beings. Hot steam blew from the tops of their heads.

Viper Ouyang was watching intently. If only the Quanzhen Sect could injure Apothecary Huang, so that he might have one less opponent to worry about when the Greats met again on Mount Hua. But their victory was by no means assured. The Old Heretic is powerful indeed, he thought to himself.

Movements on both sides slowed as the fight reached its most critical stage. Its conclusion was mere moments away.

Apothecary Huang struck out at Sun Bu'er and Tan Chuduan simultaneously. They raised their hands to block, while Liu Chuxuan and Ma Yu moved to counter his attack.

Suddenly, Viper Ouyang howled. "I'm here, Brother Huang!" He squatted and thrust his palms at Tan's back.

A force powerful enough to move a mountain threw Tan forward.

"I don't want your help!" Apothecary Huang snarled.

Qiu Chuji and Wang Chuyi thrust with their swords. Huang flicked his sleeve and blocked with his free hand, simultaneously holding off Ma Yu and Hao Datong.

"Then I will help your enemy!" Viper Ouyang cried with an amused look on his face. He struck out at Apothecary Huang's back. He had only needed to use a third of his reserves of energy against Tan Chuduan, but now he put his full force behind his attack, a wellspring of power developed over a lifetime of *neigong* cultivation and practice. It was all part of a master plan: first, neutralize one of the Quanzhen seven, thus breaking the Northern Dipper formation; then, take Apothecary Huang out with one decisive blow.

I'm done for! Apothecary Huang thought.

He summoned the *qi* to his back, in order to hold off Viper's Exploding Toad kung fu.

Viper's move was ungainly, but he knew, with all that power behind it, he was sure to prevail.

But then a shadow flashed past him. Someone cried out, threw themselves between him and Old Huang, and took the blow.

Everyone jumped back. Panting, they were amazed to see who it was who had come to Apothecary Huang's rescue: Cyclone Mei.

Apothecary Huang turned slowly to face Viper and sneered. "Old Venom, you really are a snake!"

Viper Ouyang smiled, but knew he could not stay there a moment longer. If the Quanzhen Sect joined forces with Apothecary Huang and Cyclone Mei, he would never get out alive. He turned and launched himself out the door.

Ma Yu knelt down beside Tan Chuduan and was shocked to see how badly injured he was. His body lay at a strange angle. He picked him up, only for Tan's head to flop down to one side. Viper Ouyang had fractured his spine and broken his ribs. He was not long for this world. Tears, like summer rain, ran down Ma Yu's cheeks.

Qiu Chuji drew his sword.

"Old Huang," they heard Viper Ouyang cry out, clearly some distance away, now. "Don't forget: I helped you break Wang Chongyang's formation, and I taught your treacherous disciple a lesson, to boot! I'll leave what's left of these stinking Taoists to you. We shall meet again!"

Apothecary Huang snorted. Yet more of the Venom's poison. He was trying to put the blame for Tan's death on Huang's shoulders, thereby perpetuating the enmity between the Lord of Peach Blossom Island and the Quanzhen Sect. And yet, Huang made no attempt to clear the air with the Taoists. Instead, he reached out and helped Cyclone Mei to her feet. She spluttered and spat blood. To his regret, he knew she would not live.

By this point, Qiu Chuji had rushed out into the courtyard in pursuit of the Venom. But he did not know which way he had gone.

"Brother Qiu!" Ma Yu called after him. "Come back!" He did not want his martial brother to face Viper Ouyang alone.

Qiu Chuji's eyes were ablaze as he strode back inside. Then he raised his finger at Apothecary Huang. "What has the Quanzhen Sect done to deserve your malice? You are nothing but a demon. First you killed Master Zhou Botong, and now our martial brother. Why are you here?"

"Zhou Botong?" Apothecary Huang was startled by the accusation.

"You refuse to admit it?"

Apothecary Huang, Zhou Botong, and Viper Ouyang had raced each other for several hundred *li*, but no clear winner could be determined. Then, suddenly, Zhou Botong had remembered that he had left Count Seven Hong alone in the Imperial Palace. If the Beggar was discovered, his life would be in danger.

"I have some business I must attend to," he had called to the other two men. "I'm done with this little competition!"

They knew there was no arguing with the Hoary Urchin, so they let him leave—before Apothecary Huang could ask him about the fate of his beloved daughter.

Apothecary Huang and Viper Ouyang had decided, therefore, to return to Ox Village.

Qiu Chuji quivered with rage as Sun Bu'er held Tan Chuduan's limp body, sobbing loudly.

"I am departing," Tan Chuduan said quietly.

There had been a grave misunderstanding—Apothecary Huang knew this, now—but he considered it beneath him to try to explain the situation. Instead, he smiled coldly and watched as the Quanzhen Sect gathered around their martial brother, sitting cross-legged on the floor of the inn.

"The Way is found not in beads or brush. Nature's music comes not from the flute." Those were Tan Chuduan's last words before he closed his eyes and died.

The Quanzhen Masters lowered their heads to pray. Once finished, Ma Yu took Tan Chuduan's lifeless body in his arms and went outside. The others followed him. The Heavenly Northern Dipper formation was broken forever, and, without it, they could not prevail against Apothecary Huang. Revenge would have to wait for another day.

CHAPTER SEVEN

NEW PACTS AND OLD ALLIANCES

I

APOTHECARY HUANG COULD NOT QUITE UNDERSTAND HOW he had come into conflict with the Quanzhen Sect, nor how such hatred had grown between them so quickly. There was no reason for it. Meanwhile, Cyclone Mei's breathing was deteriorating. For over a decade, he had held a grudge against her. The thought of it pressed on his heart with an unbearable weight and tears began to roll down his cheeks.

The slightest smile graced Cyclone Mei's lips. "Master," she began, "please take me back as your pupil. I wronged you, beyond all limits. Let me return to your side. I am dying. Let me serve you . . . forever . . ." Her eyes implored him.

"Yes, yes," Apothecary Huang said, fighting back yet more tears. "Just like when you were a little girl. From now on, you must obey your teacher, Flora."

Of all the evil she had done in her life, betraying her Master was her biggest regret. Now, she finally had his forgiveness. Hearing him use her childhood name made her heart flutter. Trembling with joy, she clasped his hand.

"I will always obey my Master . . . If only I could be twelve years old again. Teach me, Master, teach me . . ."

With difficulty, she knelt down and began kowtowing three times. Then she collapsed to the floor, never to move again.

Lotus had witnessed the entire, heart-wrenching scene from the secret room. If only Papa would stay a little longer; she could come out the moment Guo Jing's breathing returned to normal. She watched as her father bent down to lift Cyclone Mei into his arms.

The braying of a horse outside broke the contemplative mood.

"This is Ox Village, yes," they heard the Qu girl say. "How should I know if there is a man by the name of Guo here? Are *you* called Guo?"

"This is not a large village. Don't you know everyone who lives here?" an exasperated voice replied.

At this, the door to the inn burst open and a motley group trooped inside.

Apothecary Huang slipped behind the door, his expression grim. Here they were, the Six Freaks of the South. He had been searching for them everywhere.

Just as they entered, Flying Bat Ke Zhen'e stopped dead and then hissed, "There's someone here!" He had heard breathing behind the door. The Freaks turned. Apothecary Huang! And, in his arms, Cyclone Mei. She seemed to be dead.

The Heretic of the East had stepped out from his hiding place and was now blocking the door.

"Master Huang," Zhu Cong said, then cupped his hands and bowed. "It is our honor! The Six Heroes of the South obeyed your summons to Peach Blossom Island and went to pay our respects in person, but it seems that the Master was otherwise engaged. How fortunate that we should find you here."

Upon arrival on Peach Blossom Island, they had searched and searched for Apothecary Huang's residence, but they could not find it. In the end, they chanced upon one of the many mute servants on the island, who managed to convey to them that the Master had left.

At that moment, they came across Ulaan, grazing in the forest, by himself. Ryder Han had brought him back across the sea and on to Ox Village in their search for Guo Jing.

Apothecary Huang had been intending to strike quickly and kill the Freaks himself, but one glance at Cyclone Mei's white cheeks dissuaded him. The Freaks were her mortal enemies. I will let her finish them. It will be a comfort to her in the netherworld that she was the one to do it.

He took her wrist with his left hand and launched himself at Ryder Han, channeling his inner strength through Cyclone's claws.

Ryder Han tried to move out of the way, but he was too late. A loud crack resounded from his arm, and he felt a tingling surge through his body. He could barely move for the pain.

The Freaks were astonished. Such a vicious attack, and without a word of warning. And to use Cyclone Mei's corpse as a weapon? With a chorus of howls, they drew their swords.

Apothecary Huang held Cyclone Mei high and charged at Jade Han.

Jade watched as Cyclone's round blank eyes, long black hair and terrifying blood-soaked grimace came straight at her. Cyclone's right hand was aimed straight at her head. Frozen with fear, Jade did not move.

A long pole and a counterpoise came flying toward Apothecary Huang, who pulled back and swung with Cyclone's other arm, landing it with a thud in Jade's stomach. Jade doubled over. Ryder jumped, releasing the might of his Golden Dragon whip, but Apothecary Huang stepped forward and trapped the tip beneath his foot. Ryder Han tried to tug it free, but it was stuck. At that moment, he saw Cyclone Mei's claw coming at him. He let go of the whip and rolled backward.

At a safe distance, he felt his smarting cheek: blood. Five scratches. Fortunately for him, the deadly poison usually released from the tips of her nails had evaporated with her last breath, otherwise he would be dead by now.

The other Freaks were still fighting. They would have been defeated already, had it not been for the fact that Apothecary Huang wanted to let Cyclone Mei take revenge herself, even in death.

Guo Jing was listening with bated breath. His *shifus* were in grave danger—he could tell by their grunts and their strained, panicked breaths. He had yet to stabilize the *qi* in his Elixir Field, but he owed a filial debt to his Masters, no different to the one he felt with regard to his own parents. Holding his *qi*, he sent out a palm.

Lotus was horrified. "No! Not yet!"

Bang! The door to the secret room broke into several pieces.

The moment his palm made contact with the door, Guo Jing felt a surge of *qi* in his Elixir Field, sending a wave of heat through his internal organs. He forced his inner breath back down in an attempt to block it.

Apothecary Huang and the Freaks leaped back and turned in the direction of the sound. They were astonished, and delighted, to see the young couple sitting inside the cupboard.

At first, Apothecary Huang was unsure if he was dreaming. "Lotus, my darling Lotus, is it you?" he cried, rubbing his eyes.

Still holding Guo Jing's hand, she smiled and nodded. Apothecary Huang placed Cyclone Mei's body down on a bench, approached his daughter and sat before her on the floor. He crossed his legs and reached for his daughter's wrist. Her pulse was strong and her breathing steady. He then reached behind her for Guo Jing.

Guo Jing's *qi* had been sizzling and roiling. The sensation was so strange that he had the urge to jump up and shout to relieve the pressure building inside him. But, the moment Apothecary Huang's palm touched his, he felt the force of his senior's inner strength calm and settle his. Apothecary Huang then used his other hand to massage Guo Jing's pressure points. Within minutes, he had recovered in full.

Guo Jing jumped to his feet, scrambled out of the cupboard, bowed to Apothecary Huang and then kowtowed before his six *shifus*.

He began to tell his Masters about all that had happened since they had parted at Roaming Cloud Manor, while Apothecary Huang held his beloved daughter's hand and listened to her giggle and chatter. The Freaks tried to follow Guo Jing's story, but he was struggling to put his experiences into words. Lotus, by contrast, was a skilled storyteller. Before long, they had all slipped away to listen to her version of events, with all its dramatic twists and breath-taking turns. Guo Jing gave up and joined them instead. An hour passed in this way, as Lotus punctuated her story with witticisms and little asides, her audience drinking in every moment, as though savoring a vintage wine.

Apothecary Huang was astonished to hear that his daughter had been made Chief of the Beggar Clan. "What an odd thing for Brother Hong to do!" he said. "Maybe he is after my nickname? Does he fancy himself the Heretic of the North? Would that make me the Beggar of the East?"

Finally, Lotus brought them up to the fight that Guo Jing had interrupted. "And that's the end," she said, and laughed. "You don't need me to tell you what happened next!"

"They are scoundrels, all of them: Viper Ouyang, Lama Supreme Wisdom, Qiu Qianren, and Yang Kang. I will kill them. Come, child, you can watch the fun." Apothecary Huang's expression was tender, despite the ferocity of his words. He could not help himself; his daughter was returned to him, safe and sound.

He then looked up at the Freaks and a wave of remorse came over him. He knew he had wronged them, but still he could not admit it. "Luck was on our side. At least none of us was badly hurt," was all he could offer.

In her heart, Lotus had long felt resentful that the Freaks disapproved of her betrothal to Guo Jing. But now that Yang Kang and Mercy Mu were to be wed, their objection was moot. "Papa," she began, "why don't you apologize to the Six Heroes of the South?"

Apothecary Huang snorted. "I am off to find the Venom of the West," he announced instead. "Guo Jing, come with me."

He was not exactly thrilled to be lumbered with this dunce of a boy. *Am I, Lord of Peach Blossom Island, intelligent and sharp-witted as I am, to have such a blockhead for a son-in-law? I will be the laughing stock of the* wulin. Not only that, but Zhou Botong had let slip in a moment of characteristic recklessness that Guo Jing had stolen Cyclone Mei's Nine Yin Manual and made a copy. This had made Apothecary Huang furious. *What a dirty trick to play on his blind disciple.* But, after some reflection, he realized that Zhou Botong could not have been telling the truth. The version of the second volume Guo Jing had memorized was in fact far more complete than the one that had been in Cyclone Mei's possession. There was no way Guo Jing had obtained the text from her. Zhou Botong was famous for his distortions of the truth. Huang also had to admit that he was easily deceived; Lama Supreme Wisdom had tricked him into thinking his own daughter was dead.

All ill will he had felt toward the Freaks now dissipated. And yet, to apologize and admit to his own mistakes was unthinkable. He would have to make it up to them some other way—by helping them, if they ever found themselves in danger.

He glanced over at his late disciple, Cyclone Mei. She had sacrificed her own life to save his, out of a feeling of debt to her Master. She and Hurricane had loved each other so deeply. *If they had come to him and asked him to let them marry, he might have allowed it. There was no need to run away.* But he had to admit that his moods were unpredictable. He swung from joy one moment to rage the next. *They must have considered this and, ultimately, been too frightened to tell him. What if his daughter were to suffer the same fate as Flora, all because of his temper . . . ?* He shuddered at the thought.

No, asking Guo Jing to join him was his way of showing that he now accepted the marriage.

Lotus had understood this and was delighted. She glanced across at Guo Jing, but he appeared entirely unaware of the implication of her father's demand. "Papa," she said, "let's first go to the palace and get *Shifu* Hong."

Ke Zhen'e turned to Guo Jing. "You have persuaded the Divine Vagrant to be your Master and the Lord of Peach Blossom Island to take you as a son. We are delighted, of course. Why would we refuse? But what about the Great Khan of the Mongols . . . ?"

His betrothal to Khojin was a delicate matter that, if brought up in front of Apothecary Huang, would surely provoke his wrath. How was he to deal with it?

Just then, the door creaked and in came the Qu girl, holding a piece of parchment folded into the shape of a monkey.

"Sister, have you finished the watermelons? An old man asked me to give you this."

Lotus took the monkey without thinking too much about it.

"He told me to tell you, don't be angry, he will find you a new teacher."

Zhou Botong! Lotus glanced down at the parchment and saw that he had written something on it. She unfolded it and began reading his crooked scrawl:

The Old Urchin was a very good boy. But he couldn't find the Old Beggar.

"Why didn't he find him?" Lotus knitted her brow with worry.

Apothecary Huang was thinking. "The Hoary Urchin may be mad," he began, "but he is an accomplished fighter. As long as Count Seven Hong is still alive, he will find and rescue him. Right now, the more pressing problem is that of the Beggar Clan."

"What about them?" Lotus asked.

"Yang Kang took the Dog-Beating Cane. He may not be much of a fighter, but he's a nasty, cunning boy. He even managed to kill Gallant Ouyang. As long as the cane is in his possession, he will stir up trouble for the Clan. We should find him and retrieve it, or else the consequences could blight the Clan for generations. And it won't reflect well on you, as the chief."

Normally, Apothecary Huang would not give the Clan and their troubles a second thought. On the contrary, he would take pleasure in their misfortune. But, now that his daughter was their chief, he had no choice but to act.

The Freaks nodded in agreement.

"But we haven't seen him for days," Guo Jing said. "I fear it will be no easy task."

"Your horse," Ryder Han said, pointing at Ulaan. "Right when you need him!"

Grinning, Guo Jing ran outside and whistled. Ulaan caught sight of his master and bounded over, then rubbed his muzzle against him in delight.

"Lotus, you and Guo Jing must hurry and retrieve the cane," Apothecary Huang said. "You will soon catch up with him on that fine horse."

He turned and suddenly noticed the young woman who had just entered. There was something in her features that seemed familiar. Tempest Qu, his own disciple! "Is your surname Qu, by any chance?" he asked.

The girl laughed. "I don't know!"

Apothecary Huang had long known that Tempest Qu had sired a daughter. She should be around eighteen years of age, by now.

"Papa," Lotus cut in, "come and look!" She took him by the hand and led him inside the room behind the cupboard.

Apothecary Huang looked around and observed that its arrangement was in full accordance with his own teachings. This was surely the work of Tempest Qu.

"Papa, the chest. Look inside. I'm sure you know what they are."

But Apothecary Huang was distracted by a sideboard located in the southwesterly corner of the chamber. Behind it was a hole. He reached inside and removed a scroll. Instantly, he leaped back out.

Lotus scurried after him and peered down at the paper in her father's hands. It was tattered and covered in dust, but she could make out a few shaky lines. She began to read.

> *To the most venerated Lord Huang of Peach Blossom Island:*
> *Your disciple has acquired a collection of assorted pieces of callig-*
> *raphy, painting, and other precious artifacts from within the Imperial*
> *Palace, which I wish to present to thee, Lord, for your appreciation.*
> *I call thee Lord, not wishing to be so presumptuous as to use Be-*
> *nevolent Teacher, even if I do so in my dream-filled slumbers.*
> *I have had the misfortune to be surrounded by palace guards, but*
> *I am survived by a daughter.*

That was all he had written. The page was otherwise blank, apart from a few dark patches that looked like bloodstains.

By the time of Lotus's birth, all the disciples of Peach Blossom Island had been expelled. Tempest Qu had been the first. Lotus knew that they had all been accomplished scholars and martial artists, each in their own way. This note troubled her.

Apothecary Huang understood at once how hard his disciple had taken his banishment, and that stealing the artifacts from the palace was part of a plan to regain his Master's affection. He had taken great risks because he knew how much Apothecary Huang valued such items. Indeed, in the end, it had been his undoing. Having sustained a grave injury, he had returned home to write his will, but never finished it. A guard had followed him, and, in this hidden chamber, they had fought and killed each other.

Apothecary Huang had felt regret at his recent reunion with Zephyr Lu, and, with the death of Cyclone Mei and this new revelation, his feelings of guilt were overwhelming. He turned to face Tempest's daughter.

"Did your father teach you how to fight?" he asked gravely.

The girl shook her head, then ran to the door, closed it, and peered through the crack. Satisfied, she turned and launched into a sequence of some half a dozen moves from Jade Ripple Palm.

"Papa, she taught herself by watching Brother Qu as he practiced."

Apothecary Huang nodded and then murmured, "Tempest would

never have dared to pass on what I had taught him, as long as he was cast out from Peach Blossom Island." He paused and then added, "Lotus, try tripping her."

Lotus approached the girl and smiled. "Let's play together. Watch out!" She feinted left and then launched two rapid-fire kicks, in a move known as the Mandarin Duck. The girl was dumbstruck. One of Lotus's feet was about to connect with her right hip. She stumbled out of harm's way, only for the other foot to greet her back. The girl fell, face-first.

Seconds later, she was back on her feet. "Cheat! Let's go again, little sister," she cried.

Apothecary Huang's expression darkened. "Little sister? She is your martial senior."

The girl laughed, not understanding what he meant.

Lotus realized that her father was testing her footwork. Brother Qu's legs had both been broken, therefore she could not have picked up any such skills from him, just by watching. But, if he had trained her, he would have included such fundamental techniques.

And yet, by referring to Lotus as her martial senior, he was accepting the girl into his tutelage.

"You are a silly girl," he could not help but say.

"Call me Silly!" she exclaimed, and laughed.

Apothecary Huang scowled. "And what about your mother?"

The girl pretended to cry. "She's gone to be with Grandma."

Apothecary Huang continued to ask questions, but her answers gave him little to go on. Eventually, he sighed and gave up.

2

TOGETHER, THEY BURIED CYCLONE MEI IN THE COURTYARD of the inn. Then, Guo Jing and Lotus carried out Tempest's skeleton and interred him next to Cyclone. The Freaks considered Twice Foul Dark Wind their mortal enemies, but even they paid their respects.

Apothecary Huang stood in silence before the two graves, a hundred different feelings washing over him. "Lotus," he began sadly, "why don't we take a look at the treasures your Brother Qu collected?"

Father and daughter walked back inside and into the secret chamber.

One by one, they pulled out the items and examined them. Apothecary Huang was silent. Tears rolled down his cheeks. Eventually, he spoke: "Of all my disciples, Tempest Qu was the best fighter, with the most brilliant mind. Had his legs not been broken, not even a hundred palace guards could have bested him."

"Of course. Are you going to teach his daughter?"

"I will teach her to fight. But I will also teach her to write poetry, play the *qin*, and I'll teach her the mysteries of the Five Elements . . . All the things that your Brother Qu wanted to learn but never did. I will teach her everything."

That will not be easy, Lotus thought.

Apothecary Huang opened each layer of the chest. The more valuable the items he uncovered, the deeper the grief he felt. "These items make for pleasing diversions, to be sure, but they must never be allowed to get in the way of what is really important—that is, real ambition. Emperor Huizong was a fine painter of mountains and rivers, but he rolled them up and gifted those landscapes straight to the Jin." He took out another scroll. "Huh?"

"What is it, Papa?"

"Look at this."

The painting depicted a mountain with five sharp peaks, among which one in particular towered at a dizzying height above a ravine below, piercing the clouds overhead. A row of pine trees clung to the slope, their trunks reaching for the sun in the south, their branches laden with snow. On one side, a lone pine stood against the northern winds, old and brittle, but majestic nonetheless. Beneath it, a few vermillion brushstrokes depicted a general, practicing with his sword. His features were obscured as his sleeves danced on the wind. From his posture, it was evident that he was an extraordinary fighter. He was the only dash of color in an otherwise monochrome landscape.

There was no signature, only a poem:

> *In uniform beclad in years of dust*
> *I take in the perfume*
> *of the Emerald Hills.*
> *Never could I tire of such beauty*
> *but the moon and the hooves urge me on.*

Lotus recognized the poem from the Pavilion of Emerald Hills.

"Papa, this is the calligraphy of Han Shizhong. The poem is by the great Yue Fei."

"That's right, dear Lotus! You're so clever. The poem is written about the Emerald Hills, but the landscape there is most treacherous and is far from the paradise he describes. The painting is assured, but it lacks subtlety. It is not the work of a master."

That day, in the Pavilion, Guo Jing had traced his fingers over Han Shizhong's calligraphy. Lotus knew he would like this painting very much. "Papa, can Guo Jing have it?"

"Your heart belongs to him, now," her father said with a laugh. "Very well."

He gave it to her and then reached once more into the metal chest, picking out a necklace. "Every pearl is of exactly the same size. Most unusual." He handed it to Lotus so that she might wear it. Delighted, Lotus threw her arms around him. He pulled her close, and there they took comfort, cheek to cheek.

Lotus had just rolled up the painting for Guo Jing when she heard the urgent screech of two birds outside.

Her white condors! They were back. She bounded outside to greet her friends.

Once outside, she spotted Guo Jing standing beneath a large willow tree. One of the condors was tugging at the shoulder of his robe with its talons, trying to get him to follow it. The other was circling above, screeching. Tempest Qu's daughter was dancing around Guo Jing, clapping her hands and laughing.

"Lotus!" Guo Jing cried, as soon as he saw her. "They're in trouble; we have to save them!" He looked very agitated.

"Who's in trouble?"

"My sworn brother and sister!"

Lotus pouted. "You can go on your own."

"Lotus, don't be so childish. They need us! Come on." He ran over to Ulaan and jumped up into the saddle.

"Do you still want me, or not?"

Guo Jing was baffled. "Of course I want you. I want you more than life itself."

Clutching the reins with one hand, he reached out toward her with the other.

Lotus flashed a dazzling smile and cried out, "Papa! We're off on a rescue. Why don't you and the Six Heroes come too?" She jumped up and landed behind Guo Jing, on the back of the horse.

Guo Jing bowed to Apothecary Huang and his *shifus*, before spurring his horse on. The condors were already up ahead, crying out to show the way.

3

ULAAN AND GUO JING HAD BEEN SEPARATED A LONG TIME, but feeling the weight of his master on his back brought the little horse nothing but joy. On he galloped, as if his hooves were powered by the wind. The condors were swift on the wing, but Ulaan had no trouble keeping up with them.

Before long, the birds dropped down through a dense tree canopy and into a dark forest. Ulaan sped straight for them.

Just as they drew close, a voice came booming from between the trees.

"Brother Qiu." It was Viper Ouyang. "Your reputation precedes you, of course. I am honored to meet you and witness firsthand your consummate skill and virtuosity. What a shame you could not take part in the Contest of Mount Hua, all those years ago. May I invite the Master to demonstrate his awesome Iron Palm by offering a few of my own paltry skills?"

A howl. The treetops swayed. Then a crash echoed around them as a large tree fell.

Guo Jing jumped down from his horse and ran toward the sound.

Lotus dismounted and patted Ulaan on the head. Then she pointed back in the direction from which they had come. "Go and find my papa and bring him here."

Ulaan snorted and galloped off.

I hope Papa gets here quick, Lotus thought. Otherwise, we will have to confront Viper Ouyang on our own, once again.

She slipped between the trees, being careful not to be heard or seen. The scene that waited for her was a surprise indeed: Tolui, Khojin, Jebe, and Boroqul had each been tied to a separate tree, while Viper Ouyang and Qiu Qianren were standing facing each other. There was another man too, dressed in scale armor and bound to a tree that had recently been felled. It was the Song general who had been sent to escort Tolui. By the look of it, he had met with the force of Viper Ouyang's palm. His armor was bright with blood, his eyes were closed and his head hung limply to one side. He was dead.

Lotus looked around. The other soldiers had clearly fled.

Qiu Qianren had no desire to fight Viper Ouyang and was still racking his brains for a little trick to get himself out of it when he heard footsteps behind him. He turned and, to his delight, saw Guo Jing. Just in time! Surely he could contrive to make Viper Ouyang turn his wrath on the boy instead.

Viper Ouyang was just as surprised as Qiu Qianren. Guo Jing had been given the full force of his Exploding Toad kung fu and yet here he was, standing before them, seemingly unharmed.

"Guo Jing!" Khojin cried. "You're still alive! How wonderful!"

Lotus, too, was making her own plans. I must slow things down to give Papa time to get here.

"Scoundrels!" Guo Jing cried suddenly. "What are you doing here? Hasn't enough blood been shed today?"

Viper Ouyang smiled, but did not say anything. This would be his chance to assess the extent of Qiu Qianren's martial skills.

"Won't you show Master Ouyang the respect he is due?" Qiu Qianren piped up.

Guo Jing had listened to Qiu Qianren stir up all kinds of trouble with his lies, and this time, he assumed, would be no different. He stepped forward, bellowed, and threw a Haughty Dragon Repents.

He was now well-practiced in the Dragon-Subduing Palm, and this particular move was four parts release and six parts restraint; its power, once unleashed, was instantly withdrawn. Qiu Qianren tried to lean out of the way, but he was too slow and fell on his face instead.

Guo Jing roared and aimed a reverse palm straight at Qiu's wagging tongue. He wanted nothing more than to knock the chicanery out of him.

His hand moved slowly, but his aim was true. Qiu Qianren was powerless to fend it off. But, just as it was about to meet with his face, a voice cried, "Stop!"

It was Lotus. Guo Jing grabbed Qiu Qianren by the neck instead, lifted him up and then turned to face her. "What is it?"

Lotus was worried that, if Guo Jing hurt Qiu Qianren, Viper Ouyang might go on the attack.

"Let go! If you hit his face, the force will rebound on you and you will be injured. He is famous for this facial kung fu!"

Guo Jing, incredulous, did not realize that she was mocking the old trickster. "Facial kung fu? What nonsense!"

"Master Qiu can strip the hide from an ox with his breath alone. Quick, get out of the way!"

This only angered Guo Jing even more, but he knew better than to question Lotus, so he dutifully placed the old man back on his feet and let him go.

Qiu Qianren chuckled. "The girl knows danger when she sees it! But I have no grievance with you two youngsters. Why would I, your senior, seek to injure those beneath me?"

"Very well, then," Lotus said, and smiled. "I am a great admirer of yours, Master Qiu. I would be honored if you might share with me some of your famed kung fu. Just try not to hurt me!" She then raised her left hand, curled it into a tube, put it to her lips and blew. "This move is called Blowing One's Own Conch."

"The young lady is most bold!" Qiu Qianren said. "Master Ou-yang is a great master of the *wulin;* how dare you ridicule him!"

Slap! Lotus's hand met squarely with the side of his face. "And this one is called Brazen Cheek!"

A burst of laughter echoed from the woods. "Excellent! Another!"

It was her father. His arrival only emboldened her further. As she made as if to slap Qiu Qianren with her right hand, he ducked, only to be met with her left. He tried to block with a swipe of his arm, in a move from Palm of Connected Arms and Six Unions, but her palms fluttered before his eyes like two beautiful butterflies. Thus distracted, he left his right cheek open to another whack.

The situation was close to getting out of his control, so Qiu sent out two punches, forcing the young girl back. Then he leaped to the side and cried, "Stop!"

"What is it? Have you had enough already?" Lotus replied with a grin.

Apothecary Huang and the Six Freaks had now arrived. The sight of Tolui and the others tied to tree trunks puzzled them.

Viper Ouyang knew full well of Qiu Qianren's legendary abilities. He had, in years gone by, laid waste to the mighty Hengshan School with the use of nothing but his Iron Palm kung fu. The Hengshan fighters never again recovered their position in the *wulin.* So, how could it be that he was unable to prevail against Lotus? Was there really such a thing as facial kung fu? Viper had never heard of it, and judging by the fight taking place before his very eyes, it did not appear to be too impressive if it did indeed exist.

Viper looked up and spotted a white pouch, made from Sichuan silk, slung across Apothecary Huang's shoulders. There was a camel embroidered on it. He recognized it as his nephew's. Dread filled his heart. He had returned to the inn to find Gallant, only to stumble upon Apothecary Huang's struggle with the Quanzhen Sect. But could the Old Heretic have killed him as revenge for the death of Cyclone Mei?

"Where is my nephew?" he asked, his voice trembling.

"The same place as my disciple."

Viper Ouyang felt his body turn to ice. Gallant Ouyang had been born of an illicit encounter between the Venom and his sister-in-law. He had always referred to the young man as his nephew to save face, but in truth he was of his own flesh, his most beloved son. Gallant had been helpless, his legs injured; there was no way he could have caused Apothecary Huang or the Quanzhen Taoists any trouble. They were honorable men of the *jianghu*. Surely they could not have gone against the code of *xia*.

Apothecary Huang watched and waited. He knew the Venom would soon attack, that he would mete out upon him a righteous fury that could move mountains and shake oceans. He prepared himself for an unstoppable force.

"Who did it?" Viper Ouyang snarled. "One of yours? Or one of the Taoist dogs?" Apothecary Huang would not have lowered himself to kill a man thus incapacitated, Viper told himself. He must have had someone else do it for him.

"A young squirt who has studied the skills of both the Quanzhen Sect and Peach Blossom Island. You know him well. I suggest you go looking for him."

Apothecary Huang meant Yang Kang, of course. But Viper Ouyang turned and locked eyes upon Guo Jing. Rage was bursting from his eye sockets. He then turned back to Apothecary Huang. "Why do you have my nephew's pouch?"

"He had a map of Peach Blossom Island, which, as I'm sure you understand, belongs to me. It pains me to admit it, but your nephew was forced to have daylight on his face once again. Unfortunately, when I recovered the pouch, there was no map to be seen. What a waste of my efforts! Still, I did make sure that your nephew was given a proper resting place. Of that, I can assure you."

"Is that so?" Viper Ouyang said bitterly. He knew full well that a fight with the Lord of Peach Blossom Island would take a thousand blows or more, and there was no guarantee he would prevail. But he had obtained a copy of the Nine Yin Manual, so he would have his revenge eventually, if not today. And yet . . . if Qiu Qianren were to take care of the Freaks, Guo Jing, and Lotus, and then join him against Apothecary Huang . . . well . . . they might just succeed. The fact that he could assess the nature of the situation before him so coolly having just learned of his son's murder was itself remarkable. He must make use of Qiu's presence.

"Brother Qiu," he said. "You deal with the others. I will kill Heretic Huang."

Qiu Qianren laughed and fluttered his fan. "Very well. I will help you with Old Huang as soon as I am finished with the others."

"Excellent," Viper said, his eyes already fixed on Apothecary Huang. Slowly, he began to squat down. His adversary planted his feet in the second Heavenly Stem position.

"Kill me first!" Lotus broke in.

Qiu Qianren shook his head. "Miss, you are so adorable. It is almost unbearable . . ." Suddenly, he clutched his stomach. "Oh no, not now! What timing!"

"What is it?" Lotus asked.

"Wait a moment," Qiu replied, his face strained. "I've got the most terrible stomachache. Excuse me!"

Lotus was stunned into silence. Qiu Qianren, meanwhile, groaned and limped away. Was it a ruse? Lotus wondered. She did not dare go after him, just in case.

Zhu Cong took a piece of rice paper from his pocket and caught up with Qiu Qianren, tapping him on the shoulder. "You'll be needing this."

"Thank you!" Qiu Qianren said, and ducked behind some bushes.

Lotus picked up a stone and threw it toward the small of his back. "Go farther in!"

Qiu Qianren caught it at the last moment. "Is it the smell?" he called, and laughed. "You had better all wait for me! Don't be taking the chance to run away, now." He pulled up his trousers, shuffled a few dozen meters farther into the woods and ducked behind a row of low bushes.

"Master Zhu, the scoundrel is trying to escape!" Lotus said.

Zhu Cong nodded. "He may be brazen, but he's not quick on his feet. There's no chance of him getting away. Here," he said, and threw her a sword and a palm-shaped metal token that he had stolen from Qiu Qianren using his famed sleight of hand. Lotus had watched Qiu plunge the sword into his stomach and had known at once that it was a trick, but she had been unable to work out how he had done it. She examined it and found that the blade was retractable, made up of three parts that slid into each other. She shook with laughter. She could use this to toy with Viper, she realized.

Lotus ran up to the Venom and cried, "Uncle! I cannot take it anymore!" Then, raising the weapon in her right hand, she thrust it hard into her stomach.

Viper Ouyang and her father had been concentrating on summoning their internal strength in preparation for their duel, and had therefore missed the whole tawdry exchange between Qiu Qianren and Zhu Cong. Both men watched in shock as the young girl doubled over before them.

Just then, Lotus stood up, raised the sword once more and showed them how it worked.

Viper Ouyang's mind was racing. Was Qiu Qianren's mighty reputation built on a foundation of lies?

Apothecary Huang watched as the Venom slowly straightened his legs. He could guess what he was thinking. He then took the

Iron Palm token from his daughter. The character *Qiu* was engraved on the back, along with a wave pattern. This object was the symbol of the Chief of the Iron Palm Gang, which had its base in the depths of the inland mountains of the south. For twenty years, the bearer of this object had controlled those vast swathes of untamed land, stretching from the Nine Rivers in the east, all the way to Chengdu in the west. Was this shameless old man really the leader of such a mighty brotherhood? Still doubtful, Huang returned the object to his daughter.

Viper Ouyang peered at it from the corner of his eye, trying to hide his surprise.

"This strange thing could turn out to be a lot of fun," Lotus said with a wide grin on her face. "I'm going to keep it! That old man can't have any use for it. But this?" she added, hefting the trick sword. "I'm bored with it already. Catch!" She raised the sword as if to throw it at Qiu Qianren, but realized that it was too heavy. Instead, she handed it to her father. "Papa, you throw it to him."

Like Viper, Apothecary Huang had begun to suspect that Qiu Qianren's reputation was undeserved, and he had been intending to test the old man's skills. He placed the sword flat across his left palm, the tip pointing away from him, and flicked the handle with the middle finger of his right hand. The weapon shot forth, faster and with more force than if he had used a bow.

Lotus and Guo Jing let out a cheer and clapped. Even Viper Ouyang was secretly impressed at such a fine display of Divine Flick kung fu.

Meanwhile, the sword continued to roar straight toward Qiu Qianren as he squatted in the bushes. Moments later, it had plunged into his back, retracting shaft, handle and all.

Using his lightness kung fu, Guo Jing dashed over to take a look. He gasped, then lifted up Qiu Qianren's arrowroot shirt and waved it at the others. "The old crook is already gone!"

Using the bushes as cover, Qiu Qianren had slipped out of his jacket and hung it from a twig. Apothecary Huang and Viper Ouyang had been focused on each other, and the others had had their eyes fixed on the impending fight between the two greats of the *wulin*. He had tricked them all, once again. The Heretic of the East and the Venom of the West exchanged glances and burst into laughter. Deep down, they both felt relieved to have one less powerful opponent to have to deal with.

Viper Ouyang knew that Apothecary Huang was quick and far less gullible than Count Seven Hong. But it was rare indeed to see him relax his guard like this. How could Viper not try to take his advantage? He guffawed three times, fell silent, and then, quick like lightning, bowed.

Still laughing, his face raised to the sky, Huang promptly clasped his hands and returned the gesture.

Both men trembled almost imperceptibly.

Viper's attack never materialized. Still bowed down, he took three steps back. "Heretic Huang . . . Until we meet again!" With a flick of his sleeve, he turned.

There was a tiny twitch in Apothecary Huang's face. His arm shot out, blocking off his daughter from the Viper's sudden attack.

Guo Jing had noticed it too: Viper Ouyang had launched a secretive move similar to Splitting Sky Palm at Lotus. Guo Jing howled and threw a double punch straight at Viper's stomach.

Apothecary Huang had sent back the force of Viper's attack, but this only amplified the power in Viper's palm, which he then aimed at Guo Jing, who ducked and rolled out of its path.

Back on his feet and at a safe distance, Guo Jing gasped for air, his cheeks white with shock.

We've only been apart for a few days, and yet his kung fu has improved yet again, Viper Ouyang thought, in wonder.

The Six Freaks of the South hurried into the fray, forming a semicircle around Viper. But the Venom merely charged through their formation. Gilden Quan and Jade Han stumbled back and out of his way. They could only watch as he strode away and out of the forest.

Apothecary Huang could, of course, have joined forces with the Freaks and avenged Cyclone Mei's death, there and then. But he was proud, not to mention vain. He did not want it known in the *wulin* that he had needed their help to defeat Viper. He would rather do the deed alone. His eyes followed the Venom as he disappeared, a cold grin on his face.

Guo Jing and his *shifus* untied Khojin, Tolui, Jebe, and Boroqul. Together, they cursed Yang Kang and his deceitful, lying tongue.

"He said he had urgent business in Yuezhou," Tolui grumbled. "I gave him three of my finest horses as a gift. What a waste!"

Yang Kang had traveled with Tolui and the escort, stopping that evening at an inn north of Lin'an. In the dead of night, Yang Kang got up, intending to stab Tolui, only to find the two beggars were taking turns patrolling outside his window. Several times, he had been foiled by one of the men rounding the corner and appearing at just the right moment. He waited until dawn before finally giving up. At breakfast, he had cheated Tolui out of three horses and had ridden off with the two beggars in the direction of Yuezhou.

Unaware of what had nearly befallen them during the night, the rest of the group were about to continue northward when the two white condors turned and flew off in the opposite direction. They waited, but the birds did not return. They were intelligent creatures, and they must have flown south for a reason, so Tolui gave the order to wait until they came back. There was no urgent reason for them to set off that morning. On the third day, the condors suddenly reappeared and began shrieking at Khojin. The group packed up and followed the birds back the way they had come. That was when they had chanced upon Qiu Qianren and Viper Ouyang in the forest.

The Jin had entrusted Qiu Qianren with a mission: sow discord in the *jianghu*, so that the martial men of the south are too divided and distracted to block the Jin army's advance. Qiu Qianren had been working his magic on Viper Ouyang when he spotted Tolui beyond the trees. Recognizing him as an ambassador of the Mongols, he had joined forces with Viper and attacked him. The Mongols tried to fight back, but they were no match for the Venom.

The condors had spotted Ulaan's tracks and unwittingly led their masters straight into the jaws of disaster. Fortunately, they went in search of Guo Jing and Lotus just in time.

Khojin clasped Guo Jing by the hand and related what had happened to her over the previous few days, while Lotus watched, jealousy bubbling up inside her. She could not understand what they were saying, and it made her feel like an outsider.

Apothecary Huang noticed the strange expression on his daughter's face. "Lotus, who is this young barbarian girl?"

"Guo Jing's betrothed," she said glumly.

Apothecary Huang could not believe what he was hearing. "What?"

"Go and ask him yourself, Papa."

Zhu Cong could sense the tension in the air. He rushed forward and delicately explained to the Heretic the circumstances of the betrothal.

Unable to hold back his fury, Apothecary Huang glowered at Guo Jing. "So, the boy was already engaged before coming to Peach Blossom Island to ask for my daughter's hand?"

"We ought to come up with a plan . . . to satisfy everyone," Zhu Cong said.

"Lotus, leave this to your father. Don't get in my way."

"Papa, what are you going to do?" There was a tremble in her voice.

"I am going to kill them both! I will not allow them to humiliate us."

Lotus grabbed her father's hand. "Papa, Guo Jing says that he really, truly loves me. He never felt that way about her."

"Very well," Apothecary Huang snorted. "Boy! Kill the barbarian girl! Let us see where your loyalties lie!"

Guo Jing stared at him in disbelief. Never before had he been in such an impossible situation. What should he do?

"Already betrothed, and yet you came to me to ask for my daughter's hand? What do you say to that?"

Guo Jing's face was white. The Freaks could see that he was one small flick of Huang's finger away from fatal catastrophe. And yet, how would they be able to overcome the Heretic if he let his fury get the better of him?

Guo Jing had never been able to lie. He could only answer with the honest truth. "All I want is to be with Lotus. I can't live without her."

"Very well. Then, from this day forth, you must never meet with this barbarian girl again."

Guo Jing hesitated.

"You cannot make such a promise, can you?" Lotus said.

"She is like a sister to me. I would worry about her."

"I don't mind!" Lotus said, breaking into a gracious smile. "I know you don't love her. Of course, she cannot compare to me!"

"Then it's settled," Apothecary Huang said. "I'm here. The girl's family is here. Your six *shifus* are here. Let them all be my witness: you will marry my daughter, and not her!"

It was quite out of character for him to be so conciliatory, but there was little he would not do for the sake of his daughter. Besides, Cyclone Mei's sacrifice had also temporarily softened his heart.

Guo Jing hung his head, his mind racing. He glanced down at his belt and saw the golden dagger given to him by Genghis Khan, and the other dagger, bestowed on his father by Qiu Chuji.

My father wanted Yang Kang and I to be sworn brothers in life and death. But how can I keep this promise when he behaves as he does? Uncle Ironheart wanted me to marry his daughter, Mercy. But that can't possibly happen. The Great Khan wants me to marry Khojin. But maybe I don't have to follow my elders' wishes, after all? Why should they get to decide that Lotus and I be apart?

His mind made up, he looked up again.

Zhu Cong had finished translating Guo Jing's exchange with Apothecary Huang for Tolui. Tolui looked at Guo Jing. It was clear that he was struggling to reconcile his obligations with his heart's desire. Guo Jing did not love his sister, it was obvious. Furious, Tolui took a wolf-fang arrow from his quiver and held it in both hands.

"Brother Guo! To keep one's word, is that not the mark of a true man? You have treated my sister heartlessly. How can we, the offspring of the great Genghis Khan, trust you after this betrayal? The brotherly bond between us is broken. As for the kindness you showed in saving my father's life and mine, we will remember it and your mother will be looked after. If you prefer that she be sent south, we can arrange an escort for her. We will not neglect her, because we have given our word."

He then snapped the arrow in two and threw the pieces to the ground.

Tolui's words were testament to a steely determination and an iron will. Guo Jing felt a shiver go through him as memories of all the things they had done together on the steppe flashed before his eyes. *I agreed to marry Khojin. I gave my word. What kind of man would I be if I break it? I can't, even if Apothecary Huang kills me and Lotus hates me for the rest of her days.*

"Master Huang," he began, "my honored *shifus*, Brother Tolui, Masters Jebe and Boroqul: Guo Jing is a man of his word. I must marry Sister Khojin."

He made the announcement first in Chinese and then again in Mongolian. No one had been expecting this. The Mongolians were surprised, but delighted. The Six Freaks secretly admired their disciple for staying true to his promise—it showed backbone. Apothecary Huang, however, raised his eyebrows and smiled grimly.

Lotus was heartbroken. She paused, then stepped toward Khojin, assessing her. She had an athletic build, big eyes and well-defined features. Lotus sighed. "Guo Jing, I understand. You two are a pair of white condors from the steppe. I am merely a swallow who has grown up among the willow trees of the south."

"Lotus"—Guo Jing went to her and clasped her hands—"in truth, I don't know who is right. In my heart, I carry only you. You know that! It doesn't matter what anyone else says, I will think of you until my body is burned and my ashes are carried away on the wind!"

"Then why are you marrying her?" The tears welled in Lotus's eyes.

"Because I'm stupid. I don't know what to think. All I know is, I cannot go back on my word. But they can't change what is in my heart. I'd rather die than be parted from you!"

Lotus was deeply confused. His words pleased her and pained her in equal measure. She smiled faintly. "Dear Guo Jing, if I had known things would turn out this way, I would have suggested we stay on Rosy Cloud Island."

Apothecary Huang flicked a sleeve and gave Khojin a menacing look.

Lotus understood at once her father's intentions, and had launched herself at Khojin before he could make his attack. Apothecary Huang started to pull back as Lotus tugged Khojin from her horse.

Thwack! Apothecary Huang's hand met with her saddle.

At first, the horse did not react. Then its head sagged, its legs buckled and it fell to the ground, dead.

This was a mount bred from the finest beasts of the Mongolian steppe: muscular, robust and tall. And yet, all it had taken was one strike of Apothecary Huang's palm to kill it. The others watched in amazement, their hearts thumping. What if he had struck Khojin, as he had intended?

Apothecary Huang was stunned. Had his daughter saved her rival? If he killed the Mongolian girl, however, he knew that Guo Jing would surely turn against his beloved Lotus. So what if he does? Why should I be scared of a mere boy!

He glanced over at Lotus and saw the misery etched on her face. Yet, her expression was also tender. He could detect a hundred emotions, all mixed together. She looked just like her late mother. Losing his wife had brought on a madness in him, and, even though it had been fifteen years now, he saw her in his daughter just as clearly as if she were still with him. Lotus loved Guo Jing deeply, down into the very core of her being. She had inherited this passion from both of them. There was no changing it. He sighed.

"*Heavens and Earth they are the furnace,*" he began to chant, "*and Nature mans the grate. Yin and Yang they are the charcoal, ten thousand objects copper does create.*"

The tears rolled down Lotus's cheeks.

Ryder Han tugged at Zhu Cong's robe and whispered, "What is he singing about?"

"It's from a poem written in the Han dynasty," Zhu Cong replied. "Existence, for all creatures, is pain and suffering, like being burned in a furnace."

"A master of such martial arts, what pain can he know of?"

Zhu Cong merely shook his head.

"Lotus," Apothecary Huang said softly, "let's go home. You are never to see this boy again."

"Papa, no! I must go to Yuezhou. I'm the Chief of the Beggar Clan, now—*Shifu* said so."

"Being the chief of a bunch of beggars will only bring you trouble. There is not much fun to be had, believe me."

"I made a promise," Lotus said.

"Try for a day or two, if you must. Then, when you're sick of it, you can hand the role on to someone else." He then paused, and continued, "And what about the boy?"

Lotus glanced at Guo Jing and caught his eye. His expression was one of tenderness and love. She turned back to her father.

"Papa, if he is going to marry someone else, then so shall I. But I will only ever love him, and he will only ever love me."

Apothecary Huang smiled. "No daughter of Peach Blossom Island will be prevented from getting what she wants. Very well. But what if the man you marry doesn't let you see him?"

"Who would stop me?" Lotus replied with a snort. "I am your daughter, after all!"

"Silly girl. Your father won't live forever."

"Papa!" The tears flowed faster. "I cannot live without you!"

"So, you still accept this callous young boy?" Apothecary Huang pressed.

"Every day spent with him is a day of pure happiness," Lotus said, but her voice betrayed her heartache.

The Freaks listened in utter bemusement. Father and daughter spoke with no thought for propriety. Apothecary Huang was not known as the Heretic of the East for nothing. He cared little for the traditions passed down by the rulers of the Shang and Zhou, and despised the rites as laid out in the texts by the Duke of Zhou and Confucius. As for Lotus, she was a product of her upbringing. That she could speak so openly of marriage as nothing more than a contract, and love as love, would shock most people who heard it. Did she not understand the importance of chastity and modesty? The Freaks were more open-minded than most, but even they could only shake their heads upon overhearing such a candid conversation between father and daughter.

Guo Jing felt terrible and wished for nothing more than to offer some words of comfort to Lotus. But he was not known for his skill with words. He had no idea what to say.

Apothecary Huang looked at his daughter and then at Guo Jing. Then he raised his head to the heavens and let out a long, anguished roar. His wail echoed around the valley, startling a flock of magpies and sending them screeching up into the sky.

"Oh, magpies, build your bridge faster, so that the cowherd may see his beloved weaver girl tonight!" Lotus said.

Apothecary Huang grabbed a handful of stones and started throwing them at the birds. One by one, they fell from the sky. "What bridge?" he cried. "Passion? Love? They are nothing but fantasies. Better they die an early death!"

At this, he spun on his heel and sped off. Moments later, his dark green robe had disappeared into the woods.

Tolui had not been able to understand what had been said, but he knew that Guo Jing was standing by his promise. "Brother!" he cried out, a broad smile on his face. "You finish your business here, and we will see you once again, back in the north!"

"Keep the condors by your side," Khojin added. "Come back soon!"

Guo Jing nodded. "Tell my mother that I will avenge Papa's death."

Jebe and Boroqul also said their goodbyes, then the Mongolians mounted their horses and left.

Jade Han turned to Guo Jing. "What are you going to do?"

"I . . . I must find *Shifu* Hong."

"Yes, that is proper." Ke Zhen'e nodded. "I hear that Apothecary Huang visited our families. We must return to them as soon as possible to set their minds at rest. When you see Chief Hong, pass on our sincerest wishes for his good health, and tell him he is most welcome in Jiaxing. We will look after him, be assured of it."

Guo Jing nodded and bade his *shifus* farewell. Then he and Lotus mounted Ulaan and set off in the direction of Lin'an.

4

THAT EVENING, GUO JING AND LOTUS RETURNED TO THE palace. They began their search in the imperial kitchens, but there was no sign of Count Seven Hong anywhere. They interrogated some eunuchs, all of whom claimed that there had been no intruders over the past few days. This put their minds at ease somewhat. Count Seven may have been injured, but he was still in possession of his wits. Surely he had come up with an escape plan and was on his way to Yuezhou to meet with the rest of the Beggar Clan.

Thus satisfied, they set off westward early the next morning.

Half of China was now occupied by the Jurchen. In the east, the River Huai drew the boundary separating the Jin-controlled northern territories from the south, which remained under the rule of the Song Emperor; in the west, the two states were divided by the military stronghold Dasan Pass in the Qin Mountains.

The Song Empire, once in control of all of China, now had dominion over just seventeen provinces: East and West Zhe, the two Huais, East and West Jiangnan, North and South Jinghu, South Jingxi, the five territories of Bashu, Fujian, and finally East and West Guangnan.

Before long, Guo Jing and Lotus Huang had arrived in West Jiangnan. They were traveling along an exposed path, over a mountain ridge. Dark clouds sped toward them from the east. Midsummer storms arrive with scant warning in this part of the country. Raindrops as big as soybeans were soon beating down on them, as thunder cracked over their heads. Guo Jing scrambled to open an umbrella over Lotus, but a gust of wind ripped the canopy away within seconds, leaving him clutching nothing but a bare pole.

The sight made Lotus chuckle. "You've found the Dog-Beating Cane already!"

Guo Jing smiled, but inside he was sighing. *There's nowhere to take cover . . .* He started to remove his outer robe so that he could use it to keep the rain from Lotus for a little longer.

Lotus was moved by the gesture. "It'll be wet through before long."

"We can go faster."

She shook her head. "Let me tell you a story. One day, on a country road much like this, the heavens opened. Everyone started to run, except for one man. He kept walking at the same leisurely pace. People were curious and asked him why he didn't hurry. 'The rain is also falling on the road ahead. I will get drenched, either way.'"

Guo Jing smiled at this obvious truth.

But the tale led Lotus's thoughts to a darker place—to Guo Jing's determination to honor his word in the matter of his betrothal to Khojin, against his own heart and hers.

Our future is destined to be full of grief and heartbreak, she told herself. *Whichever path we take, we cannot run from it. Just like the storm, beating down on us here, on this exposed ridge.*

They rode on in silence. It was only when they began their descent that they chanced upon a farmstead. They knocked on the door to ask for shelter.

They were soaked through, from head to toe. Luckily, the farmers had some dry clothes that they could borrow.

Lotus was greatly amused to be given the patched garb of an elderly peasant woman. As she dressed herself, however, she was startled by an exasperated cry from the room next door.

She rushed over. "What's wrong?"

Guo Jing's face was crumpled. He held out the painting her father had given him.

Lotus took the scroll and unrolled it.

"What a shame," she muttered.

The paper and the silk mounting were rubbed and torn in many parts. Much of the ink brushwork, if not altogether washed out, was irreparably damaged. Nothing could be done to remedy it.

She cast one last look of regret at the ruined artwork as she set it down. Her eyes settled on a few faint lines of writing, next to the poem inscribed by Han Shizhong. Quite certain that she had not seen them before, she brought the painting close to her face to examine the marks.

The characters were written on the lining that formed part of the backing, visible only because the painting itself had been rendered translucent by the rain. And yet, the hidden message had also been partially washed away . . .

Studying the indistinct traces, she mumbled to herself: ". . . Fei's final writings . . . iron palm . . . middle crag . . . in the second . . ."

However hard she tried, she could not make out the missing characters. The only thing she could deduce was that, altogether, there should have been four lines, each consisting of four characters.

"Did you say 'Fei's final writings'? As in, General Yue Fei?"

"It could very well be that! Remember Wanyan Honglie thought General Yue's writings were hidden behind the waterfall by the Hall of Wintry Jade, in the Imperial Palace, in Lin'an? He found a marble casket that was supposed to contain the manuscripts, but it was empty." Lotus repeated the characters to herself several times before continuing. "These four lines must be the key to where the writings are concealed . . . When we were in Roaming Cloud Manor, Brother Zephyr and your *shifus* mentioned that Qiu Qianren was the leader of the Iron Palm Gang. Papa has also told me that the Iron Palm Gang rules over Sichuan and Hunan. Could Yue Fei's final writings have something to do with Qiu Qianren?"

"I don't trust anything, when it comes to him." Guo Jing shook his head.

"Neither do I," Lotus replied with a smile.

With no clear answers, they tucked the scroll back in their packing and carried on toward Yuezhou.

5

ON THE FIFTEENTH DAY OF THE SEVENTH MONTH, THEY entered Yuezhou, in North Jianghu. After setting the condors free on the outskirts, they dismounted and asked for directions to Yueyang Tower, the city's most famous monument.

They found a tavern next to the tower and chose a table upstairs. Once they had ordered some food and wine, they cast their eyes over the vast expanse of Dongting Lake.

The surface of the water was still and shiny, as if made from a single piece of polished jade. Mountains soared on all sides, framing the wild majesty of the scene. It was quite unlike the elegant mists and gentle refinement of Lake Tai.

Before long, their meal arrived. The food was served in exceptionally large bowls and they were given chopsticks longer than any they had ever seen before. Though their tongues struggled with the sting of the chilies that characterized the cuisine of this region, the flavors were as bold as the view.

After picking at the dishes for a little while, they turned their attention to the verses inscribed on the walls of the dining hall. Guo

Jing's eyes fell on a passage titled "Memorial to Yueyang Tower", by Fan Zhongyan. He read, mouthing silently until he reached the lines:

> *Be the first to bear the hardships of the world,*
> *and the last to enjoy its comforts.*

"What are you thinking?" Lotus asked.

Overwhelmed by the enormity of the statement, Guo Jing did not seem to hear her.

"The man who wrote this was given the posthumous title of the Duke of Wenzhong," Lotus explained. "He was more than just a man of letters. His military foresight kept the Tangut army at bay."

Guo Jing asked Lotus to tell him more. His respect for Fan Zhongyan grew as he learned about his difficult early life—Fan's father died soon after he was born, and his mother, destitute, was forced to remarry—and how he never forgot the struggles faced by the common man, even as he rose higher and higher in the Imperial Court.

Filling his bowl with wine until it was full to the brim, Guo Jing raised a toast to the great man. He then threw back his head and drank it in one long gulp.

"'Be the first to bear the hardships of the world, and the last to enjoy its comforts.' That is exactly how a hero should think!" he exclaimed.

Lotus found his passionate response endearing. "Of course, it's a very noble sentiment, but this world has too many hardships and too few comforts. Should a hero never enjoy life, even just for a moment? I wouldn't want to live like that." She fell silent for a moment, her brow furrowed. "I don't care about the world, I don't care about its comforts or its hardships. All I know is, if you are not by my side, I'll never be happy . . ."

Guo Jing, too, was thinking about their future and how they were destined to be apart. He lowered his head. There was nothing he could say to comfort her.

"I won't be happy, either," he eventually mumbled.

"It doesn't matter. It is what it is." Lotus looked up, sounding almost cheerful. "Fan Zhongyan also wrote a poem set to the tune of 'Trimming the Silver Lamp's Wick.' Do you know it?"

"Of course not! But I would like to hear it."

Lotus began to recite it:

> *"In the world of men, none reach one hundred.*
> *In youth, sophomoric; in dotage, weak.*
> *Only the time betwixt, those few short years,*
> *For fleeting fame, endure,*
> *Strung along by first in rank and gold.*
> *From such fate how can I escape?*
> *May you ask the old."*

She then explained its meaning to a confused Guo Jing.

"He was right to remind us not to waste our prime chasing fame, fortune or rank," Guo Jing said.

Lotus continued to chant softly to herself, oblivious to Guo Jing's words:

> *"As wine courses through guts wrenched by sorrow,*
> *Out pour tears of lovelorn woe."*

"Was that also written by Fan Zhongyan?"

"Yes, even that great hero loved once."

They raised their cups in a mutual salute, and drank.

As Lotus placed her cup back down, three middle-aged men sitting around a table at the other end of the tavern caught her attention. Unlike the merchants and scholars that made up the general clientele, these men had the bearing of authority, and yet their freshly laundered clothes were covered in patches.

They're probably going to the gathering of the Beggar Clan tonight, she told herself, before the chattering cicadas in the willow tree outside distracted her.

"All day, cicadas cry, 'I see! I see!'" Lotus said. "But what do they actually 'see'? Maybe even insects claim to know things they cannot possibly understand. Just like our dear friend . . . I must say, I rather miss him." She smiled.

"Who?" Guo Jing was mystified.

"Who else but our favorite lying cheat, Qiu Qianren!"

Guo Jing chuckled at the memory of their last encounter.

"What prattle!"

Lotus and Guo Jing turned to see who had cut short their merriment. A man was squatting in a corner, against the wall, watching them with a grin on his face. They relaxed when they saw his begrimed rags and sun-scorched skin.

A member of the Beggar Clan, without a doubt.

Guo Jing cupped his hands in a gesture of esteem. "Master, would you like to join us for a drink?"

"Yes." The beggar shuffled over to their table.

Lotus, meanwhile, asked for another set of chopsticks and a bowl for their guest, then poured him some wine. "Please, take a seat and drink with us."

"Beggars aren't meant to sit on benches." With those words, he dropped to the floor, reached into a rough hemp pouch on his back and pulled out a chipped bowl and a pair of bamboo chopsticks.

"You can give me your leftovers," he said, thrusting his bowl forward.

"That would be disrespectful!" Guo Jing was aghast. "We shall order whatever our elder wishes from the kitchen."

"We beggars have our beggarly ways. If I'm only a beggar in name, but not in deed, then it will all be nothing more than an act. If you wish to give alms, go ahead. If not, I'll go elsewhere."

Lotus stole a glance at Guo Jing, then at the three men in beggar-like dress. "Very well! You're right." Smiling, she took his bowl and scraped all the uneaten food into it.

Meanwhile, the beggar had dug out a few cold balls of rice from another bag he carried on his person.

As the man wolfed down his meal, Lotus counted the number of sacks he was laden with. Nine altogether, in three neat groups. She looked over to the three men; they wore the same number of pouches. Yet, they had no problem sitting on benches and feasting on an elaborate spread prepared for them by the tavern.

She noticed that they made a point of not looking in her direction, pretending not to have seen their dirty comrade. Could she even detect a whiff of displeasure?

The wooden staircase creaked, and they heard footsteps ascending. Lotus and Guo Jing turned, eager to get a glimpse of the new arrivals. Two beggars appeared—one corpulent, one skinny. The Beggar Clan members who had been so respectful to Yang Kang in Ox Village!

Right on cue, Yang Kang appeared on the landing. He caught sight of Guo Jing, hissed an order and ran back down the stairs. The plump one hotfooted it after him, while the gaunt one went up to the three men in patched clothes and whispered a few words. The men hopped to their feet and rushed after them.

All the while, Lotus and Guo Jing's guest did not lift his eyes from his bowl.

Lotus left the table and leaned out of the window, intrigued.

Surrounded by a dozen beggars, Yang Kang was being ushered westward with great deference. Once he was some way from the tavern, he glanced back and caught Lotus watching him. Lowering his eyes, he scuttled away in haste, his entourage trailing behind him.

When Lotus sat down again, their guest was licking his bowl clean. Then he wiped the chopsticks on his grubby shirt.

Taking the opportunity to observe him more closely, she noted that his face was scored by wrinkles and colored by hardship. His hands, almost twice the size of an average adult man's, were covered in blue veins bulging angrily through the coarse skin—testament to a lifetime of toil.

Once the beggar had stowed his things in one of the sacks on his back, Guo Jing stood, put palm over fist and bowed his head once more. "Please, would the elder like to take a seat, so that it would be easier to converse?"

"I'm not used to sitting on benches," the beggar said with good humor. "I know you're disciples of Chief Hong, so we are of the same martial generation, but I think the extra years I've lived give me some rank, here. My name is Lu. Surefoot Lu."

Guo Jing and Lotus looked at each other, surprised that he knew who they were.

"Big Brother Lu, what an interesting name," Lotus said, beaming.

"I'm sure you know the saying, 'A poor man without a staff will be beaten by dogs.' Well, as you can see, of sticks, I have none, but, stinky feet—I have two of those. When dogs trouble me, I plant a foot right on their cursed heads. And off they scurry, tails between their legs."

Lotus clapped at the droll reply. "I dare say the mutts scamper off at the mere sound of your name!"

"Brother Vigor Li told me how you helped him in Baoying. Most admirable. 'The sense of vocation is not limited to youth, for, without it, one lives to a hundred in vain.' It's obvious why the chief values you so."

Guo Jing stood up to thank their guest.

"I overheard your conversation about Qiu Qianren and the Iron Palm Gang. It seems you are unfamiliar with his reach."

"Please, tell us more," Lotus said.

"Qiu Qianren's Iron Palm Gang wields great influence over Jinghu and Sichuan. Its members are not afraid to kill and loot. They used to join with local officials to commit their crimes, but now they bribe the government and play the overlords themselves. Still, all that pales in comparison to their dealings with the Jin. Helping the invaders of their own country? They are nothing but traitors!"

"That old clown Qiu Qianren is a common charlatan, to be sure, but is he capable of such great and damaging deeds?" Lotus could not link this description to the man she had met.

"Do not underestimate him. His reputation is fearsome."

"Have you met him?"

"No, but I've been told that, for the past decade or so, he has been leading a reclusive life, deep in the mountains, working on his Iron Palm kung fu."

"You've been fooled. I've met him a few times, even exchanged a few moves with him. As for this Iron Palm kung fu—" Lotus broke into laughter at the memory of Qiu Qianren faking an upset stomach just to get away from her.

"I've no idea what game he's playing, but the Iron Palm Gang's power is real and they mustn't be disregarded." An earnest warning from Surefoot Lu.

"Brother Lu is right," Guo Jing said humbly, in case they had offended their guest. "Lotus loves to jest."

"Am I jesting?" She bent over, cradling her tummy, as if in pain. "*Aiiiiyaaaa*, my stomach!"

Guo Jing chuckled at her impression of Qiu Qianren, but Lotus's expression instantly changed to one of perfect seriousness. "Brother Lu, do you know the three men who were feasting over there just now?"

Surefoot Lu nodded with a sigh. "Did the chief tell you about the two factions in our Clan? The Washed and the Unwashed?"

"No," Guo Jing and Lotus answered in unison.

"It bodes ill when a group is divided. The chief has tried everything to bring us back together, but so far in vain. You may have heard that Chief Hong is assisted by Four Elders—"

"Yes, *Shifu* has mentioned that before," Lotus cut in, though she was not going to tell him how she knew—that she had been appointed to be the Beggar Clan's next leader.

"I am the Elder of the West," Surefoot Lu continued. "Those men are the other three Elders."

"So, you lead the Unwashed, and they are part of the Washed," Lotus deduced.

"How did you work that out?" Guo Jing was full of admiration.

"Look at what Brother Lu is wearing!" She then turned to Sure-foot Lu. "I don't see why anyone would choose to wear dirty clothes, though. It can't be comfortable. Why don't you wash your clothes more often? Then, you could all be the same. No more conflict!"

"You're born of wealth! Of course, you find us beggars repulsive!" Surefoot Lu stormed down the stairs before Guo Jing had a chance to apologize on Lotus's behalf.

"I know, I've offended Brother Lu. You don't need to tell me off." Lotus stuck her tongue out. "You know, I was rather worried about you, just now."

"Huh?"

"That he might kick you."

"Why would he do that? I wasn't the one who offended him."

Lotus sniggered, baffling Guo Jing even further. A moment later, she heaved a dramatic sigh.

"Remember the story behind his name?"

Guo Jing hopped up, fists raised, full of menace. "Are you calling me a dog?!"

Lotus giggled and ducked before he could tickle her.

CHAPTER EIGHT

DANGER AT THE TERRACE OF THE YELLOW EMPEROR

I

GUO JING AND LOTUS HEARD YET MORE FOOTSTEPS ON THE stairs and stopped their game. The three Elders of the Beggar Clan who had followed Yang Kang outside earlier approached their table, spread out in a line and bowed.

The one in the middle spoke first, all smiles and pleasantries. "It is not in our nature to stand by and let such wickedness pass without offering help. The vagrant Lu has marked you for death."

He was well fed and portly, and his patched garments could not obscure the airs of one who was born to a landowning family. A lush beard, speckled with gray, framed a smooth face that had never been blemished by the sun.

Lotus inhaled sharply. "What do you mean?"

"He refused to sit and share food with you, did he not?"

"Are you saying he poisoned us?"

"It is our Clan's greatest misfortune that a blackguard like him has infiltrated our ranks. He bestrewed your food with a lethal powder concealed under his nails. All it takes is one flick of his finger.

Neither god nor ghost could have detected his handiwork. It gives me no pleasure to be the bearer of this news, but the poison has already taken root in your body. In another hour, no antidote will be able to save you."

"But why, when there is no bad blood between us?"

"I would not be surprised if he found some cause to take offense during your conversation. Please, I urge you to take this remedy now. Your lives are at stake."

The man produced a small paper parcel of medicinal powder from inside his shirt and shared its contents evenly between two cups, which he then filled with wine. He urged Lotus and Guo Jing to drink up.

Of course, Lotus had no intention of taking the antidote offered. How could she not be suspicious of a stranger, especially one associated with Yang Kang?

"We are acquainted with the young lord who came and went only a moment ago," she said. "Please do invite Master Yang to join us."

"Certainly, but the miscreant's poison is most deadly. If you do not—"

"I am very grateful for your kindness." Lotus was being her most gracious self. "Please sit down, sirs, and let's drink together. I often recall the days when Xiao Feng was Chief of the Beggar Clan. What a hero! The way he fought those *wulin* masters at the Manor of Gathering Sages all by himself! And how he dispatched the villains outside the Shaolin Temple with the Dragon-Subduing Palm! And, at the Yanman Pass, he even made the Khitan Emperor snap his arrow in a pledge never to invade the Song Empire!"

The young girl's knowledge stunned the three Elders.

Count Seven Hong had recounted these tales of past deeds on Rosy Cloud Island, as they built their escape raft, so Lotus would not be ignorant of the history of the people it was her duty to lead.

She continued without waiting for a response. "And Chief Count Seven Hong . . . His Eighteen Dragon-Subduing Palms are unparalleled in the martial world. I wonder, sirs, how many of the moves have you learned?"

A flicker of awkwardness passed between the beggars. None of them had yet been granted the chance to learn even one move from their chief—though, Vigor Li, a disciple of Eight Pouches, one level junior in rank, had been taught Dragon Whips Tail.

Lotus was still not giving them a chance to speak. "You said Elder Lu was an expert poisoner, but, pardon me, his skills could not be more commonplace. Last month, Viper Ouyang, Venom of the West, invited me to taste three cups of his poisoned wine. Now, those were remarkable. I do appreciate your kind gesture. Why don't you share it between the three of you?" She pushed the cups back at them.

The smooth-faced man's smile faltered for a moment, as if he was annoyed that she had refused the tampered wine, but he recovered swiftly. Summoning his most benign expression, he said, "Since the lady has found no cause to place her trust in us, of course, we would not be so impolite as to try a stronger means of persuasion. We only have ourselves to blame that our goodwill has been thus rejected. Might I ask the sir and lady to hold my gaze and see if you can detect anything out of the ordinary?"

Their curiosity piqued, Guo Jing and Lotus looked into the man's eyes, which could only be described as two slits sat astride his fleshy cheeks.

Two marbles, set in a pig's face, Lotus thought. Nothing unusual there!

Yet, at that moment, a glow seemed to emanate from them.

"Please, sir and lady, please, focus on my eyes. You mustn't let your sight or mind wander. Now, you feel your eyelids drooping, your head spinning, your body weakening. They are the symptoms of the poison. Yes, poison. Now, close your eyes and go to sleep."

His voice was melodious—intoxicating, even. They began to feel drowsy, their limbs heavy.

A kernel of doubt told Lotus to turn her head, to avoid his gaze, but somehow she found herself unwilling to break eye contact.

"What a grand lake, and what a refreshing breeze!" the man continued. "Please, my good sir and my dear lady, you shall find rest in the gentle caress of the wind. Let yourself drift off. Allow yourself a relaxing nap. Nothing shall trouble you in the quietude and comfort of sleep."

His singsong voice grew more soporific, drawing a series of yawns from the nodding couple. When he was finished, Lotus and Guo Jing were lying face down on the table, breathing softly, in deep slumber.

2

GENTLE WAVES, LAPPING IN THE DISTANCE. A LIGHT WIND, cooling the skin. Lotus forced her heavy eyes open. The full moon was peeking out from behind the hills in the east, its glow diffused by the evening mist.

How did it get so late? she asked herself, alarmed. We were having lunch at the tavern a moment ago!

She shifted her sleep-weary body and realized with horror that she had been tied up. She opened her mouth to call to Guo Jing, but all she could feel was the rough knot of a linen cord prickling her tongue. She knew they must have fallen for the tricks of the well-fed beggar, but what manner of sorcery had he used? Nonetheless, she was relieved to see, from the corner of her eye, that Guo Jing was working to free himself.

Guo Jing seemed confident that he could rip apart the thickest of ropes using his internal strength. However, as energy coursed to his wrists and ankles, the only response he could discern from his binds was a metallic rattling. They showed no sign of tearing.

Strips of ox leather braided with cables of steel would not give so easily.

He drew deeper into his store of *neigong* power for another attempt.

Something flat, tapering, and metallic tapped on his cheek. Then it did it again. A sword?

He tilted his head back and saw two beggar youths standing nearby. There were another two by Lotus. The blades in their hands glistened.

Lotus, meanwhile, had been trying to comprehend their situation. She could not hope to escape without a good grasp of the surroundings and the people they were up against. She twisted to her side and was stunned by the sight that greeted her eyes.

She gazed out at the landscape. They appeared to be on some kind of elevation, a hilltop. The water below, shimmering in the moonlight, was partially obscured by a thin fog.

Are we on the islet Jun Hill, in Dongting Lake? she wondered. How is it possible that we have no memory of the journey?

She wriggled to face the other way. Hundreds of beggars surrounded a high platform less than a hundred meters away. They were sitting on the ground in complete silence.

The moon, perfectly round, had now moved higher above the ridge in the distance.

Today is the fifteenth of the seventh month, she recalled. The Beggar Clan Assembly! If I can pass on *Shifu*'s message, surely they will obey their own chief. But how do I remove this gag?

She waited. No one among the beggars spoke. Her patience was wearing thin, but there was nothing she could do.

Before she knew it, an hour had passed. Her numbed body had started to ache. The moon was making gentle progress in the sky. By now, it illuminated half the platform.

She thought of Li Po's poem:

> *Brushing lightly the bright lake to reveal the jade mirror,*
> *Painting with cinnabar and azurite to trace Jun Hill.*

Except that Li Po wasn't gagged and bound when he stood here, composing poetry! Somehow, she saw the humor of their predicament.

Moonbeams now grazed the large characters inscribed above the

platform: *Terrace of the Yellow Emperor.* She was reminded of her father's stories about the great rivers and lakes of China. Legend had it that the Yellow Emperor cast a three-legged bronze ritual cauldron on the shore of Dongting Lake before ascending to the heavens on the back of a dragon.

BEFORE LONG, the platform was fully bathed in moonlight.

Dok, dok, dok.

Pause.

Dok, dok, dok.

Pause.

The beggars thumped their sticks into the ground in unison. Sometimes they beat fast, sometimes slow. Some notes sounded high, others low. After the eighty-first strike, silence reigned again.

Four beggars stood up. Lotus recognized them immediately: Surefoot Lu and the three Elders of the Washed, from the tavern.

Once they had taken up their positions at the four corners of the platform, the rest of the beggars rose to their feet, crossed their arms over their chests, bowed deeply and sat down again. The men moved as one, in spite of their great number.

The rotund, wealthy-looking beggar—who had forced Guo Jing and Lotus into their current plight—began: "Brethren, calamity has struck the Beggar Clan. Ruination, indeed! Chief Hong has departed this life, in Lin'an!"

Not a sound. Only a palpable sense of shock.

One beggar fell forward. Surging waves of sobs and thuds followed, as grieving men beat their chests and stamped their feet. The cacophony shook the trees and rippled out onto the lake.

Count Seven Hong was much loved and respected by his clansfolk.

Tears streamed down Guo Jing's face, but his cries were stifled by the gag. Now, he understood why they had not been able to find *Shifu* in the palace.

Meanwhile, Lotus maintained a clear head. *The fat beggar tricked us with sorcery. Why believe him now? He has to be lying.*

"Elder Peng, who was present at the chief's departure?" Surefoot Lu's voice cracked as he spoke.

"Elder Lu, do you think someone would be so audacious as to spread such lies about our chief?" the well-fed beggar shot back. "The man who witnessed the chief's passing is here with us. Please, Squire Yang, tell our brethren about this tragic event."

Yang Kang strode forward to stand before the platform, a green bamboo cane in his hand. His presence silenced the crowd, except for the odd whimper from time to time.

"It happened one month ago, when Chief Hong was in Lin'an. He became embroiled in a martial contest. Indeed, he was surrounded . . ." He paused to allow his words to sink in.

"Who?"

"Impossible!"

"How?"

"He must have been outnumbered!"

Exclamations rose from every direction.

A month ago? Shifu was with us! He's lying! So relieved was Guo Jing that he almost forgot to be angry with his deceitful sworn brother.

Lotus cursed Yang Kang. *He is no different from that old liar Qiu Qianren, spinning tall tales about people dear to me.*

Yang Kang raised both hands to signal that he had more to say, and waited for the crowd to settle.

"Chief Hong died at the hands of the Lord of Peach Blossom Island—also known as Apothecary Huang, Heretic of the East— aided by the Seven Taoists of the Quanzhen Sect."

Yang Kang hoped he sounded convincing. His survival depended on the beggars believing this baseless claim. He had been told by Viper Ouyang that Count Seven Hong's days were numbered. The Old Beggar could not hope to survive the injury caused by Ouyang's Explosive Toad kung fu.

But Guo Jing . . . He had stabbed the young man. Left him to bleed dry in the Song Imperial Palace. How come . . . ?

When Yang Kang had seen his sworn brother very much alive, sitting with Lotus in the tavern, that afternoon, he had panicked. He sent the Elders of the Washed to capture them and dispatch them for good. He knew that, once the deed was done, it would not be long before Lotus's father Apothecary Huang, Guo Jing's *shifu* the Six Freaks of the South, and the Quanzhen Sect found out he was involved in their deaths. He was not worried about the Freaks and their mediocre martial arts. Yet, Apothecary Huang and the Quanzhen monks would be tough to deal with. If he could unleash the full force of the Beggar Clan on them . . . That should keep him safe, surely?

The names Yang Kang uttered had turned the air thick with anger and a burning desire for vengeance.

The men gathered here were notable members of the Beggar Clan and they were all familiar with the martial reputation of the Seven Immortals of the Quanzhen Sect. Apothecary Huang's name was less well known, since he had not set foot beyond the shores of Peach Blossom Island for years. Still, some of the beggars knew he ranked alongside their chief as one of the Five Greats. If these Masters banded together, it was plausible that even the mighty Count Seven Hong would . . .

"Brethren, listen to me."

From a corner of the platform, a short-limbed, stocky man spoke. He appeared to be the oldest among the Four Elders, his eyebrows and beard more gray than black.

Silence followed his request. His authority was clear.

"There are two important matters at hand," Elder Jian of the East said, once he had everyone's attention. "First, we must follow Chief Hong's instructions in appointing the nineteenth Chief of the Clan. Second, we must come up with a plan to avenge our late chief."

"Above all else," Surefoot Lu cried above the roars of agreement, "we should first honor the chief's spirit!"

He grabbed a handful of earth and shaped it into a crude figurine to represent Count Seven Hong. He placed it reverently on the edge of the platform, facing the crowd. Then he prostrated and wailed at the top of his voice. Once more, the beggars bawled at the memory of their beloved chief.

Shifu is alive and well! Lotus protested silently. You'd have known, if you hadn't tied us up for no reason. Go on! Cry! Serves you right, you stinking beggars.

Elder Jian clapped thrice and the beggars began to collect themselves. When there was some semblance of order, he spoke again: "We brethren have gathered here today on Jun Hill, in Yuezhou, to hear Chief Hong appoint his successor. Now that tragedy has befallen our Clan, we must carry out his last wish. If he left no final command, then it will be up to the Four Elders to nominate the next chief. This rule has been passed down through the Beggar Clan, generation after generation. Is it not so, brothers?"

A collective howl of confirmation.

"Squire Yang, please tell us if Chief Hong spoke any last words," the portly Elder Peng said.

The appointment of the chief was a most significant event for the Beggar Clan. The group's future depended on their leader. Not so long ago, under the seventeenth leader, Chief Shi, the Clan's sway in the *jianghu* had begun to wane. Though skilled in the martial arts, as a figurehead he was weak and muddled, and he allowed the division between the Washed and the Unwashed to widen beyond repair.

When Count Seven Hong succeeded, he meted out severe punishment for clansmen who attempted to sow discord, thus containing the infighting and enabling the Beggar Clan to regain its former position of influence.

This history was well known to the beggars in attendance. They waited for the announcement with bated breath.

Yang Kang lifted the green bamboo cane over his head with

both hands. "Chief Hong suffered grievous injuries at the hands of villains. I chanced upon the Master and gave him refuge in the vault of my house. Once his enemies were gone, I sent for the best physicians. Alas, we were unable to save him." He paused, giving the beggars a moment to mourn. "Before Chief Hong passed away, he bestowed on me this bamboo cane, along with the formidable responsibility of becoming the nineteenth Chief of the Beggar Clan."

Gasps of surprise echoed. No one had expected a young man who looked as if he had only known wealth and rank to be chosen to rule the Beggar Clan.

Yang Kang had come across the two beggars who brought him here to Yuezhou soon after he found the bamboo cane in the tavern in Ox Village. Using his charms to tease out their story, it did not take him long to realize that their obsequiousness was all due to his possession of the cane. Needless to say, all the while, he was concealing the truth of how it had come into his possession.

The beggars, in the presence of the chief's cane, answered truthfully and in great detail, so that, by the time they arrived in Yuezhou, Yang Kang had acquired a working knowledge of the operation of the Beggar Clan, as well as a good idea of its reach and influence in the *jianghu*. The finer points of the complex system of rules that governed the secret society were still unclear to him—no Clan member would volunteer such information to an outsider, even if he were the bearer of the cane—but he judged that he knew enough to risk declaring himself the next chief. After all, Count Seven Hong had been severely wounded by Viper Ouyang. How could a half-dead man travel all the way to Yuezhou to dispute his claim? Judging by the respectful way he was being treated, he was confident that, once he had been named chief, his subjects would never dare challenge his authority. So, after turning the idea over and over in his head during the journey, he came up with the foolproof tale he had just presented.

He knew that, if he stumbled over a word or blushed even for a moment, the horde of paupers would beat him to a pulp. But, with

Count Seven Hong's death all but assured, the cane in his possession and Guo Jing and Lotus Huang captured, who could discredit his story?

Since ancient times, it has been known that those who wish to achieve greatness must first endure great danger. Considering the benefits the title would bestow upon him, he judged the immediate risks to be well worth running.

THE RIFT that had grown in the Beggar Clan between the Washed and the Unwashed had divided the whole membership. The Washed dwelled in houses, feasted on meat and wine, took wives and kept concubines. All this they declared by sewing patches on otherwise perfectly intact clothes. They were often men of the *jianghu* or admirers of the Clan's upright conduct. Some joined hoping to tap into the Clan's vast networks, others because they were friends with someone already in the Clan, but none of them had ever begged on the streets.

The Unwashed were beggars in the truest sense of the word. They never made purchases with silver, ate from the same table as people outside the Clan, or fought those without martial-arts training.

The two groups were uncompromising in their views and quarreled constantly. Count Seven Hong would wear clean but patched clothes for one year and dirty rags for another, in order to demonstrate his impartiality. However, gourmand that he was, it was impossible for him to live on scraps and leftovers, so he never fully adhered to the rules practiced by the Unwashed, even though their way of life was closer to the true roots of the Clan.

Of the Four Elders, Count Seven had always turned to Surefoot Lu first on any matter. He would have long since appointed Lu as his successor, had Lu not let his temper get the better of him on several important occasions.

Understandably, the Washed members had been dreading this

gathering at Yuezhou. They had long suspected that Surefoot Lu would be next in line to take over the Clan, as he was the most righteous and the best fighter, not to mention the beggar most trusted by the chief. They were also aware that, although three of the Four Elders were of the Washed, the majority of the clansmen in the lower ranks were genuine beggars who adhered to the way of life of the Unwashed.

The Elders of the Washed were always searching for ways to improve their situation and reform the Clan in their image, but they had held back from doing anything untoward, out of respect for Count Seven Hong. When Yang Kang arrived in Yuezhou with the green bamboo cane and news of the chief's death, they saw, through their grief, their long-hoped-for opportunity to crush the Unwashed. They noticed the young man's ornate clothing and fastidiousness about food, and were confident that they could persuade him to side with their cause. So, they welcomed Yang Kang with great courtesy, hoping to learn from him the chief's final thoughts on the matter of the succession before the Assembly.

Yet, Yang Kang would not reveal a thing. He could not risk these senior figures of the Beggar Clan changing their mind about him. How could he have known that the Elders of the Washed cared little for the identity of the new chief, as long as Surefoot Lu did not ascend to the role?

The three Elders of the Washed—Jian, Peng, and Liang—seemed pleased by Yang Kang's claim to be the next chief. They shared a conspiratorial look, with the slightest nod of their heads.

"Squire Yang holds in his hands the Clan's most revered object," Elder Jian added, once he had given the crowd a moment to absorb Yang Kang's words. "If anyone among our brethren has any doubts, please come up to examine it yourself."

Surefoot Lu shot Yang Kang a sideways glance. This boy is to be our chief? To lead the brothers of the Beggar Clan?

He could hardly contain his indignation, but, though he struggled to accept the idea, he reached out courteously for the bamboo cane.

Green and glossy like jade. The very cane that had been passed down from chief to chief, there was no doubt about it.

Chief Hong must have given it to him as a token of gratitude for his attempts to save his life, Surefoot Lu told himself. Who am I to disobey our leader's wishes? I will serve this young man with courage and a loyal heart, for the sake of Chief Hong and his legacy.

With that thought, Surefoot Lu lifted the cane over his head with both hands and offered it to Yang Kang in an appropriately ceremonial manner.

"We shall obey Chief Hong's last command and bow to Squire Yang as the nineteenth Chief of the Beggar Clan," Surefoot Lu pledged, to thunderous cheers.

Guo Jing and Lotus watched in desperation, but they could not break out of their restraints. Guo Jing recalled Apothecary Huang's warning that Yang Kang would try to become the Chief of the Beggar Clan. He feared the destruction his sworn brother would wreak upon the group. Meanwhile, Lotus was waiting for Yang Kang to make a decision about how he would deal with them. Although she knew he would not let them off easily, it would give her an opportunity to improvise a response.

"I have neither the wisdom of age nor the knowledge of experience." Yang Kang was all humility. "This is too great a responsibility."

"Squire Yang need not be so modest," Elder Peng said immediately. "It is Chief Hong's last command, and we, your brethren, shall serve you with one heart."

"Indeed!" Surefoot Lu cried, full of conviction. Then, he cleared his throat noisily, and spat.

Right in Yang Kang's face. Phlegm splattered on his right cheek.

Stunned by the sudden insult, Yang Kang barely had a chance to react before he felt three more gobs of sputum land on him.

This is it! he thought, frightened and disgusted. They must have seen through my guise.

Tensing, he prepared himself to flee. He knew he had little chance of outrunning the beggars, and yet, he was not going to remain and submit himself to fate.

The Four Elders crossed their arms over their chests and prostrated themselves on the ground.

Mystified, Yang Kang, for once, was lost for words.

The beggars had, by now, ordered themselves by rank, and they approached their new chief in line, coughing and hawking.

Slime flew with each show of obeisance.

Is this their way of showing submission? Yang Kang was bewildered. How could he have known that this was customary at the appointment of a new chief? The act of expectoration was a reminder for the leader of the beggars of the treatment his followers received by society at large. As their figurehead, he must first submit to the insult suffered by all those under his command.

This spectacle brought Lotus back to the day when Count Seven Hong had named her Chief of the Beggar Clan, on Rosy Cloud Island. She remembered the speck of spittle on the hem of her skirt and his apology: "When it becomes official to the Clan, there will be a disgusting ritual, I am afraid. It will be hard on you." She had assumed he had been unable to aim his spit accurately, due to his injuries, but now she realized he had done it on purpose and his cryptic warning referred to this very rite Yang Kang was enduring. She understood why he had been vague; she might well have refused, out of pure disgust.

At long last, the beggars present had finished paying homage. "Chief, ascend the Terrace!" they cried as one.

Yang Kang eyed the platform. It was not particularly high. He knew an elegant move that would show off his kung fu. He flexed his toes, and up he flew.

Yet, to the Elders, who had honed their craft over decades, the fanciful leap contained little substance. All it had demonstrated was that the new chief was a novice of the martial arts, albeit somewhat gifted and with some training at the hands of a master. He was still young, after all.

Standing tall on the Terrace of the Yellow Emperor, Yang Kang projected his voice: "Although we have yet to apprehend Chief Hong's murderers, I have captured two of the accomplices."

"Where?"

"Cut them into pieces!"

"Make them suffer!"

The crowd erupted again.

"Bring them here!" Yang Kang ordered.

Guo Jing was also eager to find out whom Yang Kang had caught—that is, until he saw a portly beggar waddling toward him. That was when he understood.

Elder Peng grabbed Guo Jing with one hand and Lotus with the other, before hurling them down in front of the Terrace.

"Chief, allow me to speak," Surefoot Lu said. "They are disciples of Chief Hong. Why would they harm him?"

"They plotted a crime most vile." Yang Kang spat the words out. "They sought to destroy their own teacher!"

"Chief Yang saw it with his own eyes," Elder Peng added. "Are you saying he's mistaken?"

"Allow me to speak, Chief!" A man rushed to the front of the crowd. "I know them. They are heroes. Righteous and moral. By my life, they'd never harm Chief Hong."

The speaker was, of course, Vigor Li, whom Guo Jing had saved from Gallant Ouyang, back in Baoying. Li knew how fond the chief had been of the young couple.

"They are good people—good friends of the Clan!"

A younger man spoke up—Prosper Yu. He had been in Baoying with Vigor Li, where they had tried to thwart Gallant Ouyang's prurient plan to abduct Emerald Cheng.

"Speak through your leader." Elder Liang glared at the Unwashed upstarts. "You know full well you are not permitted to interrupt."

Realizing what an affront it would be to directly challenge their senior, Vigor Li and Prosper Yu stepped back, fuming in silence.

Li and Yu's protest chimed with the doubt gnawing at Surefoot Lu. They were men under his command and he trusted them.

"This lowly member of the Clan would never be so bold as to cast doubt on the chief." The Unwashed leader chose his words carefully. "Nevertheless, it is of the utmost importance that we avenge the wrong suffered by Chief Hong, and I beg the chief to extract every piece of information possible first."

"Of course! I will wring the truth out of them." Yang Kang already had a plan, and turned to his captives. "You have no need to speak. Nod if what I say is true, shake your head if it's untrue. If you try to fool us . . ." He tailed off and flicked his wrist.

Elder Peng unsheathed his sword and Elder Liang his saber. Guo Jing and Lotus each felt the sharp, cold point of a blade pressed to their back.

This was a tactic Lotus knew well. Last time she had witnessed its use was during that sweet and romantic encounter at the inn, in Ox Village. She and Guo Jing had been concealed in the hidden chamber, watching Laurel Lu try to ask Emerald Cheng to marry him. But the young lady was too shy to speak, so he asked her to answer with a nod or a shake of her head.

Lotus also remembered using the method on Gallant Ouyang, on Peach Blossom Island, when he came with his uncle, Viper Ouyang, to seek her hand. She bridled at the idea that she was about to suffer the same indignity at the hands of this treacherous snake.

Though fury had drained the blood from her face, she still had her wits about her. She needed to find a way to raise Surefoot Lu's suspicions with her responses, so that he would press for verbal answers. If she could speak, she was certain that she could convince everyone present that Yang Kang was deceiving them.

But Yang Kang also knew who he was up against. Guo Jing's simplemindedness would play into his hands, so he had him brought forward first.

"She is Apothecary Huang's daughter, is she not?" he asked loudly.

Guo Jing ignored the question and closed his eyes.

Elder Liang pressed his saber a little harder against Guo Jing's back and growled, "Yes or no?"

Guo Jing had been planning to deny Yang Kang the satisfaction of a reply, but then it occurred to him that the truth would come out, whether he answered or not. He nodded.

The daughter of Chief Hong's killer!

"Kill her!" the crowd exploded.

"Brethren, please," Yang Kang said, in an attempt to quell the masses before turning once more to Guo Jing. "Apothecary Huang gave you her hand, did he not?"

Nod.

Yang Kang pulled out the dagger tucked into Guo Jing's belt. "Qiu Chuji, one of the Seven Taoists of the Quanzhen Sect, gave you this, did he not?"

Nod.

"Your name is carved on the hilt, is it not?"

Nod.

"Ma Yu, another Quanzhen monk, taught you kung fu, and his martial brother, Wang Chuyi, saved your life. Is it not so?"

Nod.

"When Count Seven Hong was grievously injured, you were by his side, were you not?"

Nod.

Lotus cursed silently. Silly boy. Shake your head! If you keep denying, he'll have to let you speak!

Yang Kang grew sterner and fiercer with each accusation. To the beggars, each nod of Guo Jing's head was a confirmation of his crimes. They had not realized that the questions posed had little to do with any wrongdoing, and that it was all a ploy. Now, even Surefoot Lu believed that Guo Jing and Lotus Huang were guilty. He went up to Guo Jing and kicked him.

"Brethren, since they have confessed, we shall not make them suffer unduly. Elder Peng, Elder Liang, make it quick."

Guo Jing looked at Lotus and found her smiling at him.

She was content. The prospect of dying by his side comforted her. It was she, Lotus Huang, who would share him in the next life, now, and forever after. Not Khojin, the Mongolian princess to whom he was betrothed.

Bewildered by Lotus's reaction, Guo Jing tilted his head back and gazed up at the sky, looking in a northerly direction. He thought of his mother, far, far away, in Mongolia. His eyes were drawn to the glow of the seven stars of the Northern Dipper, and the sight reminded him of the fight that had taken place not long ago between the Seven Immortals of the Quanzhen Sect, Cyclone Mei, and her *shifu*, Apothecary Huang.

He had never possessed a memory for details, but, in this moment, he felt a sudden clarity. He could see before his eyes, blow by blow, how the Seven Immortals had used the Heavenly Northern Dipper formation to attack and defend, and how, by shifting positions, they had lured their opponents into the snare, before closing in on them.

So immersed was he in what he could recall from the fight, he had not noticed Peng and Liang standing over him, weapons raised.

"Not so hasty!" Surefoot Lu darted into his clansmen's way. Then, as he worked to remove Guo Jing's gag, he asked, "What exactly happened to Chief Hong? Tell me everything."

"There's no need to ask him," Yang Kang cut in. "I've told you all you need to know already."

"Chief, we need to know everything. We must hear it from everyone present, even those who have confessed."

Beads of sweat appeared on Yang Kang's hairline. He knew he could not block Surefoot Lu's interrogation, lest it reveal he had something to hide. Yet, if he let Guo Jing speak, his position would be fatally compromised.

Yang Kang's mind raced as he tried to think of a solution. To his surprise, Surefoot Lu was forced to ask the same question, over and over. Guo Jing did not seem to be hearing a word. He did not even notice his gag had been removed. He simply stared at the night sky, lost in thought.

Lotus watched Yang Kang gesture at the beggar Elders, and the blades were raised once more. If only she could do something to snap Guo Jing out of his daze.

3

SWOOOOOOSH! A PURPLE FLAME SKIMMED OVER THE LAKE. Two flashes of blue flew up into the night sky, several *li* hence.

Peng and Liang shared a look of surprise and recognition.

"Chief, an important guest has arrived," Elder Jian announced.

"Who?" Yang Kang snapped.

Jian lowered his voice: "The leader of the Iron Palm Gang." He would not wish to make the new chief seem ignorant in front of his people.

"Huh?"

"A force to be reckoned with, in this region," Jian explained patiently. "We must receive our distinguished visitors with utmost courtesy, since the leader has come in person. I fear it would not befit us to be seen with traitors. I suggest we deal with the prisoners later."

"As you say, Elder Jian. Prepare to receive our honored guest."

Not long after—*boom, boom, boom!*—three successive flares painted the sky over Jun Hill a fiery red.

Boats could now be seen on Dongting Lake, approaching the small islet. The beggars, each clutching a torch, waited in reverential anticipation.

Even though the visitors from the Iron Palm Gang were familiar with lightness kung fu, it took them a short while to reach the Terrace of the Yellow Emperor at the summit of Jun Hill.

Guo Jing and Lotus Huang were placed among the followers of the Beggar Clan, watched over by Elder Peng's men.

Lotus had been observing Guo Jing. The young man was mumbling into the starry night, his eyes glassy and unfocused. He's gone mad, she thought, before turning her mind to the newcomers. She prayed they might offer a diversion to help them escape.

Surrounded by a blaze of torches, several dozen black-clad fighters led an elderly man to the Terrace. Lotus took one look—arrow-root shirt, palm-leaf fan—and her heart sank.

Qiu Qianren!

Elder Jian strode forward and greeted Qiu Qianren with a show of ceremony. After a short, polite exchange according to the customs of the *jianghu*, he turned to Yang Kang. "This is Master Qiu of the Iron Palm Gang. His kung fu is feared throughout the *wulin*." Then he addressed Qiu Qianren: "Chief Hong has, sadly, passed into the next world. This is Chief Yang, whom we have appointed today as our next leader. He is a true hero of the younger generation. I trust a great new friendship shall blossom between our clans."

"The pleasure is all mine." Yang Kang deployed his most charming smile. He remembered this old fraud from Roaming Cloud Manor, but he made sure his face betrayed no hint of recognition.

Everyone regards you as a master, but, with this hand, I will show the world your charlatan ways, Yang Kang thought, as he reached out to greet him. He was eager to take this chance to show the beggars that a man of true prowess was now in command.

Qiu Qianren took his outstretched palm. At that moment, Yang Kang charged it with all his internal energy.

It was as if Yang Kang had wrapped his fingers over a piece of red-hot coal. He pulled, but he could not free himself. The pain traveled up to his heart. He doubled over. Two streams of tears flowed down his pale cheeks.

The four beggar Elders leaped to Yang Kang's aid.

Elder Jian, the most senior in age and rank, struck the end of his steel staff on the stone-paved ground in warning. Sparks flew.

"Master Qiu, you are our guest," he said, struggling to contain the rage in his voice. "And Chief Yang is young. What compelled you to test his martial training thus?"

"I took his hand in courtesy," Qiu Qianren replied, his voice frosty, still maintaining his grip. Then he paused and let his strength flow back down and through his hand. Yang Kang yelped in agony. "It is your honorable chief who wished to test me." He stopped speaking again and Yang Kang squealed once more. "Chief Yang was intent on crushing my old bones." Yet again, Yang Kang's shrieks punctuated his words.

Having said his piece, Qiu Qianren flung Yang Kang's hand away. Now barely conscious, the young man collapsed. Surefoot Lu caught him just before he hit the ground.

"Master Qiu, what—?"

Qiu Qianren swung his palm at Elder Jian's face.

With both hands, Jian thrust his staff forward, intending to parry the move, and Qiu grabbed at the head of the weapon. Even before Qiu's fingers had fully closed around the metal pole, an uncanny force was pushing it down and wresting it out of Jian's grasp.

Tightening his grip, the beggar, whose martial skills were not inconsequential, managed to hold on.

Just then, the air parted on Jian's left side.

Bong!

Qiu hewed at the midpoint of the staff with his free hand. The force of the blow was sufficient to tear away the skin between Jian's thumb and forefinger.

Jian had no energy left in his blood-soaked hands to cling to the staff.

Qiu snatched the weapon and swung it, using its tip to whisk away Elder Peng's saber and Elder Liang's sword. Then he drew the staff to his side. The simple movement sent his elbow squarely into Surefoot Lu's face.

In mere moments, Qiu Qianren had beaten back all Four Elders of the Beggar Clan. Shocked, the rest of the beggars clutched their weapons. They were ready to mobilize against the Iron Palm Gang. All it would take was one word from their chief.

Holding one end of the staff with both hands, Qiu Qianren flung it at a distant boulder. The steel pole pierced the rock, and the drawn-out clang of metal against stone filled the stunned silence.

Lotus Huang could not believe her eyes. Was the old cheat really so accomplished, after all? It was him all right, his features illuminated by the blazing torches and the full moon above.

He must be in league with Yang Kang and Elder Jian, she thought, searching for an explanation. The staff—there is something queer about it. Another trick.

She turned to Guo Jing. He was still staring at the sky.

Could the night's events have driven him mad? Why else would he be studying the heavens when there was a fight playing out, right before their eyes? Perhaps, in struggling to reconcile his duty to marry Khojin and his love for Lotus, he had taken leave of his senses? Forced to keep a close watch on her beloved, Lotus was unable to closely follow Qiu Qianren's antics.

But, after standing in silence for some time, Qiu Qianren spoke, drawing her eyes toward him. "Like the water in the river and the water in the well, the Iron Palm Gang and the Beggar Clan have never crossed paths. I came here in good faith. I do not understand why I was greeted with such a provocation."

Elder Jian was relieved to find restraint in Qiu Qianren's words, in spite of the iciness of his tone.

"A misunderstanding, Master Qiu," he replied, a tremble of fear discernible in his voice. "Your mighty reputation spreads across the four seas, and we, the brothers of the Beggar Clan, have always admired you and held you in the highest esteem. It is our greatest honor that you deigned to grace our Clan Assembly with your presence. Each and every one of us here wishes you only the warmest welcome. Not one of us would dream of treating you with disrespect."

Qiu Qianren held his head high and said nothing. He let the uncomfortable moment simmer before responding. "What a shame that

Chief Hong has passed through to the immortal realm. The martial world will be poorer for his loss. And what a pity that the famous Beggar Clan has appointed this young man as its new chief."

The Elders looked at each other, unsure how to reply. Yang Kang had, by now, regained consciousness. Of course, he was maddened by the insult, yet what could he do but swallow the humiliation? His hand still felt as if it were being held over a raging fire, and his fingers were swollen like thick batons of Chinese yam.

Ignoring his awkward hosts, Qiu Qianren continued, "In truth, there is a matter that brought me here today. And I also come bearing gifts."

"We look forward to learning how we can be of assistance," Elder Jian said with exaggerated humility.

"The other day, I sent a few young men to run some errands for me. Somehow, they managed to vex two of our friends of the Beggar Clan and were badly beaten. I cannot deny that their martial training was rudimentary, but if this encounter were to become known in the *jianghu* . . . well, the Iron Palm Gang can ill afford to lose face in such a manner. So, I ask you to humor this aged fellow, for I have come all this way to learn from these two kinsmen of the Beggar Clan."

"Who were the culprits?" Yang Kang cried. "Step forward and beg Master Qiu's forgiveness. Now!" It did not cross his mind that he had a duty to safeguard the well-being of those he claimed to lead. The last thing he wished to do was upset Qiu Qianren even further.

The vagrants bristled at their new chief's cowardly response. Count Seven Hong would have never subjected them to such an injustice.

Once more, Vigor Li and Prosper Yu emerged from the crowd.

"Chief, allow me to speak," Vigor Li said. "The fourth rule of our Clan states that each and every one of the clansmen should always act according to the moral code of *xia*. They must be righteous, deliver those in suffering, and aid those in hardship.

"Several days ago, Prosper Yu and I came upon our friends from the Iron Palm Gang as they were attempting to abduct a household of honest women. We could not stand by and let this act of depravity take place, so we intervened."

"It doesn't matter what happened. Ask Master Qiu for his forgiveness," Yang Kang demanded.

Vigor Li and Prosper Yu glanced at each other. If they refused, they would be defying their chief, but how could they tarnish their good names by seeking pardon from a wrongdoer?

"Brethren, if Chief Hong were still alive, he would never allow us to suffer such an indignity. I would rather die than be so abused!" Vigor Li appealed to his fellow members before pulling a blade from the rags he was wearing and plunging it into his heart. Prosper Yu knelt over him, retrieved the knife, and turned it on himself, his body falling lifeless over that of his comrade.

The beggars were seething with rage. Much as they would have liked to unleash carnage on the Iron Palm Gang, they could not break the hallowed rule of unconditional obedience to the chief.

A faint smile crept across Qiu Qianren's face. "Since the first matter has resolved itself quickly, allow me to present this to the Beggar Clan."

Qiu's men opened the chests they had brought with them, removing several dozen trays of gold, silver and glittering jewels. One by one, they were set down before Yang Kang.

The Beggar Clan had never seen such a dazzling display of wealth.

"The Iron Palm Gang keeps its bellies full, but we could never have put together such a lavish gift ourselves," Qiu Qianren smirked. "I have been entrusted by the Sixth Prince of the Great Jin Empire to bring this to you."

"Where is the Prince? I should like to meet him." Yang Kang was overjoyed at this mention of his father.

"The Prince's herald came to my abode several months ago with this offering and a message for the Beggar Clan."

So, Papa arranged this before he came south? Why does he want to court a bunch of beggars? He's never before mentioned any plans to bring them onto our side. Yang Kang nodded at Qiu Qianren to indicate that he was interested in hearing more.

"The Prince of Zhao has long admired the heroes of the Beggar Clan and bade me to personally proffer this token of friendship on his behalf."

"We are overwhelmed by the honor," Yang Kang gushed.

"Chief Yang, I must say, you are far more understanding than your old Chief Hong." A hollow laugh.

"Master Qiu, I wonder if the Prince shared any specific instructions?" Yang Kang was desperate to find out more.

"Who would be so presumptuous as to issue instructions to the great Beggar Clan? The Prince once mentioned in passing that the north, with its impoverished people and barren lands, is not quite the ground for realizing grand visions—"

"The Prince would like us to move to the south?"

"Chief Yang is most perceptive, and I must admit that I have been lacking in manners. The Prince did tell me that he could not fathom why the Beggar Clan are so partial to the bitter cold of the north, when the regions of Jiangnan and Huguang in the south enjoy such a pleasant climate and such great wealth."

"We are most grateful to receive guidance from the Prince and Master Qiu. It would be improper of us not to heed it."

Qiu Qianren had not expected his task to be so easy.

This new young chief did not show even the merest hint of reluctance, he observed with surprise. Perhaps because of the fright I have given him. Still, the beggars have been based in the north for generations, are they really so easily persuaded to uproot themselves? What if they change their minds, after I've left? I should make him promise.

Yang Kang seemed to have guessed Qiu's mind. "Today, I, Chief Yang, hereby give my word that the Beggar Clan will retreat south of the Yangtze River, and will never traverse those waters for the north again."

"Chief, allow me to speak," Surefoot Lu interjected. "We are beggars and we live on alms. Our numbers can be counted in the hundreds and thousands, our clansfolk are scattered across Song Empire lands, free to roam according to our will. Why should we be confined? I entreat the chief to think the matter thrice over."

"If we refuse this gesture of goodwill from Master Qiu, it will make us appear discourteous." By now, Yang Kang had grasped his father Wanyan Honglie's motives. The Beggar Clan had been a persistent nuisance to the Jin Empire north of the Yangtze River. Every time the Jurchen army marched south to attack the Song, the beggars would disrupt the rear guard, kill commanders, and burn food supplies. If the pests moved south, it would smooth the way for the Jin to conquer the Song.

"I shan't take a single thing for myself," he said, gesturing to the riches on display. "Elders, please divide this handsome bounty among our brethren—"

Surefoot Lu could not believe his ears. "Chief Hong is known by all throughout and beyond the Empire as the Beggar of the North. Furthermore, we, the members of the Beggar Clan, are righteous and loyal to our country and its ruler, the Song Emperor. We have been at odds with the Jurchen for generations. We cannot accept anything from those people. Never will we be forced south of the Yangtze. Never, never, never!"

Taking note of Yang Kang's darkening countenance, Elder Peng said, "Is it *your* responsibility, or the chief's, to make decisions for the Clan?"

"I shall meet my death before I go against what I know to be right," Surefoot Lu declared with pride.

"Elder Jian, Elder Peng, Elder Liang, what say you?" Yang Kang asked.

Jian and Liang both thought it unwise to move south, but Peng harbored no such hesitation. "As a subordinate, I always follow the chief's command."

His words unleashed uproar among the gathered beggars.

Yang Kang was at a loss as to how to calm the angry mob. The Elders of the Washed shouted for order, but few heeded them, as the most riotous among the crowd were the Unwashed.

"Elder Lu, do you mean to defy your chief?" Peng demanded.

"I would rather be cut into a thousand pieces than deceive my elders or defy my chief. But neither would I, Surefoot Lu, ever turn my back on the principles that have been passed down by the Clan's forefathers. The Jurchen are invaders of our realm. The Jurchen are killers of our kin. Their Jin state is the enemy of the land of my birth, the Song Empire. Have you forgotten our allegiance—our duty—as Chief Hong often reminded us?"

Jian and Liang lowered their heads, mortified.

Qiu Qianren scoffed. "Chief Yang, this Elder Lu of yours must learn to hold his tongue." He made a grab for the beggar's shoulders.

Noting how Qiu Qianren was subtly shifting his weight as he spoke, Surefoot Lu ducked down, shot between Qiu's parted legs and whipped around with three kicks at Qiu's backside, before straightening up.

True to his name, Surefoot Lu was swift and certain on his feet.

Qiu Qianren had never come upon a kung fu so undignified. Having recovered his composure, he suddenly sensed the air parting behind him. He spun around and thrust a palm.

The counterattack forced Surefoot Lu to wrench his foot away. The beggar's kicks may well have landed, but the force of Qiu's palm would have shattered his leg.

Flipping into an awkward somersault, Lu landed next to Qiu and spat. Qiu cocked his head, avoiding the phlegm. Once again, he was puzzled by the unorthodox nature of the attack.

"Enough!" Yang Kang barked.

Surefoot Lu took two steps back, but Qiu Qianren was not going to let the affront pass. He lunged, hoping to close his hands around Lu's throat like a pair of iron clamps.

The beggar sprung into a backflip, but Qiu caught him by the wrists.

Surefoot Lu knew he had lost, but he was not one to give in without a fight.

He heaved. Pushed Qiu back.

Nothing. Not an inch.

He hunkered down and rammed into Qiu Qianren's stomach.

Surefoot Lu had trained in Bronze Hammer kung fu since he was a child, and could easily make a dent in a wall with one butt of his head. In a wager with a Clan brother, he had once locked horns with a bull. He emerged unscathed; the bull, unconscious.

The slam would not cause injury, but Lu thought it would at least be enough to rock the other man back on his heels, allowing him to free himself. But, as his forehead connected with Qiu's abdomen, he felt no resistance. It was as if he had run headlong into a bale of cotton. He pulled back, alarmed. To his horror, he seemed to have drawn Qiu Qianren closer to him.

Surefoot Lu writhed and squirmed. He could not extract himself.

Qiu's stomach, somehow, was sucking him in, all while producing a fierce heat. Lu felt as if he had been plunged into a fiery furnace. His scalp sizzled, his hands were scorched.

The pain was excruciating.

"Yield!" Qiu Qianren bellowed.

"Never!"

Qiu clenched his left fist around Surefoot Lu's right hand. With a series of sickening cracks and pops, the bones in all five of the beggar's fingers were crushed.

"Yield!"

"Nooo!"

More crunching. This time, from Surefoot Lu's left hand.

Despite the pain, curses flowed from the beggar's delirious lips.

"Let's see how defiant you will be when I crush your skull!" Qiu Qianren cried.

4

JUST AS QIU QIANREN ISSUED HIS THREAT, A TALL, BROAD-shouldered young man leaped out from among the crowd and landed behind Surefoot Lu. He lifted his arm and slapped his palm down onto the beggar's backside. Loud and firm.

Smack!

A potent strength traveled through the beggar's skull, into Qiu Qianren's belly.

Smack!

Though the blow was once again on the beggar's buttocks, Qiu felt its power in his gut.

Smack!

The force sucking Lu's head into Qiu's stomach had been nullified.

Surefoot Lu took the chance to pull himself upright, but his hands were still trapped.

"You're no match for Master Qiu. Let me!" the young man cried, swiping his foot at the beggar's shoulder.

Qiu Qianren's grip was shaken. Though the kick was not aimed at him, he felt the blow at the point where his thumb joined his forefinger.

Making use of the momentum, Surefoot Lu lunged to the side. But the awkward position he had been stuck in had left him dizzy. He wobbled and crashed to the floor.

Qiu Qianren eyed his opponent. A boy, barely out of his teens, and he had already mastered the intricate skill of striking through a conduit without causing them harm. He had underestimated the Beggar Clan. He would remain on the defensive, for now.

The beggars, meanwhile, surged forward, shouting and cursing.

This insolent boy had not only killed their beloved Chief Hong, but now he had also kicked Elder Lu to the ground.

The boy was, of course, Guo Jing.

Since Qiu Qianren's arrival, Guo Jing had been focused on the seven stars of the Northern Dipper, recalling the martial formation Ma Yu and his Quanzhen brothers had used against Apothecary Huang in Ox Village.

He began to think about the formation in connection with the content of the Nine Yin Manual. Somehow, this cryptic text, of which he knew every word but understood no more than a few lines, began to make sense. Many points that he had struggled to grasp were now within his reach.

Even though he had always known that the Manual was written by a man with exceptional knowledge of the Taoist canon, and that the Quanzhen Sect's kung fu was rooted in the very same philosophy, he had never been able to connect the two fully. Until now, that is, guided as he was by the constellation above.

While the Beggar Clan Elders were wrangling with Qiu Qianren, Guo Jing had been thinking about the skill referred to in the second volume of the Manual as Shrinking Muscles, Shortening Bone. It was a commonplace technique, used by thieves and burglars to squeeze through small openings and narrow gaps, but, when advanced martial knowledge was applied, a master could use it to contract every muscle and pull the body into a small ball, much like a hedgehog or porcupine seeking protection.

When Guo Jing was on Rosy Cloud Island, Count Seven had instructed him in a section from the Manual called Transforming Muscles, Forging Bones. As his mind delved into these two chapters, the steel-reinforced leather ropes began to slacken around his wrists and ankles, before slipping off entirely. Not that he realized this was happening. His body was ten times as agile as his intellect.

The instant Elder Peng saw Guo Jing had broken free, he reached out to grab the young man, but Guo Jing eluded him with ease. It was then that Peng noticed the ropes still coiled and knotted on the ground.

How had the boy managed to wriggle out of his restraints like a weatherfish slipping between a fisherman's fingers? Peng was taken aback.

By the time he looked up, Guo Jing had already freed Surefoot Lu from Qiu Qianren's strange grip. Knowing he did not possess the skill to secure the prisoner alone, Peng cried out, "Catch him!"

Dozens of beggars responded to the call. Guo Jing's heart sank at the sight of them swinging their fists and waving their weapons, even though he knew it was because they had fallen for Yang Kang's lies.

I'll give you beggars a good beating! That will please Lotus! he said to himself.

Keen to try out his newfound knowledge of the Heavenly Northern Dipper formation, Guo Jing flexed his arms and planted his feet in the Heavenly Power position.

Standing tall and firm, he held his left arm horizontally across his chest.

Half a dozen men were upon him. Three seized him by his outstretched arm, but Guo Jing held his stance, steady as a mountain. The others joined them.

He drew his arm to his side and pivoted.

Full circle.

"*Aiyaaaaah!*"

"Ouch!"

"Bastard!"

A smack on the back. A slap on the belly. A kick up the backside. The beggars collapsed in a heap, on top of each other.

Guo Jing was about to go for Yang Kang when he saw two beggars pouncing on Lotus. Too far away to tackle them, he ripped off his canvas shoes and flung them at her attackers.

If he had not been told so many times the story of his second *shifu* Zhu Cong tossing his shoes at Qiu Chuji at the battle of Fahua

Temple, Guo Jing would never have imagined that such ordinary items could be used as a weapon.

The two beggars had lifted their blades, ready to deal the death-blow. They feared Lotus might also find a way to break her restraints, and, if so, they would lose the chance to avenge their late chief.

Just then, the air behind them gave way. Something was hurtling at them with a mighty force.

One of the attackers whipped round. A shoe caught him square in the chest. The other shoe slammed into his accomplice's back before the man even had time to turn his head.

The two beggars toppled, one on his back, the other facedown.

Closest to the action, Elder Peng was startled by Guo Jing's prowess. Only a master could throw something so soft and light with such force. He edged back.

With a flick of his hand, Guo Jing sent three more men sprawling. He then sprinted over, crouched down and started to untie Lotus's binds. Before he managed to untangle the first knot, however, scores of Clan members had already surrounded them several times over.

With the Heavenly Northern Dipper formation still in mind, Guo Jing sat down, shifting Lotus onto his lap. Using his right hand, he fought off the attacks, while his left continued to work on the knots. It was a perfect display of Zhou Botong's Competing Hands technique.

Before long, Guo Jing and Lotus were encircled by nearly a hundred men. Those at the back could not even see their captives, let alone deal any blows.

"Lotus, are you hurt?" Guo Jing asked, as he finally freed her and removed the gag. Above them, weapons clashed and men howled.

"Only numb," she answered. "And achy." She made no attempt to pull herself up.

"Lie here a little longer. I'll make them pay."

"Make sure you don't hurt my clansmen," Lotus said, with a chuckle.

"Of course!" Guo Jing gathered his internal strength to his right hand.

Pang, pang, pang!

Three men flew up and over the crowd.

Guo Jing continued to stroke Lotus's hair.

Another four became airborne.

Panic. Jostling.

"Brethren, let the Disciples of Eight Pouches deal with the traitors," Elder Jian cried from the rear.

Most of the crowd fell away, leaving just three men, who were soon joined by another five.

These eight men each carried eight cloth bags on their back. One rank below the Four Elders, they were responsible for a whole region's clansmen. There were supposed to be nine of them altogether, but Vigor Li had taken his life just before Guo Jing freed himself.

They may have been few in number, but Guo Jing could tell that these men were more formidable fighters than the other beggars.

Sensing that he was about to stand up, Lotus said softly, "Stay sitting. You can do it."

But what if they attack all at once? Guo Jing appraised his opponents and picked up one of the leather cords that had been used to tie Lotus.

He recognized only two of his attackers—the portly beggar and his stick-thin companion, who had traveled with Yang Kang from Ox Village. He would take them out first.

Guo Jing swung the steel-reinforced cord just centimeters above the ground, in a move known as the Shin Breaker, part of the Golden Dragon Whip repertoire. This was his third *shifu* Ryder Han's most accomplished kung fu. Yet, Han could not have accompanied it with the level of inner strength his student now mobilized.

The two men jumped.

In the blink of an eye, the dancing rope created a wall, shielding Guo Jing's front, back and left. And yet his right side was left undefended. His opponents saw their chance.

"No!"

Elder Jian's cry was accompanied by two loud slaps. The portly beggar and his rake-thin fellow each took a hit to the shoulder.

Their bodies flew up and sailed through the air.

The skinny beggar plowed into one of the Iron Palm Gang standing closest to the fight. His fleshy friend, flung with more heft, flew farther before colliding with another of Qiu Qianren's men.

Qiu had shown no interest in the fight until he heard the thud of body against body. That doesn't sound right, he thought, and glanced over to check on his followers.

He was incensed to see the beggars had vaulted to their feet without a scratch, while his men lay in a heap, bones broken and tendons snapped.

Just as Qiu Qianren was about to turn and confront Guo Jing, he felt a gust of air behind him. Two more beggars were flying his way. He understood that the airborne men were simply the conduit; the lethal force of the boy's inner strength was reserved for whomever they struck.

Drawing his arm back, he batted one man away, changing his course so he landed on a clear patch of dirt. With the air roaring around him, he then thrust both palms simultaneously into the next flying man's back. This powerful move was part of the Iron Palm kung fu that had secured Qiu Qianren's reputation.

Had Qiu's *neigong* been stronger, it would have canceled out Guo Jing's, probably scrambling the poor beggar's insides at the same time. As it was, Qiu struggled to keep his footing.

The man sailed through the air toward Guo Jing, before gliding to the ground and landing on both feet. He stood in a daze for a moment, then he turned and made for Guo Jing again. He was obviously not injured.

Lotus watched and realized with a shock: Old Qiu's kung fu is mediocre at best. How could the old fraud withstand Guo Jing's strong *neigong*?

A dozen moves were quickly exchanged. Two more beggars were

sent staggering from the fight before the last three fell back, accepting that they stood no chance.

Guo Jing flicked his wrist and the rope curled over two of the retreating beggars. He tugged, dragging them toward him. One final swerve of the makeshift whip and the last of the Eight-Pouch Disciples were tied and bound.

5

THRILLED, LOTUS FLASHED A GOADING SMILE AT ELDER PENG.

He must have used the dark arts of mind entrapment on us, she said to herself, recalling Count Seven Hong's description. First, you are put in a trance, and then you are forced to do whatever the spellcaster tells you to do.

"Guo Jing," she said, "does the Nine Yin Manual mention some kind of mind entrapment?"

"No . . ."

Guo Jing's answer disappointed her.

"Watch out for the smiling one," she said as he helped her to her feet. "Don't look him in the eye."

Instead, Guo Jing looked across at Yang Kang. Pinning him down with a hard glare, Guo Jing marched up to him.

Cowering among the beggars, Yang Kang had prayed to the heavens that their sheer number would be enough to subdue Guo Jing. But this had not proved to be the case, and he knew he was in grave danger.

"Elders, there are more heroes here tonight than we could possibly count. Surely we're not going to let this ingrate get away?" Yang Kang's feet were moving as briskly as his lips as he scampered over to stand behind Elder Jian.

"Don't worry, Chief. We will grind him down," Jian said to Yang Kang before turning to his fellows. "The wall formation!"

One of the Disciples of Eight Pouches stepped forward, followed by a dozen or so beggars of lower rank. They arranged themselves in a line and linked arms. Another sixteen men formed a second row behind. Then, with a loud cry, they squared their shoulders and ran at Lotus and Guo Jing.

"*Aiyooo!*" Lotus yelped as she swerved left, while Guo Jing darted right.

Two more beggar phalanxes were now bearing down on them, one from either side.

Even with his experience of leading armies on the battlefield, Guo Jing had never known such a formation. He decided to let them approach, before thrusting both palms into the beggar in the center of the line closing in on him.

But how could one man hold back a score of grown men and their collective momentum? All Guo Jing could manage, despite his exceptional kung fu and tremendous *neigong*, was to slow a few men in the middle. Those on the flanks folded in on him.

At the last moment, with the beggars all but enveloping him, Guo Jing sprung up and flew over the two rows of attackers. But, just as he touched down on the other side, a new rank appeared. He sucked in a deep breath, flexed his right foot and, once more, sailed over the heads of his pursuers.

Row upon row, the beggars plowed on. From every direction, without pause.

He jumped, but they merely rotated and came back at him.

Charge. Turn. Charge. Turn. Charge.

Wave after wave. How could he get out? Guo Jing could see no weak link to exploit. He was trapped once more.

Lotus was nimbler on her feet. Leaps and sudden quick turns were integral to her martial practice. Even so, she began to feel the strain in her body. Her heart hammered, her breathing could barely keep up.

Before long, she found herself back next to Guo Jing. She too was cornered.

Behind them, the cliff edge; in front and to the sides, files of beggars closing in.

"The cliff!" she cried.

Guo Jing sprinted over to the edge. No time to ask why.

The pursuing force ground to a halt only feet from the precipice.

Now he understood: here, at the edge, they were safe. The beggars were reluctant to come any closer, in case they lost their footing and fell to their deaths. He looked at Lotus, full of admiration, but saw only alarm in her eyes.

The beggars had reconfigured. The phalanx had lengthened to block any chance of escape. The wall had now grown into a column a dozen rows thick. It would not be possible to jump over that many men.

The beggars took one step forward. Then another. Slow but steady.

Guo Jing and Lotus were being forced, one step at a time, toward the abyss.

Guo Jing looked down. "I'll carry you." He had climbed higher and more treacherous cliff faces when he was learning internal *neigong* with Ma Yu, in Mongolia.

Lotus sighed. "They'll throw rocks."

"The Nine Yin Manual mentions something called Soul Switching." Guo Jing did not know why the passage had come to mind in that moment. "It might also involve . . . mind entrapment . . . We won't give up without a fight. If we fall, we'll *all* fall."

"But they are loyal followers of our *shifu*, their chief. Why would we want—?"

He cut her off by lifting her into his arms.

"Run!" He breathed the word into her ear and brushed his lips against her cheek.

Summoning a lifetime's worth of strength, Guo Jing threw her.

Lotus soared, borne by the clouds and ushered forth by the mist.

He's going to face them alone. The thought gripped her heart.

Bending her knees slightly, she alighted on the Terrace of the Yellow Emperor.

No one seemed to have noticed her, not even Yang Kang, who was standing a short distance away, in a corner, waving and shouting commands at the beggars attacking Guo Jing.

This is my chance, Lotus told herself. She touched her feet lightly against the ground and leaped up again.

By the time Yang Kang was aware of her, Lotus's fingertips were resting on the end of his green bamboo cane.

He yanked his end, hoping to pull it out of her grasp.

Lotus aimed two fingers, like the prongs of a fork, at his eyes. In the same instant, she swung her foot up, resting it on the shaft of the cane, which was still firmly in her grip.

Snatch from the Mastiff's Jaw: an indispensable move from the Dog-Beating repertoire. She had learned it from Count Seven Hong when he named her his successor. It was designed to recover the cane from any opponent, without fail, even if they were a superior fighter.

In this case, Yang Kang was, for certain, the lesser martial artist. And yet, in her haste, Lotus had poked him in the eyes, when she had only meant the move to be a feint to force him back.

Blackness descended over Yang Kang's field of vision. He let go of the cane, stumbled back, and fell from the Terrace.

6

"HARK, MY BEGGAR BRETHREN! STOP!" LOTUS RAISED THE cane high with both hands and projected her voice using internal-strength kung fu. "Chief Hong is alive and well. This pretender has lied to you!"

The beggars paused, unsure what to believe. It is, after all, human nature to prefer good news to bad. They turned to the young girl.

"Brethren, come! Chief Hong is safe and sound. He has been feasting on three whole chickens cooked in the beggar's style every day!"

"I am your chief. Heed my commands." Yang Kang was still struggling to see, but he could feel the effect of her words. "Push the traitor off the cliff. Then capture this liar."

The crowd roared and resumed their marching. The chief's word was law and must be obeyed, but Lotus's claim had begun to take root in their minds. Chief Hong's love for beggar's chicken was well known. Eating three whole birds a day might be excessive, but it would not be out of character.

"Look!" Lotus cried. "I have the Dog-Beating Cane. That makes me the chief."

They halted. Indeed, no one had ever known any instance of the chief losing his cane in the Clan's long history.

"We, the Beggar Clan, have always had the run of the world," Lotus continued. "And yet, today, we are being abused and insulted, right on our own patch. Two good brothers of ours, Vigor Li and Prosper Yu, were driven to an unjust death. Elder Lu has suffered grievous injury. Why?"

Half the men turned to face Lotus, wanting to hear more. She had appealed to their sense of righteous loyalty toward their fellow clansmen.

"Because of this man!" She pointed at Yang Kang. "He conspired with the Iron Palm Gang and concocted this barefaced lie about Chief Hong. Do you know who he really is?"

A chorus of "Who?" "Tell us!" and "Don't listen to her!" followed.

"He is not a Yang. His family name is Wanyan. Yes, he's the son of Wanyan Honglie, Prince of Zhao, of the Jin Empire. He's here to bring ruin and destruction to our Empire."

She looked at the hundreds of incredulous faces; for them, it seemed, the truth was a claim too far. At that moment, she recalled the metal token—shaped like a hand—given to her by Zhu Cong, after he had picked Qiu Qianren's pocket. It could come in useful. Luckily, the beggars had not searched her person and the token was still there. She raised it high, for all to see. "I took this object out of his hands just now. Look! What is it?"

The beggars rushed forward for a better look.

"The Iron Palm token!"

"Of the Iron Palm Gang!"

"Why does he have it?"

"He is their spy. That is why he carries this emblem on his person. Why else would he agree to retreat south so readily, when the Beggar Clan have been helping the poor and righting wrongs in the north for centuries?"

Yang Kang's cheeks went pale. Then, he flicked his wrist.

Two silvery lines cut through the night air, heading straight for Lotus's heart.

He was standing only a few feet away from her, at the base of the Terrace.

"Watch out!" the beggars closest to her cried.

Lotus ignored the warnings. The steel awls bounced off her chest—*clink, clink!*—and clattered to the ground.

"Wanyan Kang, would an innocent man resort to such an underhand attack?"

The beggars were awed. How was she not injured? Of course, they could not have known that, under her outer garment, she was wearing the Hedgehog Chainmail, which no weapon could penetrate.

"Who's telling the truth?"

"Is Chief Hong still alive?"

A babble of questions bubbled up. Confusion mixed with hope.

Everyone turned to the Elders. Surely they would be able to determine the truth of the matter.

Needless to say, the wall formation had long since been abandoned, allowing Guo Jing to stride unmolested through the crowd. No one paid him any attention.

CHAPTER NINE

AT THE SUMMIT OF IRON PALM MOUNTAIN

I

SUREFOOT LU HAD, AT LAST, RECOVERED ENOUGH TO SPEAK. "We, as Elders, must question them further. We must ascertain whether Chief Hong is still alive."

"We have appointed our new chief—a decision not easily revoked," Elder Peng shot back. "'Never defy the chief' is a rule our Clan has followed for generations."

Surefoot Lu refused to relent, even as the pain emanating from his fractured hands locked his jaw muscles, distorting his face into a mask of agony.

The three Elders of the Washed exchanged looks of tacit agreement and moved over to stand with Yang Kang.

"We believe in Chief Yang," Elder Peng announced. "This she-demon helped our enemies to kill Chief Hong. She is using her guile to save herself. You must not fall for her deception. Brethren, take her and make her confess!"

"Who dares lay a hand on her?" Guo Jing leaped up onto the Terrace.

No one was reckless enough to challenge the young master fighter.

Meanwhile, Qiu Qianren and his followers watched at a distance, delighted to see the beggars fighting among themselves.

"Chief Hong is feasting on delicacies from the Emperor's own kitchens in the Imperial Palace, in Lin'an, at this very moment," Lotus said, loud and clear. "He wasn't ready to tear himself away from the wonderful food, and so he asked me to take his place for the time being. When he is sated, he will return."

Count Seven Hong's gourmandizing was well known, and most of the beggars found her explanation plausible. But asking a dainty teenage girl to lead the Beggar Clan? They were incredulous.

"This Jurchen by the name of Wanyan plotted with the Iron Palm Gang to ambush me so he could steal the Dog-Beating Cane and use it to fool you. Could the Beggar Clan really be so gullible as to swallow the words of an arch pretender? Is it possible that our learned Elders have failed to see through the petty scheming of a rogue and miscreant?"

Looks of doubt and suspicion were cast at the Elders.

"If Chief Hong were still alive, why would he need you to lead on his behalf? Did he give you a token to prove your claim?" Yang Kang scrambled to hold his lies together.

"This." Lotus brandished the bamboo cane. "The Dog Beater."

Yang Kang let out a belly laugh. "Everyone saw you take it from me."

"If Chief Hong passed the Dog-Beating Cane to you, surely he would have taught you Dog-Beating kung fu. And, if he did, how was I able to take the Dog Beater from you so easily?"

Yang Kang thought Lotus was belittling him and answered in his haughtiest tone: "How dare you call it that! Do not insult the Beggar Clan's most potent scepter!"

Surely their emblem did not have such a vulgar name? Yang

Kang had expected to please the beggars with this admonishment, but all it did was reveal his ignorance—for the two beggars accompanying him would never have had the audacity to refer to the cane by name, in veneration of the authority it represented. He felt himself the target of mutinous glares amid a rising tide of fury, but he could not work out what he had said to earn them.

"Scepter?" Lotus flashed a smile. "If you want it, take it." She extended the cane, taunting him.

Yang Kang took a step toward the Terrace, before pausing to glance at Guo Jing.

"We'll keep you safe, Chief," Elder Peng said under his breath. "Let's take back what's yours." He hopped onto the Terrace, followed by Yang Kang and Elders Jian and Liang.

Surefoot Lu had also mounted the stage. He took his place near Lotus Huang, arms hanging limp by his sides. They don't call me Surefoot for nothing, he reminded himself.

Lotus was still holding out the cane, a picture of graciousness.

Yang Kang hesitated, fearing a trap. Then he placed his palm over his chest, in a defensive stance, before reaching for his prize.

She smiled and made a show of letting go. "Hold tight."

Seething, Yang Kang wrapped his fingers firmly around the cane's midpoint.

A hand darted forward. A foot flew up. Fingers in his eyes again.

And the stick was back in Lotus's grasp.

The three Elders of the Washed—Jian, Peng, and Liang—were standing next to Yang Kang, yet they could only watch, stupefied and shamed. Lotus gave them no time to react.

Lotus tossed the cane into the air. "It's yours, if you can keep it."

Yang Kang had twice been at the receiving end of Lotus's chicanery. As he dithered, Elder Jian flicked a wrist, unfurled his sleeve, and drew the cane to him.

Cheers broke out.

Only a supreme martial artist could manipulate soft fabric with such ease and precision, as if it were an extension of his arm.

Jian raised the cane above his head and presented it to his chief. Yang Kang took it in his right hand and let his inner strength course to his fingers.

You'll have to cut my hand off if you want the cane again, he said to Lotus in his head.

"Didn't Chief Hong teach you how to hold on to the Dog Beater when he entrusted it to you?" Lotus asked.

Chuckling, she tapped her feet and shot forward, straight at Yang Kang. She twirled to the side just before reaching Elders Jian and Liang, who had planted themselves protectively in front of their new chief.

As she glided past, between the two beggars, Jian flipped his palm to seize her with a backhanded Grapple and Lock.

But, the next thing he knew, she was standing toe-to-toe with Yang Kang. Elder Jian had never missed at such close proximity.

Agile as a swallow on the wing, Lotus had put on an outstanding display of the footwork from Wayfaring Fist, which she had learned from Count Seven Hong.

A swish of the cane brought the startled Elder Jian back to the moment.

A whirl of green was sweeping at his shin. He and Elder Liang jumped.

"I'm afraid the name of this move will cause offense," Lotus said with a giggle. "It's called Cane Strikes Two Dogs."

She was now standing at the eastern corner of the Terrace of the Yellow Emperor, her white dress fluttering in the breeze created by her nimble movement. In her hand, the glossy jade-green bamboo cane shimmered in the moonlight. She had snatched it so quickly that no one could say how she had done it.

"Isn't it obvious who Chief Hong's chosen one is?" Guo Jing demanded.

Thrice the beggars had witnessed Lotus whip the cane out of Yang Kang's hand, each time faster than the last. Whispers resounded. Doubt had taken root.

Surefoot Lu stepped forward. "Brethren, the techniques employed by the lady are indeed Chief Hong's kung fu."

Elder Jian caught the eye of his fellow leaders of the Washed in an unspoken exchange. Like Peng and Liang, he had followed Count Seven Hong long enough to confirm the girl's martial heritage. What could he say to counter Surefoot Lu's claim?

"Of course she is familiar with Chief Hong's martial repertoire," Jian said, after a moment. "She is his disciple."

"The Dog-Beating repertoire is known only to the Chief of the Beggar Clan," Surefoot Lu fired back. "I am certain Elder Jian is aware of that."

"It is apparent that the young lady has learned some very clever Bare Hands Seize Blade maneuvers. Nevertheless, can we say for certain that it is Dog-Beating kung fu?"

A kernel of doubt nagged at Surefoot Lu. "Miss, could you please demonstrate the Dog-Beating repertoire? If Chief Hong has indeed taught you the moves, our clansfolk shall, with one heart, declare you our chief."

"Elder Lu, I trust you have not forgotten that none of us has seen the kung fu in action—we know it only by name. How are we to confirm it?"

"What would you suggest, Elder Jian?"

Jian clapped for attention and addressed the crowd: "If the young lady defeats these hands with her cane, then I, of the family Jian, shall bend the knee and call her Chief. If my loyalty wavers, let ten thousand arrows pierce my body and a thousand sabers slice up my corpse."

Surefoot Lu snorted at the suggestion. "You're one of the Clan's most formidable masters. Your martial reputation has towered over the *jianghu* for more than twenty years. How old do you think she is? Her skill with the cane is exceptional, but is it fair to ask her to counter yours, honed through several decades of hard work?"

"Then I will put her Dog-Beating kung fu to the test!" The hotheaded Elder Liang had heard enough of these petty arguments. He lunged at Lotus with his weapon of choice—the saber.

The blade swung, the air whistled.

She smiled and tucked the cane into her belt.

Flashes of metal. Fast. Ferocious. Precise. A martial master.

Lotus leaned a mere fraction to the side. The sharp edge glided past her—three times.

She did not move her feet once.

"You think you are worthy of the Dog-Beating Cane?" She beamed at the beggar, noting how he had avoided her vital points. With the smile still hovering on her lips, she struck at him with her left hand, while her right grabbed at one end of the curved sword.

Rage flooded Elder Liang's senses. He, a famed master, well known and revered in the *wulin*—how could he allow a mere child to defy him so?

Hewing sideways and hacking down, he charged at Lotus with deadly intent.

"Elder Liang! No lethal blows!" Jian had come around to the fact that there was something to Lotus's claim and was feeling less animosity toward her. It was now crucial to rein in his fiery companion before he injured her.

"I don't mind." Lotus giggled once more.

Punch, kick, elbow, jab. Lotus flittered and fluttered around the older man, raining down moves from a dozen different martial repertoires upon him.

The beggars were bedazzled by her rapid-fire display.

"Lotus Palm!" a Disciple of Eight Pouches gasped.

"Oh, Bronze Hammer Fist!" another beggar exclaimed.

She launched the next before each move was named. The voices started to overlap.

"Wayfaring Fist—"

"Iron Broom Kick—"

"Conquer with Ease!"

Count Seven Hong had always dreaded the bother that came with taking on disciples and training them. So, over the years, he had only shared a crumb of his knowledge here, a morsel there, as reward for members who had performed commendable deeds on behalf of the Clan. Easily bored, he also disliked teaching the same kung fu again and again, so his favored clansmen each picked up a different skill.

Lotus, however, was the exception. Delighted by her cooking, Count Seven Hong had shared with her several dozen different moves from different martial repertories during the month they spent together in the town by the Yangtze River. Though she learned fast, she was only training for fun. Often, after a handful of repetitions, she would want to move on to something new. Count Seven also found explaining intricacies a chore, so Lotus was able to emulate the moves, but had yet to grasp their nuances.

Now, with the Clan's eyes on her, she was consciously showing off the martial knowledge bestowed by Count Seven Hong.

Liang's command of the saber was, without a doubt, masterful. In normal circumstances, Lotus would be struggling, but her infinite array of strange moves had left her opponent's head spinning. The beggar Elder decided to err on the side of caution, weaving a tight net of protective maneuvers across his torso.

Lotus let her arms fall into a resting position over her chest and grinned. "Admit it."

Liang had yet to draw on the full scope of his knowledge. How could he concede the fight so soon? He dropped his defensive stance and turned the saber's edge outward, its tip raised.

Down he hacked, twisting the blade sideways.

Lotus stood perfectly still. She made no move to tilt or lean away. She waited.

"No!" Elder Jian and Surefoot Lu cried simultaneously above the shouts and gasps from the crowd.

Liang drew his arm up as soon as he realized Lotus had no intention of evading the blow, but to pull back fully on a strike as potent as this, at such close range, was next to impossible.

The blade sliced down on the young woman's left shoulder.

Liang knew that, even though he had withdrawn his *neigong* energy, the sharpened steel would slice through her flesh. He had been too rash—

The lightest tap. Three inches from the wrist. His Gathering Convergence pressure point.

Numbness.

The saber clattered to the ground.

Orchid Touch.

Placing her foot on the weapon, Lotus cocked her head and grinned. "How about now?"

Elder Liang stared at her, stunned. How had she survived unscathed? The wise thing to do now was retreat. So back he hopped.

"Remember, she is Apothecary Huang's daughter." Yang Kang tried to claw back support. "She wears Hedgehog Chainmail. No weapon can cut through it!"

Elder Jian furrowed his brow at this new piece of information.

"Hmm? What do *you* think?" Lotus said, beaming.

Surefoot Lu shot a warning look at the young woman, hoping that she would be content with her triumph. He could tell that her inner strength was limited. Were it not for her dizzying martial repertoire, her wit and her armor, she would have come out of the fight as Liang's equal, at best. Against Jian, the most accomplished among the Elders, she would not stand a chance.

Of course, she ignored his signal and offered Jian a yet more dazzling smile.

Lu was desperate to stop this unnecessary confrontation, but he had expended all his powers trying to withstand the agony radiating from his hands. He could not summon the energy to speak. He could only stand there, drenched in the cold sweat brought on by the whole ordeal.

Slowly, Elder Jian looked up and fixed his eyes on Lotus. "Miss, I should like to exchange a few moves."

Guo Jing had been observing the older man. Composed and relaxed, he moved with a grounded poise that stemmed from a deep foundation in the art of *neigong* inner strength.

I can't let Lotus put herself in danger, Guo Jing thought, as he pulled from his robes the leather cord that had been used to restrain him, and strode forward.

He flicked his wrist. The makeshift whip unfurled with frightening speed, lashing at the boulder Qiu Qianren had impaled with Jian's steel staff.

Leather curled around metal.

"Up!" Guo Jing gave a sharp tug.

The staff shot from the rock like a bolt of lightning and flew straight at Jian.

The beggar Elder knew any attempt to catch it would result in shattered bones.

"Out of the way! Quick!"

As he leaped aside, barking a warning to his clansfolk, he saw Lotus reach out, tap the bamboo cane's end on the midpoint of his hurtling staff and guide it gently to the ground.

This move from the Dog-Beating repertoire was called Crush the Dog's Spine.

"Let's play!" Lotus said with a chuckle.

Jian was astounded. I will be admitting defeat the moment I begin to concede an inch, he told himself as he bent down to pick up his staff.

He bowed, holding his weapon upside down. "Please be merciful with the cane."

Elder Jian's gesture was well known throughout the *wulin* to signify wholehearted deference to a martial elder. It demonstrated his admission that he did not consider himself skilled enough to fight on an equal footing, and was instead seeking to learn.

"No need to stand on ceremony; I fear I am the lesser fighter, here." Lotus extended the cane and flicked Jian's metal staff the right way up with a Flip the Dog Belly Up.

It was not an overstatement to describe Elder Jian's staff, which he had wielded for decades, as an extension of his person. Yet, one light touch of the bamboo cane and its tip was now spinning toward his temple. The beggar locked his wrist to halt the momentum, narrowly avoiding making a fool of himself before the fight had even started.

Since Jian had declared himself inferior, he followed the martial custom that dictated the weaker party should initiate the first three moves.

Balancing the staff on his shoulder, Jian tipped the steel bar back before swinging it down.

Stones Flogged for the Qin Emperor, a move from the Staff of Demented Frenzy repertoire made famous by Sagacious Lu, a hero of the Marshes of Mount Liang.

Lotus knew she had to be careful. Even a glancing blow from the metal pole might result in internal injury, for all the protection afforded her by the Hedgehog Chainmail.

Answering with the Dog-Beating kung fu, she edged her way forward between flashes of steel.

Thick as a child's arm, the metal staff weighed at least thirty *jin*. The bamboo cane looked flimsy in comparison. Yet that apparent weakness was its greatest strength. Weighing no more than a dozen *taels*, it could be wielded with ease.

In no time at all, the Dog-Beating Cane had woven a net of attack so tight that the staff could find no room to strike.

At first, Elder Jian avoided direct contact with the Dog-Beating Cane, fearing he might shatter the Beggar Clan's symbol of authority. But, within a dozen or so exchanges, the little green stick was jabbing and poking at every vital point up and down his body. He pulled his weapon close, using every scrap of kung fu knowledge and combat experience he had accumulated over the decades to block the onslaught.

Guo Jing watched in awe. He had seen Lotus employ Dog-Beating kung fu several times before, but even he found it impossible to anticipate her next move. His thoughts soon strayed to the man who taught her this intricate kung fu, Count Seven Hong.

Wherever you may be, *Shifu*, I hope you are on the mend, he prayed silently.

Lotus shifted her grip down the cane. Pinching it in the middle with just three fingers, she twirled it playfully in a circle.

Though somewhat flummoxed by this sudden show of apparent frivolity, Elder Jian recognized that this was his chance. Hoisting his weapon, he speared it at Lotus's left shoulder.

A swivel of her wrist, and the cane took a sharp twist, its tip coming to rest one foot beneath the top of the metal pole.

Instantly, Jian felt his arm being drawn outward, his weapon straining against his palm. The light touch of the cane had turned the thrust of his attack back on him. Tightening his grasp, he struggled to regain control of his staff.

Jian's retreat only brought his opponent closer. Alarmed, he switched to a different kung fu, then another. Yet, seven or eight martial repertories later, the bamboo cane still clung as if glued to every move of the steel staff.

Dog-Beating kung fu utilized eight types of attack: Trip, Hack, Coil, Jab, Flick, Draw, Block, and Spin. As the duel continued, Lotus settled into a series of Coil moves, curling the cane around the staff like a vine winding its way up a tree. The tree trunk could grow tall or wide, but it could never untangle itself from the vine's grip.

Elder Jian made several more attempts to free himself, all to no avail. Concentrating his *neigong* energy in his arms, he switched to the Mighty Vajra Staff technique. The air growled with each swing of the steel staff, but the cane continued to trail every sweep and strike like a shadow. Though it appeared that Jian was pulling Lotus along, he was, in fact, being stifled by his own struggle to free himself from the influence of the bamboo stick.

Jian had unleashed half of the repertoire's moves, but it was having no effect. He was now certain of Lotus's claim.

Just as he was about to pull back and admit defeat, he heard Elder Peng's voice: "Grapple and Lock the cane."

"Go on, try it!" Lotus whipped into a succession of Spin attacks, which forced Elder Jian to follow her instead.

The Dog Beater was a whirlwind of green, spinning between the five major acupressure points along the beggar's spine: the Unyielding Space, on the back of his head; the Wind Mansion, on the nape of his neck; the Great Hammer, where the neck joined the shoulders; the Spirit Tower, between his shoulder blades; and the Suspended Pivot, at the base of his backbone.

A touch on any of these points by the cane would be lethal—or would cripple him, at the very least.

Jian understood the danger he was in, but he was so harried that he could not even lift his staff for his own protection. He pressed forward, hoping to create some space in which to turn, but the green storm had engulfed him. The cane's point would not stop flitting over his five vital points.

The beggar had only one option left. He must escape.

The instant he reeled away from one blow, the next one would fall on him. The faster he tried to evade it, the faster the cane chased him. He ended up running round and round in an ever-expanding circle.

Lotus, meanwhile, was in her element. She swapped the cane between her hands without turning her body or shifting her feet, and yet she did not for one moment let the tip stray from the vulnerable points on the beggar's back.

By now, Elders Lu, Peng, and Liang had hopped down from the Terrace to give Jian more room, but it did him no good. The beggar ran another half a dozen laps before crying, "Mercy, Miss Huang! I yield!"

"What did you call me?" Lotus asked, with another bright smile.

"I bow to the chief."

Jian wanted to put his words into action, but the Dog-Beating Cane was still dancing around his back. His robe was, by now, drenched through and beads of sweat were dripping from his beard.

At last, Lotus felt vindicated. Beaming, she pulled back with a flick of the cane, tapped it instead on the steel staff and flung it upward. Once more, she had used Jian's own power against him, sending the momentum back into his staff.

The heavy weapon flew up high into the sky.

Elder Jian bowed deeply, relieved that he had been spared. The rest of the beggars followed, bending low as they saluted their chief. They had all been convinced by Lotus's mesmerizing skills.

Jian took a step forward to spit in her face, but, casting his eyes over her jade white complexion glowing with a coral blush, and her features delicate as spring blossom, he hesitated, then swallowed the phlegm back down.

Just then, the air parted above his head.

A shadow flitted onto the Terrace and caught Jian's steel staff.

Elder Peng: the beggar who had captured Lotus and Guo Jing using the dark art of mind entrapment.

Lotus was pleased for the chance to seek redress. She pointed the cane at the Purple Palace pressure point, just above his sternum. Her plan was to intimidate him using the Spin technique, aiming for the vital points on his chest and forcing him into a clumsy retreat, making him out to be an even bigger buffoon than Jian.

But Peng stood his ground, crossed his arms, and bowed. What was the point of fighting this young woman when his kung fu was inferior to Jian's?

Lotus touched the cane on his acupressure point, but held back her inner strength. "What do you want?"

"I bow to the chief."

Lotus glared at him. The moment their eyes met, her heart fluttered. She turned away at once, but curiosity got the better of her and she stole another glance.

A radiance was emanating from his eyes. A glow that reached deep into her being. She could not look away, so instead she squeezed her eyes shut.

"Chief, you must be tired. Rest a little." His mellifluous tone was soothing.

Exhaustion washed over Lotus. She could hear a voice in her head: *It's been a long night.*

Her eyes sore and her throat parched, she felt drained.

"Peng, what do you think you're doing?" Elder Jian could see that Peng was trying to hypnotize her. He had honored the young woman as the Chief of the Beggar Clan; it was now his duty to protect her.

Peng smiled at Jian. "The chief needs to rest. She's worn out. You mustn't disturb her."

A small part of Lotus was aware of the peril she was in, but her body had given in to the fatigue. It wanted her to close her eyes, to sleep. It would not have cared if the skies were about to crash down upon her. Her body needed rest.

Guo Jing's words from before suddenly broke through her semi-conscious state.

"Soul Switching . . . tell me more . . ." She felt as if she had been jolted from a dream.

Guo Jing had been watching Lotus closely, poised to strike a deadly blow against Elder Peng if he used that infernal skill of his again. He rushed over and whispered the description from the Nine Yin Manual into her ear.

She listened carefully. The principle of Desist and Observe.

Desist: control of the heart. She ran the lines one by one in her head. *Desist: embodiment of the essence.*

She closed her eyes. Drawing on her wealth of martial and literary knowledge, she inhaled. Breath and mind joined as one. With each fresh gulp of air, her body calmed.

Elder Peng watched her eyelids droop and her breathing slow. She must be asleep now, he told himself. Thrilled with his success, he readied himself for the next step of his scheme.

Just then, Lotus opened her eyes and smiled at him.

Pure joy.

The corners of his mouth turned up. He was floating.

An indescribable feeling spread through him. A lightness of being. A laugh burst forth before he could comprehend what was happening.

Lotus was impressed: The Nine Yin Manual lives up to its reputation. I've overpowered him with a mere smile.

Flushed with triumph, she grinned wider still. She was curious to see its full effects.

Elder Peng realized he was in grave danger and tried with every fiber of his being to still his heart, but it was impossible to claw back control in his panic-stricken state.

He caught a glimpse of Lotus's smirk and cradled his belly as he convulsed with another wave of laughter.

Ha ha ha . . . he he he . . . ah-ha-haa-haaa . . . aaah-ha-aaa-yaaa-ooo . . .

Chortling ever louder, his voice spread out across the lake in a cacophony of hooting and bellowing.

The beggars looked at each other. What was so funny?

"Elder Peng!" Jian tried to restore order.

Peng pointed at Jian's nose and doubled over, shaking merrily.

Jian rubbed his sleeve over his face, feeling self-conscious.

The sight made Peng guffaw even harder. He backflipped down from the Terrace and rolled on the ground in hysterics.

The beggars sensed something was wrong. Two of Peng's most trusted followers rushed over to help him back onto his feet. Shrieking with laughter, the beggar Elder pushed them away.

Before long, gasps could be heard amid the cackling. Peng's face was turning purple as he sank deeper into this uncontrollable fit.

In normal circumstances, Soul Switching only resulted in drowsiness, but Lotus had used it against Peng just as he was trying to entrap her, when he was at his most vulnerable.

"Chief, allow me to speak." Elder Jian bowed and stayed bent over as he spoke, to show his submission. He feared Peng would soon be suffocated by his uproarious state. "Elder Peng has been insolent and deserves to be punished. And yet, we beg the chief to be magnanimous."

As Surefoot Lu and Elder Liang chimed in with their entreaties, Peng was still squeaking and squawking in the background.

Lotus turned to Guo Jing. "Enough?"

He nodded.

"I will let him go, on one condition. No one is to spit on me."

"The chief's word is our command," Jian said immediately. Time was now of the essence if Peng's life was to be saved.

"Go on, jab his pressure point." Lotus chuckled, happy to be spared the disgusting ritual of being anointed as Beggar Chief with the Clan's saliva.

Jian jumped down and struck two of Peng's acupressure points. The laughter ceased immediately. Peng's eyes rolled into the back of his head as he gulped great mouthfuls of air. He was thoroughly defeated.

"Well, I do rather need a rest now," Lotus mused. "Hey, where's Yang Kang?"

"Gone," Guo Jing answered.

"What?" She jumped up in frustration. "How? Where?"

"There." He pointed toward the lake. "With Qiu Qianren."

Lotus gazed into the distance and saw a set of sails resting close to the horizon. They had too much of a head start. Although annoyed, she understood why Guo Jing had not stopped Yang Kang— he still honored the friendship between their fathers and their own sworn brotherhood.

IN FACT, Guo Jing had only noticed Yang Kang was gone when it was too late.

Like everyone else, Yang Kang had been watching the contest between Lotus and Elder Jian intently. When he saw how Jian struggled so soon, he knew he would have to get off the island if he was to have any hope of staying alive. Carefully, he edged over to the envoys of the Iron Palm Gang and asked for their help.

Qiu Qianren had also realized that the teenage girl would soon succeed in her claim as the Chief of the Beggar Clan. It would do him no good to stay, outnumbered as he was, especially as he would have to deal with her companion's redoubtable kung fu. He signaled to his entourage and slipped away before the fight was over, taking Yang Kang with him.

Some beggars did observe the Iron Palm Gang's retreat, but the Clan's commanding figures were too involved in the fight to take heed, so they let the uninvited guests slip away.

LOTUS HUANG raised the Dog-Beating Cane high. "I shall help Chief Hong look after our Clan's affairs until his return. Elder Jian, Elder Liang, lead the Disciples of Eight Pouches east to meet Chief Hong. Elder Lu, you will stay here to recuperate."

The crowd erupted in cheers.

"What should we do about him?" Lotus pointed at Elder Peng.

Jian bowed and did not straighten up until he had said his piece: "Brother Peng's transgression was grave and he must be severely punished. Nonetheless, I beg the chief to think on the deeds he has done for the Clan over the years and spare his life."

"I knew you would speak on his behalf." Lotus shot Jian a look, but there was also a hint of a smile on her face. "Fine, he has laughed enough. Let him be demoted . . . He shall become a Disciple of Four Pouches."

Peng and the three remaining beggar Elders thanked their chief in unison. Deflated and full of regret, Peng removed five bags from the nine he wore on his back.

Once the erstwhile Elder had trudged toward the rear, to be with the others of his rank, Lotus continued to address the Clan. "It is not often that our brethren come together; there must be many affairs to attend to. But, before we proceed, we must give Vigor Li and Prosper Yu a worthy burial.

"I can see that Elder Lu is the best among you, so you shall obey him in all matters of import for the time being." A moment later, she added, "Elder Jian and Elder Liang will provide assistance," so no one would try to undermine Surefoot Lu's authority.

"I'll bid farewell, now—we have other affairs to attend to—but I shall see you all in Lin'an before long." With those words, Lotus took Guo Jing's hand and headed down toward to the shore.

The beggars guided them to the pier and stood to attention as they watched the boat carrying their new chief vanish into the mists.

2

GUO JING AND LOTUS ARRIVED AT THE YUEYANG TOWER JUST as dawn was breaking. Ulaan and the condors were waiting patiently for them on the shore.

Lotus gazed at the early morning sun breaking away from the ripples, its colors reflected in the lake and the sky. It was a majestic sight.

"Between the lips are mountains far, in the mouth is the Yangtze long— vast, gushing and infinite. The glow of dawn, the shade of dusk, ten thousand shifting scenes.

"Fan Zhongyan captured the view so well," she said. The description was from "Memorial to Yueyang Tower." "We have to stop and take a look. Let's climb to the top."

Together, they scaled the Tower and watched the sun rise over Dongting Lake. The events from the night were still fresh in their minds, and yet, for a while, they did not speak of them, making conversation about nothing in particular instead.

Suddenly, Lotus's face darkened. "I haven't forgiven you."

"Huh?"

"You know exactly what I mean."

Guo Jing scratched his head, unable to recall what he might have done wrong. "Please—please, tell me."

"Why were you prepared to leave me by myself when the beggars tried to push us off the cliff? Do you think I could have gone on living without you? Don't you know by now how I feel?" Tears began to fall down her cheeks.

Guo Jing took her hand and clasped it to his chest, too overwhelmed to reply. "You're right," he said eventually. "If one of us is to go, we should go together."

Lotus sighed, but her reply was cut short by the sound of footsteps. A man appeared at the top of the stairs. He was glancing left and right just as the young couple turned to see who it was. They could not believe their eyes.

Iron Palm Water Glider—Qiu Qianren.

Guo Jing hopped to his feet and stood in front of Lotus protectively, but, to their surprise, Qiu merely grinned, waved and flew back down the stairs.

"Was he scared of us?" Lotus said. "What an odd man. I will find out." And she began to run after him.

"Be careful!" Guo Jing rushed to follow, but, by the time he reached the bottom of the Tower, they were both gone.

"Lotus! Lotus! Where are you?"

What if she had fallen victim to Qiu's merciless kung fu? The possibility terrified Guo Jing.

Though Lotus could hear the panic in Guo Jing's voice, she chose to ignore him. She wanted to find out what Qiu Qianren was up to first. If she replied, the old fossil would know she was on his trail.

She tiptoed after him at a safe distance as he made his way around the outer perimeter of a large mansion, pausing as he turned a corner at its northern end. She would wait a little before catching up with him.

Qiu Qianren guessed Lotus must be following him from Guo Jing's cries. He turned the corner and stopped.

They both waited, and listened. Nothing. Then, at the same moment, they both crept up to the corner.

Lotus was confronted with a vision of wrinkled, pockmarked skin, just like that of Dongting Lake's famous mandarins.

Qiu Qianren was greeted by a face as delicate and ravishing as the blossoms on the banks of the River Xiang.

Their noses almost touched.

Panic flashed across their eyes.

Yelping, they spun round and bolted in opposite directions.

Although wary of Qiu Qianren's kung fu after his display the night before, Lotus could not let him slip away so easily. She sprinted most of the way around the mansion's outer wall, fleet of foot thanks to her lightness *qinggong*; she was planning to spy on him from the eastern corner.

Qiu Qianren, it turned out, had had exactly the same idea. Once more, they almost rammed into each other—this time, by the screen wall opposite the mansion's south-facing main gate.

Lotus stood facing him. She could not risk turning, because that would open her back to his attack, but if she could keep him talking until Guo Jing had found them, then she would not be in any significant danger.

She smiled sweetly. "Uncle Qiu, what a small world! We meet again."

"Indeed, and so soon after we parted ways in Lin'an! I trust the young lady has been well?" Qiu Qianren returned her pleasantries with an equally pleasant grin.

So, you're back to your old lying ways, Lotus said to herself. Don't you remember seeing me last night, at Jun Hill? Well, well, whatever you say, I'll answer with the Dog Beater.

"Guo Jing, now's your chance!" Lotus called at the top of her voice.

Qiu Qianren whipped around in alarm.

No one.

Only a gust of air against his shin.

He had been duped. He jumped.

Lotus swung the bamboo stick low, using Count Seven Hong's Trip technique.

Qiu Qianren dodged the blow, but he had no idea that the cane would whip back at him so rapidly, nor that it could create a rush of parting air that would crash against him like the waters of a mighty river.

Trip. This one word described ten thousand subtle variations. The quicker Qiu Qianren jumped out of the way, the faster Lotus flashed her cane, to the point that any observer would see nothing but a whirl of green where once a young girl and an old man had stood.

At the eighteenth sweep of the stick, Qiu Qianren was a fraction too sluggish. A whack on his left shin was followed by his right ankle being hooked out from under him.

Thump! He found himself lying flat on the ground.

"No, stop, hear me out!" he yelled.

Beaming, Lotus pulled back. He hopped to his feet, but, just before he was about to land, he was met with a flick and a strike from the Dog-Beating Cane. Once more, Qiu Qianren lost his footing, again landing on his back.

By the sixth tumble, Qiu Qianren had learned his lesson. He would stay down, with his belly pressed flat to the ground.

"Get back up."

Following her command, he leaped up and yanked at the drawstring of his trousers.

It snapped.

He grabbed his waistband.

"Shoo, or I'll let go!"

For once, Lotus was speechless. Never in her life would she have imagined a martial master and the leader of one of the *jianghu*'s most influential gangs resorting to such a sordid ruse.

She decided she would rather not take the risk.

"Pah!" she muttered under her breath as she retreated.

Qiu Qianren roared with laughter.

Amused by the absurdity of it all, she had to admit, albeit grudgingly, that she had been outwitted.

Qiu Qianren was about to chase Lotus away, far enough that she would not turn back to pester him, when Guo Jing appeared between them.

The young man guarded his chest with one arm as he drew a languid semicircle from his hip upward with the other.

Qiu Qianren had seen enough to be sure that, if the boy's left palm joined the right, as though he was cradling an invisible orb, a force quite unlike anything he had ever known would burst forth.

He started to laugh, then gave out an almost undignified squeal.

"Ignore him," Lotus called. "Strike!"

Guo Jing was still wary of the man's Iron Palm, for its intensity and complexity was equal to that of the most prized kung fu of Zhou Botong, Apothecary Huang, or Viper Ouyang. He knew it would be a mortal mistake to underestimate his opponent at such close proximity. And yet, he gathered his *qi* in the Elixir Field, relaxed his body and prepared to strike.

"Little ones, Grandpa here has been overindulging and has given himself a bad stomach, yet again," Qiu Qianren said, still holding his trousers up by the waistband. "Once more, I must beg your pardon."

"Strike him," Lotus urged as she backed away.

"I know what you young 'uns are thinking. You won't let it rest until old Grandpa shows his true colors. Well, the problem is, my tummy has been having a mind of its own of late. Especially at crucial moments like these. But I have an idea. Listen carefully, now. If you want to prove your mettle, meet me at the foot of the Iron Palm Mountain in seven days."

Irritated by his patronizing tone, Lotus reached inside her clothes for her needles. She was waiting for him to lose himself in his prattling, so that she could unleash a Skyful of Petals. Would he still refer to himself as jolly old Grandpa then? But, on the other hand, what if she struck his hands by accident and made him lose his grip . . . ? As she deliberated over what to do, she was struck by a sudden realization. Iron Palm Mountain . . . The secret message in the painting!

"Dragon's den or tiger's lair, we'll be there!" She paused for a moment. "How do we find you?"

"Go west from here. Through Chengde, Chenzhou, then up the Yuan River. Between Luxi and Chenxi, you'll find a mountain that looks like all five fingers of one hand are pointing up to the heavens. That is Iron Palm Mountain. The terrain is treacherous and Grandpa's kung fu most fearsome, so you have been warned. You can always apologize to me now, instead. There's no need to put yourselves in danger."

Lotus was overjoyed. His description was just like Guo Jing's painting!

"May we meet again within the week." She accepted the challenge with exaggerated politeness.

Qiu Qianren nodded, then crunched up his face as if in pain. *"Aiyooooo! Aiyoooo!"* And off he dashed, clinging to his waistband to preserve his modesty.

3

"LOTUS, I DON'T UNDERSTAND," GUO JING SAID.

"What is it?"

"Why does he pretend to know so little kung fu? He could have overpowered us easily. Remember when he struck me in the chest at Roaming Cloud Manor? If he had used the same *neigong* then that he did last night, I wouldn't be standing here today. Why does he put on this silly act?"

Lotus nibbled on her thumb as she pondered these questions. "I really have no idea. I tripped him over again and again with the Dog Beater, just now. He was defenseless . . . Maybe the move with the beggar's staff was some kind of sleight of hand?"

Guo Jing shook his head. "He crushed all the bones in Surefoot

Lu's hands. He also met my attack head-on. What he did requires real learning; he couldn't have faked it."

Lotus pulled a pearl hairpin from her hair, sat on her heels and started scribbling on the ground. After a while, she sighed. "I don't know what the old fossil is playing at, but I'm sure we'll find out when we get to Iron Palm Mountain."

"But shouldn't we head back to Lin'an to look for *Shifu* instead? That awful old man is probably playing another trick on us. Why go to Iron Palm Mountain?"

"Remember the hidden message in the painting Papa gave you?"

Guo Jing scratched his head, trying to recall. "We don't know what it says. The rain washed away half the characters . . ."

"You still haven't worked it out?"

Guo Jing was stumped. "You know what I'm like. Just tell me. You obviously have worked it out."

Lotus scratched four broken lines in the dirt. "Though there is a missing character in the first line, it can only be *Yue Fei's final writings*. I was struggling with the second line, but it must be *shan*— mountain!"

"Are you saying . . . the first two lines . . . that General Yue Fei's writings are in Iron Palm Mountain?" Guo Jing clapped his hands together. "Let's go now! The Iron Palm Gang have betrayed their homeland by joining forces with the Jin. We can't let them give Yue Fei's writings to Wanyan Honglie! What about the last two lines?"

"Qiu said Iron Palm Mountain is shaped like the five fingers of a hand, so the third line probably is *Beneath the middle crag.*"

Guo Jing applauded. "You *are* smart! What about the last line?"

Lotus was now speaking more to herself than to Guo Jing. "*In the second . . . the second . . .* What could that be?" She tilted her head and her long hair fluttered. "I can't work it out. I'll try again when we get there."

TOGETHER, THEY rode west with the condors, passing through Chengde, Taoyuan, and Yuanling. Before long, they had arrived in Luxi. Yet, when they asked the locals for directions to Iron Palm Mountain, the townsfolk simply shook their heads.

Disappointed, they decided to stay in Luxi for the night. That evening, Lotus asked an inn boy about the local sights. The young man rattled off a long list, yet there was no mention of Iron Palm Mountain.

Lotus pursed her lips. "How dull! Sounds like this little place has no areas of natural beauty."

"Luxi may be small, but the scenery around Monkey Claw Mountain is incomparable!" The man was clearly rankled.

"Monkey Claw Mountain? Where's that?" Lotus kept her tone casual. It could be just the place they had been searching for.

The man turned to the door with a terse, "Pardon me."

Grabbing the back of his shirt, Lotus pulled him back into the room. She placed a *sycee* ingot of silver on the table.

"Yours, if you tell me everything about Monkey Claw Mountain."

The serving man reached out. "Really? Mine?"

Lotus nodded with a smile.

"I will tell you, but don't go there. Evil men dwell up there. Death awaits any soul who strays within five *li* of Monkey Claw Mountain."

Lotus caught Guo Jing's eye. She could tell he had had the exact same thought: the Iron Palm Gang!

"Does this mountain have five peaks, shaped like the claws of a monkey?" Lotus blinked innocently.

"Indeed! The five summits are lined up like this." The man opened his palm, fingers pointing skywards. "The middle one is higher than the peaks either side. The most curious thing is how each crag is split into three segments—just like our fingers."

"Segment!" Lotus leaped to her feet. "In the second segment!"

"Yes!" Guo Jing cried in joy.

The man gaped at them.

Lotus asked him a series of questions about how to get there, only letting him go when she was entirely satisfied.

Cradling the silver with both hands, the man skipped out of the room, delighted with his unexpected good fortune.

"Come on!" Lotus was raring to go.

"It's only sixty *li* away, it won't take Ulaan long to make the journey. Why don't we make our pilgrimage in the morning?"

"Pilgrimage?" She laughed. "We're on a mission to take back Yue Fei's writings!"

"Oh." Guo Jing felt very silly. How could he have forgotten?

LOTUS AND Guo Jing slipped through the window and took Ulaan from the stables without anyone at the inn noticing. The condors flew ahead as they galloped southeast along the route described by the inn boy.

Clumps of foliage at chest height sprouted from both sides of the rugged mountain path. It would have been a difficult journey, had they been on foot, or on a lesser horse.

In no time, they had covered forty *li*. Looming ahead, five vertiginous tors towered above them, their tops shrouded by scattered clouds.

When they reached the foot of the mountain, they gazed up at the craggy summits that seemed to tear angrily at the moonlit sky, as if someone was thrusting their hand right up into the belly of the heavens.

"The middle peak is just like in the painting." Guo Jing was thrilled. "Look! It's even got pine trees at the very top."

Lotus chuckled. "All we're missing is a general practicing with his sword. Why don't you go up and give it a try?"

"Too bad I'm not a general."

"I'm sure Genghis Khan will . . ." She trailed off.

Knowing what she meant, Guo Jing looked away. He did not have the courage to look her in the eye.

AFTER SETTLING Ulaan and the condors, and checking there was no one in sight, Guo Jing and Lotus began to ascend the middle crag on foot.

Circling to the other side, they scaled the rock face with their lightness kung fu until they reached a narrow path. They followed the track for several *li*, winding back and forth, and eventually arrived at a dense pine forest. Before they could decide whether to explore the woods or continue upward, they saw light glimmering between the branches. Their eyes met. Without saying anything, they crept in silence toward the source.

A few steps later—*whoosh!*—two men, clad in black, burst from the trees, their glinting weapons pointed straight at their faces.

If we fight these men, the Iron Palm Gang will know we're here and it'll make stealing Yue Fei's final writings more difficult. Lotus weighed their options as she recalled the hand-shaped token she had taken from Qiu Qianren. Removing it from the inside pocket of her robes, she showed it to the black-clad men without saying a word.

They took one look, stepped aside and bowed.

Swift as lightning, Lotus twirled the bamboo cane and tapped their pressure points. Neither man could move. She then kicked them into the undergrowth and stole toward the light, with Guo Jing following close behind.

Candles and lamps were glowing at both ends of a stone house. They tiptoed to the western side and peeked through the window.

Vapor rose from a large wok that was sizzling over red-hot coals. A boy, dressed head to toe in black, tended the stove. His small body worked the bellows with all his might. Another boy in a similar outfit noisily scraped the contents around the bottom of the pan with a metal ladle.

A grizzled old man sat cross-legged in front of the fire, his eyes closed in concentration. He was inhaling the steam from the wok, his breathing deep and slow.

Qiu Qianren, dressed in his signature arrowroot shirt.

Before long, wisps of hot air began to rise from the crown of his head. He stretched his arms high—heat seemed to be issuing from the tips of his fingers, too.

All of a sudden, he leaped up and plunged his hands into the wok.

The sweat-soaked child at the bellows somehow found a new burst of energy and pumped faster.

Qiu Qianren stood motionless at the stove. The leader of the Iron Palm Gang was clearly not impervious to the heat—it was his will alone that kept his hands buried in the hot pan.

At length, he drew his arms back and thrust his palms out. They smacked loudly against a small sandbag suspended from a roof beam by a slender piece of string.

But the bag did not even quiver.

Guo Jing was astounded. To hit it without making it swing requires the most exquisite kung fu. This man is a true master.

Meanwhile, Lotus was certain that this was another show put on to fool any onlookers. She would have said something, had they not had more important things to do—that is, finding Yue Fei's final writings.

They watched Qiu Qianren repeat the move over and over: temper the hands, strike the bag, then back to the stove again.

Lotus was aching to discover how he made steam rise from his head and fingertips, but she could not see any device that might help to create such an illusion. She recalled how Zhu Cong had exposed his stunts at Roaming Cloud Manor.

If Zhu Cong was here, he would see through the old sham at once, she said to herself. Even I can admit that he is far more perceptive than me in these matters.

Since they could glean nothing more from Qiu Qianren's ritual, they crept over to a window on the eastern side of the house.

Lotus and Guo Jing were shocked to find Yang Kang inside, and, next to him, Mercy Mu. What had brought her here? they both wondered, as they eavesdropped on the conversation.

Yang Kang was being his most charming self, all sweet nothings and empty promises. He was trying to convince Mercy to marry him as soon as possible, but the young woman would not be swayed. She refused to consider their union until Yang Kang had killed Wanyan Honglie and avenged the death of his birth parents—her godfather and his wife.

"My dear, don't you understand?" There was a hint of accusation in Yang Kang's tone.

"Understand what?"

"Wanyan Honglie is under permanent protection. How could I find the opportunity to do it, on my own? But when you become my wife, I can pretend to take you to pay your respects to your new family. We'll have no problem getting close to him and we can do it together. For certain, success will be ours!"

Mercy lowered her head.

His logic seemed to have persuaded her. A blush began to spread across her cheeks.

Sensing that she was relenting, Yang Kang grew bold. He reached out for her hand and let his fingers glide over her skin, while his other arm snaked around her waist.

Lotus was furious. She would not stand by and let Mercy fall for Yang Kang's lies. She had to do something.

4

"WHO COMES HITHER WITHOUT MY SUMMONS?" A GRUFF VOICE barked before Lotus could warn Mercy. She whipped round, as did Guo Jing.

Standing before them, illuminated by the light of the moon, was Qiu Qianren.

Something felt different. The man had always put on an air of grandeur, and yet it could not mask the slippery look in his eyes. Now, his expression was grave.

He swaggers even more on home ground, Lotus noted. He must have heard our arrival and staged the show with the wok.

Lotus grinned brightly. "Uncle Qiu, we come in peace. We promised to arrive in seven days. We're not late, are we?"

"What nonsense is this?" His tone was tetchy, if not exactly hostile.

"Have you forgotten?" Lotus was still in excellent humor. "I hope your stomach has recovered. If not, I suggest you consult a doctor before we begin, or else . . ." She trailed off and giggled.

Qiu Qianren answered with a growl, drawing back his palms to strike.

Lotus stood her ground. She was giddy at the prospect of her Hedgehog Chainmail doing its worst.

"Move!" she heard Guo Jing shout.

A gust rushed past her ear as Guo Jing launched a Dragon-Subduing Palm at Qiu Qianren.

An overwhelming force crushed her shoulders. She knew she should move aside, but she could not, for her body had already been cast up into the air.

She careened backward. Her breath caught. Darkness descended.

Qiu Qianren's brief contact with Lotus's steel armor was enough to leave his palms bloody. Momentarily dazed by shock and anger, he was only roused by a powerful strike from his adversary.

Their internal energies clashed in a loud *pang*.

The force drove each side back three steps.

Qiu Qianren found his footing instantly. Guo Jing swayed before regaining his.

During their encounter on Jun Hill, Guo Jing had thought they were equals, but now he knew he was the weaker party—his feeling of strength had all been down to his new insight into channeling internal energy through the Heavenly Northern Dipper formation.

Scooping Lotus up into his arms, Guo Jing sensed the air split behind him. He had no desire to fight—all he wanted was to remove Lotus from danger. Cradling her with one arm, he let rip a Dragon Whips Tail, without turning to face his assailant. This move from the Dragon-Subduing Palm was designed to throw off an attack, and Guo Jing's desperation imbued it with an even greater potency.

Once more, their inner strengths collided, and this time it was Qiu Qianren who almost lost his foothold. Feeling the tears in his palms acutely, he raised his hands in the moonlight. Bright red blood oozed from the wounds.

At least the spikes weren't laced with poison, Qiu Qianren thought with relief.

Guo Jing took the chance to secure Lotus in his arms and scamper toward the middle crag. He had managed to give himself a head start of several dozen paces when the battle cry was raised.

He looked downhill.

A sea of torches. A throng of men clad in black.

He had no choice but to head toward the peak.

He ran with his swiftest lightness *qinggong*, hoping to find refuge. All the while, he did not feel Lotus stir even once. He put a finger under her nose.

Nothing. He felt nothing.

She had stopped breathing.

"Lotus!"

No answer.

"Lotus!"

Still no reply.

Guo Jing's pace slackened briefly, and Qiu Qianren—leading a dozen of the Iron Palm Gang's strongest fighters—began to gain on him.

I could probably fight my way down, Guo Jing said to himself. But it would be too great a risk with Lotus so badly injured.

He left the trail in haste, sprinting in a straight line toward the summit. He had had plenty of practice climbing cliffs and racing up mountains in Mongolia, and in no time the gap between him and his pursuers had doubled.

Without slowing, Guo Jing pressed his cheek to Lotus's to gauge how she was doing. She was warm. His heart felt a little lighter.

He called out her name again. Still, no response.

Guo Jing was not far from the peak, now. He guessed that his enemies already had him surrounded. His only hope of getting out of this predicament was to find a place to revive Lotus first.

He cast his eyes around and noticed a dark spot, around ten score paces uphill, to his left. It could be the mouth of a cave. He took a deep breath and scaled the short distance. It was indeed a cave, as he had hoped. The entrance was reinforced by a stone arch.

Guo Jing carried Lotus inside and set her down tenderly. He pressed his hand on her Spirit Tower pressure point, between her shoulder blades. He channeled his inner strength and delivered it through this vital point to smooth her *qi* and calm her breathing.

Members of the Iron Palm Gang were now gathered halfway up the crag, their shouts growing ever more thunderous.

Before long, Guo Jing heard a guttural "*Ahhhh!*" and knew Lotus must be coming to.

"My chest hurts," she said weakly.

"Don't worry. We will rest here for a little while."

Relieved, Guo Jing made Lotus more comfortable on the floor and moved to the cave's entrance, his palm held in readiness over his chest. He would fight to the death to protect Lotus.

He peered outside.

A ring of fire. Half a *li* downhill. Scores of Iron Palm Gang members, each carrying a torch.

One man stood alone ahead of this blazing wall. Qiu Qianren.

Their flames cast enough light for Guo Jing to make out their angry faces, distorted by their fierce battle cries. And yet, not one of them took a step toward him. It was as if their feet were nailed to the ground.

Why weren't they charging up to the cave? Seeing no sign of an advance, Guo Jing returned to Lotus's side.

Just as he stooped down to her, he heard a muffled swishing sound.

It was coming from deeper inside the cave.

Footsteps?

Swinging his arm to shield his back, Guo Jing straightened up and spun around.

The darkness of the cave stared back at him. He could not see how far it extended, nor could he make out what had caused the noise.

"Who's there? Come out!" he yelled.

His own voice answered him, echoing off the rocky walls.

Silence.

Then someone cleared his throat and laughed.

Qiu Qianren?

Guo Jing struck the flint and tinder he always carried. A man was striding toward them from deep inside the cave.

Arrowroot shirt, palm-leaf fan, grizzled hair, hoary beard... Qiu Qianren the Iron Palm Water Glider.

I just saw him outside. How did he get in here? Guo Jing asked himself in disbelief. He felt a chill spread across his back—his shirt was soaked in cold sweat.

"Well done, little ones, you found me," Qiu Qianren said with a chuckle. "Such courage, such determination. Most admirable." Suddenly, a frosty expression descended over his features. "But this is a secret hiding place of the Iron Palm Gang. No one is allowed inside. Ye who enter shall meet their death."

Guo Jing was still trying to comprehend Qiu Qianren's words when he heard Lotus ask, her voice feeble, "Why did *you* enter, then?"

"Erm... I haven't got time for tittle-tattle. I have a matter of some import to see to." Qiu Qianren made for the exit.

It was not in Guo Jing's nature to initiate an attack, but neither did he want to take risks, with Lotus so badly injured. What if the old man launched a sneak attack as he ran past?

He thrust both palms at Qiu Qianren's shoulders, in a move he learned from Quick Hands Zhu Cong, his second *shifu*.

As predicted, the old man raised his hands to block.

Guo Jing immediately folded his forearms and rammed his elbows into Qiu Qianren's chest.

This was typical of Zhu Cong's kung fu—opening with a ruse that masked the sting to come. So subtle and hidden was the actual blow that most opponents failed to detect it.

Guo Jing intended to wind the old man, but it occurred to him, before he dug his elbows in, that the push back contained no power, unlike the blows exchanged moments ago outside Yang Kang and Mercy Mu's room.

While Guo Jing was still trying to make sense of Qiu Qianren's sudden impotence and decide how he should respond, his hands twirled, of their own accord, locking his opponent's wrists.

Qiu Qianren writhed and tugged. His response had no effect whatsoever, except for exposing the depth of his kung fu—or, rather, the lack of it.

Now Guo Jing was certain he was the stronger fighter. He relaxed his fingers for a fraction of a second, then pulled.

Qiu stumbled headlong into Guo Jing, his arms flailing helplessly.

Guo Jing finished by tapping the Yin Capital pressure point at the base of Qiu's sternum, and the old man collapsed in a heap on the ground.

"My lord," Qiu Qianren gasped, "why do you toy with me thus, when you are standing on a knife-edge?"

The cries of rage and defiance outside had been growing louder with each passing minute.

"See us down safely," Guo Jing demanded.

Qiu Qianren's face crumpled and he shook his head. "I can't even vouch for my own life. I can't promise you safe passage."

"Order your followers to stand aside. Once we are down from this mountain, we will let you go, unharmed."

Qiu Qianren looked even more miserable. "Young boy, why can't you let me be? Look outside and you will understand."

Though wary of some trick, Guo Jing did as he was asked. What he saw left him stunned. Before the line of torches stood a man, cattail-leaf fan in hand, shouting at him.

Qiu Qianren.

He turned back quickly to the man lying on the floor. The same face.

"How . . . ? How . . . ? There are two of you?"

"My silly boy, don't you see?" Lotus was barely audible above the noise coming from outside. "There are two Qiu Qianrens. One is a master of kung fu, the other a master of falsehood. They look exactly the same. This one is the liar."

Guo Jing struggled to comprehend this revelation. Eventually, he asked Qiu Qianren, "Is that true?"

"If the young lady says so," the old man said gloomily. "He is my twin. I am the eldest, and I was the strongest, too—until my little brother's kung fu overtook mine."

"Which one of you is Qiu Qianren?"

"Does it matter? What difference does it make if Qianren is my name or his? We are very close. We have shared the same name since childhood."

"Tell us! Who is Qiu Qianren?" Guo Jing urged.

"He is the impostor, of course!" Lotus cut in.

"Then what is your name, old man?" Guo Jing pressed.

Knowing he stood no chance against Guo Jing, Qiu had to answer. "My late father did give me another name—Qianzhang. I don't much like the sound of it, so I have never used it."

"Your name is Qiu Qianzhang." Guo Jing could not suppress a chuckle.

"I can call myself any name I want. What's it to you?" The old man showed not the slightest sign of awkwardness or embarrassment. "Ten feet make one *zhang* and seven feet make one *ren*. So, my name, Qianzhang, has three extra thousand feet over the name Qianren."

"I think Qiancun—a thousand inches—would suit you better," Lotus teased.

"Why do they just shout and not come up?" Guo Jing asked.

"No one dares move without my command."

Guo Jing was not sure whether to believe him or not.

"The crafty old fox won't speak the truth unless we show him our colors." Lotus's voice was still muted. "Jab him at the Heaven's Vent."

This pressure point, at the base of the throat, between the collarbones, was known to bring forth an unbearable itch, as if ten thousand ants were crawling under the skin.

"*Aaaahhh . . . aaaahhh . . .*" Qiu Qianzhang yowled. "You evil, wicked—"

"Tell us everything. Then we'll free you," Guo Jing said.

Qiu Qianzhang took a deep breath to focus his mind, and began.

5

QIU QIANZHANG AND QIU QIANREN WERE IDENTICAL TWINS, just as Lotus had surmised. When they were children, their appearance and temperament were so similar that no one could tell them apart. When they were thirteen, Qiu Qianren had saved the life of Leader Shangguan of the Iron Palm Gang, and the older man shared all his martial knowledge with him by way of thanks.

Qiu Qianren worked exceptionally hard, so that, by the age of twenty-four, his skills had surpassed those of his Master. One year later, Shangguan named Qiu Qianren his heir and the next Leader of the Iron Palm Gang. Shortly after that, he passed away.

A steadfast Song patriot, it was Shangguan's lifelong wish to help the troubled Empire recover the territory lost to the Jin. Qiu Qianren, by contrast, was only interested in using his martial knowledge to make a name for himself. Before long, he was famed across the *wulin* as the Iron Palm Water Glider, one of the five masters to receive an invitation to the Contest of Mount Hua.

However, since Qiu Qianren knew he could not beat the Quanzhen Sect's Wang Chongyang, he declined to take part, and, for the next two decades, led a hermitic existence on Iron Palm Mountain, honing his martial skills. He was determined to be crowned the

Greatest Martial Master Under the Heavens at the second Contest of Mount Hua.

As the brothers worked on their martial training, the divergences in their personalities started to show. One worked incessantly, the other gave up as soon as he realized he had no natural talent for it. One lived deep in a remote mountain far away from the rest of civilization, the other scammed his way through towns and cities across the land, trading on his brother's fearsome reputation to get by. And so, it was Qiu Qianzhang whom Guo Jing and Lotus had met at Roaming Cloud Manor, but Qiu Qianren whom they had encountered at the Beggar Clan Assembly at Jun Hill, as well as outside the stone house earlier that night. Since they looked and dressed exactly the same, Lotus had mistaken one for the other, and had paid a hefty price for her error.

This cave had been the final resting place for generations of Iron Palm Gang leaders. It was customary for them to climb up to the second segment of the middle crag to await their fate when they realized death was nigh. Ordinary Gang members were forbidden even to come within a certain distance of it, on pain of death. If the leader passed away elsewhere, a follower would be tasked with the great honor of carrying the leader's remains to the burial site, before slitting his own throat in the cavern as an ultimate act of devotion.

Through sheer luck, Guo Jing had stumbled upon this sacred place and gained some respite from the pursuing force. The Iron Palm Gang shouted and cursed, but no one dared take one step onto forbidden ground. Even the leader could not enter, unless he was planning never to return. Qiu Qianren could only use his mighty kung fu to project his voice from below.

What had brought Qiu Qianzhang to the cave, then? The dying leaders of the Iron Palm Gang were known to travel on their final journey with their favorite weapons and antiques, so that their beloved objects could keep them company in the afterlife. Over time, a sizeable hoard had been amassed.

Following the setbacks and insults he had suffered over the past few months, Qiu Qianzhang's mind had turned to the treasures in the cave. He knew that sharp blades would not improve his kung fu, but they would give him an edge when defending himself. Since Guo Jing and Lotus's arrival was imminent, now had seemed as good a time as any to see what he could find in the cavern. He also figured that the fear of this hallowed place would keep the Iron Palm Gang members far enough away so that no one would notice him trespassing. Yet, the very people he was hoping to arm himself against had brought the whole Gang almost to the door.

Guo Jing was lost in his own thoughts as Qiu Qianzhang finished his tale. We're safe here for now, he told himself. The Iron Palm Gang won't cross into this sacred site, but we have nowhere to run, either. If we go up, we meet only clouds, and if we go down, the whole Gang will be waiting . . .

"Go inside and take a look." Lotus's voice interrupted his thoughts.

"Let me check on you first." Guo Jing found a branch and lit it. He unfastened her robes gingerly and peeled away the Hedgehog Chainmail from her shoulders.

Two black handprints marked her otherwise unblemished skin.

She would have died instantly if not for the armor, Guo Jing thought with a shudder. It looks as if the blow she has suffered is more serious than the one I took from Viper Ouyang. Perhaps we can use the same healing technique from the Nine Yin Manual?

"Hey! You said you'd stop the itching!" Qiu Qianzhang called to Guo Jing.

Guo Jing was so consumed by the sight of Lotus's injuries, he did not hear his captive.

"Don't worry." Lotus gave a wry smile. "Let him go."

Lotus's voice brought Guo Jing back to the present. He released the bind on the Heaven's Vent acupressure point, and the relief for Qiu Qianzhang was instantaneous. Guo Jing refused, however, to restore the old man's mobility, and left him lying on his back, huffing and puffing.

Having found a longer branch to use as a second torch, Guo Jing said, "I'll go inside quickly. Will you be all right here, on your own?"

"The old fossil will keep me company. Go!" Lotus tried to sound cheery, but in fact she was in great pain. Her body alternated between flushes of extreme heat and icy cold shivers.

Guided by the flame, Guo Jing stepped cautiously into the darkness. After following the tunnel through two turns, he arrived at an enormous chamber. A natural cave, it was ten times the size of the man-made entryway.

A dozen or so skeletons were dotted around the space. Some were sitting up, others lying supine. Each had made the journey into the world beyond in a different way. Some bones were scattered, others still maintained the outline of the human form. There were even relic urns and spirit tablets to commemorate the deceased. Swords, secret weapons, and other treasures clustered around each group of remains.

These were the great heroes of yesterday, Guo Jing thought, stirred by the scene. Today, they are nothing more than piles of bones. Still, at least they have each other's company, here—much better than lying buried underground, all alone.

Weapons and antiques had never held Guo Jing's interest. Right now, with Lotus on his mind, they were nigh on invisible. But, just as he turned to leave, a wooden casket caught his eye. It was sitting on a skeleton that was leaning against one wall of the cave.

There appeared to be an inscription on the lid. He crept over to take a closer look.

The Secret to Defeating the Jin.

Guo Jing mouthed the phrase to himself. Could this be General Yue Fei's last writings?

Timidly, he reached out and took hold of the casket.

Craaaaaack!

The skeleton lunged at him.

Guo Jing leaped back. The bones clattered to the ground.

He bolted, running as fast as he could until he was back among the living. He planted the torch in a crack in the floor and helped Lotus up, so that she was leaning against him. Together, they opened the box.

Two thread-bound volumes.

Guo Jing started thumbing through the slimmer one. It contained petitions and memorials Yue Fei had written to the Emperor, calls to arms and declarations of war, essays and commentaries, as well as lyrics and poetry. Every page was an impassioned affirmation of his loyalty, faith, and devotion toward his homeland.

Guo Jing kept making noises in agreement and admiration as he read.

"Read them aloud to me," Lotus murmured.

Guo Jing opened to a short text entitled "Pledge at the Temple of the Five Mountains":

"Since the upheavals in the Central Plains, invasions came from the east and the north. I made my pledge in the lands beyond the Yellow River, rising up in Xiangtai. I enlisted in the army on the day I tied my hair and came of age, and have since fought in more than two hundred battles. Though I have yet to make it far into the eastern wilderness, to purge the nests and hideouts of our enemy, still, I have had the pleasure of avenging at least one of the ten thousand wrongs done to my country.

"Now, once more, I lead a lone brigade, marching out of Yixing. At the battle of Jiankang, we defeated our foe at one beat of the war drum. My sole regret was failing to crush them outright, so not a single horse of theirs could retreat. For now, I train my troops and rest my soldiers, kindling our fighting spirit and steeling our hearts for the next encounter.

"Forward we look to the next battle, the next chance to win honor for our country, to traverse north across the vast sands, to bathe our nemesis' court in blood, to slaughter every invader of our people, to welcome the return of our two Emperors through the gates of our capital,

to take back our lands, to forge a new territorial map. Forward we look to our Imperial Court ruling without concern, our lord and ruler reposing at ease. Such is my hope.

"*Penned by Yue Fei who was born in the lands beyond the Yellow River.*"

Though Guo Jing mispronounced some characters he did not recognize, he delivered the passage from the heart. These few lines contained a lifetime's worth of hopes for the patriotic general, and that very same fire was burning in his chest, just reading them, now.

In any other situation, Qiu Qianzhang would have made some snide remark. Yue Fei's blind—nay, pig-headed—loyalty had always grated on him. Such foolishness to stand against the changing tide of history, he thought. Well, it's not a mistake I'd ever make.

And yet, he bit his tongue and instead nodded as if in vehement agreement. "Excellently written. Excellently read. A hero's words from a hero's lips. Excellent! Excellent!"

In his immobile state, he would say anything to keep Guo Jing in good humor, anything to keep the young man from tapping his Heaven's Vent again.

"Papa always wished to have been born a few decades earlier, so he could have met this great hero . . ." Lotus trailed off, remembering their last exchange. "Can you read some of his poems?"

Guo Jing turned a leaf and read out loud "River Run Red" and "Layered Hills," which she knew well, of course. Then he turned to "Temple of Jade Brilliance" and "For Zhang Yuan," both of which were new to her.

The young couple were deaf to the shouting and cursing outside. By the light of the flickering torch, Guo Jing read out Yue Fei's last poems. Lotus listened, her head resting on Guo Jing's lap.

"This one is called 'The Dragon-Dwelling Temple of Poyang.'

> "*The temple at the Hill of Soaring Rocks,*
> *Where the woods are tranquil and the springs serene.*

> *Coats of precious gold, the likeness of buddhas,*
> *Caps of snowy white, the heads of aged monks.*
> *Over the pond, the moon's chill grows.*
> *Among the pine, autumn with the night blows.*
> *With these words I come to bid the dragon,*
> *Bring forth the rain to wash the people's woes."*

Lotus thought she could hear the wind rustling and birds calling above the racket outside, and a chill engulfed her body. She snuggled up to Guo Jing—gently, lest the Hedgehog Chainmail prick her beloved.

"General Yue never, for one moment, forgot the suffering of the common people. Truly, a great hero!" Guo Jing said, to no one in particular.

"What's in that one?" Lotus asked.

Guo Jing picked up the other volume and read the first few lines. "This is . . ." His voice wavered in excitement. "Battle strategies! This must be what Wanyan Honglie was trying so hard to find. Thank the heavens it didn't fall into his hands."

The book opened with six lines:

> *Cautious with recruitment and appointment*
> *Diligent with drilling and training*
> *Just with punishment and reward*
> *Clear with commands and orders*
> *Strict in discipline and rules*
> *United in triumph and hardship*

Just when Guo Jing was ready to turn to the next page, he realized the only sound to be heard was the whistle of the wind between the crags.

The shouting had ceased.

For the first time since they had taken shelter inside the cave, an eerie silence had descended.

6

A SERIES OF CRACKS AND POPS BEGAN TO BREAK THIS SHORT-lived stillness, drowning out the murmuring of the night breeze. It was a noise they all knew well.

The splatter and splutter of wood catching fire.

"Thank you, little ones, for a painful death!" Qiu Qianzhang lashed out. He had quite forgotten that he had been honoring them as heroes only moments before.

Guo Jing laid Lotus carefully on the floor and hurried to the entrance of the cave.

He stood looking out, gobsmacked.

Fire.

Walls of glowing hot flames. Pressing in on them. Engulfing every tree and shrub in its path.

Everything was ablaze.

They're going to burn us alive! Guo Jing realized with horror.

He crammed Yue Fei's papers back into the casket and stuffed it inside his shirt, before lifting Lotus into his arms.

On his way out, he kicked the cursing Qiu Qianzhang in the midriff to release the bind on his pressure point and thus restore his mobility.

There was only one way open to him—the summit.

Guo Jing scaled the several hundred feet to the peak with ease. Qiu Qianzhang scampered after him, since he too had nowhere else to turn.

Guo Jing set Lotus down and sighed.

The flames licked and lapped at everything in their way. It was only a matter of time before they reached them.

"General Yue's name, Fei, means 'to soar,'" Lotus said, out of the blue. "His courtesy name was Pengju, 'lifted by the winged *peng*.' We could instead be 'lifted by the condors'?"

"Huh?"

"The condors. They could carry us down."

"Brilliant!" Guo Jing hopped to his feet. "I hope they're strong enough."

"Better to die trying . . ."

Sitting down cross-legged, Guo Jing calmed his mind and pooled his *qi*. He let the energy circle in his Elixir Field, in his lower abdomen.

Moments later, he let out a whistle. It shot far into the distance—a powerful demonstration of the Quanzhen Sect *neigong* he had learned from Ma Yu, now fortified by lessons from the Nine Yin Manual.

Though Guo Jing was several *li* above sea level, his voice traveled down the mountain with ease. Almost at once, two white dots appeared in the night sky.

Borne on the wind and illuminated by the light of the moon, the condors had recognized their master's call, which was still echoing between the crags.

Guo Jing helped Lotus take off the Hedgehog Chainmail and lifted her onto the back of the female condor. He then undid one of the long sashes tying her dress together and wound it around the bird, in case Lotus was too weak to cling on.

Once satisfied that Lotus was secure, he mounted the male condor and looped his arms around the bird's neck.

Guo Jing gave the signal and the condors spread their wings.

Seconds later, they were airborne, gliding smoothly through the night sky.

Guo Jing's fear that they would be too heavy for these magnificent creatures was unfounded.

In spite of the pain she was suffering, Lotus was not ready to pass up a chance to taunt Qiu Qianzhang.

Pressing lightly on the condor's neck, she directed the bird to fly just meters above the desperate man, to give him an eyeful of their fantastic escape.

"My lady, take me, please!" Panic, awe, envy. "Save me!"

"She's not strong enough to bear two. Ask your little brother for help. You've got three thousand feet over him, after all."

Giggling quietly, she gave the condor a tap and away they flew.

"But all these treasures will burn with me!" Qiu Qianzhang cried.

Curiosity got the better of Lotus.

The bird swooped down close and Qiu Qianzhang cast himself off the peak. It was his only chance of survival.

He knew that, if by some miracle he managed to descend through the fire unscathed, he would still be walking straight into death's embrace, for he had set foot in the Iron Palm Gang's sacred site, where no living soul was allowed—he had broken the Iron Palm Gang's hallowed rule that even the leader, his own twin brother, could not defy.

The fire had, by now, blocked the entrance to the cave.

Jump. Get on the condor . . . It was all he could think. He grabbed at Lotus.

The extra weight sent all three into free fall.

The condor beat her wings in desperation. But she kept falling.

Qiu Qianzhang tried to peel Lotus's arms from the condor to take the bird for himself, but he had no idea she was bound to it.

Lotus fought back with what little strength she had, her movement limited by the very sash keeping her secure.

Seconds before they crashed into the valley, moments before they plummeted to certain death, they heard the call of the male condor. He swooped, diving head first alongside his mate, his steel-hard beak pecking at the crown of Qiu Qianzhang's head.

The old man flung his arms up to bat away the attacking bird. The next thing he knew, he was tumbling through the air, until all that remained of him was a desperate wail as he plunged into the depths of the valley.

The female condor cawed with joy at the lightened load. She arched her pinions and, before long, the condors were gliding wing-to-wing, soaring north, their masters clinging firmly to their backs.

APPENDIX

NOTES ON THE TEXT

PAGE NUMBERS DENOTE THE FIRST TIME THESE CONCEPTS OR names are mentioned in the book.

P. 25 GRINDING HIS INK

Traditionally, ink in China is formed into sticks or cakes, using soot, animal glue and sometimes also incense to create a perfume. These are then ground against special smoothed and carved pieces of stone, along with a few drops of water. According to Chinese literati culture, the ink stick, ink stone, brush, and paper form the so-called Four Treasures of the Study. The earliest examples of ink made this way appear to date back to the twelfth century B.C.

P. 96 JADE EMPEROR

The Jade Emperor is the supreme deity in the Chinese tradition, a representation of mortality, but, importantly, not the creator of life. No such creator-God exists in Chinese thinking. In Taoist practice in particular, the Jade Emperor commands the other gods in the pantheon, rewarding and punishing their actions every year, as if holding court in a palace on earth.

P. 98 IN ARTIFICE THERE IS SUBSTANCE, IN SUBSTANCE THERE IS ARTIFICE

This comes from the standard gloss on Sun Tzu's *The Art of War* and echoes the Taoist and Buddhist dichotomy between fullness and hollowness and the nature of the Void. And yet, Sun Tzu is also committed to the importance of lying and trickery in warfare. Elsewhere, Sun Tzu writes, "He will conquer who has learned the artifice of deviation. Such is the art of maneuvering."

P. 103 KONG MENG DONG SONG

These characters, when put together in Chinese, sound just as comical and nonsensical as they do in English. The fact that each line consists of rhyming sounds makes a mockery of Chinese poetic tradition, using the four characters per line and four lines per verse model, which is one of the standard building blocks of Chinese prosody.

P. 167 A SIGN CARVED IN WOOD

The Chinese have, since ancient times, viewed a person's penmanship to be revealing of their character as well as their artistry. As such, the calligraphy of significant people has been preserved for millennia by tracing them onto pieces of wood or stone, carving out the characters and, in some cases, painting them in a solid color so that they might be read more easily. In this way, a tablet or sign could contain the work of two significant figures: the person who composed the text and the person who literally wrote it using brush and ink. This ancient practice does in fact still persist in contemporary China, and it is not at all unusual to see examples of the calligraphy of Chairman Mao or Deng Xiaoping gracing the entrance to university campuses or other official buildings.

P. 171 ZHONG KUI, THE JUDGE OF THE UNDERWORLD, THE KITCHEN GOD AND THE EARTH GOD

Zhong Kui is known as the vanquisher of ghosts and demons, having been given the role by Yanluo, the ruler of the underworld. He is reputed to keep order over some eighty thousand ghosts.

After death, the Chinese believed that one's soul would face judgment. The Judge of the Underworld, here, is one of the deities believed capable of carrying out such judgment.

The Kitchen God is the most important of the domestic gods in the Chinese tradition. On the twenty-third day of the twelfth lunar month, just before Chinese New Year, the Kitchen God returns to the heavens to report on every household's activities. The Jade Emperor then uses this information to decide who he will reward or punish over the coming year. Appeasing the Kitchen God, therefore, is of utmost importance.

The Earth God—literally "the Lord of the Earth and Soil" in Chinese—is a heavenly protector of a community. Each locality will have its own Earth God, and local inhabitants will bring him offerings and even stage birthday celebrations for him to enjoy.

P. 216 HORSETAIL WHISK

The horsetail whisk is a weapon made by tying hair from a horse's tail to a longish handle. Originally designed to whisk away insects without hurting them, it is in fact supposed to be a compassionate weapon, fully in keeping with the Taoist and Buddhist belief that one should not harm living creatures. Traditionally, when a Taoist disciple left their temple to live as a wandering monk, their master would gift them a horsetail whisk. Should they be tempted to return to a secular life, the whisk would remind them of their spiritual calling.

427

P. 239 BLACK APOTHECARY

The surname Huang can be literally translated as "yellow," so calling himself the Black Apothecary is a play on his own name.

P. 270 UNBRIDLED HEART I AM NOT WEIGHED, BY EITHER SHAME OR GLORY

These lines come from a poem written by the real historical figure Qiu Chuji.

P. 284 SOME SPEND YEARS IN ISOLATION

This poem has been slightly adapted by Jin Yong from the original, written by Yuan Dynasty poet Cheng Tinggui (A.D. 1289 to approx. A.D. 1362) for his friend, a Taoist, who had been living alone for decades on a boat. Many interpret the first two lines, "Some spend years in isolation, cultivating only unkempt hair and eccentricity," as a dig made by the Quanzhen Sect Taoists at Cyclone Mei, or even at her master, Apothecary Huang.

P. 296 THE WAY IS FOUND NOT IN BEADS OR BRUSH. NATURE'S MUSIC COMES NOT FROM THE FLUTE

These lines also come from an original poem written by the real historical figure Qiu Chuji.

P. 419 FIVE MOUNTAINS

China's five most culturally significant mountains are Mount Tai 泰山 in the east, Mount Heng 衡山 in the south, Mount Hua 華山 in the west, Mount Heng 恆山 in the north, and Mount Song 嵩山 in the Central Plains. They have been the locations for imperial pilgrimage, and are each associated with one of the five cosmic deities of Chinese religion. Mount Hua is the very same mountain upon which the martial greats had their Contest, and Mount Song is home to the Shaolin Temple.

P. 422 COURTESY NAME

In times past, educated Chinese men assumed a courtesy name *zi* 字 when they turned twenty. This would be the one used in polite company, as opposed to the name given to them by their parents at birth, known as a *ming* 名.

P. 422 *PENG* THE MYTHICAL BIRD

The *peng* 鵬 is a gigantic mythical bird, similar to the roc or garuda, that can also fly great distances. In some versions of the myth, once airborne, it does not land for another six moons. It is, therefore, often used as a metaphor for the act of reaching higher knowledge or enlightenment, or achieving great deeds.

JIN YONG (1924–2018) (pen name of Louis Cha) is a true phenomenon in the Chinese-speaking world. Born in Mainland China, he spent most of his life writing novels and editing newspapers in Hong Kong. His enormously popular martial arts novels, written between the late 1950s and 1972, have become modern classics and remain a must-read for young readers looking for danger and adventure. They have also inspired countless TV and video game adaptions. His death in October 2018 was met with tributes from around the globe.

Estimated sales of his books worldwide stand at 300 million, and if bootleg copies are taken into consideration, that figure rises to a staggering one billion. International recognition came in the form of an OBE in 1981, a Chevalier de la Légion d'Honneur (1992), a Chevalier de la Légion d'Honneur (2004), an honorary fellowship at St. Antony's College, Oxford, and honorary doctorates from Hong Kong University and Cambridge University, among others.

ANNA HOLMWOOD translates from Chinese and Swedish into English. She was awarded one of the first British Center for Literary Translation mentorship awards in 2010 and has since translated novels and short stories for publication and samples for agents and rights sellers. In 2011 she co-founded the Emerging Translators' Network to support early career translators, and served on the UK Translators Association committee in 2012. Anna was editor-in-chief for Books from Taiwan from 2014 to 2015, and has previously worked as a literary agent, representing some of China's top writing talent. She is now a producer alongside her translation work.

GIGI CHANG translates from Chinese into English. Her translations include classical Chinese dramas for the Royal Shakespeare Company and contemporary Chinese plays for London's Royal Court Theater, Hong Kong Arts Festival, and Shanghai Dramatic Arts Center.